Little Hickman Creek Series

Loving Liza Jane

A Novel

Sharlene MacLaren

WHITAKER
HOUSE

Publisher's note:
This novel is a work of fiction. References to real events, organizations, or places
are used in a fictional context. Any resemblances to actual persons,
living or dead, is entirely coincidental.

Loving Liza Jane
First in the Little Hickman Creek Series

To contact the author, Sharlene MacLaren:
e-mail: smac@chartermi.net
website: www.sharlenemaclaren.com

ISBN: 978-0-88368-816-8
Printed in the United States of America
© 2007 by Sharlene MacLaren

1030 Hunt Valley Circle
New Kensington, PA 15068
www.whitakerhouse.com

Library of Congress Cataloging-in-Publication Data
MacLaren, Sharlene, 1948–
Loving Liza Jane / Sharlene MacLaren.
p. cm. — (Little Hickman Creek series)
Summary: "Feisty Liza Jane Merriwether discovers that God is the ultimate Matchmaker
when she moves to Little Hickman Creek, Kentucky, to become the new schoolteacher;
she meets a widowed farmer who falls in love with her, but he has already sent for a
mail-order bride"—Provided by publisher.
ISBN-13: 978-0-88368-816-8 (trade pbk. : alk. paper)
ISBN-10: 0-88368-816-6 (trade pbk. : alk. paper)
1. Teachers—Fiction. 2. Widowers—Fiction. 3. Mail order brides—Fiction.
4. Kentucky—Fiction. I. Title.
PS3613.A27356L68 2007
813'.6—dc22   2006100116

2 3 4 5 6 7 8 9 10 11 12 ⨺ 14 13 12 11 10 09 08 07

A hero reminiscent of Lancelot and a heroine as stubborn as Annie Oakley make *Loving Liza Jane* an engaging romance.

—*Ane Mulligan*
Reviewer for noveljourney.blogspot.com

Loving Liza Jane, the first installment in MacLaren's Little Hickman Creek Series, is a sweet and involving story of two people so determined to do God's will that they sometimes forget to seek what it might be. The relationships are touching and deep, the characters are believable and inviting, and the town of Little Hickman feels like home....*Loving Liza Jane* is a great choice for any lover of romance or historicals.

—*Roseanna White*
Senior Reviewer, *Christian Review of Books*

When I first received *Loving Liza Jane,* I thought it would be just another prairie romance novel....However, this was not the typical story at all, and though it contained the basic sketch of characters, it strayed from the usual outline. I enjoyed the variation from typical plot scenarios and experienced more than a few surprises in this one!

The author made this novel shine....Wonderful story! I can't wait for the sequel!

—*Michelle Sutton* (pen name)
"writing truth into fiction"
http://edgyinspirationalauthor.blogspot.com

Loving Liza Jane is a delightful romantic excursion into "yesteryear," a story that reads like *Anne of Green Gables* meets Laura Ingalls Wilder.

—*Kevin Lucia*
www.titletrakk.com

Dedication

To Kendra and Krista,
Precious daughters,
Cherished friends.

Chapter One

August, 1895

*T*wenty-one-year-old Eliza Jane Merriwether, better known as Liza, had never been one for self-pity. No sir, if things didn't go her way, which often they did not, she simply sucked in a deep breath, held her head high, gathered up her skirts, of which there were many, and marched forward, gaining fortitude with every step.

This, however, took the cake, tested her endurance, if not her dwindling courage, to its very limits. More than once, she'd had to ask God if He was sure about the direction He was sending her, and every time she received some form of affirmation. Still, she couldn't help but speculate.

The hot August sun beat down on Liza's shoulders, its relentless heat seeming to burn a hole straight through the material of her cotton gown. Dust gathered on her brow and eyelids, the grime mixing with beads of perspiration that she fruitlessly dabbed at with her now soiled handkerchief.

Just where was this town of Little Hickman, Kentucky? And how many more bumps along the dirt track, which the driver had taken the liberty of calling a road, must she submit herself to before reaching her destination? If there was one rut, there had to be at least a million, every one into which she was certain Mr. Brackett had managed to drop a wheel.

"Hang onto yer hat, little lady," called the driver as they flew over another bump. Too late, Liza grabbed for her fancy bonnet, only to watch it fly to the dusty earth below, turn over onto its side, and roll like a wheel into the nearest mud hole.

"My hat! Stop, Mr. Brackett. I need my hat."

"Sorry, ma'am; ain't got 'nough time to go back. 'Sides, the thing is flat-out ruin't by now." His words were lost to the hot, driving wind, as he veered into the next rocky bend, making no effort whatever to slow down his rig, if anything, encouraging his team of draft horses to gather more speed.

"What? Well, I never! I purchased that hat at Wentworth's Department Store in Boston along with this fine dress just before departing. Surely you can imagine how much I paid for it." Of course, she wouldn't mention the fact that after days of wearing it she would have liked to have dispensed with it altogether.

Mr. Brackett inspected her, his beady eyes narrowing to mere dots on his round, bulbous face. His jowls waggled with every bounce of the springs beneath his rotund body; and although Liza tried not to stare at him, she couldn't help but notice how much he resembled an overgrown ox.

"Lady, where we're headin' you ain't gonna be needin' no highfalutin' hat," he said with a laugh just before slowing the horses' pace. The one called Puddin' snorted appreciatively and threw his head sideways.

"I'd appreciate it if you'd keep your opinions to yourself," she said, sitting ramrod straight to accentuate the statement.

Mr. Brackett's bulging arms flopped to and fro as he handled the reins. Throwing her a swaggering, mostly toothless grin, he said, "I'll keep that in mind, miss." To this, he laughed so hard and loud that spittle flew from his mouth and with it a shot of the foulest breath she'd ever whiffed.

Liza took advantage of the next several miles of quietude Mr. Brackett afforded her by glancing out over the colorful landscape, grasslands dotted with wildflowers, low mountains in the distance, an outlying pasture accommodating a sprinkling of cows and horses, a ramshackle barn, and a deserted meadow that looked to have once been farmland.

To say her trip from the Cape had been an easy one would have been an outright lie. Still, she couldn't deny it'd been interesting; certainly, it warranted a newsy letter to Aunt Hettie and Uncle Gideon upon her arrival. Of course, she would leave out the parts about sleeping next to a grizzled old man on the overcrowded train, refusing to eat one more sliver of beef jerky and cold beans offered by Mr. Brackett when there was nothing else to choose from, and coming upon a rattler when she'd run into the bushes to relieve herself. Aunt Hettie would have a conniption fit if Liza were to enlighten her on every aspect of her journey.

Why she'd thought it necessary to purchase a new outfit for her travels was beyond her. Everything was all but ruined; add to that her now missing hat. She'd so wanted to arrive in Little Hickman making a good impression. Oh, she'd make an impression all right, but it would be far from good if folks were prone to make judgments based on appearance. They would want a proper, genteel lady to teach their children, not someone completely disheveled, as she now obviously was. Well, bother! They'd hired her to be the new teacher sight unseen. They would just have to accept what arrived.

"How much farther is it, Mr. Brackett?" she asked, fanning her face with the fingers of her long white glove. She'd long ago realized the futility in wearing such impractical articles of clothing in the sweltering August temperatures.

"How many times you gotta ask that question, miss? I done told you we'd be there by nightfall."

"Well, pardon me, sir, but it is going on six o'clock, and I have not yet come across one sign that would indicate we are nearing our destination. How do I know you're even driving in the right direction?"

He chuckled quietly. "You won't be seein' any sign until we're near on top o' the place. As for whether I'm goin' in the right die-rection, l'il woman, I 'spect you'll have to trust me on that."

"My name is Miss Merriwether, and I'll thank you to address me as such," she said as her temper flared in a decidedly unchristian manner. "Since I am Little Hickman's new schoolteacher, I should think you would show me a bit more respect."

He snorted loudly. "Oh, you got my respect all right. But you'll need a lot more 'n that to make do as Hickman's new schoolmarm."

Liza twisted the fingers of her soiled white glove and shot an upward glance at the man beside her. "What do you mean by that?"

He snickered before swatting a pesky fly away from his face with one of his giant hands. "Ya ain't the first teacher Hickman's hired, and ya won't be the last." He spat on the side of the road, and Liza wrinkled up her nose at his uncouth behavior. "Hickman's hired three in the last three years."

"Three?"

"Yep." Loosening up on the reins a bit, he rested his beefy elbows atop his knees before exploding with another round of laughter. "I guess that ole biddy, Mrs. Winthrop, failed to inform you 'bout Hickman's history of teachers."

"History?" Something told her she shouldn't have voiced the one-word question.

Mr. Brackett took her in with a sweeping look. "Why, a pretty little thing like you oughta know you cain't handle a bunch of ruffian boys. Hellions they are, yes indeed. There's Clement Bartel for starters; he's mean and nasty that one. Then there's Gus Humphrey, Sam and Freddie Hogsworth—twins they are, and Rufus Baxter, just to name a few. Troublemakers, ever' last one of 'em. They done run off the first woman-teacher Hickman Creek ever had, and the two men that follered her. Gone—like the dust off a used saddle.

"Guess it don't make no never mind whether the Board o' Education hires a woman or a man; you'll be gone 'for the rooster crows on the third mornin'. Yep, you got yer work cut out for ya, little wom—er—Miss Merriwether."

Liza swallowed down a lump the size an apple and feigned nonchalance. "Well, I'm sure it's not nearly as bad as you're letting on, Mr. Brackett." Then tucking a stubborn strand of loose golden brown hair behind her ear, she concluded, "It's not as if I don't have prior experience in handling children." Of course, she doubted looking after Mr. and Mrs. Handy's two small children qualified in terms of educational experience. After all, she'd only recently obtained her license from a small teacher college in Boston.

"Children? Hah! Them boys don't hardly qualify as children, 'specially Clement and Rufus. They're plenty big enough to drive their paw's rigs and farm the land. Them boys is plain lazy about learnin', and gettin' into trouble is one way of breakin' the boredom."

"Well, if they're bored, I'll just have to find a way to make learning fun for them." To that, she folded her hands and set them in her lap, as if the simple act should settle everything.

"Well, you just do that, Miss Merriwether. It'll make my Eloise tickled pink to hear that. There weren't nothin' fun 'bout learnin' with them other ones far as I know."

Liza's ears perked up. "Eloise? You have a daughter, Mr. Brackett?"

"Shore 'nough. She's eight, my Eloise. Right smart, too, you'll see. And sweeter than a teaspoon o' honey. Sure do love that l'il angel o' mine. 'Course, you probably won't be around long enough to get to know her." He raised an eyebrow in challenge.

"Oh, I'll be around, Mr. Brackett, you can bet on that."

She'd had to prove to Aunt Hettie that she'd made the right decision in coming to Little Hickman. Now it seemed she also had to prove it to Mr. Brackett and herself.

Minutes seemed to roll into hours as the wagon tipped and turned along the dirt path. Conversation between the two of them withered into dead silence, save the chirping of birds and the continual squeak of rusted springs in the wagon bed. Just as Mr. Brackett had stated, there were no signs pointing the way to Little Hickman.

Liza had about given up hope of ever reaching their destination when her eyes lit on an old dilapidated wooden board nailed to a rotted tree stump. Hand-painted letters, crookedly situated, spelled out the words **Little Hickman Creek** and under that, **Welcome**.

Liza glanced at her surroundings, curious when Mr. Brackett stopped the wagon outside a small ramshackle building and began to dismount.

"Is this it?" she asked, certain the actual town had to be around the next bend.

He gifted her with another of his toothless grins and winked. "You seen the sign, didn't you, Miss Merriwether?" Walking around to her side of the wagon, he reached a hand up to help her down from her perch. She took his callused hand and stepped to the hard earth, nearly losing her balance in the process, her wobbly legs refusing to hold her in one spot.

"But…" Giving the place another fleeting look, she noted several crudely built structures.

"This here is Main Street," said Mr. Brackett. "Over yonder is Flanders Food Store where you'll be gettin' yer food supplies an' such." He pointed to a basic little building sporting a crooked sign. "Next to that is Emma's Boardinghouse."

"Further up is Winthrop's Dry Goods, then the mercantile, and around the bend is Grady's Sawmill. That there's the school," he added as an afterthought, pointing to a little white structure two or more blocks away. The schoolhouse, although small, looked to be the nicest and the newest building in the entire town. She gave an audible sigh.

A rickety, planked sidewalk trailed along one side of the road where she made note of two curious bystanders in muddy farm clothes who had halted in their steps to peruse Mr. Brackett's arrival. One tipped his hat at Mr. Brackett before continuing his conversation with the other. A rickety wagon carrying a woman and her child passed by, the swayback horse pulling it looking ready to drop in his own dusty tracks.

Several other horses stood tied to a hitching post outside a tawdry looking building. At first glance, she thought it was an eating establishment, but common sense told her it was more likely a saloon when she heard twangy piano music and saw a round, flabby fellow come swaying through the swinging doors and promptly vomit on the sidewalk. Turning her head away, she fought down her own brand of queasiness. *Lord, help me if this is to be my new home.*

"Winthrop swore she'd be here to meet you," said Mr. Brackett, a hint of apology in his tone as he searched the street. "Don't know where she could be." He pointed at a crooked bench in front of a nearby building. "Go sit a spell."

She must have worn a look of sheer panic, for he hesitated only briefly before waving her in the direction of the bench. "I said sit."

Too tired to argue, she walked to the bench and dropped into it.

"Havin' second thoughts, are we?"

"Absolutely not," she assured, bristling at his ill-mannered tone. That she was indeed having second thoughts was something she would keep to herself. Certainly, Mr. Brackett would be the last to discover her inner turmoil.

While she waited on the straight-backed bench in front of a square little building, she turned to peer through the front window. Layers of dust covered the pane, but despite the haze, she managed to identify the place as Little Hickman's Post Office. Closed now, she could see the front counter, marred and dirty, and beyond that, several empty slots into which Liza presumed the postal clerk sorted incoming and outgoing mail. Several "wanted" posters hung haphazardly on one wall, along with a crooked sign advertising a Sunday Picnic. "Evryone Wulcome!" The malformed letters and incorrectly spelled words reaffirmed in Liza's mind how much the town of Little Hickman needed a decent teacher.

"Hello there! Yoo-hoo, Mr. Brackett, is that you?"

Mr. Brackett was just crossing the dirt road when a tall, portly woman, finely appareled, approached him briskly from the opposite sidewalk, her full skirts dragging along behind her as she held to her wide-brimmed, feathery bonnet. She carried a dainty parasol in her other hand, and Liza quickly decided that the woman's fancy getup did not seem to mesh with the backdrop of falling-down buildings and dirt-packed roads. Nor did it blend in with the woman's coarse features. However, it did make Liza mourn the loss of her own beautiful hat lying facedown in a mud hole some miles back. She had the distinct notion that this woman would have placed a great deal of importance on Liza's new hat. Hastily, she stood to her feet awaiting introductions.

"Just the person I was lookin' for," Mr. Brackett said, failing to sound pleased.

Hurrying across the road, the woman dismissed Mr. Brackett with a curt nod and immediately turned her attention to Liza. "Well, I declare, would this little mite be Miss Merriwether?"

"That it would," answered Mr. Brackett, coming alongside Liza.

"Why, you're no taller than some of your prospective students, Miss Merriwether. I had hoped, I mean I expected..." The woman looked her up and down with worried eyes, then took two full steps backward as if to gain a better perspective. Liza squared her shoulders and stretched to her fullest height. But what was the use? She was all of five feet two inches tall in her Sunday-go-to-meetin' shoes.

"Is there a problem?" Liza faltered.

"Oh, begging your pardon, young lady. What foul manners I have." To this, she tittered nervously, her owl-like eyes drilling holes into nearly every inch of Liza's petite frame. Then, offering her gloved hand, she said, "Iris Winthrop. You will remember me as the president of Little Hickman's Board of Education."

Liza smiled as best she could and fought down nervous butterflies. "Of course. So nice to finally make your acquaintance, ma'am," she said, taking the offered hand and wincing under its firm, hot squeeze and vigorous shake.

After having spotted a public notice in one of Boston's newspapers advertising the need for a teacher in beautiful Kentucky, Liza had put the matter to prayer. Within the week, she'd applied for the position, asking God to close doors as He saw fit. Since then she'd received exactly three letters of correspondence from Mrs. Winthrop, the final one containing an offer of employment, the teaching contract, a payment schedule, meager as it was, and information pertaining to her arranged housing. It appeared every door had opened wide for the new teacher's entrance.

Although Liza had jumped with joy at the opportunity, her aunt had seemed to view it more as a death sentence. "Kentucky?" Aunt Hettie had cried, "but it's so desolate and uncivilized there. I'm afraid you'll be taking on a mission project instead of a respectable teaching position."

"Aunt Hettie, I've prayed about this, and I truly believe this is where God wants me to go. You must look at this as an opportunity for me to spread my wings."

To that, her aunt had frowned sorrowfully. "If your parents were alive I know they would agree that you should think this through more logically."

"Trust the Lord, Auntie. He will take care of me. Remember Mark 5:36 says, **'Be not afraid, only believe.'** We must claim that verse as ours."

Now, looking about the town of Little Hickman Creek, Liza couldn't have explained for the world why she'd been so all-fired determined to fill the position as teacher. Had she misinterpreted God's leading? The place looked as unproductive as a wobbly pump handle. Even the lazy, scrawny dog meandering across Main Street affirmed her worst fears. Aunt Hettie had been right; Kentucky was an uncivilized place.

Even so, she couldn't ignore the yearning she'd had to set herself free of Aunt Hettie's loving, yet constrictive, apron strings and Uncle Gideon's watchful eyes. Oh, they'd been wonderful guardians to her, taking her in so willingly after she'd lost both her parents to a house fire that she had survived thanks to an alert neighbor. But now, at twenty-one years old, she was ready to experience life on her own. If living in this town didn't help accomplish that, she didn't know what would.

"Well, my dear, you must be exhausted. How was your train ride from Boston?"

The trip had been anything but pleasant, the long hours grueling, the heat sweltering, but she wouldn't let Mrs. Winthrop believe she was unaccustomed to a little hardship.

"Everything went very smoothly, thank you," she said, praying the woman wouldn't detect her fabrication of the truth.

Foolishly, she'd thought that her twenty-five-mile ride from the train depot with Mr. Brackett would be a blessing in comparison, but riding atop the mud wagon's buckboard alongside the sweaty, unkempt man had been just as excruciatingly uncomfortable as the overcrowded train ride, if not more so.

All she wanted to do now was settle into her new surroundings, unpack her large trunk and satchel, and finally take advantage of the opportunity to relax. A cool bath would suit her fine, she decided, wiping beads of sweat from her brow even as she hurriedly scanned her surroundings. Indeed, she was anxious to explore the school, but sheer exhaustion dictated tomorrow would be soon enough.

"Well, fine then," Mrs. Winthrop said, continuing to peer down her nose at Liza before favoring her with a puny smile. "Where is your luggage?"

"My trunk is on the back of the wagon."

"Mr. Brackett, do get Miss Merriwether's bags," she ordered.

"You got my pay—Ma'am?"

Liza noted Mr. Brackett took pains to draw out that last word, his obvious distaste for the woman seeming to seep from his pores.

"Begging your pardon?"

He gave a churlish grin, yanked a filthy handkerchief from his hip pocket, and mopped his equally filthy forehead. "You heard me. I been on the trail for more hours 'n I care to count. I'd appreciate my pay first."

Liza squirmed where she stood, uncomfortable witnessing their private squabble.

"Oh, for goodness sakes, Mr. Brackett, you are about as restrained as a cornered rooster."

"And you are a toffee-nosed, highfalutin' hen."

"What?" The question came out in a squawking fashion. "Well, I never! You have the manners of a—a contemptible varmint."

"Please," Liza cut in, feeling the fool. "Mrs. Winthrop, would you please pay the man—if that was indeed the arrangement?"

Mrs. Winthrop and Mr. Brackett glared at one another until Mrs. Winthrop finally reached into her small beaded bag and withdrew a folded envelope. Handing it over, she scolded. "I should think you'd have considered carting Miss Merriwether from Lexington an honor, Mr. Brackett. She is, after all, Hickman's new schoolteacher."

"Oh, it was an honor all right, but that don't mean I don't need money for puttin' food on the table for my little Eloise," he said, tucking the envelope into his shirt pocket.

"Humph," the woman said. "You shouldn't be raising that poor child without a mother. Clyde and I would gladly have…"

"I know what's best for my Eloise, and you best remember that."

Turning his back to both women, he climbed into the rear of the wagon. Emerging moments later with Liza's huge trunk, he let it drop to the hard earth. Liza watched as a puff of dirt and dust rose on all sides and winced at the thought of her precious china teapot shattering into a million little pieces.

To that, he bounded off the back of the wagon, tipped his hat at Liza, spat on the ground at Mrs. Winthrop's feet, and sauntered away. "Say hello to poor ole Clyde," he called as an afterthought.

"I'll do no such thing," she retorted under her breath, brushing her skirts with her gloved hand, as if to sweep away the germs that remained from the unpleasant encounter. "What an uncouth man he is. I do apologize for his terrible behavior." Eliza noticed that she didn't mention her part in the fight. "I would imagine your journey with him was most unpleasant, but I couldn't seem to find another man that wasn't caught up with his harvesting and whatnot. Of course, there was Benjamin Broughton; I might have called on his services, but no, that would not have been appropriate. Besides, I'm told he has his hands full out at his place. No, I'm afraid Mr. Brackett was my only option. My poor sister, God rest her soul, never should have married that frothy, ill-mannered man."

"Is Mr. Brackett your brother-in-law?" Liza asked, mystified.

"Unfortunately, yes, and now that uncivilized man is trying to raise my sister's daughter. Imagine! Since Clyde and I have no children, we would serve as fine guardians to that forlorn child."

"But I'm sure Mr. Brackett loves his daughter dearly."

"In these parts, love isn't enough. Besides, we have the wherewithal to see to her future needs what with Clyde's bountiful inheritance."

"You can still offer financial help, can't you?"

The woman threw her a look that said Liza had overstepped her boundary.

"Sour puss won't accept any support from us," she said in a huff, moving toward the back of the wagon where Liza's trunk lay on one side. Liza found herself picking up her skirts and hurrying after the woman.

Staring down at the oversized crate that carried all of Liza's belongings, Mrs. Winthrop heaved a sigh. "Well, I suppose we best try to…"

"You get off my porch, you scalawag!" The shrill-sounding order came from across the street.

Curious, both women turned their gazes in the direction of the commotion.

The same scruffy man Liza had observed just moments ago emptying the contents of his stomach onto the sidewalk was having words

19

with a tall, slender woman holding a long-handled broom in one hand and a frying pan in the other.

"You despicable, tobacco chewin', boot-lickin' loon! O'course you can't have a room in my hotel. I am trying my best to run a respectable business here. You go hang yer fiddle back up at Miz Guttersnipe's place. You fit in right well over there!"

"But M-Miz Guttersnipe ain't near the c-cook that you are," the man stammered, his glazed-over eyes revealing his confusion.

"Get!" the woman insisted, pounding him on the head with the iron pan and forcing him off her porch with the broom.

"I'm gittin', I'm gittin'," he cried, covering his head with his arms as if that would protect him from the beating he was taking. Losing his footing, he stumbled, then fell, on his way down the steps.

"Get up, you ole fool," she hollered, battering his head with the straw end of the broom.

Staggering to his feet, he wobbled away, cursing as he went, his bloodshot eyes looking dazed and uncertain.

Once the lady was sure he was gone, she laid the frying pan on a nearby rocker and took to sweeping off the porch, as if she hadn't a care in the world.

"Who is that?" Liza asked with awed wonder.

"That, my dear, is Miss Emma Browning. She runs the town's only boardinghouse. Miss Guttersnipe, on the other hand, runs a—well, a hotel of ill repute, if you will. It's over yonder."

"And who was...?" Liza pointed at the swaying figure heading up the street.

"That despicable man was her father, Ezra Browning, the town drunk. Or, might I say, one of them."

"Her—father?"

"That's correct. Now, shall we see what we can do about moving this trunk?"

Confounded, Liza bent to grip the trunk on one end by its handle while Mrs. Winthrop took the other.

"You ladies needin' some help there?" asked a kindly voice from behind.

"Oh, Mr. Collins, how very nice of you."

Although the scrawny man didn't look much stronger than the two of them put together, Liza welcomed his offer of assistance.

"Where to?" he asked.

Mrs. Winthrop turned and pointed a finger at the hotel. "Miss Browning's establishment."

"Oh, but I thought I was to have a place of my own," Liza hastily put in, bending to share the handle with Mrs. Winthrop while Mr. Collins took the other end. "The contract clearly stated…"

"I'm afraid the old Broughton place is not quite ready yet. You'll have to stay at Miss Browning's in the interim."

"I see."

Sighing, Liza did her best to lift her end of the trunk and move in the direction of the boardinghouse. Her spirits suddenly fallen, she fought down tears of frustration.

Lord, whatever have I gotten myself into?

Chapter Two

*P*apa, I found two eggs!" Seven-year-old Lili Broughton rushed through the door all smiles, her little hands each carefully holding out a warm egg.

Early rays of sunlight stretched their spindly fingers through the dusty windowpane and came to rest on the red and white checkered tablecloth. August warmth penetrated the walls of the sturdy cabin, making standing by a heated cook stove all the more laborious.

"Now that's a good girl," Benjamin Broughton said, bending to take the eggs from his daughter and giving her a loving smile. "Did the old girl give them up willingly?"

"Soon's I walked in the coop she moved aside for me, Papa, as if she was pure delighted to be rid of those uncomfortable lumps beneath her belly."

Ben Broughton gave a hearty laugh before pointing at the open door. Adept at reading her father's silent commands, Lili ran to the door and shut it with a none-too-quiet approach. She twisted her lip guiltily at his reproachful gaze. "Sorry," she muttered.

"We need to keep our voices down, sugar. Molly is still sleeping, and I'd like to keep it that way."

"She sure cried a lot last night."

"She's growing more teeth."

"Again? Ain't she always doin' that?"

"You know better than to say *ain't*. It is not a part of our everyday language, Lili. And, no, Molly is not always growing teeth. It just seems that way."

"When's she gonna quit?"

"I don't know. I imagine once she gets a mouthful."

"Well, she can't keep growing teeth forever. I didn't."

"Lili…"

Ben stretched taut muscles where he stood and mindlessly massaged the back of his neck with one hand while cracking an egg with the other. Lack of sleep had taken its toll on his body, never mind the fact that he was only twenty-nine years old and should be able to handle it. Raising two youngsters, one in diapers, and the other a rambunctious, precocious seven year old, was no easy task, particularly when he had a farm to operate.

Dropping a hunk of grease on the hot fry pan, he watched it sizzle. "You only found two then?"

"Two?"

"Eggs."

"I din't look for more, Papa. You said you needed two more eggs to add to the rest, so that's all I got."

He grinned into the pan. "We'll go out after breakfast and fetch the rest, pumpkin, providing Molly continues sleeping."

Few moments passed before Lili started up again. "Freddie Hogsworth says it all the time."

"What?"

"*Ain't.* Among other things, of course."

"Well, I wouldn't want you going around repeating *anything* Freddie Hogsworth says," he told her, hiding a grin beneath his yet unshaven face. "I don't think I'd trust that boy as far as I could pitch him."

"You could pitch him far, Papa. You got muscles that are bigger than any man I know."

Ben laughed again. "And you have a tongue that loves to waggle, young lady."

Lili giggled and turned three circles on the planked floor. Ben heard the grit beneath her high-topped shoes and winced at the idea of having to sweep it yet again. The cabin had always shone like a whistle when Miranda was alive. Something twisted in his gut with the simple reminder of sweeter days. *Best not to dwell too long in that dark place,* he told himself.

"What we gonna do today, Papa?"

"You and Molly are going to Mrs. Granger's house later so I can work the fields till dusk."

Without looking, Ben knew his daughter's shoulders slumped where she stood. "Why can't I never come with you?"

"Ever—why can't you ever?" he corrected, sprinkling salt, pepper, and a bit of milk into the egg mixture, then using a long wooden spoon to combine the ingredients. "And we've been over this before. The fields are no place for a little girl. I'd be worried the entire time." Turning briefly to study his daughter's sullen expression, he added, "And that would slow me up."

"But Papa, Mrs. Granger don't have no little girls."

"Any…She doesn't have any little girls," he corrected again. "But she has Charles."

"He's a boy. 'Sides, he's too old to play with. All her other kids is long gone."

"Well, true. She has all those barn cats and that poor excuse of a dog, though. You like them, don't you?"

"Yes, but they ain't kids." He fixed her with a scowl.

"Aren't," she corrected.

"Well, before you know it school will be starting. Then you'll have lots of friends to play with."

"Is she here yet?" Lili asked.

"Who?"

"The new teacher."

Keeping up with Lili's chatter was always a chore. "I wouldn't know. I imagine she'll be arriving any day now."

"Is she still gonna stay in Grandpa Broughton's old place?"

"If I ever find time to fix the roof, mend the porch steps, and buy new windows, yes." The list of things to do to the tumbledown place to make it livable seemed endless. A body would have to be desperate to want to live in it. Still, his was the only farm near town that included a vacant cabin, and so he'd felt obligated to offer it since his daughter attended the school and required an education. Unfortunately, his offer included volunteering to make it fit for human habitation. The place hadn't been lived in for nearly ten years, unless you counted all the critters and varmints that had willingly taken it over.

The other teachers had always lived with families, but much to Mrs. Winthrop's dismay, this particular teacher, Miss Merriwether, had insisted on her independence. Of course, Mrs. Winthrop had thought it highly inappropriate that a lady live alone, particularly the school-teacher, and even Ben had inwardly scoffed at the notion. The wilderness was no place for a self-governing female. He'd already decided that the lady was undoubtedly some fastidious, uppity spinster from the city used to having her way. Probably stubborn to boot.

As it turned out, it mattered little what Mrs. Winthrop, or any-one, thought about her living arrangement. Hickman needed a school-teacher, and since no one else had applied for the job, the school board had voted to invite Miss Merriwether.

"Is she gonna live with us until you finish it?" Lili asked, sliding onto a nearby stool.

"Good grief, Lili, what would ever make you ask such a question?"

"Ain't she ar 'sponsibility?"

"Don't say ain't, Lili, and no, she certainly is not *our* responsibility.

I simply offered your grandfather's old place if and when I find the time to fix it up. Until then she'll stay at Emma Browning's boardinghouse."

"Will she be mean and grumpy?"

"Who?" He was still thinking about old Mrs. Winthrop.

"The new teacher."

"I shouldn't think anyone would be mean and grumpy to you," he offered, giving her a slow grin and turning the eggs over in the pan. "Now hop down and set the table, would you?"

"Mr. Lofthouse was mean and grumpy to everyone," Lili said as she walked to the cupboard to take down a couple of plates.

"Well, that was Mr. Lofthouse."

"And the teacher before him, Mr. Abbott, was only a tad better. But he had that ugly black mark on his face. Did you know that hair grew out of that thing?"

"Hair? Sweetheart, a person can do nothing about a birthmark."

"I know, but it was hard to look at that man, 'specially when he got up close. I wonder if the new teacher will have a birthmark," she said, hugging the clean plates to her shirt.

"I doubt it."

"I wonder if she will be pretty," she said.

Ben smiled at the little chatterbox. "God made everyone different, Lili. It'd be good if you kept that in mind. Looks are not everything, honey. In fact, they're not even important."

"Mr. Lofthouse wasn't too bad to look at, but he couldn't make no one behave," she charged, seeming to ignore his strategy for teaching a timely, godly lesson on love and acceptance.

"Anyone. He couldn't make *anyone* behave."

"I know. That's why they had to fire him."

"I believe he quit, pumpkin."

"Do you think the new teacher will quit?" she asked, finally laying a plate on the table.

"I couldn't say."

"I wouldn't want to teach them mean boys what sit in the back."

Deciding to let her grammar slide, Ben took a tin plate from the table behind him and stacked the eggs atop it. "Those Hogsworth twins ever give you any trouble?"

"No, Papa, but they sure do like to stir things up. Once they brought a snake into school and stuffed it right inside Mr. Abbott's coat pocket when he wasn't looking."

Ben stifled a chuckle. "I'm sure that created a stir."

"Mr. Abbott's face went pure white with shock when he stuck his hand inside and came out with that slimy thing. When he tossed it across the room, it landed smack on Eloise Brackett's desk. She screamed from here to kingdom come, Papa."

He laughed quietly. "I imagine she did."

"I wouldn't have minded if it'd landed on my desk, Papa. I'm not ascared of snakes."

"You're not *afraid* of much of anything, young lady," Ben said, tapping the end of her freckled nose with his finger.

Taking their seats a moment later, father and daughter clasped hands at the table. "Whose turn is it to say the morning prayer?" he asked.

"Yours, I believe," Lili said, her authoritative tone signifying she'd been keeping track.

"Well then, I'll take your word for it," Ben said, grinning at her freckled face before bowing his head.

"Dear Father," he prayed, "we thank Thee for the food You've put before us. Please watch over Lili, Molly, and me today as we go about our business. You know exactly what our needs are, Lord, and

27

we trust Thee to meet them according to Your timeline.

"Help us, Father, to live according to the commandments that Thou hast set before us and to be ever mindful about showing the love of Jesus to our neighbors.

"Please give us generous hearts and kind spirits.

"In Thy name we pray…"

"And be with the new schoolteacher!" Lili cut in before he'd managed the final amen.

Ben couldn't hold back his spontaneous chuckle. "Yes, Lord, and be with the uh, new teacher, Miss…uh…"

"Miss Merriwether, Papa."

"Yes, Miss Merriwether." Sneaking a peek at his daughter for good measure, he quickly added, "I believe that's all—for now—Lord. Amen."

Smiling appreciatively, Lili hastily released his hand and took to her breakfast like a famished piglet.

Ben took advantage of her silence to ponder his day.

There were fences to mend on the back forty, a lame horse to tend to, Bessie and Sarah to milk, hogs to feed, and fields that needed plowing and harvesting. And then there was that matter of his grandfather's old house up on Shannon's Peak. Just when was he supposed to find the time to make the necessary repairs to that so that the new teacher could move in?

Pardon me, Lord, he inwardly amended, *but I wish when You created me, you'd have thought to add a spare hand. I could use an extra about now.*

Shoveling a forkful of eggs into his mouth, he watched his daughter. She had her mother's hair, golden curls that had a way of shimmering in the light, then changing hues with the slightest toss of her head. And those freckles. My, but she had a faceful of them. There'd only been a few decorating Miranda's pert nose, but Lili's face was

 28

peppered. Unfortunately, they coincided with, perhaps lent to, her mischievous behavior. Then there was that lone dimple on her left cheek, positioned in exactly the same spot as Miranda's had been.

Miranda. How he missed her. But time and sheer busyness, not to mention God's faithfulness and grace, had a way of smoothing over the hurt. Little by little, every new day brought him one step closer to wholeness. Still, he had a long way to go, and he doubted he would ever truly love another woman—even if he chose to remarry. Women as sweet as Miranda only came along but once in a lifetime. Nevertheless, there was the matter of his daughters; they needed a woman's touch. And that was a matter he could no longer continue to ignore.

What was he going to do when his daughters, particularly Lili, started asking the sort of questions intended for a woman's ear? Even now, he had a difficult time dealing with Lili's overwrought emotions. One moment she was laughing hysterically, and the next, drowning in a puddle of tears. Plain reason told him she would only grow more complicated. All women did. To his knowledge, no man had ever mastered the internal workings of the female mind. And as if Lili weren't enough, God had seen fit to drop another daughter into his lap just fourteen months ago—while taking the one woman who had the means for raising his little girls.

He wasn't bitter. He'd passed through that stage in his grieving process and discovered afterward how much better off he was for not lingering there. Bitterness got him nowhere. Besides, he'd had little time for it. Neither had he taken the time for self-pity, much as he could have enjoyed wallowing in that particular venue. Self-pity was a luxury, something he couldn't afford with two daughters to raise and a farm to maintain.

No, the practical side of things kept him moving in a forward direction. The problem was, all signs pointed to his inability to continue his forward progress. For the past several weeks, it appeared he was stuck in muck up to his eyebrows, spinning his wheels, and getting nowhere. If anything, the farm was suffering. Already there were crops wasting only because he hadn't the time to work them properly.

Even Mrs. Granger was petering out on him, complaining of aches and pains she'd never had before, confessing to him that taking on two children when she'd already raised nearly a dozen of her own was a bit more than she could handle at this stage of her life.

"I'm not as young as I used to be, Ben," she'd said nearly two weeks ago after he'd put both girls on the wagon, then gone back into the house to pay her. "I promise I will help you for a bit longer, but only until you manage to find someone you can count on permanently."

"I thought I could count on you permanently," he'd protested.

Her frown told him he'd thought wrong. "I'm getting up there, Ben. Heavens' sake, child, I watched *you* grow up."

It was true; she was an old family friend, the epitome of a good neighbor. She'd nursed his own sick mother when she'd come down with an uncommonly high fever, had even sat with her and clutched her hand until she'd breathed her last. Consumption was what they'd called the lung-destroying disease that took his mother. Not long after her fateful death, his father had fallen ill and perished from something similar.

Orphaned at fourteen, Ben had moved in with his crusty, eccentric, yet somehow lovable Grandfather Broughton, even though he'd claimed impoverishment. When the old man died, however, Ben discovered a suitcase full of money stashed beneath his grandfather's rusted bedsprings, squashing all rumors of destitution.

The find had been a bittersweet blessing, for it put Miranda and him in a much better financial position to begin their marriage. Still, he'd figured his life would never be quite the same without the old man. He'd put a stamp on his heart that would forever affect his life's decisions. "God first, boy. Remember that," he'd repeatedly said.

"You could always court Emma Browning," Mrs. Granger had said, pulling his thoughts back to their conversation. "She's very pretty, don't you think? And she has a good heart. Granted, she's a bit on the wild side..."

"Mrs. Granger, Emma is a tiger on the loose. I like her enough, but I'd certainly never marry her! And that father of hers is a drunken dolt."

Mrs. Granger nodded. "You're right, of course." Deep in thought, she pursed her lips, then blossomed with a ready smile. "What about the widow Riley?"

"The widow Riley is ten years my senior, Mrs. Granger, and well, plump—she's plump." Plump had not been a good choice of words. Whopping might have better described her, but he had more class than to be completely forthright when it came to another's looks.

"Well, you can't be too choosy, Ben. You have motherless daughters. How much longer do you think you can properly care for them?"

"That's why I've hired you, Mrs. Granger."

"And I've told you that you need to start looking elsewhere, Benjamin. Besides, my Althea is expecting another baby any day, and she's asked me to come to St. Louis to look after the rest of her brood."

"But you just said you're getting too old for this."

"Althea is my daughter. I can't refuse my own children." As if a light had just come on, Mrs. Granger brightened. "I have it. How about looking into a mail-order bridal service? They advertise those kinds of agencies out east, you know."

At that, he'd laughed outright, finding the entire notion bizarre and completely illogical. Men and women married for love, not convenience, didn't they? Besides, he wasn't even sure it was the Christian way of going about finding a woman to care for his daughters.

But a few days later he'd seen the advertisement at the post office where John Holden kept a supply of newspapers from such places as New York and Boston, and he'd had time to rethink his position.

"MARRIAGE MADE IN HEAVEN AGENCY"
CHRISTIAN Women Seeking God-Fearing Men.
Will Marry Sight Unseen Providing the Match Suits.
Prefer Courting First, However.
Prospective Groom to Pay for Prospective Bride's
Transportation and Room and Board
Until Said Marriage Is Performed.

Under the eye-catching caption was a list of names of women, all desperate, no doubt, and their varied attributes. Included were such things as date of birth, physical features, background information, family history, personal talents and interests, and a host of other tidbits that would satisfy any male anxious enough to find a wife.

Ben had laughed most of the way home that day wondering to himself what would drive someone to such extremes as to advertise her need for a husband. But then, hadn't he been equally irrational for hovering over the ad for as long as he had, even going so far as to imagine what some of these spurned spinsters looked like? They couldn't be shy, he mulled, for what timid woman would be so bold as to market her availability? Nor could they be exceedingly attractive, or some man would surely have snatched them up before they'd had the chance to apply at the agency.

So why exactly had he hastily ripped the ad from the paper and stuffed it into his pocket? For all he knew, the outfit could be running an illegal racket. Under the guise of "Christian-based agency," they could be stealing overtly enthusiastic men blind. And he could be one of them! Try to explain that to Mrs. Granger when he came crawling back to her begging for more time, admitting he'd been swindled by an imaginary marriage market.

On the other hand, the organization could be completely legitimate, doing its best to find husbands for otherwise unmarriageable women because of their deadbeat personalities, or worse, unsightly facial birthmarks that grew hair!

But then looks didn't matter. Hadn't he just told Lili that this morning?

Later, after dropping off a disgruntled Lili and a fussy Molly at Mrs. Granger's place, he headed up Shannon's Peak to have a look at his grandfather's old cabin. Might as well determine what else needed fixing, make a bank withdrawal, and purchase some essential supplies. The fields would have to wait another day.

Chapter Three

*L*iza rolled over on her mattress of lumpy feathers and glanced overhead at the discolored ceiling. Across the room a window curtain waved about, signifying a gentle wind, even though no evidence of moving air quite reached her. Tossing the sheet off her warm body, she studied her surroundings before rising.

A lone chest of drawers marked with age stood against a paint-chipped wall. Atop it rested a flowered chamber set, a pitcher and cracked basin, and on the wall above the chest hung a faded and distorted mirror in a beaded metal frame. A round, rather misshapen, colorful rug covered a good share of the gouged wood flooring, probably covering the worst of its blemishes. Next to the bed stood a wobbly table housing one kerosene lamp and a vase of dying flowers. Liza groaned then draped an arm across her forehead. If this was the best the town could offer in boardinghouses, the rest of the town sorely lacked class. Of course, she'd known that as soon as they had rolled into the place last night.

"Breakfast!" came a squalling voice from downstairs. Liza immediately identified it as that of Emma Browning, her pretty but rough-edged landlady. Apparently, the kitchen was directly beneath her room. "Anyone interested better set yourself at the table within the next five minutes, or all this food will go to my hungry dog and cat!"

As if a freight wagon pulled by a mule team had just plowed through Emma Browning's Boardinghouse, the entire place shook with the feet of hungry occupants as they opened and closed doors and then skittered down the flight of creaky stairs.

Apparently, Emma Browning meant business when she announced breakfast.

 34

Not nearly as inclined as her housemates to meet the breakfast deadline, Liza lifted herself from the bed and momentarily dangled her feet over the edge, worrying herself silly about nothing and everything. Would there be enough teaching supplies in the little schoolhouse? How many students could she expect? And why was she Little Hickman's fourth teacher? Moreover, why wasn't her house ready for her? Surely, she'd been adamant enough about wanting her independence.

At least Aunt Hettie would be relieved to find she'd been dropped off at a boardinghouse. "There is safety in numbers, my dear," she would say.

Without further thought, Liza decided that besides investigating the schoolhouse first thing this morning, she would seek out the cabin intended for her use and, if need be, do the work herself to make it livable.

Liza rose and shuffled across the room, heading for the chamber set first where a full pitcher of water awaited her. It should be room temperature by now, she ruled, snatching a washing cloth and towel from the top of her opened trunk. Thankful that at least a fresh bar of soap lay in a dish beside the basin, she took it up and began her morning ablutions. Just then, there came a quiet knock at her door.

Startled, she jumped back and drew the string of her nightdress more securely about her. "Yes?"

"Miss Merriwether? It's Emma Browning. Aren't you coming down for breakfast?"

"I—I'm not quite presentable. I guess I slept longer than I'm accustomed to doing."

"It was a long journey for you, ma'am. I would expect you need your rest. How about I bring something up to you later?"

"But I thought..."

"Don't pay me no never mind. I have to be downright merciless with those no-good mongrels downstairs. They spend their days laborin' on farms or at Grady's Sawmill and their evenin's cavortin' and gettin' corned, then 'spect me to feel sorry for 'em. You, however, are a guest, and I would never hand over your breakfast to my dog and cat."

Liza thought she detected a hint of humor in the woman's voice. So she'd been right about her after all; there was some give to Emma Browning. Perhaps she wore her thick cloak of resistance for good reason. Perchance she'd learned a few hard lessons about basic survival from her drunken father.

Liza didn't have the heart to tell her that her keyed-up stomach might not handle food at present, so she murmured a quiet thank-you and listened for Emma's retreating footsteps before she finished getting ready for her day.

After a hasty breakfast of cornbread and coffee, which Liza took in the dining area rather than in her room, she inquired of the other boarders about the schoolhouse.

"It doubles as a school durin' the week and a church on Sundays. The circuit preacher makes his rounds but once a month, and the rest of the time a lay person delivers the words," said Mr. Dreyfus, the only guest among the others seated around the long rectangular table who appeared interested enough in conversation.

"I see," answered Liza. "I suppose I'll need to check with Mrs. Winthrop about getting inside the school. I want to see about available supplies and equipment."

"Place is pretty sparse," said Mr. Dreyfus. "That was one of John Lofthouse's complaints, that and those Hogsworth twins, Rufus Baxter, Clement Bartel..."

"No need to worry Miss Merriwether about them boys now, Mr. Dreyfus," Emma interrupted. "School hasn't even begun."

It was the second time Liza had heard about the rowdy boys of Little Hickman Creek, and she found herself pushing down nervous qualms. She would find a way to deal with the behavior problems of these disorderly boys when the time came. Now, however, there were other more pressing issues.

"Where might I find the cabin I'm to live in?"

A bearded fellow, whose name she hadn't caught, produced a hearty laugh. "You mean that old Broughton place?"

"That would be the one," she said, stiffening at his sardonic manner.

"The place ain't hardly worth fixin'," he said. "It's been years since that old coot, Broughton, died. Don't know why his grandson even offered the place. It was in disrepair before Broughton passed on. It's gonna take a heap o' work fer Benjamin to make it fittin' fer a lady."

"Well, has he at least begun the work?" she asked, annoyed with the fellow's honesty.

"Cain't say."

"Is anyone else lifting a finger to help?"

"Cain't say one way or t'uther 'bout that neither," he answered between bites.

"Didn't anyone know I was coming?" she asked, frustration rising rapidly.

"Lady, we all got jobs to go to," said a wily looking character with dirty overalls and scraggly beard. "If we was married with kids, it'd be one thing, but we ain't. 'Spect the people with youngins oughter be the ones offerin' the helpin' hands."

"What about your sense of pride and community?"

All seven men sitting around the table gave her a blank look, as if she'd just asked them exactly how many miles it was to the moon and back.

"Oh, for gracious sakes, at least you can tell me how to find the place," she said, her patience thin as a pence.

"You'll have to go rent a rig at Sam's Livery if you wanna git out there," offered Mr. Dreyfus.

"Can't I walk there?"

The men all shared a laugh. "Shore. If ya don't mind wadin' up to yer thighs 'cross Little Hickman Creek."

"Or she could walk the extra half-mile to where the bridge crosses over it," suggested Mr. Dreyfus. "Hain't been no bridge built yet over by where the Broughtons live."

"The rig'll git her there quicker," offered yet another. "Them horses is used to the trek."

"Where is the cabin?" Liza asked again, her nerves fraying faster than a loose thread on a homespun quilt.

"Come out to the porch and I'll point the way," said Emma, whose sudden return to the dining room seemed a welcome respite. "You men finish up yer breakfast so I can clean up this place," she ordered, waiting for Liza to join her on the porch. To that, every man picked up his fork, as if the jail warden himself had issued the command.

Liza wasn't accustomed to driving a wagon such as the one Sam Livingston had presented her with at the livery. Unlike Uncle Gideon's fine upscale runabout back in Boston, this one had a hard seat and loose springs that made for a terribly rough ride. Several times, she'd had to grip the edge of her seat with one hand while hanging on to the reins with the other in order to keep from tumbling off. Although it was a tad better than the muddy wagon Mr. Brackett had transported her in to Little Hickman, it still felt as if her brain were rattling every time she came to a bump or a gully. Add to that the uncommon heat of noonday, and she was about as miserable as she could remember ever having been. Still, she pressed on, determined not to let a little discomfort spoil her adventure.

After taking the proper turns in the crude, two-track path that followed the contour of the land, and passing the landmarks Emma had aptly named "The Tree with Two Trunks" and "The Three Pines Standing in a Row," she arrived at the narrow stream called Little Hickman Creek. Bringing the team to a halt at the edge of the water, she studied her surroundings. There was no denying its untarnished splendor. Rolling hills and plentiful green-blue grass covered the earth like rich, lavish carpet. Distant horses and cows grazed side by side on a neighboring rise, lending to a sense of rightness deep in her soul.

After some time, she snapped the reins to nudge the team across the water, praying that the wagon would stay upright. As if they'd negotiated the tiny river a hundred times before, they entered the water and came out on the other side with ease. Greatly relieved, she had only to round a cluster of oak trees up ahead before reaching the cabin.

As Liza had expected, Emma's directions proved accurate. Amidst huge shaded oaks and overgrown brush, at the top of a ridge that Emma had branded Shannon's Peak, stood a weatherworn cabin. At first glance, Liza halted the horses and merely gawked at the dilapidated spectacle. At worst, it would fall over tomorrow, or perhaps at *best*, she concluded sourly. She hadn't expected *pretty*, but she hadn't expected a decaying old shack either. Did they actually expect her to live in this place?

Just south and at the foot of the ridge was a neat cabin with sheds and a barn. The Broughton place, perhaps?

Urging the horses forward, they took the incline with little effort. "Whoa," she called out as soon as they'd reached a horizontal clearing suitable for stopping the wagon. Twisting the reins around the front panel, she pulled on the brake handle, lifted her skirts, and dismounted, then made the trek the rest of the way up the hill.

Mounting two rickety porch steps and finding the front door ajar and crooked on its hinges, she entered with care, fearful of falling through loose boards.

To say she was shocked by her discovery would have been too mild. Layers of dust, no less than half an inch deep in places, covered every square inch of the three-room structure. Cracks in the floor revealed the earth below, and gaping holes, indicating long ago windows, now served as doorways to the elements, not to mention any wild creatures that had a mind to enter. Worse, excrement in various stages of deterioration covered the floor, emitting the foulest of odors. Liza gasped for air then pinched her nose shut.

On one wall of the main room stood a stone fireplace with a rusted-out kettle hanging from an inside hook, and beside that, ancient chopped wood randomly stacked in an old wood crate. In front of the fireplace, a three-legged table rested on its side, its missing leg lying nearby showing signs of having been dinner to some wild creature.

Advancing with caution, Liza bent to pick up a dilapidated chair, as if putting it right might somehow improve the overall look of the place.

Warped cupboards hung at a slant on an adjacent wall. Was this to be her kitchen? Stepping closer, she spotted a deep sink with a pump handle where she supposed the water from the well pumped through a pipe and into a makeshift drain hole. At least there was an indoor pump, she ruled. Of course, the way her luck was running, the well would likely be dry.

"Lord, forgive me, but what's happened to my wonderful sense of peace?"

Her only response was the skittering of a tiny gray mouse on a mad rush for the open door. Liza covered her gaping mouth with both her hands to hold back a shriek and turned back toward the kitchen, shuddering.

Nearly black from soot and grime, the only evidence that the sink had once been white was the tiny tracks of a varmint, no doubt that same little creature she had just encountered, or at least his close cousin. Regardless, the very notion that she might have to share the place with rats, mice, and squirrels made her shiver despite the menacing heat.

She scoffed and decided that the only thing that could make this place less appealing would be discovering a corpse in the next room. She decided to see for herself, even if it meant risking life and limb.

"Looking for something?"

Liza whirled around at the cavernous voice and squelched a scream, shocked to see a giant of a man with jet-black hair and a matching day-old beard standing in the doorway.

"Who are you?" she managed to ask, her heart thundering.

"I think I should be the one asking the questions since you're on my property," he replied, prickly as a porcupine.

"Excuse me? This was to be my residence, but I can see I was merely dreaming," she shot back. "This place isn't fit for swine, although it would seem something has found it quite habitable."

As if realization had suddenly struck, he crossed his arms and stared down at her. "You?"

"Pardon me?" she asked, brushing at her skirts. Besides being big, the man looked fierce, his shaded expression giving way to intense blue eyes, a stark contrast to the black hair.

"You're—Miss Merriwether?" he asked with a hint of amusement.

"I am," she answered, holding her head as high as her five-foot-two-inch frame allowed.

For no good reason the man started laughing, his mirth fairly filling the barren little cabin.

Rather than ask what could be so funny, Liza nursed her mounting annoyance and prayed for patience. "And who might you be, sir?"

Still laughing, it took a moment before the beast of a man settled down long enough to answer. "Name's Benjamin Broughton, ma'am. Ben will suffice," he said, offering a hand, which she didn't take. "I must say I had someone entirely different pictured in my head for Miss Merriwether."

Liza noticed that he had a slight British accent. "Well, I'm sorry to disappoint you, Mr. Broughton."

"No need for apologies," he hastened, finally dropping the hand he'd offered. "It's just that, well, you're so young and…small."

"I am twenty-one years old," she answered briskly, figuring it best to keep her guard up. Aunt Hettie had warned her countless times about placing her trust in total strangers.

"Twenty-one now, are you?" He bit his lip, probably to hold back another round of laughter. "Have you ever taught school?"

"Not that it is any business of yours, Mr. Broughton, but I recently finished my schooling and acquired my teaching certificate."

"I see. So you haven't any real experience."

"That should be of no concern to you."

"Ah, but it is. I have a seven-year-old daughter, you see. As a matter of fact, your name came up in conversation with my Lili just this morning."

"In reference to what, may I ask?"

"Well, let's just say my daughter is rather curious about you. The other teachers, well, never mind." His eyes twinkled with merriment.

"I shall look forward to meeting her—and your wife, of course."

In the twinkling of an eye, his expression clouded, but rather than comment, he turned his gaze on his surroundings. "Place is going to take a bit of fixing."

"A wagonload is more like it, Mr. Broughton. It appears that you didn't expect I'd follow through with my commitment, but here I am."

"Yes, here you are." One corner of his mouth angled upward.

"Mrs. Winthrop never so much as hinted that there would be a problem with my housing. Had I known the condition of this cabin, I would not have signed a teaching contract." She gave the place another quick look.

His laugh was low. "Perhaps that's why she didn't tell you. Hickman needed a teacher, and you were the only one who applied."

"I'm beginning to understand why."

"Mind telling me what you have against staying in town?" he asked.

"Very simply, I believe it's time I gained my independence, Mr. Broughton."

"Ah, yes, twenty-one is well past time for that." Again, his midnight blue eyes hinted at humor.

"In most circles, twenty-one is considered marriageable." She felt her back go straight.

He rocked back on his heels. "Approaching spinsterhood, are we?"

Appalled, she ignored the jibe. "When do you expect to have this place ready for me?" The mere question seemed absurd in light of the amount of work it would take to refurbish the rustic cabin. As if to rub in the fact of her rueful circumstances, she kicked a piece of rubble out of her way and watched it sail across the room.

"That anxious to move in?"

"If you must know, I don't relish the notion of having to live with a band of ill-mannered, unkempt, slothful men."

"Hmm. I see your point, the Browning establishment."

"Miss Browning herself is quite charming," she hastened. "Nothing against her."

"Of course not."

Liza ambled toward the bedroom, away from his watchful eye. Fortunately, this room held no disappointing discoveries. In fact, its window remained intact, much to her surprise. Strange how a little thing like a window could please her so. On the furthest wall stood an armoire. While it had seen better days, it would serve her well for storing what items of clothing she'd brought with her.

As if reading her mind, Mr. Broughton nodded at the piece. "That old cupboard came over on a boat from England. My grandfather brought it when he and Grandmother migrated to America. It's a good, sturdy piece of furniture."

"I can see that." She moved closer to sweep a hand over its dusty exterior. "You descend from England, then?"

"I do. In fact, I came over with my parents when I was about ten."

"That would explain your accent."

"People say they detect a slight one."

Although the room lacked bedsprings and a dresser, she didn't mind. With the money she'd been saving from previous jobs and that that Uncle Gideon had given her to get started with, there would be enough to purchase inexpensive bedroom furniture and a few other essential pieces for the rest of the house. It appeared she would need a table for certain and at least two chairs, one for her, and one for a guest—if she ever made a friend, that is.

"This room won't require as much work," she said, her spirits slightly lifted. Although the floor was warped, it didn't show any cracks between the boards. A good rug would cover up the worst of its flaws.

Mr. Broughton stepped into the room then, ducking in the doorway, the full height of his body shadowing her petite frame. Never before had she felt so exceedingly small. She turned her attention to the rest of the room, giving him plenty of latitude to move about.

"No, it's the rest of the place that will take some work. Now that you're here I'll call on Thom Hayes and Willie Jenkins to lend a hand. It will take some time, however."

"Now that I'm here? Hadn't you thought I might want to move in upon my arrival?"

He chuckled. "I guess things don't get done near as quickly in these parts as they do where you're from, ma'am. Patience is a virtue, you know. Or haven't you heard that?" The twinkle was back again, along with a twisted grin.

"Of course I've heard it. I believe you'll find it in the Bible."

His laughter intensified. "The Bible, you say? Do you read it much?"

"Of course. I read it every day," she said, deeply annoyed.

"Ah, that's good to know. Hickman will do well to have a Christian teacher for a change."

She straightened, well pleased that he'd commented on her spiritual status.

"How familiar are you with the Word of God?" he asked.

She shifted her weight, nervous under his perusal. "Enough, I suppose."

One keen eye favored her with a wink as he clasped his hands behind his back. "Well, if you were as familiar as you claim, you would know that the old adage does not come from the Bible but from Chaucer's writings, *The Canterbury Tales*. But perhaps that was what you meant to say?"

Liza's face colored. "I suppose you've cornered me on that one, Mr. Broughton. I don't claim to be a literary historian. I see I shall have to brush up on my facts if I am to converse with you."

"Not at all," he answered, further amused. "I doubt you're the only one who has ever mistaken the origin of some well-known phrase." He dipped his head politely, an act that put her on the defensive, particularly since his roguish smile seemed accompanied by mischief. What was this man about?

Tamping down the temptation to expel a nasty comeback, she merely asked, "How long before you begin work on this place?"

"I've already told you, it will take a few days. I have fields to tend to, my children to look after, supplies to be bought..."

"I should think your wife would watch over your children," she blurted.

Again, the shaded expression surfaced, but he offered no explanation.

"As for your fields and the supplies, I could offer you some money..."

He held up a hand to halt her. "Not necessary."

"If I'm to live here, I intend to do my part. If that includes paying you for the repair of this—this..." Helpless to find a single word to describe the place, she left it unfinished.

"The matter will be handled."

"Regardless, I don't intend to live off the fruits of others."

"You won't be. You'll be working it off by teaching our children," he argued.

"Well, then I'll help you do the work. It's only right," she stated.

"I think not," he said, a muscle in his jaw flicking.

"Why not? I can do hard labor."

He gave Liza a quick once-over. "Pardon me, ma'am, but you're a mite of a woman."

"I'm perfectly capable of doing any job you might hand over to a man."

With that, he burst into a round of riotous laughter, the sound bubbling from his chest and seeming to bounce off the cabin's rickety walls. She supposed it had been an absurd statement, but certainly not that funny.

When he finally composed himself enough to speak, he merely said, "I'll be starting on the work sometime this week—or next." Turning, he headed for the door to the cabin.

"This week or next? But—why not today?" she asked, following directly on his heels, frustrated that he didn't see the matter as urgent.

He stopped in midstride and turned. "Patience is a virtue, ma'am. Remember?"

"I remember, and for the moment, I have all the patience I can possibly muster. I have just traveled several hundred miles to reach this place, Mr. Broughton. I would appreciate a home of my own to settle into before school starts."

He cocked his handsome head at her. "Ah, well, that could be a problem." Then, glancing out the hole in the wall where once a window had been, he asked, "You see those fields out there?"

"Of course," she answered, following his gaze.

"There's corn out there that needs harvesting. Some of it is rotting already. Corn is not my only crop, either. There's plowing and haying, not to mention cows that need milking, and a couple of hogs to fatten up before slaughtering day."

When she failed to show him sympathy, he looked toward the ceiling with a sigh. "What I'm trying to say, Miss Merriwether…what is your first name?"

"Eliza—Eliza Jane. Liza to my closest friends. Miss Merriwether to *you*," she tacked on.

He narrowed his midnight blues on her. "What I'm trying to say, *Liza*," he carefully articulated with a hint of spite, "is that you came at a busy time in my life."

"Well, excuse me, Mr. Broughton."

"Ben will suffice," he reminded.

"School will be starting soon, and since you knew I was coming, I should think you would have planned ahead."

He bowed his head and murmured something. A hasty prayer, perhaps? "I'll gather some men and start as soon as possible. That's all I can tell you.

"I'll have to find someone to watch my girls," he added as an afterthought while turning around. "The woman who watches over them is leaving soon."

"I should think your wife…"

He offered her a cynical look. "I am no longer married, so you can stop referring to my wife. She died over a year ago."

The simple statement stopped her in her tracks. "Oh," was all she managed for the moment.

Chapter Four

I have a classroom to organize and lessons to prepare for, but I suppose I could find time to help with your children," she offered, folding her hands at her petite waist.

He noticed that several strands of golden brown hair had pulled loose of the little knot she'd piled on top of her head. He wondered what she'd do if he simply tucked them back behind her ear. "No need. I'll manage my personal affairs."

He had to get out of here, he told himself. The cabin was downright stifling, and the little woman inside it didn't help matters. He hadn't wanted to mention Miranda's passing, but now that he had, he prayed her name would not come up again.

"Do you have anyone in mind—to watch your children, that is?"

"No—yes—no; well, sort of." He couldn't lie. "I have several women in mind I'm about to approach on the matter." The truth was he had a few, not several. "They all have broods of their own and I'm thinking that adding two more to the litter won't make that much difference to them."

There was the Johnson clan up the road. Mrs. Johnson had five little ones and another on the way. He seriously doubted she'd want to take on two more, but it couldn't hurt to ask. Then there were the Bergens, the next farm over. They had four, but they were all very young. Their son, Thomas, a mere nine, was the oldest of the children. Mrs. Bergen likely had all she could handle right now.

He'd thought about the widow Riley, but he was afraid, after the suggestion Mrs. Granger had made about courting the woman, she just might get designs on him. There was always the mail-order bride concept, but that option was a last resort.

Liza tilted her head at him, as if to assess his situation. "Are you certain? The truth is, I want you to finish this place, and if watching over your children will speed things up, well…"

"No. Mrs. Granger will be around a bit longer, and as you said, you have to tend to your classroom."

"How old are your children, Mr. Broughton?"

"Molly is fourteen months and Lili is seven. They're a handful, but very smart."

The teacher's face brightened. "I'm sure they are." Then, catching a hurried glance out the window, she said, "Well, I best be going. I have important things to see to."

They exchanged strained smiles.

"I'll stop by in a few days to check your progress," she added. "I should think you'd be well on your way by then."

Demanding little woman.

He watched her gather up her skirts and march down the slanted pathway toward her rented rig. She'd have to buy one of those get-ups if she planned to move out here. The three-mile walk was simple enough on warm, sunny days but downright bone-chilling in the winter months.

He wondered if she had a clue of what lay ahead. Something told him she would learn as she went. She seemed made of tougher stuff than he'd expected. On the outside she was sweet and fragile looking, but on the inside he suspected her blood was mixed with grit and gravel.

"Good-bye, Mr. Broughton," she said from her high perch on the wagon.

Leaning against the little cabin's exterior, he managed a grunt and a simple nod of the head. He could see already that the woman was going to rub him the wrong way.

As Eliza Jane Merriwether maneuvered the wagon back toward town, he mumbled a hasty prayer. "Lord, give me strength."

That evening, after putting both his girls down in the little room next to his, Lili on the cot, and Molly in the crib, he took a strong cup of coffee and pulled a chair up to the table.

The day had been sweltering, but nighttime breezes now wafted through the open windows of his sturdy house, cooling and lending comfort. He tipped the chair back on its hind legs and hoisted his feet atop the table, something Miranda would never have allowed. Even as he did so, he had to push down a guilty conscience. He could almost hear her scolding tone now. "Benjamin Broughton," she would say, "you get them boots off that table straightaway. We're gonna be eatin' ar breakfast on that table."

A slow smile formed and lingered as the memories did.

He'd met his Miranda at a barn dance when he was nineteen. The entire town seemed to have shown up for the affair, the night-time celebration of the day's barn raising. Glancing about the place that night, and looking for his buddies, Rocky Callahan and James Buchanan, he'd spotted Miranda Franklin instead. It was the Franklin family who'd lost their barn to a fire along with countless livestock. As was the custom, the men and boys from all across the region showed up the following week to raise another barn. He and his aging grandfather had been among them.

He'd caught glimpses of the Franklin girl that day and thought she'd noticed him, too, but always when he'd sent a special nod or smile her way, she'd dropped her head in a skittish manner, picked up her flouncy skirt, and turned away, as if a mere glance at him were too embarrassing. She was a shy one back then.

51

Well, that night he meant to change things. There she was standing as pretty as a picture in front of the punch table, golden curls hugging the curve of her neck, a fitted, flowery dress accenting her tiny waist. Mustering up all his courage, he'd approached her, afraid she'd run the other way. But she hadn't. Instead, she'd smiled and given him a curtsy. One look into her clear blue eyes had been like seeing the ocean for the very first time. Pricked by Cupid's arrow, he'd felt the pangs of young love.

Ben smiled at the simple remembrance. It hadn't taken them long to figure out they belonged together, and so they'd married in June of the following year.

That was ten years ago, although it felt like two entire lifetimes. He was a mere twenty-nine, but he could have been forty-nine for all the pain and suffering he'd endured in her passing. She'd been sickly during her second pregnancy, and when the complications of childbirth set in, there was little the doctor could do for her. Her resistance was too low, Doc Randolph had said. In the end, she'd bled to death and left him with an infant daughter and a six year old that he hadn't the slightest notion how to care for.

Now, here he was, fourteen months later, barely managing. If nothing else, he'd learned to place his faith and trust in his heavenly Father.

Reaching for his tattered Bible, he opened it to the passage he'd been studying. In the margin, he'd scrawled, **"The sorrows of death encompassed me, and the pains of hell found me: I found trouble and sorrow. Then called I upon the name of the LORD; O LORD, I beseech thee, deliver my soul. Gracious is the Lord, and righteous; yea, our God is merciful. Psalm 116:3–5."**

He'd penned the words just after putting his newborn infant into her crib and his wife in her grave. Emotions he'd labored long and hard to keep under lock and key had gushed forth that night, as if a mighty dam had finally broken free. In his misery, he'd sought strength in God's Word and found it.

"Papa?"

Ben went into automatic alert at the sound of Lili's small voice. Booted feet hit the floor as he lay his Bible back down and turned to face his daughter. She stood in the doorway, golden curls mussed and sleep still evident in her eyes.

"What's the matter, pumpkin?"

"I can't sleep," she mumbled, crossing the room.

"Why not?"

"Molly's makin' noises," she complained.

"What kinds of noises?"

"Snorey ones."

Ben smiled. "At least she's sleeping for a change," he reminded.

"Can I sit on yer lap?"

Without giving him the chance to reply, Lili climbed up and snuggled into the crook of his neck.

"It's late, Lil, and you know how you are in the morning when you don't get the sleep you need."

"I promise not to grouch—too much," she said.

He smiled over the top of her head and smoothed down a few hairs that insisted on going straight to his mouth.

"I'm also too excited," she added.

"Now, what would you have to be excited about?" he asked, rubbing little circles into her back.

"Miss Merriwether. What else?" Her voice fairly chirped with enthusiasm. "Aren't you excited?"

Ben closed his eyes and sought a suitable reply. "I wouldn't say *excited* is the proper choice of words." At present, the woman represented work to him.

After picking up building supplies in town and talking several men into coming out to help him, Ben and the others had set about refurbishing the old Broughton place immediately. One thing was certain; this was not a simple project. Matter of fact, the further they got into it, the worse it got. It seemed everything from the roof on down needed some sort of repair.

"Why ain't you excited?" Lili asked, curling into him.

"I've asked you not to use that word."

"Well, then why *aren't* you?"

"Well, of course I'm happy that you will start school as scheduled. Isn't that enough?"

"What does she look like, Papa?" she asked, ignoring the fact he'd dodged her question.

How could he explain to Lili that her new teacher was pretty without risking disrespect to her mother's memory? "She's—fine—I suppose."

"But how does she look? Did you notice any ugly birthmarks?"

Ben laughed outright, the mere thought of an ugly mark on the refined Miss Merriwether somehow cheering his mood. "No, Lili, none that were visible."

Satisfied, she asked. "Was she mean and grumpy?"

He supposed that all depended on who you asked, but he had to come up with a better answer than that. "I'm sure to you she will be everything and more than you ever dreamed possible in a teacher."

Lili drew back and granted him a wide-eyed look of joy. "Jumpin' Jehosephat! This is good news!"

"Lili, where do you come up with your vocabulary?" Ben scowled, at the same time fighting the urge to smile.

"I'm plain thrilled that you liked her," she said, ignoring his question.

 54

"I didn't say I..."

"When can I meet her?" she cried.

"Huh?"

"Can we drive the buggy into town tomorrow so I can meet her face-to-face?"

"What? No, Lili. Papa has many chores to do tomorrow, one of which is fixing up Grandpa Broughton's place so she can move into it."

"Just think of it, the new teacher will be our neighbor. I will be the envy of the whole entire school."

"Lili, it is not nice to create envy in your friends, particularly if you want to keep them," he gently scolded.

Ben glanced out the window and up at Shannon's Peak. The cabin was near enough that when his grandfather had lived there Ben could see the smoke rise up from the chimney, see his shadow pass across the window on a moonlit night, and catch the sight of his glowing lamp in the window when he sat next to it in the morning to read from the old family Bible. Would he once again watch out his window for the first hint of light on Shannon's Peak?

"Well, when can I meet her?" she pleaded.

"School will start soon enough."

"But I want to meet her before—so I won't get the jitters."

He smiled. "You weren't nervous last year, were you?"

"Not on the first day," she admitted, fidgeting with the hem of her cotton nightgown, "but I was petrified on the second day, 'cause I found out Mr. Lofthouse was mean and grumpy."

Ben sighed. "Lili, I'm sure you have nothing to worry about." After meeting Miss Merriwether, he could rest assured his daughter would be in safe hands. The teacher might have been a little crisp and outspoken with him, but he was sure she had a love for children. Of course, he couldn't tell Lili that because it was just a hunch.

"Well, can I meet her anyway?"

Her persistence was beginning to annoy him. "I just...well, per-haps I can drive you into town one day soon." He knew just as soon as she batted those golden lashes and gave him that droopy look there'd be no letting up until she'd met the infamous Miss Merriwether.

"Oh, thank you, Papa. Tomorrow?"

"No promises."

He was an easy target, and he knew it. Her slender arms moved around his neck and tugged until she'd gotten his face down close enough to plop a wet kiss across his cheek. "I love you, Papa. You are the best Papa in the world."

"All right. I can see where this is heading. It's time you hopped back into bed. Morning will be here before you know it."

"Can I have a drink of water first?"

"Suppose you have to beat a path to the outhouse. Too much water will do that to you."

"Then I'll wake you up to take me."

"That is just what I was afraid you'd say." He tousled her hair and gently placed her on her bare feet. Her sleeping gown was getting shorter, indicating a growth spurt. "When did you grow those extra inches?" he asked, frowning.

She stretched to her full height. "I am seven, going on eight."

"You just turned seven last month."

"I'm still going on eight," she corrected.

He smiled and stood to his feet, mulling about how proud Miranda would be of Lili. "Let's get you that cup of water."

The next morning brought dark storm clouds. With no trace of a sunrise in sight, it appeared as if a storm was imminent. Ben tossed the bedcovers off him and rose with a start, distant thunder bringing him to full awareness. He pulled on the same pair of old work pants he'd worn yesterday, but grabbed a fresh shirt off the stack of halfway folded ones he'd laid on top of the chest of drawers.

The concept of a mail-order bride struck him anew. At least the place would shine once more if he had a woman around. Not to mention there would be breakfast on the table when he came in from milking Bessie and Sarah and feeding the livestock. Washday would become her duty, and she could mend his shirts and darn his socks. Most important, she would love the Lord. The agency advertised only Christian brides.

Lord, what am I thinking?

The stench of last night's burnt biscuits, pork gravy, and navy beans with brown sugar still lingered heavily, turning his stomach. He wrinkled up his nose as he passed the unscrubbed kettle still sitting on the cook stove. There was barely time to clean up the place what with all the chores awaiting him in the barn and out in the fields—and now over at the cabin. What had he even been thinking when he'd offered the broken-down place? At first, it'd seemed a generous move, even charitable, but now he questioned his sanity.

"You goin' out to the barn, Papa?" The familiar little voice forced him to turn.

"Lili, go back to bed. It's not even six o'clock yet. I'll be in to rustle up some breakfast after I've tended to the animals. It's going to rain and I want to finish as many of the outdoor chores as possible."

She dropped her lower lip. "I can help."

"I prefer you stay inside with Molly. She may wake up, and I'll need you to keep watch."

"But I helped you gather eggs yesterday while she slept," she argued.

"This is different. I have a good deal more to do right now than gather eggs."

"But, Papa…"

"Lili!"

Brought up short by the unfamiliar harshness in her father's tone, her eyes welled up. Without another word, she walked slowly back to bed.

Another time he may have contemplated changing his mind, but not this morning. He hated that he'd hurt her feelings, of course, but it was high time she learned she couldn't always have things her way.

Playing the part of both parents wasn't easy. Armed with fortitude, he closed the door behind him and headed for the barn.

❄ ❄ ❄ ❄ ❄

"Benjamin, what in blazes was ya thinkin' by offerin' up this place to that new schoolteacher?" Thom Hayes was standing at the top of an unstable ladder handing Ben more roofing supplies.

Ben gazed at him from the roof's peak. Thankfully, the weather had held off till now, but every minute was touch and go the way the dark clouds loomed. Air so still and close made the warm, early morning temperature seem that much worse.

He gave his friend a rueful smile and wiped his brow with the back of his hand. "Thom, I've asked myself the same thing more than once."

"Well, I'd say it was mighty generous," Willie Jenkins shouted up. Hammer in hand and pocket full of nails, he set out to repair the tiny porch. "A little screw-headed maybe, but downright generous." Ben chuckled and reached for the additional roofing materials.

"Appreciate the kind words," he shouted down.

"Mighty sticky this mornin'," Willie added, staring up at the sky.

"We're in fer a storm," said Thom.

"Let's pray it holds off till I finish the worst of this patching."

 58

Approaching hoofbeats came over the rise just beyond the creek crossing, putting a stop to the conversation.

"Someone's comin'," Willie announced.

"I see that. Anyone recognize them?" Ben asked.

Two men on horseback, saddlebags bulging, galloped into view.

"Looks like Jeb Gunner and Sully Thompson. Word must've got 'round that we was needin' some extra help out here."

Ben settled into a sitting position and removed his hat to run his hand through his scruffy, longish hair.

"Hullo there!" shouted Willie. "What brings you two out here?"

"What's it look like?" Jeb asked, his ready grin revealing a few missing teeth. Bringing his horse to a stop, he dropped the reins and slid easily from the saddle. "The missus told me I best get out here to help else she'd consider givin' my supper to the hogs." He immediately went for his saddlebag and lifted the flap. "Brought out some extra tools."

Ben laughed. "Sure are grateful for the offer. As you can pretty well tell, we have our work cut out for us."

"Whoo-eee!" Sully moaned. "This here is what ya call a project!" Still sitting atop his mount, he repositioned himself in the saddle and scanned his surroundings, lazily resting a hand atop the saddle's horn. Rotted and warped floorboards, already pulled up from inside the house, lay scattered about the ground, while fresh cedar boards stood neatly stacked against the house. Here and there lay bits and pieces of debris that someone had tossed haphazardly, knowing there'd be a huge bonfire later. Taking off his hat, Sully slapped it hard against his knee. Even from his place on the roof, Ben could see the dust fly helter-skelter. Among other things, dust was something all farmers had in common.

"Looks like you spared no expense on them boards," Jeb noted, glancing at the fresh cedar slats.

Ben couldn't explain himself, but when he'd gone to the sawmill and seen the puncheon floor boards, mere split logs with their faces a little smoothed over with an axe or hatchet, stacked beside the smooth cedar, there'd been no contest. How could he expect a prim little schoolmarm to walk barefooted across boards that would fill her feet with splinters? To think he'd gone soft was a fear he harbored, so he hoped the matter would pass over quickly.

"Got a decent price," he mumbled.

"Yeah? You got cedar floors in yer own house?" Jeb asked the question, but all the men waited for his reply.

Ben exhaled noisily. "No, I don't have cedar flooring. I have oak slats. What difference does that make?"

A lifted eyebrow on Sully's crusty face hinted at amusement. "Yer awful touchy on the subject. It was a simple 'nough question."

Ben could have kicked himself for his overreaction. Maybe it was because he wasn't completely sure himself why he'd splurged. "I suppose I'm feeling the pressure of getting this place finished. We all have crops that need our attention. I figured if I purchased quality stuff I'd be less likely to have to make repairs on the place later."

"Makes good business sense," Willie muttered.

"Yer right about us all havin' crops that need tendin'," Thom said. "I got fences to mend on the east side of my property, an ailing horse, and cabbage fields what need weedin'."

Each one added to his personal list of ongoing tasks until they'd exhausted the subject. Sully finally climbed down off his horse and headed inside the house. "This pump work?" he called from the kitchen area.

"Well's good, pump needs priming," Ben answered. "Water's probably rusty from lack of use."

"Cupboards are hangin' crooked. Chimney got any cracks?" he asked.

"Not that I know of."

"Sink's black. Ceiling looks a little warped."

Ben smiled. "Did you come out here to work or to grumble? We already know this place is a shambles without your rubbing it in."

"Just pointin' out a few things."

"Yeah, well, you'd do well to get to work. Never know when that schoolteacher might show up. Wouldn't set well with her if you didn't look busy," Ben said, setting a roofing nail in place.

"You met her yet?" Jeb asked after hauling out the old three-legged table and adding it to the pile of rubble.

"I have." Best to keep his answers short, he determined.

"What did you think?" That from Jeb Gunner.

Ben smiled to himself. "What does it matter?"

"Just curious. She look tough enough to handle the likes o' them Hogsworth twins or Rufus Baxter?"

Ben laughed. "That remains to be seen. She doesn't appear to be much taller than my Lili, but I have a feeling she'll give them a run for their money regardless of her size. She struck me as a regular spitfire."

"That's so."

"Well, now, ain't this interestin'?" Sully chimed from below.

"What's that?" Ben hollered back.

"Just found me a brand new picture fer hangin'. 'Twas stashed on the top shelf of this here wardrobe. Nice country scene with a river runnin' through, pretty mountains in the background. Words inscribed on it are *Patience Is a Virtue.*"

Ben set to driving each nail faster and harder. He should have left the picture at home. He might have known someone would come across it, even if he'd done his best to hide it.

"Where'd it come from?" Willie asked.

Ben yanked a few more nails out of his hip pocket and fastened another shingle in place.

"Ben?"

"What?"

"You buy this picture for the schoolmarm?"

"No, I bought it for the cabin," he clarified.

"Ah, the cabin," Sully said with a chuckle. "Mighty nice gesture."

Chapter Five

*L*iza trudged through mud up to her ankles on her way out to the necessary behind the little schoolhouse. Why nature seemed to call at the most inopportune times she couldn't say. Drenching rain soaked through to her scalp and saturated every inch of her clothing. And it was not the sort of rain that looked as if it'd be letting up anytime soon. At least it had held off until mid-afternoon, giving her plenty of time to walk to the school, survey the surrounding properties, and wash the six classroom windows from the outside. She'd spent the rest of the afternoon inside her classroom taking inventory of her stock, meager as it was, dusting shelves, rearranging books, and going over class lists.

Two little white sheds, one with the word *Girls* painted in black on the door and the other, *Fellows,* stood at the back of the property. Hurrying along the beaten path, she glanced out over the open fields before throwing wide the door, thinking she had glimpsed two shadows lurking behind some trees, but too distracted to pay the matter much attention.

Moments later, muffled footsteps approached. Disconcerted, she waited for any kind of clue to the indistinguishable sounds but came up with nothing. She thought about asking who was there, but the very notion seemed silly, if not downright awkward. Perhaps whoever passed had no idea she was even inside; thus, asking would bring about undue embarrassment. No, it was better that she wait things out. In time, they were sure to move on. Besides, who would linger long in this rain?

But as the minutes ticked away and she continued to hear scuffling sounds and quiet movement, it appeared whoever was out there was up to no good. They seemed to be running around the outhouse and every once in a while tapping against it.

"Hello?" she finally called out, standing and straining to find a crack in the wall where she could get a bird's-eye view. Unfortunately, they'd built the structure in such a way as to ensure total privacy. Liza found herself cursing the good craftsmanship. "Who's there?"

Rain continued pelting the roof, but it didn't blot out the stifled giggles and guffaws coming from the other side of the outhouse. She knew without a doubt that some kind of plan was in the making. She also knew it was the sort she wouldn't approve of.

"What's going on out there?" she demanded. Still no verbal response, just quiet laughter, the kind that came from rascally boys. Somewhat afraid for her safety, yet confident someone was playing a simple, harmless prank, she pushed at the door, intending to face the troublemakers head-on. However, the thing refused to budge.

"All right, this has gone far enough. Open this door," she said, exuding all the authority she could gather.

More spurts of laughter.

"Apparently you find this funny," she said. "I can assure you I will not punish you if you simply let me out. In fact, we'll all have a good laugh. How does that sound? Are you my future students?"

No answer. Even worse was the pounding of retreating footsteps and continued distant laughter.

"Hey, where are you going?" she called out, as if they would pay her any mind. "Come back here."

Frenzied, she pushed and pounded on the door, even called out to anyone who might be passing by despite the rain. Although embarrassed by her situation, she did not relish the thought of spending the night here. Surely, someone would come along.

As the perpetrators' laughter disintegrated, she found herself standing in stunned silence, the onslaught of rain somehow lending to her sense of isolation and despair.

With a frown, Liza closed her eyes to ponder her situation and then spun in a circle as if to stir up her thinking capacity. But thinking was not that easy in the confines of her odor-filled environs.

❄ ❄ ❄ ❄ ❄

"Will Miss Merriwether be at Miss Browning's Boardinghouse, Papa?"

"I would think so, pumpkin. It's well after supper. Unless she's gone out calling."

"Has she made lots of friends?"

"I wouldn't know."

With the rain coming to a stop, Lili had talked her father into allowing her to ride into town with him to gather up a few supplies. Molly bounced happily on his knee as they rolled along. In her finagling, Lili had also managed to convince him to take her to visit Miss Merriwether. If it hadn't been for the fact that the sun had peeked out, the air had dried and cooled considerably, and Molly was in chipper spirits, he'd have frowned at the notion. However, he did need more roofing nails for the cabin, additional screws, and some different hinges for the new door he was installing. He just hoped old Mr. Johansson was still open for business at the mercantile. The man kept the strangest hours.

"What color is her hair?" Lili asked out of the blue.

"What?"

"Miss Merriwether's hair."

Uncomfortable with trying to explain the teacher's fair looks, he said, "You'll find out soon enough."

"Don't you even know?" she asked, eyes filled with disbelief. Molly sang a happy tune of her own making as the wagon took each bump and curve in the well-traveled road.

Ben kissed Molly on the top of her blond head and smiled down at Lili. "I told you everything I'm going to tell you, sugar. You will have to make your own conclusions as to your teacher's looks when you meet her."

"Oh, I just know she will be pretty," she cried, exuding excitement.

Sighing, he asked, "Lili, what does it matter how she will look?"

"Mama was pretty. I just want to look at another pretty lady."

Ben's heart fell clear to his toes then crawled slowly back into position. How should he respond to a remark like that? Lili rarely talked about her mother, although he'd certainly never discouraged her. Sometimes he wondered if she'd put her mother out of her mind completely. A child's early memories didn't often stand the test of time, but Lili's comment eased his mind on that theory.

"Well then, I suppose you won't be disappointed," he managed to say.

The town was bustling with activity for early evening. Perhaps it was the fact that the hot temperatures had let up, lifting folks' spirits. Several men stood clustered on the sidewalk in front of the post office, conversing, while their womenfolk carried on their own conversation in front of Flanders' Food Store up the road.

A couple of dogs chasing after a cat crossed in front of the wagon, and Ben had to pull back on the reins in order to allow their frantic passage. He passed by Sam's Livery and waved at Rocky Callahan, who was just leaving. Rocky was an old friend who'd come upon some hard times of his own, having lost his wife to smallpox some three years ago; and, as if one loss wasn't enough, his four-year-old son had died from a high fever mere months ago. The man's face never had regained its ready smile. It was one thing to lose a beloved wife, but a child as well? Rocky had stopped coming to church altogether, making Ben wonder if he'd lost his faith along with his family.

Johansson's Mercantile bore a *Closed* sign, but the man himself sat on a rocker outside his establishment. Ben drove his rig up to the hitching post, climbed down with Molly in his arms and Lili close behind, and then wrapped the reins around the post.

"Mind if I pick up a few supplies inside?" Ben asked.

"Sign says closed," Eldred Johansson said, pointing.

"I can read," Ben said with a grin, "but I thought since you were sitting right here that perhaps you wouldn't mind…"

"Well, now that you put it that way, I suppose I could open for a few minutes more. Just for you, mind you."

"Much obliged, Eldred."

The aged man stood to his feet, then delivered a mischievous look. "'Sides, I do think I have a few extra candy sticks in my drawer just longing to go to some sweet little girls."

"That so?" Ben asked, playing along.

"Papa…" Lili whispered, squeezing his hand.

The wagon filled with supplies to last at least a few more days, the Broughton family headed in the direction of Emma Browning's Boardinghouse. Lili sucked daintily on her strawberry candy stick, while Molly went at her orange one with a vengeance, slobbering and wiping her sticky fingers on Ben's Levi's every time the need arose.

At the front door, Emma greeted the three of them with a smile. Wearing a plain gown that gathered at her trim waist, she wiped her brow with the back of her hand and laughed as soon as she laid eyes on them. "Well, my, my, look who's here. How ya'll been?"

Ben returned the smile, suddenly and unexpectedly nervous at the prospect of asking to see Miss Merriwether. He didn't want any rumors passing about him coming to call on the new schoolteacher. "We're just fine, Emma. You?"

"Me? Gracious, I'm good as can be considerin' I got me a crop o' hooligans stayin' under my roof. Sure do wish I could get some decent men to come and stay for a change."

Ben laughed. "You could always say no to the worst of them."

"Oh, I do, believe me. I weed through 'em much as I can. Matter o' fact, I sent old Ezra Browning on his way the other night. Sent him off to Guttersnipe's place. That man was just a swimmin' in his ale. Couldn't have made it back to his own place if he'd had a rope tied around him and someone pulling him there."

It amazed Ben how she referred to her drunken father as if he were just another lout off the street. He'd heard tales of her upbringing, even remembered as a kid the cuts and bruises she'd endured at her father's cruel hand. But the truth was she'd come through it tough as nails and with a seemingly good-natured outlook.

Of course, she was standoffish with men, and with good right. To his knowledge, she'd never courted a single soul, although she certainly was pretty enough to win most any man's notice. Most had come to accept her for who she was—engaging from a distance but downright lethal if you got too close.

Ben, however, rated differently. He'd never approached her on any level but friendly. Thus, she'd let down her defenses with him, allowing for a sort of affable alliance between them.

"Would you like to come in?"

"Is Miss Merriwether here?" Lili shot out before Ben even had the chance to explain their sudden appearance on Emma's doorstep.

"Lili, I was getting to that," he said, laying a hand on Lili's head and willing her to keep quiet. Then, giving Emma an apologetic look, he said, "Lili's been very excited about meeting the new school-teacher."

Emma smiled and bent down so her face came within inches of Lili's. "Why, look at how you've grown. I hardly even recognized you, honey."

Lili smiled and stood tall. "Thank you, Miss Browning. Is she?"

"What? Oh, Miss Merriwether?" She stood back up and lent her index finger to Molly, who hadn't stopped working on her candy stick for one second. Molly spared a sticky hand for Emma's finger and passed her a quick smile that revealed two front teeth the color of her orange stick. Emma smiled at Molly, then turned a serious eye on Ben.

"Miss Merriwether hasn't been here since mornin'," she whispered. "I'm gettin' nervous, Ben. I would've thought she'd at least come back for supper, particularly since she didn't take any lunch along, even though I offered to send her off with somethin'."

"Where'd she go?" he asked, mildly concerned.

"As far as I know she was plannin' on workin' at the school. But that was hours ago."

"I'm sure she's off visiting someone."

"Don't think she's made any friends to speak of yet," Emma replied.

"Maybe she decided to walk the streets, get to know folks."

Emma looked doubtful. "She was a woman on a mission, if you know what I mean. She intended to put some hours in at that class-room of hers, but I didn't think she'd be gone all day."

"I'll go have a look around."

"Oh, would you? That'd be mighty nice of you. Why don't you leave the girls here? I'll keep them occupied."

69

"Thanks." He transferred his sticky younger daughter into Emma's arms. As long as no one threatened to steal her candy stick away, Molly was happy to go with most anyone. Lili, on the other hand, had a mind to stick with him. Her hand went immediately into his.

"I'll go with Papa," she voiced.

"Lili, I'd rather you stayed here with Miss Browning," he said.

"But what if you can't find Miss Merriwether? What if something's happened to her? What if she needs me?"

Ben smiled. "I'm sure she is perfectly fine. As soon as I locate her, I'll bring her back here to meet you."

"I have some toys stored away in that box over there just for those special occasions when youngin's come around. Help yourself," Emma said, pointing to a large trunk across the parlor.

That was the only invitation Lili needed. Investigating a box full of toys she'd never seen before was a hard offer to turn down. Ben winked at Emma. "Thanks," he whispered. "Now stop worrying. I'm sure Miss Merriwether is fine. I'll check the school first. She just might still be working in the classroom."

Emma pushed him out the door. "Then go tell her she's put in a long enough day and it's time she came back here for some nourishment and rest."

Ben chuckled. "I—don't think she would take to my using that sort of tone with her. I've already discovered the woman has a mind of her own."

Emma laughed. "Well then, you've discovered more about her than I have, Benjamin Broughton. I fear she'll move into that cabin of yours before we have the chance to get acquainted."

❋ ❋ ❋ ❋ ❋

Liza shifted on the hard seat and dabbed at a few more useless tears. Her throat felt parched and dry from all her squawking and squealing for help. A lot of good it had done her. So far the only visitors she'd had were a sniffing dog and a squirrel or two. Even the dog meandered off, obviously disinterested in her dilemma, although she'd been desperate enough to try to convince him to run for help. "You dumb mongrel!" she had called after him when his sniffing ceased and he sauntered away.

Her emotions had run the gamut. Countless times she went from expectation to doom all in the span of a few seconds. Every time she heard the sound of distant galloping hooves or the racket of a wagon's passing she jumped to her feet and yelled for help, only to have her hopes smashed to smithereens. More than once she'd given in to tears then just as quickly brushed them aside. It wouldn't look good to her rescuer to find her blubbering like a helpless little fool. He'd go straight to Mrs. Winthrop and tell her the school board had failed. No, it was best to keep her head about her.

When daylight turned to dusk, however, her emotions turned inward, more weighty and reflective. She had no way of knowing what time it was, as she'd taken off her wristwatch before washing windows. What if no one found her? What if she had to spend the night in this disgusting place? Worse, two nights! Three! Perchance Miss Browning thought Liza had slipped inside the house unawares and was in her room reclining. But why would her proprietor check on her whereabouts? Liza was not the responsibility of Emma Browning.

Stories, unimaginable, formulated in her mind along with grotesque pictures of herself when at last they discovered her pathetic, rotting body. "New Teacher Found Dead in Outhouse," the headline would read. "Funeral Pending Until Further Notice."

71

And how would Aunt Hettie and Uncle Gideon feel once they learned the truth and then had to explain it? Folks would ask, "What took her, Hettie? Was it the plague? Consumption? Malaria?" Aunt Hettie would cover her mouth with the corner of her handkerchief and cry crocodile tears. "No, no, not that," she would wail. "It was the outhouse, yes, it was. The one in the back of Little Hickman's schoolyard!"

Liza's lower lip quivered at the thought.

"Dear Lord, what am I to do?" she asked.

The thought struck her that she'd spent more time fretting about her hopeless set of circumstances than praying about them. Now, in addition to the fear and panic that hovered overhead, she had a fresh batch of guilt to deal with.

"**Fear thou not; for I am with thee: be not dismayed; for I am thy God: I will strengthen thee; yea, I will help thee; yea, I will uphold thee with the right hand of my righteousness.**" She began to recite aloud every verse she'd committed to memory during her Sunday school days, thankful now for the persistent Mrs. Grunthum, who'd forever looked down her long, pointed nose unhappily if anyone dared come to class unprepared.

Patience is a virtue. The silly idiom came back as a cruel reminder, but why did the face of Benjamin Broughton have to accompany it?

"**Rest in the Lord, and wait patiently for him.**" The memorized passage rolled off her lips. "I'm trying, Lord, but this is Liza, your naturally impatient child, the one who often thinks she knows so much until You show her the error of her ways. I know You have a plan for me, Father, but does it have to include sitting in this outhouse?"

Patience is a virtue. There it was again. She folded her arms and made a sound of disgust when she clicked her tongue against the roof of her mouth. As Hickman's new teacher, she should have known about Chaucer's writings. Why did it have to take a burly, albeit handsome, farmer to set her straight?

She'd heard that the circuit preacher was riding into town next Sunday. If she was still alive next week, she intended to arrive early enough to sit in the front row. That should tell Mr. Broughton that she took her faith seriously. The fact that she'd mistaken an ancient idiom for a passage of Scripture was insignificant. After all, God knew her heart. What did it matter what some striking Englishman thought of her?

As the minutes turned to hours, Liza leaned her back against the hard wall. Drowsy in spite of her state of affairs, she allowed her eyes to close. The rain had long quit, and with it came a stillness, the only sounds she heard being the distant hoot of an owl or the snap of a branch overhead. If she were back at Emma's house in bed she would have enjoyed the serenity of the moment. But now the silence merely haunted her.

She must have temporarily dozed, for she found herself jumping to alertness at the sound of someone's approach. It seemed paramount to yell for help, but on the other hand, the rabble-rousers responsible for getting her into this fix just might be the ones drawing closer. Was locking her in this place just the first step to what they planned to do with her once nightfall came?

Fear mixed with her blood, sending quivery chills up and down her body. She swallowed down a hard lump and took a settling breath. "Who's there?" she said in a voice that hardly qualified as a whisper. Strange how she'd screamed and squawked all afternoon in the daylight, but now that night had fallen, an all-new feeling of dread had come to make its home in her.

"Is anyone in here?" came a male voice. A strangely familiar voice at that.

73

"Yes." Liza felt hope rise up in her chest.

"Liza? Miss Merriwether?"

It was him! Or was she growing delusional?

"Yes," she exclaimed, jumping to her feet and hopping up and down, as if there was a need to let him know she was inside. Suddenly she was pounding on the door. "Let me out, let me out. Hurry!"

"Well, just a minute. Hold your horses."

"What? Hold my horses? I'll have you know I've been in here for hours on end. And you have the nerve to tell me to hold my horses?"

Even over the sounds of his walking around the shed two, three, four times, she heard his low chuckle. How he could even think of laughing at a time like this was beyond her. "I have to get this rope untied," he explained, his voice too calm. She wanted to scream at him to work faster. Oh, for a breath of fresh, clean air.

It wasn't until the door opened and she looked into the face of her rescuer that she remembered what she must look like. She'd come out in the drenching rain; her dress had soaked clear through to her skin; her hair had fallen away from its tight little knot; her eyes were no doubt swollen from hours of on-and-off crying spells. Oh, what must he think?

But none of that mattered one iota, for as soon as she laid eyes on him she flew into his arms.

Chapter Six

*H*ey, what's this?" Ben asked, putting an awkward arm around the hysterical woman.

Ben couldn't explain the relief he felt at finding Miss Merriwether. He'd spent a full hour walking through town, peeking inside windows, even knocking on a few doors to ask if anyone had seen her. But no one had. When mild concern evolved into outright worry, he began to pray that God would keep her safe wherever she was.

About the time he had decided to walk over to Sheriff Murdock's office and report her missing, he determined to have one last look at the schoolhouse. He'd made a thorough search inside the building earlier, but he hadn't thought to look around the yard, certainly not in the outhouse.

The storm had given way to a clear, starry night, and with it, a bright moon to shed an evening glow—enough so that he'd been able to see the rope tied securely around one of the little shacks out back, the one marked *Girls*. At first he'd thought the rope was there to keep people out. For all he knew the school board had ordered it closed for maintenance. Maybe they planned to move it to a new location. But if that were the case, why hadn't someone locked the other one up as well?

When he'd drawn nearer and detected a sound inside, he knew he'd found the elusive Miss Merriwether, particularly when she started ranting at him to hurry things along. Relief mingled first with amusement, then confusion, and finally disgust. Who would do such a thing?

"Are you all right?" he asked, momentarily putting her away from him.

"No," she exclaimed, going right back into the circle of his arms. "I thought I was going to die in there. I even imagined the newspapers reporting my death. And then my funeral. And then poor Uncle Gideon and Aunt Hettie."

"Who?"

"Never mind." She sniffed and wiped her nose on his shirt.

She was a sight to behold with her hair having fallen into total disrepair, her dress hanging in a mass of wrinkles, her eyes and nose red and swollen, and the whole of her looking about as attractive as any female he'd ever laid eyes on.

"Do you have any idea who locked you inside that thing?" he asked. He didn't quite know how to react to this woman in his arms. It'd been so long since he'd held one.

"No, but if I did I'd have their hides hanging on the nearest clothesline."

At last she pulled away from him and straightened her skirt as best she could. He guessed she'd been sitting on it for the better share of the day.

"Any ideas at all?" he persisted.

"I told you, no. I couldn't see a thing. I tried to find a peephole or a crack, but they've sealed that place up good and tight. In fact, I was beginning to wonder if my lack of oxygen in there would steal away my life before I had the chance to starve or languish from thirst."

He found himself smiling at her colorful embellishment. "I don't think that would have happened. There are air vents right overhead," he told her, pointing. "See those openings?"

Refusing to look where he pointed, she placed both hands on her hips. "It is quite clear that you do not share in my plight even one little bit. That was a most uncomfortable situation to be in, Mr. Broughton."

Ah, so now it was back to formalities. That was fine with him. Besides, he had no business looking at the schoolteacher in any way but friendly. Nor did he have any business remembering what she'd felt like in his arms mere moments ago.

"I'm sure it was and I sympathize entirely, truly, I do."

"Then why are you smiling?"

He straightened his face. "You amuse me, that's all."

"Humph." She turned and started to walk, so he followed after. "I know there were more than one."

"More than one?" he asked, confused.

"Perpetrator," she clarified. When he caught the calculating tone in her voice, he knew the weaker side of Miss Merriwether had suddenly vanished.

"Well, that's something to go on. It was a group effort then."

She stopped and stared at him. "You aren't laughing at me, are you?"

"Absolutely not. I just find it ironic that you haven't even had your first day of school yet, and already there are problems. Are you sure—?"

"Don't even suggest I go back to Boston, Mr. Broughton. I am here to stay. At least for the year. That is what I agreed to when I signed the contract, and I shall not go back on my word."

With that, she resumed walking, holding her head high. He hurried to catch up.

"That's good. You'll need that stubborn streak running through you when you meet up with some of your students. I've heard stories that would curl your toes."

"Well, I've had about all the toe curling I can stand for one day, thank you. I believe I'll go back to the house and have a nice hot bath."

"Not so fast," he said, taking her by the arm. "You and I are going to pay a visit to the sheriff's office first." He started hauling her in another direction.

"What?" She stopped dead in her tracks and yanked her arm from his grasp. "I will not report this incident."

"Why not? Pranksters played a nasty trick on you. If you don't report it, they'll think they've won. They'll stop at nothing to wear you down, run you out of town. It's happened to three other teachers in the last three years."

"Well, it's not going to happen to me. And I'm not going to report this to anyone. I happen to think that if I report it, they'll get an even bigger laugh. Not only will it make me the laughingstock of Little Hickman, but they'll have the satisfaction of knowing the sheriff isn't going to spend more than five minutes on a silly little incident like this."

"Silly? Aren't you the one who was crying hysterically just moments ago and soaking the front of my shirt?" He pointed to the wet splotch in the middle of his chest.

She looked only a little embarrassed. "Well, I've come to my senses," she said, sticking out her pert little chin and resuming her steps.

"Really."

"Yes. You and I and—those hooligans—are the only ones who know about this incident, and I wish for it to stay that way, Mr. Broughton."

"But that's ridiculous," he argued, matching her gait. "A crime was committed."

"That was no crime. It was a childish prank. I intend to find out who was responsible, but I won't bring the law into it."

"And how do you expect to find out?" he asked, growing irritated with her stubborn streak.

"I haven't quite determined that, but I will. Give me time."

They walked the rest of the way in silence.

Emma Browning met them on the front porch, her worried expression quickly replaced by a wholehearted smile. "Oh, Miss Merriwether, I was so concerned about you. Where have you been? And look at you!" Emma held a sleepy Molly in her arms. A wide-eyed Lili stood beside her.

"I've been at the school," Liza said.

"My goodness. Since this morning?" Emma exclaimed. "I don't think the school board expects you to spend every waking minute there. You must be tired and hungry."

Liza smiled at Emma's constant chatter. "I'm perfectly fine, Miss Browning, although I am a tad hungry and thirsty."

"Why o' course you are. It will only take me a moment to warm some stew." She handed Molly over into Ben's arms, then gave Liza a stern look. "You'll call me Emma."

Liza smiled. "All right then."

That settled, Emma hurried inside, leaving the rest of them standing on the porch.

"Papa, is this really her?" Lili whispered, tugging on his arm, her gaze traveling from him to Liza and back to him.

"It is. Miss Merriwether, meet my older daughter, Lili, and my younger one, Molly." Molly had snuggled into the curve of her father's neck, quite disinterested in the newcomer.

The first thing Liza did was bend over so that her height matched that of the inquiring child's, although she didn't have to bend far. "I'm very happy to meet you, Lili. Your father tells me you will be one of my students."

At first Lili appeared speechless, perhaps even shy, as her eyes roamed the full length of Liza's small frame. "I'm almost as big as you."

"You're tall for your age and I'm rather short for mine. I guess that makes us quite a pair."

"Are you old enough to be a teacher?"

"Lili." Ben laid his hand atop Lili's blond head.

Liza laughed. "Do I look that young?"

"Yes. But at least you're pretty. I asked Papa if you were, but he wouldn't say. I knew she'd be pretty, Papa." The child's outspoken manner had Ben squirming where he stood.

"Lili, don't embarrass Miss Merriwether."

Liza stood up and took Lili's hand. "I'm not embarrassed. In fact, I think I shall make a point to seat you close to my desk for those occasions when I might need an encouraging word or two."

Lili brightened. "Did you hear that, Papa? Perhaps I'll wind up being her favorite little girl."

Liza laughed again. "Well, you never can tell."

"I will pound your erasers for you every day if you like, and straighten up the classroom, and pick up slates, and—"

"How about we discuss classroom responsibilities later?" Liza suggested with a smile.

"It's running late, Lil," Ben interrupted. "We best be going."

"But, Papa, Miss Merriwether and me just met."

"Miss Merriwether and *I* just met," he corrected.

"I thought you met a couple days ago," Lili said, confused.

Liza laughed outright. "I think your papa is right; I need to get some rest. It's been a very—long day." She threw Ben a knowing look, and he couldn't resist the urge to chuckle, though it still bothered him that she refused to report the incident. He was tempted to go to the sheriff on his own, but he'd halfway agreed to keep the matter quiet.

"Lili, you go climb in the wagon. I'll be along shortly."

"But, Papa..."

"Go." Sometimes all it took was one word and a stern look to make his message clear. This was one of those moments. Offering one last smile to her new teacher, Lili turned and headed for the wagon. "I'll come visit you again if Papa brings me, Miss Merriwether," she called.

"You do that, Lili," Liza returned. Then to Ben, "She is charming."

"I hope you find her so in a couple of months."

"I've no doubt I will." She reached a finger to Molly's cheek, then looked at Ben and whispered, "I want to thank you for rescuing me."

"You're welcome."

"I suppose I was a tiny bit hysterical at first."

"You had the right to be."

She looked surprised. "Really?"

He gave her a thin smile. "You should talk to Sheriff Murdock. I think he'd give the matter more than a five-minute investigation."

"Perhaps. But I meant it when I said I want this to remain under your hat."

Hesitating as he thought that over, he finally said, "I'll agree, but on one condition."

"What is that?"

"If even one more such incident occurs, or you are threatened in any way whatsoever, you will go straight to the sheriff."

"And if I don't agree?"

"Then I shall have to take the matter into my own hands." With that, he tipped his head toward hers and, with his index finger, tapped her lightly on the tip of her nose.

She stepped back, as if the tiny touch of his finger had emitted a shock. "I suppose that is reasonable, Mr. Broughton."

"Do you ever intend to call me Ben?"

"No." She gave him a sheepish look. "You are, after all, the parent of one of my students."

"Which would make it quite improper, I suppose?"

"Precisely."

He chuckled. "You are quite a lady, Miss Merriwether."

❄ ❄ ❄ ❄ ❄

Thankfully, the next several days passed without incident. Liza busied herself in her classroom, dusting, scrubbing the hard plank flooring, washing windowsills, sorting through old files and notes from former teachers, and learning what she could about her forth-coming students.

From what she had determined, she was to have two first graders, three second graders, two third graders, three fourth graders, three sixth graders, and five students that ranged between the ages of twelve to fifteen, all of whom were working at varying levels. If her figuring were accurate, she would greet exactly eleven boys and seven girls on the morning of Monday, August 26.

The schoolhouse was situated at the end of Main Street, easily within walking distance of Emma Browning's place. It was a tall, rectangular building with a steep, gabled roof, white clapboard siding, and three uniform windows on each of the longer sides. The front of the schoolhouse had three steps going up to a wide front door, while the back of the schoolhouse had a much narrower door. She expected the students would use that door for such times as taking trips to the necessary, going out to the small playing field, or hauling in coal with which to feed the fire. In the winter months they would use the front door for entering and exiting since the coat hooks were stationed there.

In the course of conversing with Emma, Liza had learned that local farmers and a few handy businessmen had joined together some five years earlier to erect the structure, building it in its entirety in less than a week. In addition to building the schoolhouse, they had also borne the work and cost of providing the outhouses. Once these were completed, the town had raised sufficient funds with which to purchase new textbooks and a few desks. Apparently they'd considered the remainder of the secondhand desks sufficient, although Liza would beg to differ on that point. Most were wobbly and marred from years of use. There were exactly thirty desks, and so she'd determined to put to the side those that were in the worst shape and use them for storing items such as extra readers, teaching supplies, and writing tools.

Liza knew that once she moved out to the Broughton cabin she would need to consider some mode of transportation but had decided not to worry about it until colder weather set in. Until then she would walk, making the extra half-mile trek to the creek's crossing. Perhaps she would meet up with Lili on the way, and they could keep each other company.

It was Saturday morning. Dazzling sunlight cast its glow through the open classroom windows, throwing lazy shadows across the floor and heating up the room. Liza was preparing to take the trash barrel to the outside receptacle when she heard the schoolhouse door open. Whirling around, she discovered Mrs. Winthrop standing in the entryway.

"Mrs. Winthrop!"

"I thought I would drop by to see how you're handling things. I've heard from various sources that you're spending every waking minute in this place." Mrs. Winthrop set about examining the room in its entirety.

Liza gave an uneasy laugh. "I wouldn't go so far as to say every waking minute, but it is true that I've spent a good deal of time here. I've much to do to prepare for my first day of school."

"Yes, it is coming up, isn't it? Do you think you shall be ready in another week's time?"

Liza's stomach knotted at the thought. "Yes, I'm quite certain I will be."

If anyone looked the picture of wealth and refinery, Mrs. Winthrop did in her long, shirtwaist gown of deep purple. The leg-of-mutton sleeves looked hot and uncomfortable, but they were in vogue according to a fashion magazine Liza had had occasion to browse through while still living in Boston. A matching hat with a frilled flap called a *bavolet* attached to the back of it to protect her neck from the sun, covered her head, where Liza could only imagine a tightly pulled back bun. To add to her stylish look she carried a small bag in one hand and a purple parasol in the other.

Certainly, she was the best-dressed woman in a town that appeared not to have much in the way of possessions. Liza knew nothing about her other than that her husband owned the town's only dry goods store. One thing she did know was that Mrs. Winthrop insisted on propriety, and so it also made her wonder what the woman thought of Liza's own simple calico dress with the missing button, the three-quarter length sleeves, and the apron front.

"I see that you have cleaned this place up with particular care." Mrs. Winthrop walked to the windowsill and rubbed a palm along the wooden surface.

"I have tried," Liza replied.

The woman managed a smile. "Yes, well, very good. Are you finding everything you need, then?"

"Yes, I believe so."

"I would imagine there aren't nearly as many teaching supplies as you would like. Heaven knows I have tried to convince this town to do better in the way of supporting its school."

"We will make do." There were plenty of stone slates and chalk, several reams of old paper, and a good supply of lead pencils. Liza had been happy to find that the majority of the textbooks were in decent shape. In the tall cupboard at the back of the room she had discovered a number of *Comly's Spellers,* the *Introduction to English Reader,* plenty of arithmetic and geography books, and several penmanship books. Of course, they showed wear, but not one was missing pages.

"I should think you would be comfortable in the winter. The stove is rather new, added when the building was built." Mrs. Winthrop seemed especially proud of that fact. "The farmers tried to reinstall the old one, but at my insistence, the town purchased a new one. It only seemed fitting in light of the fact that the building was freshly built."

"I appreciate that, Mrs. Winthrop. It's hard to believe on a hot day such as today that we will ever need a stove, but I'm sure we will."

"Our winters can grow very bitter, my dear. But I'm sure you're used to that—coming from Boston."

"Yes."

"We don't get much snow, but the frigid temperatures can be particularly loathsome."

The woman lingered, and Liza wondered if she had more to say. Not wanting to dismiss her intentionally, Liza merely picked up the wastebasket she'd earlier meant to carry outside.

"Oh, I should also remind you that tomorrow is Sunday."

"Yes, I'm quite aware," Liza replied.

"You shan't be working on the Lord's Day, I would hope."

"Of course not."

"The service will be held here, as you know," the woman said, lifting her shoulders.

"Yes, I've been told."

"There are benches out in the building at the back of the property. At 7:00 a.m. several of the church elders will move the student desks to the back of the room and make way for the benches. I hope that won't be too much of an inconvenience for you."

Liza offered up a smile but noted Mrs. Winthrop didn't return one. "Not at all."

"I will be here to supervise, of course," she added with a hint of authority.

"Thank you. I appreciate that," Liza said.

"I would expect to see you in service, of course. After all, the teacher of Little Hickman has a reputation to uphold. But then, no doubt you recall all the rules of etiquette that you agreed to adhere to when you signed the contract."

"Naturally. I will do my best not to disappoint you." Liza prayed her mounting irritation didn't show.

Mrs. Winthrop gave just a hint of a smile. "Well then, I suppose I should allow you to get back to work." With that, she waved and headed out the door, seeming to leave a chilly draft in her wake.

At suppertime, Liza locked up the schoolhouse, knowing that Mrs. Winthrop had a key with which to unlock the building for the elders in the morning. The neighborhood was peaceful and the main street quiet. Here and there, people passed her on the wooden sidewalk, nodded their greetings, offering warm smiles.

Perhaps life in Little Hickman would be pleasant after all.

Chapter Seven

*L*ili, it's time we headed for town. Church will be starting in less than thirty minutes."

"Is Reverend Miller going to preach today?" Lili bounded out of her room all smiles. Her hair ribbons were crooked again, but it couldn't be helped. Ben had had a difficult time as it was getting both girls moving this morning. The uncanny heat of the night had seemed to steal away a good share of everyone's sleep.

"As far as I know," he said with a smile.

Reverend Miller had been circuit riding for well over fifty years. To Ben's knowledge, the man serviced three other churches, traveling from one town to the next every week, and paying visits to sick parishioners all over the region throughout the week. The man easily surpassed seventy and suffered from chronic heart problems. Ben worried that he would keel over on some deserted country road, and no one would discover him till spring.

As far as Ben was concerned, Little Hickman had grown big enough to support a preacher of its own, and he'd been hoping his longtime friend, Jonathan Atkins, might assume the position. Jon had recently completed his seminary degree and moved back to town.

Of course, there were bound to be those who would balk at the idea of having to increase their giving. A full-time preacher would require a salary. It would seem there were some in the church who had not yet caught the vision that God was bigger than any of them could imagine. Just the same, he meant to bring up the matter at the next church council meeting.

"Do you suppose he'll have a peppermint stick in his pocket?"

Ben gave his daughter another grin. "He usually does. But don't ask him for one. That would not be polite."

"I know that, Papa. Usually I just go up to him and smile very pretty, and that is all it takes to get him to reach into his pocket."

"Lili," Ben said in a scolding tone while fighting back a smile, "where do you learn such impish ways?"

Shrugging, she laughed and skipped out of the house, leaving him to tend to a whimpering Molly.

The schoolhouse was packed to the gills this morning. Whether it was because people wanted to check out the improvements inside, or whether they were hoping to get a look at the new teacher, Ben couldn't say. He wanted to believe it was because folks were anxious to worship God on this hotter-than-usual August morning.

He spotted Miss Merriwether almost immediately. There she was, bright as could be in her rose-colored gown and prim little hat. She'd found a place in the very front row and, although he wouldn't have minded greeting her, he certainly wouldn't make a point to do so. At least there were several folks gathered around her to make her feel welcome. For that Ben was happy.

"Papa, there's Miss Merriwether," Lili said, tugging on his arm as they made their way past other worshippers to sit on a bench about halfway back.

"So I see."

"Can we go sit with her?" she asked midway down the pew.

"No, Lili. We will sit here."

"Can *I* go sit with her?"

"We will sit as a family."

Molly began to fidget as soon as they sat, and Ben told her in a whisper to behave, bringing about a batch of tears. Frustrated, Ben shifted her on his lap and jostled her, but she wouldn't be comforted. When Molly's cries intensified and she started kicking, several heads turned, particularly those of the women. Somehow he managed to ignore their blatant stares and kept up with his incessant bouncing.

To Ben's relief Carl Hardy went to the front and led the gathering in the singing of the first hymn. Ben sang out in his deep bass voice, hoping to drown out the sounds of his anxious child. Lili paid no mind to her sister's whimpers, more bent on getting a better view of the much more exciting Eliza Merriwether.

At the close of the five-verse song, Molly was still going strong. In fact, she'd geared up for her second round by the sounds of it, her blotchy, puffy face and runny nose a clear indication of her sour mood. "Lili, stay here," Ben instructed quietly. "I'll try to calm Molly outside. I'll be back as soon as I can."

"Can I go sit with Miss Merriwether?" Lili whispered loudly.

Pausing in the middle of the row, and knowing he was blocking the view of everyone behind him, he nodded in haste. He was in no position to argue with her, and Lili knew it. He would have to speak with her later for having manipulated him unfairly, particularly when he'd already told her no. Of course, he'd also told her they would sit as a family, and now here he was deserting her.

Ben paced outside the building in an attempt to calm Molly. A woman would know what to do, he ruled. *Ridiculous.* No woman knew his Molly the way he did. She was simply going through a persnickety stage, as he'd heard one woman refer to these cranky times, and no amount of fussing by any woman would change that fact. Still, the notion that two heads were better than one came to mind and stuck there.

"God, what would You have me do?" he muttered heavenward, mopping his wet brow as he marched about. Seeing a shady oak tree to stand under, he made for the spot while talking in low tones to Molly.

Life was anything but easy these days with the farm chores never ending, the housework mounting, those feelings of failure as a single parent spiraling, and now the pressure to finish the cabin. He was only one man. How was he supposed to pull it all together?

"Be still and know that I am God…" The familiar verse of Scripture buried itself in his consciousness, and he thanked his heavenly Father for the gentle reminder. Still, it didn't solve the problem of Molly's hysteria and his own sense of helplessness.

"Peace I leave with you…" Another wonderful reminder of God's faithfulness and ability to care for his needs if he would simply let them all go into His hands. Easier said than done, he ruled, as he sat down and then leaned against the aged oak's trunk.

At long last, Molly settled into his chest and heaved a couple of long, deep sighs. He suspected she'd slept as restlessly as he had last night. "Feeling better?" he asked in a gentle tone, rubbing her soft cheek with his callused hand. As if in answer she looked up at him and managed a weak smile. "Now you decide to smile," he said with a chuckle. "What got into you?" he asked, reaching into his back pocket for a handkerchief with which to wipe her eyes and runny nose. Pulling it out, he also pulled out a rumpled piece of paper. After wiping her face, he unwrapped the piece of paper to study its contents.

MARRIAGE MADE IN HEAVEN AGENCY

It was the classified ad he'd run across in the post office a couple of weeks ago. Was it some kind of sign from God that he'd drawn it from his pocket in the churchyard? He studied the ad again, noting each woman's name with particular care and then her individual specifications. *Specifications* seemed an odd word to use in describing each woman's character, rather like searching out a prize horse.

Each one of these women claimed to be God-fearing, even going so far as to describe briefly their testimonies of faith, although the space given them to do so was sorely lacking.

Molly crawled off his lap and began to toddle around the tree, bending to pick up a small stick and then tossing it back in favor of a different one. Ben watched her momentarily and then went back to the advertisement.

The name Sarah Woodward cemented itself in his mind. He'd studied each entry carefully and always his eyes traveled back to hers.

My name is Sarah Woodward. I am a fine, upstanding Christian woman looking for a Christian man with whom to build a home. I am an enthusiastic person who is not afraid of work. I dearly love children. I stand five feet six inches tall, and am what you would call fine-boned, aptly filled out, and well bred. I have red hair that people often refer to as flaming and blue-green eyes, better known as hazel, I suppose.

I enjoy housekeeping duties and am an especially excellent cook. I shall do my best to make some Christian man a fine wife.

**Please contact this agency at the above noted address for further information. Any one of these women will be happy to correspond prior to making traveling arrangements. All impending costs will be the responsibility of the prospective groom.

Ben folded the paper neatly and put it back into his pocket. What was he doing by holding on to this silly advertisement? Did he actually think that sending for a bride was a workable solution? On the one hand, it would solve the issue of caring for his children and managing the household chores. Mrs. Granger was leaving for St. Louis in a matter of days. On the other hand, what if this Sarah Woodward turned out to be completely incompatible?

Flaming red hair…hazel eyes…tall and curved. She sounded like his Miranda, except for the red hair.

Was that it, then? Was he looking for a replacement for his dead wife, someone whose looks, work ethic, and personality matched those of Miranda Broughton? The notion both shamed and enticed him. Of course, it wouldn't be fair to Miss Sarah Woodward if he spent his days comparing the two of them. Then again, she'd never know if he didn't let on.

It would be good to have a woman around the house again.

And the more he thought about it, the more appealing it sounded.

The clip-clop of an approaching horse stole his attention. Quickly he sought out Molly and found her intent on something near her feet, clumsily trying to bend over it without toppling.

"Hullo there, Benjamin," came a booming voice.

Surprised to see Rocky Callahan reining in his horse, Ben pulled himself up from his place under the tree and walked toward his friend, keeping one eye on Molly as he did so.

"Hi, Rocky. Arriving for church, are you?" At close range he noted dark circles beneath the man's eyes. As rough-hewn and brawny as he was, the pain still showed in his weary expression.

"Naw. Thought I'd ride into town and see if Sam is at the livery. I got to pick up some shoes he's been working on for one of my horses."

"I see." Choosing his words carefully, Ben squinted up at the fellow, the bright sun's rays blocking all but his broad physique. "How have you been, Rock?"

 92

Ben thought once again that he knew the pain of losing a wife, but he couldn't imagine life without his daughters. Not a day went by that he didn't thank the Lord for both of them, as difficult as it sometimes was raising them on his own.

"I've been better."

Distant memories registered of Miranda and him socializing with Rocky and Hester before either of them had started families. They'd been so happy back then, playing games on weekends, talking and singing, laughing and joking, and never dreaming of what lay ahead. It was a paradox of cruel proportions that both he and Rocky had lost wives in their late twenties. Even crueler that Rocky had lost his only child to an incurable fever that took days to run its course. Whenever he thought of it, Ben's heart ached.

"I don't pretend to know what it's like to lose a child, Rocky," Ben said, taking another wistful look back at Molly, who by now had plopped herself in a pile of dirt. "But I do relate to the pain of losing a wife."

"Yeah, well, I guess you know that it's not easy."

"I do." Ben looked at the toe of his boot and kicked at a stray leaf. "What have you been doing with yourself? You've made yourself pretty scarce. I looked for you at the church picnic last month."

"I got no cause for celebration."

"Maybe not," Ben reasoned, praying for the right words, "but a lot of folks missed you just the same." Rocky's horse spooked and sidestepped, giving Ben a better angle with which to study his friend's long face. "Truth is it'd do you good to come around more. It can't be healthy for you to stay holed up out there at your place day after day."

Rocky cursed under his breath. In his own human state even Ben had slipped a time or two with his tongue, but he'd never heard Rocky use a blasphemous word as long as he'd known him. The realization stunned him, but he didn't let on. Instead he berated himself for not keeping better track of how his friend was feeling.

"You know, Rock, sometimes you just have to lift your head up and look to God. He's the best source of strength I know."

Rocky sneered. He gazed out over the horizon as if to measure his words before spewing them. "Don't preach to me about God's love, Ben," he said evenly. "I heard it all before from folks. Hardly a day goes by but what my own Ma don't come out and hound me to get back to church."

"She only wants what's best for you."

Unlike Ben's worldly-wise upbringing, Rocky's had been sound both spiritually and otherwise. Ben hadn't found God until his late teen years, after he'd met and fallen in love with Miranda. In fact, he had her to thank for introducing him to the Lord. Oh, his grandfather had known God, of that he was certain; but it had taken the love of a pretty young woman to set his mind straight on eternal matters.

"I reckon, but I could do with less preaching. Everyone seems to have all the answers. 'Why, it was the Lord's will the way He took Hester and your boy home before their time,'" Rocky said sarcastically, nodding in the direction of the church. "Do folks in there actually think I find those words comforting?"

"I don't know what they think, Rock. Mostly they don't know what to say, and so they figure anything is better than nothing."

Rocky shrugged. "I'd rather they'd leave me alone."

Ben took an unsteady breath. "I don't believe you mean that."

Rocky took off his hat and dashed his fingers through thick, dark strands of hair, then situated the dusty thing back on his head. A soulful rendition of "Amazing Grace" wafted through the open windows of the church. "I best be going."

"Come on out to the house sometime," Ben offered. "My cooking isn't much, but I'd be obliged if you'd join us for supper. I been working on my grandpap's cabin for the new schoolteacher. I could use an extra hand."

"New schoolteacher, eh? I heard she arrived." He looked out over the distant terrain. "My Joseph would have been five years old this fall," he continued. "S'pect he would have been starting school."

Knowing it was pointless to comment, Ben simply nodded. "Might do you good to get your mind off your troubles for a change."

Rocky snapped back to attention. "Yeah, I might swing by sometime." But even as he spoke the words, Ben knew they weren't genuine. Tipping his hat at Ben, he gave a mechanical smile. "Good seein' ya, Ben."

And off he rode, bigger-than-life shoulders drooping, body swaying, as he turned his horse in the direction of Sam's Livery.

❈ ❈ ❈ ❈ ❈

Reverend Miller was a round little man with scant white hair combed over the top of his head to give the appearance of more hair. His searing eyes, filled with wit and wisdom, seemed to reach into a body's depth, making the already warm room seem all the hotter. He spoke with such passion that beads of perspiration formed on his brow and dripped slowly down his wrinkled face, creating little droplets at the bottom of his chin and eventually falling onto the pulpit below. Liza imagined a little pool of salt water mixing with his sermon notes, blurring the inky words.

A few rows back discontented children squirmed and whined until the sounds of shushing parents quelled their cries. Liza could hardly blame the youngsters for their restless behavior. The room had to be pushing ninety degrees.

The stench of body odor wafted over the slow-moving air current, forcing Liza to go for her handkerchief. She cleared her throat and glanced down at Lili Broughton, who had sidled up next to her, claiming Liza as her friend.

"We should all think of our life on this earth as an assignment," the reverend said, his now twinkling eyes resting on Liza. She shifted in her seat, waiting for what would come next. She noticed he didn't mince words.

"There's more to Christianity than meets the eye, my friends," he challenged. "Serving Christ means serving others as well."

"I'm sure the good teacher here would agree that assignments require extra time and commitment. Isn't that right, miss?"

Liza smiled and nodded, feeling the eyes of the congregants fall to her.

"Well, dear people, the same is true of God. One day you will stand before Him and He will issue you a final exam. The Bible says in Romans 14:10–12, 'For we shall all stand before the judgment seat of Christ. For it is written, As I live, saith the Lord, every knee shall bow to me, and every tongue shall confess to God. So then every one of us shall give account of himself to God.'

"Our heavenly Father wants each of us to pass that exam." Again, Reverend Miller looked at Liza. "It's always nice to be on the teacher's good side now, isn't it?" Laughter filled the room, and Lili sidled in closer.

"Because God, our teacher, wants us to spend eternity with Him, He has already told us what questions we can expect on this exam. How wonderful it would be if every teacher would give us the questions in advance. We would know exactly what to study for." A couple of snickers followed.

"What's the questions, preacher?" asked a small voice from the third row. Folks tittered with amusement at the child's barefaced curiosity. Liza hoped the young fellow was a future student.

"Well now, I'm getting to that, son," Reverend Miller said with a ready grin. "The first thing God will want to ask is, did you believe in His Son Jesus Christ." He looked out over his parishioners, as if to size each member up. "He won't ask you about your background, your degree of wealth, or your job. He won't ask you how many times you darkened the church door, and He won't even ask you how much money you put into that offering plate. No sir. The only thing that will matter to God is, did you accept the gift that His Son Jesus offered you, and did you learn to love Him and trust Him with all of your heart?

"According to John 14:6, **'Jesus saith unto him, I am the way, the truth, and the life: no man cometh unto the Father, but by me.'**"

The entire room grew so silent you could have heard two flies in conversation. "And that is the first question God will ask."

"What's the second question?" the same little child asked.

"Ah, yes, the second question." Reverend Miller tugged at his plump, round chin. "I suspect He will ask you what you did with your life—your gifts, your talents, your relationships. Did you spend all of your energy on yourself, trying to please just you? Or did you pour out your life on others? Did you strive to be generous and thoughtful, putting others before yourself? Or did you live only for your own pleasures?

"Tough assignment?" he asked, invoking deep thought. "It's up to you to make good choices, my friends. God wants you to spend eternity with Him. Be sure you are ready with the right answers when He asks you the questions."

The Reverend's words stayed with Liza, even as folks circled around her after the service to introduce themselves. Later, she would take the time to ponder his words more carefully. Yes, and she would make a point to study her Bible more diligently. God knew she needed every ounce of wisdom available before beginning the school year.

Lili stayed close by as folks, too many to count, gathered around to meet the new teacher. There were the Haywards, an elderly couple; the James family, with twin toddlers and, from the looks of it, another on the way; the Bentleys, newly married; and several others whose names she hadn't caught.

Just when Liza thought she'd met most everyone, a slender woman approached from across the aisle. "Miss Merriwether, I'm Bess Barrington. You'll be teachin' my youngins, Erlene and Thomas. My girl's six and my Thom is eleven." The woman quickly pulled her children out in front of her. Erlene offered up a shy, tiny-toothed grin, while Thomas merely tipped his chin with practiced politeness.

"Hello. I shall look forward to getting to know both of you better," Liza said.

"If you have any problems at all, you be sure to let me know, you hear?" Mrs. Barrington said. "The husband and me believe in a good education, and we expect our kids to behave themselves."

"Well, I appreciate that. I'm sure we'll do just fine." Since Thom looked especially embarrassed, Liza gave him a reassuring smile, after which he dipped his head to study his worn-out shoes.

"And this here is Sarah Jenkins. She's thirteen," Lili announced when a freckle-faced girl broke through the circle. Brown hair parted in the middle fell in two long braids, and a bright smile revealing crooked teeth seemed only to add to the girl's charm.

"I'm happy to meet you, Sarah."

"I been itchin' to meet ya, but my ma and pa told me I best be patient. They said school would start soon enough and then I'd be swimmin' in homework instead o' the creek."

"Well, I should hope there'll still be time for swimming when school starts, Sarah. I'd hate to think we'll let all that lovely autumn sunshine go to waste."

Everyone shared a light laugh. "Well now, it's nice to see that the new teacher is getting plenty of attention." Reverend Miller's friendly voice cut through the laughter as he inched his way to the center of the affable crowd.

"Reverend Miller!" shouted Lili. The man smiled knowingly and then reached deep into his pockets. Moments later, he pulled out a handful of candy sticks, and several eager little hands opened wide for the generous offering.

Warmed by the gesture, Liza smiled widely. "I enjoyed your sermon, sir."

"I thank you for that, ma'am. I hope it was taken in the manner in which it was intended." His bright eyes scanned the circle of worshippers as several nodded and mumbled their assent.

"It sure was, Reverend," replied a tall man on the outside of the circle. All eyes and ears turned toward the mellow-sounding voice, including those of Liza. She couldn't remember having met the rather lanky yet sturdy-looking fellow with sandy hair and sun-browned skin. "We all needed to hear those fine words of challenge and insight."

"Well, Jonathan Atkins. Surely is good to see you again, son. Just look at you. How have you been? Are you finished with your schooling, then? Have you met the new teacher?" It was plain the Reverend was partial to him the way he endlessly crooned.

"I couldn't be better; yes, I am; and no, I can't say that I have," he replied in one concise sentence, friendly as could be, poking his way through the parting crowd until he came face-to-face with Liza, his long-fingered hand outstretched to take hers. A keen smile revealed straight, white teeth. "But I should like to now."

99

His grip was firm, his acutely blue eyes penetrating in much the same way as those of the preacher. Liza's immediate instinct was to withdraw, but she let him hold her hand until he dropped it gently to her side. "I'm pleased to meet you, miss," he said with a hint of a southern drawl that also contained a certain quality of refinement. A southern gentleman, she mused.

"Jonathan has been away at seminary," the reverend announced. "And a fine Bible scholar he's become," he hastened to add.

"We sure are proud of him," chimed in a scrawny fellow with tattered shirt and worn workpants. "He growed up in these here parts and come out lookin' clean as a whistle. All edjekated and ever'thin', 'magine that."

Jonathan laughed heartily. "These folks are slightly biased, as you may have noticed. Please don't mind them. It's a pleasure to meet you. I hope you're adjusting to life in Little Hickman."

His friendly demeanor and casual reaction to the rash of compliments was indeed refreshing. "Yes, thank you."

"You hail from Boston, do you?" he asked. Apparently, someone had already enlightened him as to her background.

"I do."

"Nice town. I've only been once, mind you. A dear friend of mine attends the University. I must say its beautiful waterfront and historic value impressed me a great deal. I should like to return some day."

Awed by his genteel manner and speech, Liza found herself staring into his compelling eyes, drawn by the warmth of his smile. "Yes, it is a lovely place. I always enjoy talking to people who have visited so that I may hear their observations."

"Perhaps we will talk more then," he said with a smile.

"I should like nothing more."

His eyes flashed with warmth. "Then it's settled. I'll call on you soon."

"Jonathan." The smooth voice from behind captured everyone's attention.

"Benjamin!" Benjamin Broughton stood on the fringes of the crowd, a sleeping daughter in his arms. For reasons unbeknownst to Liza, her heart wobbled at the sight.

"Excuse me, miss," Jonathan said, leaving her side to amble through the masses in the direction of Mr. Broughton.

"Ben, you old brute, you."

The two went into a bear hug, mercilessly squeezing the child between them, but not disturbing her slumber in the least. Ben shifted her to one arm and took up talking with Jonathan. At that, the crowd dispersed, including Lili, who immediately went to her father's side after bidding Liza good-bye. Liza saw the leave-taking as an opportunity to slip out the back door.

She might have escaped unnoticed, except for Mr. Broughton's final words.

"Miss Merriwether, thank you for allowing my Lili to sit next to you in church. It came in mighty handy for me."

She detected only a hint of a smile. "You're entirely welcome, sir."

"You might stop out at the cabin in the next few days. I believe you'll be quite surprised at the progress."

"Really?" She'd fully intended to check on the matter sooner but had found herself caught up in school preparations instead. "I appreciate that."

Jonathan Atkins raised nicely shaped brows. "The old Broughton cabin, I presume?"

"That's the one," Ben said.

A gleam of interest sparked in Jonathan's eyes. "Rather lonely out there, isn't it, miss?"

"I shall enjoy my solitude," she countered.

The hearty laugh that followed originated deep in his chest. "Solitude. You hear that, Broughton? Miss Merriwether wants her privacy. You'll see that she gets it now, won't you, Ben?"

Ben's face colored for reasons Liza did not understand, and because his reaction flustered her, she lifted her skirts and made for the door.

Chapter Eight

*L*iza maneuvered the team of horses over the narrow bridge that spanned the width of Little Hickman Creek, breathing a sigh of relief when she reached the other side. She'd opted to go the additional half mile to see if the rickety bridge would handle the rig, and now that she'd accomplished the feat, traveling the extra distance seemed worth her while.

The late-August sun cast unremitting heat onto her back and shoulders. Her wide-brimmed hat shaded her face nicely, but did nothing for the rest of her. Nevertheless, the sights and smells of late-blooming lilies and a menagerie of wildflowers lifted her spirits as she steered the team of two on their way, her body swaying and shifting precariously on the high seat with every tip and turn of the wagon's axle.

Four days had passed since she'd spoken to Mr. Broughton about the progress he'd made on the cabin. It was high time she saw it for herself. With the groundwork set for the startup of school, she would take the next few days to relax and mentally prepare for the first day.

Upon first glance at the little cabin sitting atop Shannon's Peak, she took in a quick gulp of air and reined in the team. Somehow, it seemed to stand a little straighter with its brand new door, fresh, shiny windows, and new roof. She caught herself smiling and holding a hand to her heart. Could it be? It hardly seemed like the same place she'd first spotted two weeks ago. Apparently, Benjamin Broughton had taken her seriously after all.

Several horses were hitched to a fence post outside the cabin, and the sounds of hammering, loud talk, and scuffling about inside the little house greeted her as she drew nearer in the rig. She called the horses to a halt at the same horizontal clearing where she'd stopped before, tied the reins around the brake stick, and then quickly grabbed her skirts and jumped down from her perch.

A lumbering man emerged from the cabin just as she made for the newly fixed porch steps. "Well, hullo there, miss. Might ya be the renowned Miss Merriwether?" Twinkling eyes showed under a low riding hat, while a smile peeked through his graying, rather shaggy beard.

Liza smiled in return and lifted her skirts to climb the stairs. "Yes, sir, I am," she said. "I've come to check on the progress of my future home."

"Well now, ain't that somethin'?"

"Who're ya talkin' to, Andy?" asked a voice from inside.

The man turned toward the door of the cabin. "The new schoolteacher. She's come to inspect our work." Creases formed at the corners of both eyes, giving Liza the impression that he was teasing.

"Well, invite her in."

The man named Andy stepped aside, tipped his hat, and issued a silent welcome with his outstretched hand.

Once inside, what she saw both amazed and pleased her beyond words. In fact, she had to fight the urge to pinch herself to see if she might be dreaming. Everything about the place was different from when she'd first laid eyes on it, from the sparkling windowpanes to the new wood floors, from the new kitchen cupboards to the recently scrubbed sink. Even the smells had changed from dingy and musky to fresh and clean.

"Speechless, are we?" said a husky voice.

She whirled around and came face-to-face with Mr. Broughton, his overpowering stance catching her off guard so that she took a step back. Large, booted feet positioned themselves several inches apart, fisted hands perched on either side of his tapered waist, and one thick eyebrow arched in question.

"I—I, well, yes, I suppose I am."

"I suspect that's a first for you."

"Excuse me?"

Muffled snickers filled the room, forcing Liza to look about her. At least six pairs of eyes peeked around corners, gazed down from ladders, or peered at her from across the open space.

"Ben done recruited us to help him get the job finished so's you could move in right quick. He said you were a might, ahem, determined." This from a rather thin man dressed in dusty overalls. "Name's Sully Thompson, ma'am. I believe you'll be havin' my youngsters in your classroom. Todd and Samuel. They's seven and nine." That said, he extended a grimy hand.

Liza put on a smile and took his hand, finding it sweaty and rough. "My pleasure, Mr. Thompson. I thank you kindly for volunteering your services." Her eyes took in her surroundings.

"Oh, weren't no volunteering about it, ma'am. Ben here practically dragged us all here by our ears. Said we was to show up if'n we had any kids attendin' the school," said yet another man. He started descending the ladder as he spoke. "Different fellas been out here most ever' day. We all got plenty ta do on ar farms, but we figure this here's a worthy cause, and the quicker we finish, the faster we can all git back to ar own jobs, includin' Ben here." Then he let loose a light chuckle. "'Sides, ain't none of us wantin' the schoolmarm ta get her dander up any more'n necessary."

Liza felt her face color at the mere insinuation of her earlier annoyance with Mr. Broughton. Had he told them all about her initial anger at finding the cabin in total disrepair? Worse, had he enlightened them on the outhouse episode as well?

"Well, just the same, I appreciate your help, whether it was voluntary in nature or otherwise," she said rather coolly, afraid to appear overtly thrilled with the cabin's outcome on the chance that Mr. Broughton might view her actions as kowtowing. If there were to be an apology made on her behalf, she would give it in private.

"Yer happy then?" Andy asked in a hopeful tone.

"It's, well, more than I ever imagined." And it was. The more she studied her surroundings, the more delighted she became. She began to walk around the room then, oblivious to the watchful eyes that followed her every move. She would add her own finishing touches, of course. Curtains, rugs, a tablecloth, pictures—pictures. Just then, she noted a framed painting hanging on the wall beside the bedroom door.

"What's this?" she asked, moving closer. The artwork was a scenic, lush valley surrounded on all sides by low mountains and luxuriant, grassy hills. A cluster of deer drank from a clear blue mountain stream and grazed in verdant meadows. A brass plate at the bottom of the frame carried the title "Patience Is a Virtue." Alongside that the name of the artist.

Patience is a virtue. A blush crept up her neck, making her wish for a high collar to wrench across the heated, blotchy spot. She knew exactly why the painting hung there, and, although it was a beautiful piece of art, it would serve to remind her often of her earlier show of *impatience* with Benjamin Broughton and her lack of Bible knowledge. When she mustered the courage to look at Mr. Broughton, she found him equally flustered.

"Ben informed us all the paintin' was a gift to the *cabin*, ma'am," said Sully Thompson with a spark of amusement. "He wanted to make that clear when I first discovered it restin' facedown on the top shelf of the closed cabinet."

"Sully." Ben's sudden harshness seemed sufficient to put the men on warning. In fact, each one set to picking up tools and heading for the door.

"Time for us to take a quick waterin' break. Excuse us, ma'am," said Andy, brushing past her while courteously tipping his hat. "Come on, men."

"Nice meetin' ya, miss," offered yet another whose name she hadn't learned.

One by one, each man filed out until it was only Mr. Broughton and she, his great hulking presence fairly taking up all the air and surrounding space.

Liza turned her gaze toward the picture. "It's a lovely painting that you've bought—for the cabin."

"Sully should have kept quiet about it."

"It will be a good reminder to me of my lack of tolerance and staying power. I do tend to rush ahead of myself."

"It wasn't my intention..."

"And I think you've found a good place for it. A person can surely spot it from any angle."

"It can be moved into the other room," he assured.

"No, it's—perfect where it is."

"I discovered it in Johansson's Mercantile. It seemed fitting in light of, well, our earlier discussion." He threw her a meaningful look.

"Yes. Well, it was foolish of me to think the phrase came from the Bible."

"Not at all. It was a simple mistake."

"Well, no matter; it's true I need to brush up on the Scripture. I'm afraid the Lord has much work to do in me," she confessed.

Mr. Broughton's hands went to the back of him and he rocked just slightly on his booted heels, a smile breaking through. "I believe we all can say the same for ourselves."

His intense gaze set her to walking about the little cabin once more, her shoes seeming to glide across the newly installed floor and making her relish in the thought of walking across it barefoot.

107

"The place is shaping up nicely, don't you think?" he asked, his deep voice resounding off the walls of the empty cabin.

"Yes, absolutely." She skimmed her palm across the kitchen workspace, happy when she found the wooden surface smooth to the touch. Even the sink and little cookstove next to it, which were marred from years of use, were clean. She tried to picture which man had labored so in the cleaning of it. Was it Mr. Broughton?

"We tried to fill in all the cracks in the walls so that you'd scarcely notice any drafts come winter. The fireplace should heat the place up nicely." It was a massive thing with stone frontage from floor to ceiling, and it took up an entire wall. "I believe you'll—"

"Mr. Broughton," she quickly interrupted. "I simply must apologize for my previous behavior. It's true; I do tend to overreact."

"Is that a fact?" Crinkle lines carved into the corners of both eyes indicated he was prone to teasing.

"Well, you saw how I was after I'd been locked up in that outhouse."

He gave a rich sounding laugh. "Hysterical."

"Have you managed to contain that secret, by the way?"

"Reluctantly so."

Relief flooded through her veins. "I appreciate that." Moments of silence followed as she continued moseying through the cabin. "The place is wonderful. I should like to move in the day after tomorrow."

He seemed to think that over. "There are a few more items to finish, after which I suspect you could begin moving in. Do you have furniture?"

"No, but I will—after I place an order with Sears and Roebuck. There is a catalog at Johansson's Mercantile." She spun circles to scan the room from every imaginable point of view. "I shall need to buy a table and chairs and perhaps a writing desk. Yes. Oh, and I'll need to purchase a new bed and perhaps a chest of drawers. The armoire will suit me fine in the interim, of course. Rugs, yes, I need rugs, although the floor is lovely. I never imagined.

"And curtains. I saw the perfect calico pair at Winthrop's Dry Goods just yesterday.

"A few towels and a tablecloth will dress up the kitchen nicely; well, that is, once I buy a table, and…what?"

Mr. Broughton was laughing at her. "Nothing. You're getting ahead of yourself again. Do you really think you'll be ready to move in day after tomorrow? You don't even have anything to sleep on."

"I shall sleep on the floor and enjoy every minute of it. I packed plenty of quilts and such."

He laughed again. "You are something."

Now it was her turn to laugh. "Aunt Hettie used to say I could get myself into trouble quicker than a worm at the end of a fishing line."

Mr. Broughton smiled. "That's the second time I've heard you mention your aunt. Where are your folks?" He folded his thick arms, propped a broad shoulder up against the wall, crossed his booted ankles, and studied her from across the room.

"They died in a fire. A neighbor managed to rescue me, but before he could run back inside to wake my folks the roof collapsed. My mother's sister Hettie and my Uncle Gideon raised me from that day forth."

A look of sorrow washed across his face. "It must have been horrible for you."

"I was very young, a mere baby."

"I see. It's good that you don't remember." Something in his expression denoted deep-set pain. It made her want to ask about his wife, but she held her tongue. Emma Browning had been kind enough to indulge Liza just this week in a few of the facts surrounding Mrs. Broughton's unfortunate death after giving birth to Molly.

"Have you found someone to care for your children yet?" It seemed a safe enough topic.

The question seemed to shake him from a state of introspection. "Oh, well, I have found a solution of sorts." He pulled himself away from the wall and advanced to a window across the room, the one overlooking the creek.

"That's wonderful," she said, staying put by the deep sink, watching him lean into the window. "A woman from town then?"

He turned. "Why do you ask? Are you interested in the job, Eliza Jane?"

Flustered by his straightforward tone and carefree use of her two Christian names, she put a hand to her throat. "No, of course not."

"I didn't think so," he said, smiling. He seemed to admire his handiwork as he ran a hand over the windowsill. "I've come to a decision over the past several days. I suppose you could say the job of refurbishing this cabin has hastened my decision, made me more aware of my circumstances. My children need stability, you see."

Liza bit into her lip without thinking. "Of course. What will you do?"

"I've decided to send for a mail-order bride."

"A w-what?" she asked, her voice breaking.

"A bride," he stated as matter-of-fact as you please.

"Someone you don't even know?" The notion seemed ludicrous.

"That's right."

"But that seems risky," she pointed out.

"It is a Christian organization," he clarified.

"And you assume that makes it right?" she asked, frantic for no good reason.

"I've just told you; my daughters need stability—and a woman."

"I should think you could find someone in these parts."

 110

He grinned at her from his rather self-important stance, then turned it into a cynical chuckle. "Did you have someone in mind?"

"Absolutely not, Mr. Broughton."

He sauntered away from the window. "Well, I'm wiring some money to the agency tomorrow."

"Tomorrow? But that's so soon. What if she is quite homely?"

He laughed again and Liza realized she was beginning to accustom herself to the husky, jovial sound. "I won't marry her on the spot, Liza," he said. He'd done it again, used her Christian name as if it were second nature. "The agreement is that I will court her from the start while employing her services."

"I see. But that hardly seems appropriate, employing her services."

He raised his jet-black eyebrows. "I plan to make arrangements for her to stay at Emma's place. In fact, she can take over the room you will vacate."

What was that tight feeling that made breathing so difficult? "I see. What does Lili say about—this arrangement?"

Deep frown lines creased his forehead. "Lili doesn't know yet."

"That hardly seems fair, Mr. Broughton. Lili seems a very impressionable child. I should think—"

"It doesn't matter what you think, now, does it?" He issued the fact as cool as could be, shutting her up on the spot. He moved to the door, the heels of his boots seeming to accentuate his point as they echoed in the empty room. "The fact is, I need a wife," he added, turning just slightly, annoyance evident in his voice. "And the sooner the better I think."

❋ ❋ ❋ ❋ ❋

Ben patted the envelope stored safely in his hip pocket, then checked to see that the letter he'd written to the agency was there as well. He intended to deposit money in the bank first, then wire the desired amount to the Marriage Made in Heaven Agency. If nothing else, the drive in had demonstrated his point of needing a wife. Lili had been crying profusely ever since they left the farm because he'd told her they would not be stopping off at Emma Browning's place to pay a visit to Miss Merriwether. Molly had been crying as well, but for reasons that only God Himself understood. He'd left the kitchen in a shambles and dirty clothes on the floor.

To make matters worse, he had a splitting headache, and he suspected the stress of unmet deadlines, failing crops, an ailing horse, and unfinished chores contributed greatly. Yes, he needed a wife.

He'd spent a good share of last evening reading Scripture and seeking God's direction regarding bringing a woman into their household. In the end, he'd simply asked the Lord to drop a giant stumbling block in front of him if the idea of sending for a mail-order bride was entirely wrong. And now it would seem that instead of a stumbling block the Lord had filled him with plenty of reasons for needing a woman. Simply put, he was at the end of his rope as far as single parenting went.

To top matters off, Mrs. Granger had announced that the day after tomorrow would be her last for watching the children. She was heading for St. Louis on the next available train out of Lexington. In fact, she was considering a permanent move. "Nothing much holding me here in Little Hickman, Ben," she'd said. "My family's gone, spread from here to kingdom come. My daughter's been itching to find me a place near her. I believe my son Charles and I will scout out the area while I'm there."

Ben liked Mrs. Granger. She'd always been a good family friend. But truth be told, he'd miss her dependability almost more than her friendship. She'd been a steady force for his children, Lili in particular, always loving and gentle in her treatment of them.

"Well, I'm happy for you," he'd said begrudgingly. "Naturally, we will all miss you dearly."

"You know I feel the same."

So what was he to do in the interim? Sarah Woodward wouldn't arrive for several weeks, and then only if she agreed to all his stipulations—caring for his children and the housework, staying at the boardinghouse, and attending church regularly. He was certain the latter was the least of his worries.

What if she is quite homely? Liza's words came back as a fresh reminder of yesterday's heated discussion on the topic. Of course, looks were not an issue, he told himself. Still, he could hardly abide the thought of marrying someone entirely unseemly in looks. Miranda had been beautiful by anyone's standards. The contrast would be hard to take.

It's not fair to keep the news from Lili. She's impressionable. He hadn't expected the schoolteacher to be so forthright in her opinion, but he supposed she did have Lili's best interests in mind, Lili being her student and all. And he had to admit she did have a point. He would have to let his daughter know of his intentions sooner or later.

As if on cue, Lili sniffed loudly, forcing him to turn his gaze on her. She sat on the far end of the seat, facing straight ahead, Molly snuggled in between them. "Have you ended your crying spell yet?" he asked too harshly.

Apparently, Molly thought he spoke to her, for her whimpering started up again. "Molly, what is it? Are your teeth bothering you again?" He drew a handkerchief from his shirt pocket and swiped it across the child's runny nose. Then, slipping an index finger into her mouth, he found swollen gums and discovered the molar responsible for her pain. To top matters, her cheeks were unusually hot. "Maybe we best stop in to see Doc Randolph while we're at it."

"Then could we go see Miss Merriwether?" Lili asked.

"We've been over this before. You don't need to visit her every time we come to town." Though it was more *Ben* who needed to avoid the little lady.

"But I haven't seen her since last Sunday."

"And you shall see her on Monday when you start school." He wasn't about to tell her the teacher was moving into the little cabin tomorrow. Lili would be on Miss Merriwether's doorstep making a pest of herself from the very beginning. In fact, he would have to lay down some ground rules regarding visiting the teacher when the time seemed right.

His patience ran as thin as water as he slowed the horses at the town's entrance. Sitting in a ramshackle chair, Sam Livingston waved a gnarled hand when Ben passed the livery. He forced a grin and waved back.

The clip-clopping sounds of horses' hooves filled the air while the stench of manure, dust, and Madam Guttersnipe's bitter ale carried over the soft breezes. He suspected the Madam had raked in a goodly profit last night by the looks of the littered sidewalk outside her establishment. The notion made him scoff with disgust.

"What are we doing here?" Lili asked when he pulled up in front of the bank. Her tone denoted no change in temperament.

"I'm depositing some money. You stay here with Molly."

"But I want to go with you."

He heaved a sigh and mentally counted to ten. "Lili, you are trying my nerves with your incessant need to argue this morning."

She sat back with an even deeper frown and then crossed her arms.

"Watch your sister," he ordered, climbing down and heading for the bank, nerves a jangle.

Chapter Nine

A covering of dark, menacing clouds blanketed the little town of Hickman on Monday morning, the first day of school. Swirling butterflies skittered through Liza's stomach, threatening to mess with her breakfast of buttered bread, apple slices, and black coffee. And if she was nervous, she wondered how her students must feel. The fourth teacher in four years. Surely, most of them were just as apprehensive.

As for meeting many of her students, she already had, save the troublesome Hogsworth twins, Rufus Baxter, Clement Bartel, and Gus Humphrey. In some cases, one or both parents had shown up with their youngsters at the school last week to make her acquaintance, or she'd met them in church on one of the two Sundays she'd attended. All in all, she was both excited and apprehensive as to how everything would go.

"Lord, give me strength and wisdom for this day," she prayed aloud as she set about straightening desks that she had earlier lined up in four perfect rows. Small desks to the front, larger ones to the back.

As if in response to her prayer, a quiet kind of confidence began to settle in. "I can do this," she whispered. What was that verse she'd just learned from the fourth chapter of Philippians? **"I can do all things through Christ, which strengtheneth me."** Yes, that was the one. She would cling to it throughout the morning.

She'd risen almost at the crack of dawn, well before she'd seen any movement downhill at the Broughton house. Of course, she'd seen a lighted lamp out in the barn and supposed Mr. Broughton was tending to his livestock, so certainly he was up. The mere image of him moving about had created inappropriate patterns of thought. What had she been thinking? And what right did she have to dally in her brand new, shiny window looking out over the expanse into a dimly lit barn? Surely, he never thought of her in any way but ordinary, so she must do the same. After all, the man was getting married.

Married. To a woman he'd never even met. She could barely fathom the concept. In fact, the notion frightened her altogether. It would be just her luck to wind up with a regular oaf—plump, lazy, and mean, to boot.

Moving into the little cabin had been pure joy. Although she'd come to take pleasure in Emma Browning's friendship, and even admired her for her undeniable spunk and fortitude, she'd been anxious to launch out on her own, to gain her independence. Wasn't that why she'd left Boston in the first place? Of course, she missed her aunt and uncle dearly, but every day that she'd spent in Little Hickman had affirmed her decision. No question about it; God had brought her here.

Several folks had helped her move into the little cabin, simply showing up at Emma's place that morning, bringing gifts of food and offering their assistance. There were Elmer and Bess Barrington and their two children, Thomas and Erlene; and Andy and Eileen Thompson and their sons, Todd and Samuel. Even Mrs. Winthrop stopped by for a short visit, long enough to mention that Liza's lack of furnishings should have kept her at Emma's place. But Liza refused to let the comment darken her spirits.

Then there were her new neighbors on the other side of the Broughtons—the Bergens. They, along with their nine-year-old son, Thomas, had shown up about noon bearing jars of stewed tomatoes, peaches, a bushel of apples, sacks of flour, sugar, beans, and a fresh batch of apple cider. Add to that the two wooden chairs they'd offered her, a pretty rag rug, and a new set of curtains, and Liza was overwhelmed with gratitude.

Benjamin Broughton managed to keep his distance, merely waving to her on a trip out to his barn. She suspected he would have ignored her altogether were it not for her calling out to him first. The man was strange, friendlier than a young pup one minute, and completely unobtrusive the next.

Lili, on the other hand, was at Liza's beck and call. She suspected the child was pushing for first place in the teacher's heart. If her father was in the least bit maddening, she found his daughter charming and lovable. Full of antics and lively speech, the girl proved pure entertainment. Yet when Liza had told her to head for home, she'd never balked or complained. Charming, yes. That summed the child up quite nicely.

"Good morning, Teacher," said a kindly voice from behind.

Spinning around, Liza was delighted to find Jonathan Atkins standing in the classroom doorway. He wore a pair of blue trousers and a short-sleeved linen shirt. His sandy-colored hair fell lazily across his forehead, giving him a look of mischief.

"Mr. Atkins!"

"Please, Jon will do," he corrected. A bright and genial smile graced his nicely shaped mouth, complementing his square-set jaw.

"All right, then. What brings you to the school this cloudy morning, Jon?"

They'd visited only briefly on the sidewalk yesterday, but he'd promised to look her up soon. She found him to be an effortless conversationalist. Moreover, the fact that he wanted to discuss her fair city made him even more interesting.

"I needed a ray of sunshine, and so I figured I'd find it here."

She blushed at his obvious flattery and then patted down invisible wrinkles on the skirt of her yellow-flowered cotton dress.

"You do look lovely, and if I were several years younger I'd be plum excited about starting school today."

She laughed. "Thank you. I needed a boost of confidence this morning."

He sobered instantly. "You have nothing to worry about, you know. You'll do just fine."

"I dearly hope so. I've heard more remarks than I care to remember about a certain few boys I will be having in my classroom."

"Don't let them scare you, Liza. Those boys need to know that someone loves them first off. If I have the right names in mind, and I believe I do, they haven't had the best upbringings. Some of these families up in the hills live in squalor, and that's putting it kindly. You may even have to plug your nose a time or two when you pass by certain desks."

That part didn't bother her. If anything, her heart melted for those less fortunate. She only hoped she could be enough for them. What if she discovered their needs went beyond her meager resources? Liza walked to the window and gazed out at the road. In just a few minutes, students would be strolling toward the school from every direction carrying their lunches in baskets or pails, and perhaps toting school bags. Expectant eyes would look to her for reassurance. She wanted to greet them with hope and a smile. She turned toward Jonathan.

Perhaps he read worry in her expression, for he hastened forward. "The real reason I've come is to offer up a prayer for you—if you'd allow me to, that is."

Taken aback and humbled by his kindness, Liza swallowed down a lump of gratitude and blinked back a tear before it fell. She hadn't realized until now just how much she needed the prayers of others, particularly those of a man of the cloth.

"I'd be much obliged," she said, sincerely meaning every word.

❋ ❋ ❋ ❋ ❋

"Oh, Papa, my stomach is tied up tighter than a ball of yarn. I hope my hotcakes don't come up on me—or on my desk."

Ben chortled as he gazed down at Lili; Molly again nestled between the two of them, much more contented since starting on the soothing medicine Doc Randolph had prescribed for her swollen gums, runny nose, and fever. "Now, why on earth would you be nervous? You know Miss Merriwether better than all the others."

"I know, but I don't know all them hard books."

Ben smiled and took advantage of the uncommon peace and quiet of morning, enjoying these few moments with Lili before he dropped her off for her first day of school. Without warning, he wondered if the teacher's stomach had tied itself in knots as well.

"Miss Merriwether won't expect more from you than you're capable of."

"I know what I have to learn this year 'cause I heard it from the ones in grade two last year."

"Well then, you have it made, don't you?"

She thought that over. "I learned some multiplication facts from Sarah Wilde last year, but she moved." She made it sound as if the one and only child she could gain some prior knowledge from had left her in the dust.

"You'll make new friends who will help you along."

She patted the cloth towel atop her lunch basket. "What'd ya put in here, Papa?" Her mind was off and running in various directions.

He winked at her. "You'll find a jam sandwich, a jar of peaches, a piece of Mrs. Granger's pie, and a jar of apple juice."

"Is that enough?"

He gave a light laugh. "I suspect if it's not I'll hear about it tonight."

"Can I walk home with Miss Merriwether tonight?"

"That's a long hike for you."

"She walked it this morning."

And he'd felt guilty for not offering to take her in the wagon when he'd seen her set out about half past six, her yellow skirts flying, the rim of her bonnet flapping in the gentle breeze. He could only imagine the golden brown tendrils of hair coming loose from that bun before she reached town. Oh, she'd been a remarkable sight all right, marching down that grassy hill purpose driven and ready for business.

Moments later, he'd shaken himself back to reality when he recalled the letter he'd just sent to the Marriage Made in Heaven Agency, along with the wired money. He had no business watching the petite little schoolteacher head for work from his barn window when he intended to marry another. *Sarah Woodward.* The name seemed nice enough. He could only hope and pray he'd read the Lord correctly.

"Well, can I walk home with Miss Merriwether?"

"I suppose we'll have to check with her on that, sugar. She may have to stay late tonight since it's the first day of school. I wouldn't want you imposing."

"I wouldn't be. Besides, she already invited me."

The glimmer in Lili's eye told him she'd been looking for just the right moment to broach the subject.

"I suppose you hinted at the idea?" he asked, half scolding.

"Nope! She just up and came out with it. But she did say I needed to ask permission first."

"Well then...I suppose it can't hurt to keep her company. However, I don't think it's a good idea to make it a habit."

"I won't," she promised.

The schoolyard seemed full of parents and children, each making their way up the wide steps to the front door. Molly's plump body supported under one big hand, Ben held Lili's hand with the other until they reached the door.

"Good morning, students," said a cheery Miss Merriwether as students filed past in silent surrender to the opening day of school. *Is this the quiet before the storm?* he wondered. He couldn't help but smile at the look of sheer delight on Liza's face. Apparently, she'd lost her nervousness.

"Good morning, Mr. Broughton," Liza greeted him with composure. Ben couldn't quite tell if she felt as calm as she looked. "And good morning to you, Miss Molly," she said, pinching one of Molly's chubby cheeks. Molly giggled and smiled happily for a change and then reached out her fingers to touch the teacher's face.

"Miss Merriwether," Ben returned, trying not to look too hard at her. "I brought you something," he added, handing Lili over to her.

Liza took her hand. "Lili, I'm so happy to see you. It will be so nice to have your friendly face to look at whenever I need cheering."

Lili looked less than confident as her eyes followed a trail around the room, searching out familiar faces. When she did spot someone, she dropped Liza's hand, waved at the other child, and scooted off to say hello.

"I understand you've invited Lili to walk home with you tonight."

"I did. Did she ask your permission?" Liza asked. He towered over her, her prim features looking up at him.

"She did, and I consented. I trust she was truthful when she said it was your idea."

Liza smiled, and the sight of her perfectly shaped lips framing gleaming, straight teeth stabbed him square in the gut. "Of course. I'll have her home before supper if that's all right with you."

"That's fine." He studied her fading smile as she scanned a roomful of students and adults.

"You look a trifle worried." Ben dipped his head so that he came within inches of her face. She exuded some kind of flowery fragrance, rocking his senses and making him want to station himself right next to her for the rest of the morning.

121

"Actually, I feel much better than I did, particularly since Jon prayed for me."

"Jon?"

"Yes, he's right over there." Ben looked where she pointed and discovered his childhood friend standing across the room visiting with several parents.

"Ah, I see him," Ben said. "I'll have to go say hello."

Jonathan Atkins' genuine smile and friendly demeanor had always had a way of drawing people. So he'd come to wish Liza well and to pray with her. Ben scolded himself for not having thought of it himself. In fact, he hadn't even prayed aloud with his own daughter, and she'd had the jitters. It would have been a perfect opportunity. Suddenly, he felt like an insensitive brute.

"Have you known Jon long?" she asked.

"We made a connection almost immediately when we first met as kids," Ben told her, his eyes going from her to Jon.

"Well, he seems like a very kind and nice man," she replied.

Ben searched her face. Had Jon already won her notice? And what if he had? He himself had just sent for one Sarah Woodward. He'd best not worry whom Miss Eliza Jane Merriwether set her cap for.

"Good morning, everyone!" All eyes turned toward the crisp voice of Iris Winthrop. She'd situated herself on the platform at the front of the schoolroom, hands folded tightly at her waist. "Students, take your seats, please. Parents, may I have your attention?"

All manner of pleasant chatter ceased as the staunch and snappish woman took control. "She has my attention," Ben whispered good-naturedly.

Liza tipped her face upward and threw him a half amused, half scolding look.

He turned his mouth down in a hasty frown and immediately straightened, as if duly reprimanded.

"Thank you all for coming out on this first day of school," Mrs. Winthrop said, as if she were standing in a large lecture theater addressing a roomful of strangers. Not even a hint of a smile cracked her hardened face.

"We want to welcome the new teacher, Miss Eliza Merriwether, who comes to us from Boston. Besides a host of knowledge, I am sure she will introduce a world of culture and sophistication to our children, something I'm afraid this town sorely lacks." At that, she cleared her throat and pulled back her already perfectly straight shoulders. Several indiscernible mutterings rose up about the room.

"Let us hope that this year of education will prove advantageous for one and all."

Someone snickered loudly. "Oh, yeah, we'll take advantage all right." The male sneer came from behind. Ben turned in the direction of the voice, but Liza ignored the jibe and remained face forward.

Slumped over in an adult-sized desk at the back of the room and laughing quietly was Clement Bartel. His long legs stretched out under his desk, and his face was dirty. Nearby was Rufus Baxter. It was hard to say which of the two was responsible for the unnecessary quip, but Ben would have liked to cuff him for making it. Looking about, he spotted just about every parent but the Bartels and Baxters. It figured.

Of the two boys, Ben thought Clement looked the more unprincipled. He was a big fellow with shaggy brown hair and unkempt clothing. The flannel shirt he wore bore holes, as did his worn-out overalls. Infuriation ran deep at the thought of him or any young man giving Liza even one drop of trouble in her classroom.

Mrs. Winthrop's voice droned on as he contemplated all the things he might say to the hooligans at the back given half a chance, and then he saw people moving about and quietly making for the door. He caught the tail end of the woman's speech. "…With that, I wish you all a good day."

The next thing Ben knew, someone ushered him out the door before he had the chance to say good-bye to his daughter, or wish Liza well, or tell her he would pray for her today.

The presence of low-lying clouds emitted a dewy denseness to the air. Ben sucked in a breath, noting the thick smells of nearby horse dung.

"Muggy today," someone muttered, moving past him.

"Yes, it sure is," he agreed, forcing a friendly tone.

"Ben!" called the voice of Jonathan Atkins. "Got time for some coffee?" The man approached with his usual smile in place.

Ben waved a greeting. "I'd love to, my friend, but I have to head over to Emma's place."

"Emma Browning?"

"That's right," Ben replied.

"Mind if I walk along?"

"I'd be pleased to have the company," Ben told him.

Jon put a hand to Ben's shoulder as they started out, sneaking a peek at Molly and smiling. She turned her face in to Ben's shoulder.

They headed in the direction of town. "Well, so what's the story on Emma Browning? Does she attend services?" Jon asked, seeming interested.

"Not often."

"That's too bad. Any ideas why that is?"

Ben shifted Molly's dead weight to the other arm. "I'd call Emma a skeptic," Ben answered. "She's bitter, particularly toward men and God. I figure that growing up with that abusive, drunken father of hers is what gave her the cynical outlook."

"Abusive, you say?" Jon's eyes went from curious to compassionate.

"Yeah. Don't you remember she used to come to school with bruises?"

"I moved to Hickman about the same time as you, but I guess I don't remember too much about school. I had my own set of problems to deal with." He of course was referring to his own rather topsy-turvy home life. The difference with Jon was that he'd found God in his early years due to Reverend Miller's kindly, fatherly influence; Emma had found strength within herself, building a thick wall of resistance in order to survive.

"Yeah, I remember that," Ben said.

Jon kicked a stone clear across the road. "Emma was a pretty thing back then. I imagine she's downright beautiful now."

"I take it you haven't seen her since coming back to town." Jon shook his head. "Well, I can tell you she's pretty on the outside, but underneath that façade there's a raging tigress."

"No kidding. So why are you going to see her?"

Ben should have known the question would surface. Unsure how much to divulge, he waited for the right choice of words. "I need to ask her about room availability."

"Oh? You thinking of moving out now that the pretty teacher has moved next door?"

Ben rolled his eyes at his friend, sensing Jon was toying with him. "No, I have—well, I'm expecting some company."

Jon sidestepped and playfully jabbed him in the arm as they went. "Really? You, a visitor?"

"Why is that so hard to believe?"

"I figured I was your only friend," Jon teased. "Who is he?"

Ben braced himself. "It's not a—he."

Jon halted and hastily grabbed hold of Ben's arm. Molly laughed as Ben was pulled back. "What are you saying?"

"I'd rather not say anything, if you don't mind." Ben removed his arm from Jon's grasp and resumed hasty steps.

"Come on, this is me, your old buddy. What's going on?"

Ben stopped again, faced Jon head-on, and simply blurted out the entire story of Mrs. Granger's departure, his need for immediate assistance, how he'd stumbled onto the marriage ad, and the steps leading up to his decision.

"You're getting a wife? But Miranda hasn't been gone more than…"

"It's been well over a year, Jon. Look at me; I'm toting a fifteen-month-old baby all over town when I should be working at my farm." To that, Molly let loose a giggle, as if she'd fully understood his remark. Jon instinctively reached up and tweaked her petite nose.

"I understand that, but a wife? I mean—someone you don't even know. Think about it. What if she's…?"

"Quite homely? Or has a birthmark with hair growing from it? Forget I said that," Ben added when Jon sent him a clear look of confusion.

"So it's settled. Did you pray about this?"

They passed a little bakeshop and whiffed the aroma of fresh-baked bread. "Of course I did," Ben said, annoyed that Jon would even ask. "And God hasn't exactly thrown any bricks at me to halt my progress."

"Sometimes all He asks from us is a little common sense, Benjamin."

"And I happen to think I'm using a lot of it right now. The truth is, I can't continue in this mode. My daughters need a mother, and that's that."

Seeming desperate to talk some sense into him, Jon's words started running together. "How do you know this—this future bride of yours even wants to be their mother? Most brides don't want to share their grooms with anyone for a while."

The subtle hint at intimacy stirred up an uncomfortable ball of nerves in the pit of Ben's stomach. Funny, he hadn't actually thought about sharing his bed with her.

"You think too much," Ben said in rebuttal.

"And you think too little!"

After both men mulled in silence for the next several yards, Jon finally spoke. "I guess I should be happy, you know, about this whole wife situation."

Ben delivered Jon a look of irritation. "Why is that?"

The young preacher smiled greedily. "At least now I don't have to wonder whether or not you have eyes for the teacher. Mighty pretty lady she is."

Ben concentrated all his attention on a mangy looking dog straight ahead. "It wouldn't take you long to notice that now, would it? Even that preacher's license in your pocket hasn't dissuaded you from looking."

"I'm not blind," said Jon with an impish grin.

Ben's eyes followed the mangy dog until it went behind a building and into an alley. "Well, she's not your type."

Jon laughed heartily. "Listen to you. I didn't mean to get your dander up. You're the one who brought up the matter of marriage."

"Fine." The swine was trying to trip him up. "My dander's not up," Ben added coolly. "Here's Emma's place."

"Mind if I go in with you?" Jon asked.

Rather than answer him, Ben took the porch steps, knowing Jon would follow.

Jon opened the door for the baby-toting father and slapped Ben on the back. "After you, Romeo."

Chapter Ten

The morning went amazingly well. Now that the suspense had ended regarding the infamous Hogsworths, Rufus Baxter, Gus Humphrey, and Clement Bartel, Liza decided to concentrate her efforts on remaining positive and upbeat. For the most part, the young men, all sitting in the back, appropriately slumped over for her benefit, had been rather quiet and self-contained. She attributed it to Jon's morning prayer. Perhaps she could convince him to come every morning at the start of the day.

She'd determined to keep the first day's lessons light and fun. They started the day by playing a game with arithmetic problems that even the younger children could solve. Next, they took time to share summer activities and then followed that up with a penman-ship lesson, copying a segment of the U.S. Constitution. After a hur-ried recess break, Liza settled in with one of her much-loved books, one she thought destined to be a classic, *Black Beauty*. The children sat in rapt wonder as she read the first four chapters of Part One. Even the Hogsworth twins sat up straighter, seeming to set the tone for their counterparts.

By noontime, the clouds had not yet lifted, but as the rain held off, she saw no reason that the children could not go outside once more. After issuing rules regarding eating their lunches at their desks, practicing good manners, and screwing down the lids on the ink wells tightly to eliminate the risk of leakage, she instructed them on the proper behavior for outdoor recess.

To keep the process simple she'd listed each rule on a large slate, using an alphabetical system that she hoped to have them memorize in time. Some of the rules were: *Always be kind*, *Bullying is unacceptable*, *Come in at the bell*, *Don't push and shove*, *Everyone deserves fair treatment*, *Fair play is expected*, and so on. The children seemed to take to the rules immediately, and even the rowdies at the back of the room sauntered past her with nary a comment.

However, she had the strangest feeling that the quiet waters were only temporary; somehow, the day's hovering dark clouds seemed an ominous foretelling.

After quickly scarfing down her own lunch, she stepped out the back door and onto the porch landing to watch the children at play. At the far end of the schoolyard, a ball game was in the making, as two captains shouted out players for their teams. Not far away, preteen girls huddled close, giggling and tousling their braids when Thomas Barrington and Andrew Warner made quiet remarks in passing. Liza smiled at the innocence of childhood, recalling her own happy, carefree youth.

Oh, Lord, please help me to do the job I've been hired to do here, she quietly prayed. *Make me worthy of my calling.*

"You shoulda been there, Gus. It was durn near the funniest thing I ever did see," said a male voice on the other side of the building, immediately putting Liza on alert. The boy's sentence ended on a high-pitched squeak indicating one of the pitfalls of male puberty.

"Yeah? What'd she do?" asked the voice that could only be identified as Gus Humphrey.

"Screamed to the heavens, she did! Demanded we let 'er out. Even promised not to punish us if we did." Everyone seemed to get a chuckle out of that.

"'Twas the funniest sight we ever seen," came another voice almost identical to the first, although this one lacked the squawk of male adolescence.

129

"How'd you do it?"

"Brought us some rope from Pa's barn. Worked great to tie the door shut."

"Musta stank somethin' awful in there," said a younger, purer-sounding voice, something in his tone signifying respectful awe.

Liza gasped, then piled both of her hands on top of her mouth.

"How long was she in there?" asked Gus.

"Don't know exactly. When we come back that night to let 'er out, the door was wide open. Someone must've heard her squawkin' and come to her rescue."

More laughter followed.

Liza tiptoed down from her perch, careful to move slowly so as not to make the porch steps creak. Advancing to the side of the schoolhouse with particular care, she made for the bend at the building and crept around it, not surprised at all to find the Hogsworth twins and Gus Humphrey. She was surprised, however, to find seven-year-old Todd Thompson standing amidst the huddle. Each boy carried on as if he'd just heard the funniest yarn of the century.

"Well, hello, boys," Liza greeted just as sweet as sugared jam.

The tight little cluster of boys jumped apart. Their gaping mouths returned no greeting. Instead, their faces went from hearty to glum in less time than it would take to melt a snowflake in June. Little Todd Thompson looked the most surprised, his eyes showing every bit of the whites around his honey-brown pupils.

If she hadn't been so angry, she might have laughed at the boys' predicament.

"Lovely day, don't you think?" Each one nodded in sober silence, lining up as if she'd told them to fall into place on the double. She brushed slowly past them, taking care to look directly into each one's eyes, noting with dismay that no one but Todd required her to look downward to see into them.

A fleck of the jaw and a twitch of a cheek told her what she wanted to know; they were nervous, and for good reason. Their secret was out. Judgment day was upon them.

She glimpsed at a dreary summer sky. "Despite our lack of sun, we can't complain about the temperature now, can we?"

All four boys shook their heads, awaiting their sentence, their faces drained of color.

"Well?"

Wrinkled brows hovered over pleading eyes, as each one pondered how to respond to her one-word question.

"Don't you have anything to say?" she asked, studying their serious faces. Finally, Gus Humphrey opened his mouth to speak.

"I ain't...What I mean to say, Miss, is that..." His pathetic start had Liza almost feeling sorry for him. Almost, but not quite.

"Miss Merriwether, I got a—a powerful need," said Todd, his eyes suddenly gone hazy and bloodshot while he held back tears, his booted feet now marching in place like a beaten down little soldier.

Amusement climbed to the surface, but she pushed it back down.

"Well, what exactly is keeping you from heading out to the privy, Todd?" she asked, simple as could be.

As if he'd just been stung by a giant honeybee, he made for the outhouse, holding the front of his pants as he danced along. The other boys watched him go with longing in their eyes. "Now then, you were saying?" she asked Gus, her eyes drilling holes into his pitifully worried ones.

He cleared his throat and started again. "I—I was about to say that I—wasn't even th—."

131

"Oh my," Liza said, hastily checking the dial on her wristwatch. "I'm sorry to break this up, boys. I'm sure we might have had a rather informative conversation." To this, she cleared her throat. "But, well, just look at the time." She tapped her watch with her fingertips.

"Huh?" Gus asked, clearly mystified.

"I must get inside to plan the afternoon lessons. You boys scoot out to the yard now, or you shall miss the remainder of your play-time."

She headed back for the corner of the building, waiting for the boys to soar past her. When no one moved, she turned around, only to find three boys with blank expressions. "Well, stand there if you must, but time is wasting." She gave them a smile, lifted her skirts, and headed back inside, her heart lifting in exuberance with every step she took.

✳ ✳ ✳ ✳ ✳

Ben studied the looming clouds as he followed the carved path from barn to house. Distant thunder and streaks of lightning filled the western skies. The rain had managed to hold off the entire day, but now it looked as if they were in for a drenching. Inside the house, he hitched his flannel shirt over a long nail by the door and hung his hat beside it. A stiff breeze had cooled the afternoon air.

Moving to the basin, he pumped in a goodly amount of water, doused his hands and face, lathered them up, and then hurriedly rinsed and dried himself. He would go pick up Molly at Emma's first and then swing by the school. No way would he allow Liza and Lili to walk home in weather such as this.

Emma had promised him a room for his prospective bride and even volunteered her services to care for Molly until the woman arrived, claiming she would welcome the change of pace that caring for a little one would bring.

Dumbfounded by her offer, yet relieved beyond measure, Ben thanked her. "I promise you it won't be long," Ben had said. "I'm sorry I can't tell you the precise day of her arrival, but I'll pay you a fair price for your trouble," he added.

Emma had waved him off with the promise. "What are friends for, Ben Broughton, if not to lend a hand?"

Everything seemed to be working in his favor, he decided.

Although Emma had thought his notion of a mail-order bride extreme, she hadn't tried to talk him out of it as Jon had. If anything, she'd agreed his situation warranted a solution. "Perchance this is just what you need, Benjamin, a woman to help you carry the load."

"Perchance what he needs is a brain in his head," muttered Jon from behind. Ben did his best to ignore him, and Emma only half acknowledged the remark.

The entire exchange between Ben and Emma had taken less than five minutes, with him handing Molly over to her and promising to return shortly with everything she would need for the week, and Jon watching from the sidelines, his expression dour.

"Tell me something, Miss Browning," Jon finally said, emerging from the shadows and leaning over the counter to better eyeball Emma. "Don't you think the idea of this marriage is a bit ridiculous?"

With nary a flinch, the woman had matched his gaze, her back as straight as a finely hewn pine board. "Benjamin Broughton is a reasonable man, Mr. Atkins, or should I say Reverend?" She'd raised a sculpted brow at Jon, something in her steely eyes holding out an unseen warning. "He certainly is capable of making his own personal decisions, don't you think?"

"Even reasonable men make poor choices, Miss Browning," he had added, equally challenging.

133

The hushed verbal match made Ben wonder if the two of them had forgotten he existed in the same room.

She swept Jon over with a scathing look. "I couldn't agree more. However, in the case of Mr. Broughton, I believe he has more sense than your average, ahem, levelheaded man."

Whatever she'd intended by the statement, she'd managed to put Jon Atkins off with it. Perhaps it was her expression, something in the way she'd defied him with a mere look, her blue-eyed, China-doll face a direct conflict with her frozen glare. Whatever the case, Jon seemed rankled afterward, which was strange coming from a man adept at making a typical female swoon under his charm. Moreover, the notion that Jon had met his match in Emma Browning gave Ben a fair amount of satisfaction.

The road to town seemed filled with children hurrying home from school. If it weren't for the dark clouds, he'd have allowed Lili to walk home with Liza, but no telling what the skies held. No, after picking up Molly he would swing by the school and insist they accept a ride.

A bolt of lightning streaked across the sky at that precise moment, followed quickly by a crash of thunder. Ben jerked in spite of his usual sense of calm, thankful that he'd thought to use the fold-up top. At least they would all stay dry on the journey home.

By the time he reached Emma's, the rain fell in sheets, nearly blinding him. Throwing the reins over the hitching post, he made a dash for the covered porch. Emma opened the door as soon as he lifted his hand to knock.

"No need to knock, Ben. This is a public establishment, not my private living quarters. I live upstairs, remember?"

He gave a sheepish grin as he wiped the rain from his shoulders and stomped his feet on a rag rug. "I'll try to remember that. How was Molly for you?"

"As perfect as an angel," she said, pointing to the crib set up in the room off the parlor. He could see even from a distance that his baby slept soundly. Even the next round of thunder did not rouse her.

"Sounds like quite a storm," Emma said, peeking out the parlor window.

"It's coming down hard now. I best get over to the schoolhouse and fetch Liza and Lili. I dearly appreciate this, Emma," he said, heading for the little room where Molly napped. "I don't know what I would have done if you hadn't offered."

"Don't give it a thought. Bring her by in the mornin', preferably after I've served my guests their breakfast."

"I'll drop her off after I take Lili to school. How would that be?" He lowered his voice to a whisper when he drew near his sleeping baby.

"Fine."

Ben gave Emma a quick perusal. He noted that she'd tied her blond hair back in its usual bun. Several strands had escaped it, however, indicating that she'd done her share of bending and reaching during the day, probably tending to Molly.

No one could ever accuse Emma Browning of being lazy. Her faded cotton dress bore plenty of stains, evidence of her work-filled days. Still, the raggedy garment fit her curvaceous frame perfectly, making him suddenly wonder just why it was she'd never married. Surely, men found her attractive enough. Even he had noticed her lovely features, although he'd never voiced it. No point in misleading her.

"How's the teacher settling in?"

Ben hadn't so much as welcomed Liza into the neighborhood, having decided that walking over there just might be a breach in propriety. "I expect well enough."

To avoid Emma's silent appraisal, he bent to lift his sleeping

135

daughter. Molly stretched and curled into his embrace, her downy blond head snuggling deep into the curve of his neck, her little hands tucking between her and Ben's broad chest. Soft breathing meant he'd barely disturbed her. Never would he tire of holding his daughters in his arms like this, no matter how old they became.

Throwing a blanket over her, he smiled over the top of her head and mouthed another thank you to Emma before heading out the door and into the rain-soaked afternoon.

The schoolyard looked deserted save a scruffy, long-haired cat hunched under the porch steps seeking shelter from the storm. Jumping off the rig's platform, he threw the blanket over Molly's head and made a run for the schoolhouse, hoping to find the teacher and Lili waiting inside. Yet, when he turned the doorknob, he found the building locked up tight.

Sighing, he ran back to the wagon and again climbed aboard, uneasy about the notion of them walking in open fields in the midst of an electric storm.

Deafening thunder reached his ears just as streaks of lightning lit the darkened skies. Keeping the blanket over his now fussing baby, he tipped his face into the driving, blinding rains and turned the rig around, heading for the dirt trail that led toward home, hoping to come upon the wayfaring pair.

❄ ❄ ❄ ❄ ❄

Liza and Lili hovered in the cave to which Lili had led them. "Ain't it just plain wonderful in here, Miss Merriwether?" Lili asked, her adventurous spirit almost contagious.

Almost, but not quite.

Liza managed a weak smile while watching the torrential rains through the cave's small opening. Pools of water collected on the outside, but because they'd had to step up to the opening, they were free of any danger of getting any wetter than they already were. One thing was certain; the cave had served its purposes for keeping them safe and dry. She could only hope that Mr. Broughton would understand when she delivered his daughter later than she'd promised.

"It's—well, lovely, I suppose," Liza said in response, adjusting her position on the rocky floor, seeking out a place with which to find some measure of comfort. "I dearly hope nothing else has sought shelter in here." Liza looked behind her, dismayed to find nothing but inky blackness that seemed to go on forever. "How far back does this cave go?"

"I don't know. Me an' my friend Lenora Humphrey found it last summer."

"Gus's sister."

"Yes. She ain't nothin' like her brother though."

Liza wondered how Lili's father, with his refined English inflection, handled his daughter's Kentucky accent.

"*Isn't*, Lili. You mustn't say *ain't*."

"She isn't like her brother," Lili conceded. "We are nearly best friends, Lenora and me. But I also got Eloise Brackett for a best friend, and Rosie Bartel, and then there's Sarah Jenkins," she rattled on, "but she's thirteen, which is a might old for a best friend."

"Age doesn't matter that much if you have things in common," Liza said, leaning into the cool, rock-strewn wall and temporarily closing her eyes to ward off a bullying headache.

"My papa is twenty-nine. He's really my best friend."

Liza had wondered about his exact age. Now she needn't wonder anymore.

"As it should be."

"Is your papa your best friend?" Lili asked.

"My papa died, but I suppose he would have been."

137

"You don't have a papa?" The child's eyes grew wide with disbelief. "Do you got a mama?"

"Nope, I'm afraid not. I lost them both to a fire—when I was very young."

Wondering if the girl would now demand details, Liza braced herself.

"Who adopted you?"

Liza laughed lightly. "Well, my aunt and uncle never actually adopted me, but they raised me and treated me exactly as if I were their daughter, and I love them very much."

"Do you miss them?" Lili asked in rapt wonder.

"I certainly do. But I'm happy I came to Kentucky to be your teacher."

Comfortable silence filled the next few moments until another round of thunder shook the ground. Liza drew the child into her embrace, happy when Lili didn't resist.

"I don't have a mama, either." The words came out on a hoarse whisper.

Liza's heart took a tumble. "I know that. And I'm very sorry for your loss." She fingered the child's long golden braid.

"Papa says that there ain't no point to being mad at God about takin' ar mama, either, because God knew 'zactly what He was doing."

"I believe he was right in telling you that," Liza said, swallowing hard.

"God took my mama to heaven just as soon as my sister was born." Lili sucked in a long, laborious breath after letting loose of the words. "But I don't blame Molly!" That she added in particular haste.

"Well, of course you don't. I'm sure no one would accuse you of such a thing."

"One time Andrew Warner said, 'I bet you wished your sister wasn't born.'"

"Oh, Lili."

"I kicked him," she announced matter-of-factly. "And then he cried and ran to Mr. Lofthouse."

Liza certainly didn't condone violence, but in this case, it seemed warranted.

"Then what happened?"

"Mr. Lofthouse didn't do nothin'—anything," she self-corrected. "When I told him what Andrew said to me, he just told that boy to leave me alone."

"Well, that's good."

Another lull filled the space between them, Lili's hot breath seeping through the material of Liza's sleeve. "Sometimes I wish my papa would find me a new mother." Liza's breath hitched at the unexpected declaration. "But then I feel guilty when I think it."

Apparently, Lili's father still hadn't disclosed his plan to send for a mail-order bride, and it peeved her plenty. Did he plan to wait until the woman arrived to make the announcement? She couldn't imagine what it would feel like suddenly to be introduced to your new mother. However, the matter was none of Liza's business. Hadn't Mr. Broughton clearly stated as much when she'd tried to interfere?

"You shouldn't feel guilty," Liza said simply. "It's natural for a little girl to want a mother. I don't know what I'd have done if it weren't for my aunt Hettie."

"I would want her to be pretty, of course," Lili said.

"Of course."

"My mama was real pretty. Was your mama pretty?" Big blue eyes met Liza's gaze.

139

"All the pictures I've seen of her indicate that she was. And my father was handsome."

"My papa's handsome, don't you think?"

The question set her off balance. "Yes…Yes, I think he's very handsome." No point in hiding the plain truth.

Lili stretched her neck so that she could better see into Liza's face. Then she studied her with particular care. "If I got a new mama, I would want her to look 'zactly like you."

"Oh, Lili, I do believe that is the nicest thing anyone has ever said to me."

"Maybe you could marry my papa someday. I could ask God to make it happen."

Liza held her breath. One thing she'd learned early on about Lili Broughton was that her mind traveled nearly as fast as the speed of light.

"Sweetie, I'm not sure you ought to pray for that."

"Why not? Don't you think God answers prayers?" Lili's eyes grew to boulder size.

"Well, yes, I believe He does, but sometimes we have to be careful what we ask for."

With a confused look, the child continued, "Papa says that God will give us everything that we ask for if it lines up with His will, and if it's something that we need."

"Lili! Liza!" A distant male voice carried on the wings of another ear-splitting crash of thunder.

"That sounds like Papa!" Lili squealed, crawling to the opening.

Liza's heart thumped unevenly.

"Papa! Papa, we're over here! Miss Merriwether and me are havin' us a friendly little conversation."

Liza worried her bottom lip with her teeth. Oh dear, the way Lili made it sound, they were having a regular picnic. All that was missing were the fancy little sandwiches and a platter of cookies. She began to question whether she should have allowed Lili to talk her into stopping. Yes, they'd found necessary shelter, but, on the other hand, if they'd just trudged along, they would likely have been home by now.

How long had Mr. Broughton been out searching for his daughter, and would he hold Liza responsible for detaining her?

Worse, in what kind of mood would he be once he found them nestled in a cave?

Chapter Eleven

*B*en let loose a long-held breath and thanked God from the bottom of his heart when he heard his daughter's voice, then saw her waving wildly, leaning out of a hole in the side of a rock formation at the foot of a huge stony slope.

Kentucky was known for its many caves. He might have known Lili would discover this low-lying one, nearly covered up completely by overgrown brush, and stationed well off the beaten path. It was smart of them to seek shelter. He wondered if Liza had been the one to suggest it.

He clucked at the horses to hurry them along, eager to make sure both the teacher and Lili were fine.

As if sensing something exciting lay in store, Molly poked her head out from under the dampened blanket. "We found them, Mol," Ben whispered with a smile.

"Gaaaa-gaaaa!" Molly babbled in response, flapping both her arms under the blanket.

"That's right. Thank You, God."

He'd already circled the trail twice and had been about to go back into town and report his daughter missing to Sheriff Murdock. It would be the second time since the teacher's arrival in Little Hickman that he'd been tempted to pay the sheriff a visit. It made him wonder if trouble didn't follow the teacher. Even her aunt had said Liza could find it faster than a worm at the end of a fishing pole.

"Papa, Miss Merriwether and me been talkin' about lots of things," his daughter said as he drew nearer. Lightning struck and, moments later, another round of thunder erupted. It would seem the storm planned to hold on.

"Have you now?" Ben reined in the team at the front of the cave.

"Yeah, and I told her I'm going to ask God…"

At that, the schoolteacher hastily moved Lili aside and poked her head out the opening.

"Mr. Broughton, I can explain. The rain was absolutely drenching, and then what with the thunder and bolts of lightning, well, I…*we* thought that finding shelter was of utmost importance. Lili remembered this cave that she and Leonora Humphrey had discovered last summer. And so she led me to it, even though I went rather reluctantly. I knew you would wonder…"

"Miss Merriwether, the important thing is that you're both safe. Now stop your jabbering and climb aboard my wagon. It's not completely dry in here, but the top does ward off the worst of the rains."

"Yes, sir, we shall do that straightaway."

The creek had expanded considerably, making Ben wonder what tomorrow would bring if the rain refused to let up. He'd seen Little Hickman Creek swell to river proportions in less than twenty-four hours with continuous rain. If that were the case this time, it could become impassable. Even the bridge upstream could wash away with heavy rains. He pulled the horses to a halt at the bank and studied the situation.

"Mr. Broughton, shouldn't you consider going the extra half-mile to the bridge crossing?" Liza called from the back seat. Relentless water pounded on the wagon's tarp-like ceiling, doing little to keep them all dry. Much of the precipitation seemed to be falling sideways since the wind had picked up, making the conditions worse than ever.

"Don't know how safe that would be. It's a rickety structure, and what with these torrential rains, I'm afraid it might not hold. I believe I'd rather take my chances here."

"Do you often get rains this heavy?"

"It's a might unusual to see it come down so hard and so fast," he answered, looking straight ahead.

"I'm scared, Papa." Lili's voice held high-pitched alarm.

"Don't be, sugar. I won't let anything happen to you. Liza, will you take Molly, please?"

"Of course."

Molly went willingly when Ben lifted her over the seat. The exchange took but a second, but in that brief time, their eyes connected and held. He glimpsed concern and so he whispered, "Everything will be fine. You'll see."

She nodded and managed a brave smile.

Turning around, he muttered a prayer for protection, then tapped the reins, urging the horses forward. As if sensing the danger, they advanced with caution, swinging their mighty heads from side to side and snorting their objections.

"Yah!" Ben hollered, slapping them harder. "Yah!"

One step, two steps, three—they hit the fast-moving waters and quickly sank up to their bellies. How deep was it? No matter, it was too late to turn them around.

Neighing with fright, the horses stopped in their wake, but Ben rejected their stubbornness and urged them into the water's depths, resorting to the whip more than he would have liked. Obeying, they resumed the trek, snorting their fury at being forced into the cold water.

The wagon tipped precariously, and when they reached the halfway point, water began seeping into the bottom of the carriage.

Lili let out a scream, but Liza must have muffled it with her hand, for the child quieted quickly.

"Almost there," Ben called while fighting to keep calm himself, feeling the crushing weight of responsibility for his passengers as the waters trickled in, flooding the floor. "Almost there," he repeated.

The well-trained horses kept their footing and reached the other side, their hooves vibrating the earth as they stomped and clomped on the muddy banks, continuing to pull until the wagon cleared the powerful waters. Once out of harm's way, Ben called the horses to a halt, threw the reins over the brake stick, and whirled around in his seat.

"Everybody okay?"

Liza sat stiff as a corpse, her eyes bulging with moisture, her face devoid of color. Lili's head was buried in the teacher's side, her eyes clamped tightly shut against the cotton fabric of Liza's clinging-wet dress. Only Molly looked at peace with herself and the world as she poked her head out from under the blanket.

"Paaaa," Molly cried, sending Ben a toothy grin.

At that, Liza cracked a smile of her own, following it up with a nervous giggle.

Very slowly, Lili emerged from her cocoon. "Are we alive?" she asked Ben, her eyes wide with astonishment.

Ben threw back his head and let out a peal of laughter. "Yes, pumpkin, we are all quite alive."

Liza brought her hand up to stifle a giggle, but soon out-and-out laughter sprang forth, producing tears that mixed with her already rain-dappled face.

Before long, Molly joined in, and then Lili, although neither of them quite saw the humor for what it was.

Once the joviality died down, Ben turned around and slapped the reins. "It's time I got us all back home."

Not until he'd driven several yards down the mud-sloshed path did he realize he'd included Liza when he thought of home.

Rather than take Liza to her cabin, he directed the horses into his own drive, pulling them to a stop at the front door. Jumping off the side, he raised his hands up to Lili so she could jump down. She scampered hastily into the house, darting raindrops as she fled and sloshing mud in every which direction.

Ben took Molly from Liza's arms next. "Don't move. I'll be right back," he promised, his eyes snagging hers.

In a minute he returned, only to find the stubborn woman already dismounting, her back to him as she lifted her skirts to find her footing. Clasping her on either side of her tiny waist, he set her on the ground, noting that she wasn't much heavier than his Lili.

Openly flustered by his handling, she glanced around the soggy yard. "I'll just walk up the hill. Thank you for the ride, Mr. Broughton."

"Come inside," he ordered, seizing her by the arm.

"Oh, I couldn't. It wouldn't be proper."

He laughed. "Now is not the time to worry about propriety, Eliza Jane. You're soaked through to the skin, and you need to dry off."

"I can dry off just as well at my own place."

"Come inside," he urged, giving her another tug. "We'll soon be swimming if we stay out here much longer."

"Well, all right, but only until the rain lets up."

Just as Ben closed the door behind them, lightning scratched its evil talons across the darkened sky once more.

❀ ❀ ❀ ❀ ❀

With Lili's coaxing, Liza agreed to stay for supper, even helped make the food selections: Boston baked beans and bacon slices, collard greens, canned peaches, and warmed biscuits. While she tried to make herself useful in the kitchen, Lili at her side, Mr. Broughton laid out some garments he'd fished from a drawer and insisted she put on while he tended to the horses and a few other outside chores.

Although she'd shunned his suggestion at first, knowing the clothes must surely have belonged to his wife, she couldn't help but notice how uncomfortable she felt in her sopping wet dress. Lili had already hastily changed into something else and had even changed Molly's wet diaper and day dress without her father's prompting. It seemed foolish to remain the only one in wet clothing.

"Well, if you're sure," she said, not allowing her gaze to linger on his deep blue eyes, instead letting it fall to the carefully folded violet dress that lay on the table.

"Of course I'm sure," he said, standing in the open doorway, his huge frame all but blocking the view to the barn and beyond.

When she still didn't move, he offered her a ready smile. "It'll be too big, but at least it's dry." Then to Lili, "Supper's smelling mighty good."

"It'll be ready when you come back in, Papa."

He gave Liza one last look. "I'll be back shortly." With that, he closed the door behind him and jogged off across the open yard.

The dress was indeed big. Shoddy might describe exactly how she felt in it. The hem dragged behind her, skimming the floor, no doubt doing a fine job of collecting dust. She'd managed to roll up the sleeves several times, but could do little with the oversized waist and bodice. However, it was dry, and that was the important thing. Mrs. Broughton must have been a splendidly well-formed woman, Liza surmised.

Dinner conversation centered around the continuous rainfall, the events of the school day, including lunch and recess play, and Lili's lively description of the wondrous cave in which she and Liza had found shelter. Mr. Broughton gave her his full attention, every so often capturing Liza's eyes in his, the twinkle there telling Liza he wasn't nearly as interested in what Lili had to say as he let on. Still, Liza thought it wonderful the way he let Lili prattle, as if every word she uttered were of utmost importance.

"And do you have homework tonight?" Ben asked, finally finding a spot in Lili's long line of nonstop chatter to insert the question.

"Nope!" Lili beamed across the table at her teacher. "Miss Merriwether says the real studyin' won't start up till next week. She's givin' us a week to get arselves adjusted."

"Is that so?" Ben asked, laying down his spoon and going for a few sips of apple cider, watching Liza over the top of his tin cup while he swallowed.

Liza found his gaze disarming so she turned her attention back to the smiling Lili.

"I'm sure that set right with the rest of the classroom," Ben remarked.

"Everyone cheered real loud. Oh, and Miss Merriwether's readin' *Black Beauty* to us, Papa. It's about a beautiful shiny horse that has to leave his mama and papa at the farm where he grew up. Are you goin' to read more tomorrow, Miss Merriwether?"

"I certainly plan to," Liza answered, wiping a speck of something from her chin with her finger, realizing too late that she should have used the napkin provided her.

Benjamin glanced outside. "I seriously doubt there will be school tomorrow."

"What? But how can that be?" Liza asked, alarmed.

His mouth dipped into a frown. "Little Hickman Creek is rising fast." He glanced at the window, where water coursed like rivers down the glass pane. "If that rain doesn't let up soon, the entire valley could flood. Fortunately, Shannon's Peak is high and we're set far enough back, but I'd bet my grandmother's bonnet that the bridge won't hold past midnight."

"But—how will I get to school?"

"As I said, you won't be going anywhere tomorrow. Until we can fix the bridge, I'll drive you across."

"No." The word escaped before she had time to consider the alternative.

One of Ben's dark eyebrows shot up. "No?"

"I won't impose on you any more than I already have. You're busy enough with your own troubles. You've said so yourself."

He nodded. "Do you have another plan?" He leaned forward, his big arms taking up the better share of the tabletop. "Surely you've thought ahead to proper transportation. What did you have in mind, particularly when colder weather sets in?"

"I had thought to buy a horse."

"Fine. I'll drive you until you find yourself a decent animal to ride." He seemed adamant.

"I could ask Sam Livingston if he has anything to offer," she said.

"Sam's low on inventory right now. It should improve by springtime," Ben replied.

"Oh." Liza tried not to show her disappointment.

"He might work out a rental system with you," Ben added, "but he doesn't have much for sale."

"Papa, we have a horse Miss Merriwether can use." Lili's cheery voice cut into Liza's sagging mood.

"Maggie is lame right now."

"What about Charlie and Lucy?" she asked.

"Charley and Lucy are draft horses, not suitable for riding, Lili. Besides, they're towing horses."

"I ride 'em," she said proudly.

"Only when I lead with the rein."

"What about Tanner?" Lili asked, refusing to give in.

"Tanner is a rambunctious stallion. He needs a firm hand."

"I have a firm hand with a horse," Liza intercepted. She'd grown up riding at Uncle Gideon's sister's coastal ranch.

Ben shook his head. "You don't know Tanner. He's a real charger. Full of vim and vinegar."

Liza bit back an argument that begged to come forth. Now was not the time, she told herself. Besides, there were more pressing issues at hand. Still, the desire to prove herself to the man seemed almost more than she could bear. His natural assumption that she was incapable was like a burr in her side.

"Well, the fact remains I don't want to put you out," she said in response, taking a sip of cider to help gather her wits.

"You won't be putting me out, Liza." He'd done it again, used her given name. Of course, he had no idea what effect the simple familiarity had on her. "I plan to drive Lili, anyway. You may not be able to get to the school as early as you'd like, but as long as the bridge is down, you won't have much choice."

"But—how will you get across the river?" Liza asked.

The corners of his eyes crinkled when his face gave way to an impish grin. "Same way as I did tonight, I expect."

Lili's face immediately brightened. "That was an adventure, Papa. I won't be half as scared the next time."

Ben chuckled. "You were plenty worried tonight, sugar."

"I know, but I'll be braver next time. I won't even close my eyes."

Across the table, Molly blabbered on her own from her highchair, completely enthralled with the sound of her own voice. Liza tried to picture a strange new woman entering this sweet little house, taking over the household duties.

150

"You're sure the bridge will be down?" she asked, anything to deter her wandering thoughts.

He nodded. "I'll go out first thing in the morning and check it, but it's almost certain to be unsafe even if it is still standing. Thom Bergen mentioned the possibility of erecting a decent bridge at this end. His wife's been nagging him for a good long while now. It's not a bad idea, particularly with your arrival on this side of the creek."

"I don't want to be a nuisance," said Liza.

"Don't worry about it. It's something that's needed our attention for some time."

After clearing the table, Liza offered to wash the dishes. Lili took up a towel and volunteered her services with the drying. While they set about in the kitchen, Ben removed Molly, who by now had managed to fill her entire front with breadcrumbs and beans. She was a comical sight, and when Liza laughed, Molly gladly joined in, happy finally to be the center of attention.

When Ben finished wiping the baby down from head to toe, he excused himself and took her into the side room that the sisters shared, announcing that it was well past Molly's bedtime.

"Lili, do you know where the broom is?" Liza asked as soon as he disappeared around the corner. The least she could do was work off her generous supper. From the look of things, the floor had not seen a broom for several weeks; crumbs, caked-on dirt, and various spills littered the long, flat timber boards. After that, she would see to scrubbing down the spattered countertops where evidence of long-ago food spills still lingered.

"It's in the lean-to," Lili said, walking to the small room just off the kitchen area. Coming back with straw broom in hand, she offered it to Liza, then tilted in close. "Papa hates to broom the floor," she whispered. "That's one of his worst chores."

Liza winked and whispered in return, "I can't imagine that there are many men who would claim to love it." Lili giggled as if she and the teacher shared the best secret.

Once she'd finished sprucing the place up, swept the floor, dusted a couple of shelves, and scrubbed the table and kitchen workspaces until they shone, Liza put Lili to work on a world map jigsaw puzzle on the floor in front of the stove. Rain continued pelting the roof of the Broughton's sturdy house, making Liza wonder how her own new roof was faring.

Although she knew she should trudge up the narrow path to the top of Shannon's Peak where her little cabin sat nestled amongst overgrown bayberry plants and rosebushes in need of pruning, she was none too interested in getting drenched all over again. Besides, there was something comforting about sharing a roof with a kindly neighbor in the midst of a formidable storm. She told herself that his handsome features should have no bearing on the fact that she wished to extend her stay as long as possible.

With that thought in mind, she knelt over Lili's sprawling figure to study the unfinished puzzle and was about to put a wooden corner piece in its rightful place when Mr. Broughton emerged. She felt his presence before she saw him, knew he watched with shrewd eyes. "I didn't expect you to clean the place up, Liza." His voice seemed unusually low.

"It was the least I could do," she said, straightening to meet his gaze, the puzzle piece still in hand. She fondled the coarse wood with both hands, suddenly nervous under the man's perusal. Thankfully, Lili paid them no mind as she continued examining the puzzle with care, deciding which piece to pick up next. She lay on her stomach, elbows propped, chin on both palms.

Ben Broughton's eyes scanned the length of Liza, as if seeing her for the first time. Did he suddenly regret having lent her his wife's dress? "Miranda was much taller than you—and more—well, filled out," he concluded awkwardly.

His words brought an immediate blush to Liza's cheeks, but she refused to let him see. Instead, she tipped her head downward to give herself time to recover. "I appreciate the dry clothes—even if they are a bit too big."

Ben's gaze lifted to the sounds of rain pelting on the roof. "The rain hasn't let up," he muttered.

"I should probably head for home. I'm afraid I've outstayed my welcome," she said, her nerves a jangle.

He chuckled lightly. "You worry too much."

Liza glanced down at Lili, still engrossed with the puzzle. "It's a lovely puzzle. Lili tells me you made it for her. Where did you find such a wonderful map?"

His gaze dropped to the puzzle. "A peddler came through town. He had it on hand along with a myriad of other strange goods."

There had to be at least a hundred different pieces to the puzzle, making Liza wonder at the work and effort he'd put into carving out each detailed section.

As if he'd read her mind, he added, "Making it helped to occupy my mind while the baby slept. Miranda had passed on not long before, and there was no time for self-pity."

"It must have been a very difficult time for you when—she died." She kept her voice low.

His eyes flashed with untold emotion. "She died only moments after delivering Molly—thriving one minute and hemorrhaging the next. That's what took her. There wasn't anything the doctor could do."

Liza's own eyes betrayed her when they filled with tears. "I'm so sorry," she whispered.

153

Both of their gazes went to the child, so enthralled with the puzzle that she hadn't heard a word of the adult conversation.

They stood in silence, listening to the thunderous storm, watching the rain drizzle down the windowpane in crooked pathways.

When she could stand it no longer, Liza asked, "Do you sometimes find yourself questioning God?"

He grinned down at her. "It's good to question, I think. I shall be honest and say that, like any other normal human being, I've questioned His purposes, yes, but I've discovered it does me no good to linger there. Only when I truly thanked God in my dire circumstances did I begin to find peace in the midst of them. I don't believe we really experience God's richness until we've suffered some losses."

He walked to the window to peer out more closely at the raging storm. Without forethought, she followed. When she stepped up next to him, she couldn't help but notice he smelled of soap and baby powder, and the simple finding melted her from the inside out.

"I admire your faith, you know. It's wonderful that you can look at life so positively. Many in your shoes would shake their finger at God in anger," Liza said, her voice quivering.

He turned away from the window, his gaze shifting to Lili. "I have a friend named Rocky Callahan who is doing that very thing right now. He lost his wife three years ago to smallpox, and more recently, his only son to a raging fever."

"But that's so sad."

Ben's pensive look told her he agreed. "I've been praying that God would soften Rocky's hardened heart."

For reasons Liza couldn't understand, she felt compelled to rest her hand on Ben's forearm. His muscles bunched beneath her touch. "I will pray for him, as well," she promised.

"Thank you," he said, his deep, mellow voice massaging her senses, his eyes trailing a path to her hand and then her face until she felt his gaze penetrate clear to her heart.

Without warning, he raised his hand to remove a loose strand of hair from her face. "I've wanted to do that for some time, you know," he said. The touch of his fingers, as they barely brushed past her cheek, sent an upward chill that began at her toes and moved straight to the top of her head, vibrating her very core. She might have moved if it weren't for the fact that his midnight eyes held her captive.

"You have?"

He nodded, then began rolling the loose strand between his fingers, seeming to study it. "I think God has sent you to Little Hickman Creek for a reason, Eliza Jane."

The endearing manner in which her name rolled off his tongue made her shiver. Moreover, it was nearly her undoing when his mouth curved into a warm smile.

"Really?" she asked, her voice unsteady with the single word.

Another nod of the head was all she got by way of response, and she might have pressed him for more were it not for the sudden banging on the Broughton's door.

Ben reached the door in two long strides, then flung it wide. There on the other side stood Jonathan Atkins, drenched as a drowned cat, and looking just as surprised to see Liza in Ben's house as she was to see him.

Chapter Twelve

*S*o you're safe then," Jon said, eyes on Liza as he stood in the pouring rain.

"Of course she's safe. What are you doing here?" Ben asked as he pulled his friend inside and quickly closed the door. Water fell from Jon's clothing to form little pools that refused to soak into the oil-treated wood floor.

"Hello, Mr. Atkins," Lili said, looking up when she heard the commotion.

"Hello there, Lili. Aren't you a sight for sore eyes? What do you think of this storm?"

"I think it's fun," she replied happily.

Jon laughed then bent down and tousled Lili's blond head before he looked at Ben and Liza. "Mrs. Winthrop sent me to tell Liza there'd be no school tomorrow."

"I figured as much," Ben said. "How's the creek faring? I'm surprised you made it across."

"The creek's swelling fast. The bridge won't last much longer."

"You had best stay here for the night," Ben suggested.

Jon smiled. "I was hoping you'd invite me." Then to Liza, "I stopped at your cabin to pass along the message and was alarmed to find your place dark." Throwing Ben a hasty glance, he added, "I might have known Ben here would take good care of you."

Ben shifted his weight, eager to right the awkward situation. Instinctively he wondered if Jon had seen him through the rain-spattered windowpane when he'd touched Liza's hair. If so, the man would never let him live it down.

"I had to pick up Molly at Emma's place, and so I stopped at the school to bring Lili and Liz—Miss Merriwether—home as well. The storm was raging by the time school let out."

"Perfectly understandable," Jon said with an even tone, his eyes flickering with suspicion.

"It wasn't safe to be walking in those conditions," Ben added.

"Of course it wasn't." He clasped his long fingers together in front of him and rocked back on his heels.

"I knew Lili would be frightened," Ben maintained, searching for the right words.

"I wasn't scared, Papa," she chimed in, "—not until you nearly drowned us."

At that, Jon's eyebrows shot up. "Drowned?"

"We were in no real danger," Ben assured.

Jon heaved an imaginary sigh. "Ah, well, that's good. It would be difficult to explain yourself to the school board if you drowned the teacher after the first day of school."

Ben forced a smile. "It was nothing like that." He failed to see the humor that Jon apparently saw. "The horses were—unsure, that's all. But as you can see, we made it safely across in one piece."

"Yes. I can see that, and it's good that you brought Liza here—where you could keep an eye on her," Jon answered, eyes twinkling.

Moments lapsed before Liza broke the silence with a cough. "Well, I really should be going up the hill."

"Nonsense," Jon said. "No need to leave on my account."

"Oh, but I've been here…" A blast of thunder blotted out her next words and Ben considered it providential.

"I'll walk you," Ben quickly offered, his eyes fastened on Liza.

But Jon swiftly countered. "I won't hear of it. Look at me. I'm already as wet as a skunk. Why should you subject yourself to this weather, my friend, when it would be just as easy for me to see the lady home?"

"I am quite capable of seeing myself home," Liza said with a trace of stubbornness. "I don't need coddling."

"You're not walking up that hill alone," Ben announced, "coddling or no."

"You are absolutely right," Jon said. "And that is exactly why I insist on taking her." With that, he extended a looped arm, inviting Liza to put her hand there.

Hesitating only briefly, she gave Ben a hasty look before accepting Jon's offer. "Well, all right then." Her eyes moved to Lili next. "Goodnight, Lili," she said, avoiding Ben altogether. "If it's not raining tomorrow, you may pay me a visit. That is, if your father doesn't mind."

Lili squealed with delight.

Moments later, the door closed behind the pair, and Ben heard them set off on a run up the hill. He watched from the window until their shadowy figures vanished from view. He could do with less of Jon's gallantry, he mulled.

"Do you think Mr. Atkins likes her, Papa?"

Ben made an abrupt turn toward Lili. "What? Well, I wouldn't know, sugar. I suppose he might."

Lili sighed loud enough for Ben to hear. "If she marries him, she won't be my teacher anymore."

"Lili, you're getting ahead of yourself."

Ben stared out over the dark expanse wondering if they'd made it to the top of Shannon's Peak yet.

"You could always marry her first!"

Smothering a groan at his child's outspokenness, he asked, "Where do you come up with such things?"

"It just popped into my head."

He laughed lightly, suddenly wondering what she would think if she knew about his plans to marry one Sarah Woodward.

"Well, you best think of other things—like popping into bed!" Lili stood up, leaving the incomplete puzzle on the floor. "But what if Mr. Atkins marries her before you get the chance?" Her question came out on a high-pitched whine.

"If I decide to remarry, it will be to a woman of my own choosing."

"Don't I get to help you choose?" she asked, her blue eyes round with hope and longing.

In spite of himself, Ben laughed aloud, then bent to tickle his daughter. She shrieked with pleasure. "Shh, you'll wake your sister, and neither of us wants that."

With that, he pushed her gently in the direction of her room.

More than two hours passed before Jonathan Atkins reentered the Broughton house. Constant pacing and peering up at the well-lit cabin on Shannon's Peak had Ben's nerves stretched taut as a drum. "Where on earth have you been?" he bellowed when Jon casually entered, hung his coat on a hook by the door, and headed for Ben's fine leather chair, the one he'd ordered from Philadelphia and waited four long months to receive by freight.

"Had you worried, did I?" he asked, a self-satisfied look on his face. Incessant rain still pounded against the roof. "Got any coffee?"

"I thought you were just going to walk her up the hill. You've been gone for two hours!" Ben cried, ignoring the request, agitated for reasons he couldn't quite pinpoint.

Jon lifted a wet sleeve to peruse his wristwatch. "Hmm, I guess I have. Time flies in the presence of fine company. Especially the company of a pretty Easterner."

"What have you been doing?" Ben persisted.

Amusement flickered in Jon's eyes, his mouth quirking at one corner. "Talking. I guess you don't have any coffee."

"What about?"

A deep-timbred chuckle rolled out of Jon's chest. "Ben Broughton, if I didn't know better I'd say you were jealous, which makes no sense considering you're soon to be married."

Ben sat down on a straight-back chair across from his friend, the reminder of his impending marriage taking the wind right out of his sails.

Jon steepled the fingers of both hands and fixed his eyes on Ben. "We talked and sipped on cider, if you must know. She's a wonderful conversationalist, asked me about college and seminary, my hopes for taking a church parish, my family—or lack thereof—my friends out East. She spoke of Boston, her acquaintances, the unfortunate passing of her parents, and a number of other things. We even discussed spiritual matters. She's quite a beautiful woman, and dedicated to serving the Lord."

What if Mr. Atkins marries her before you get the chance?

"You look as if you've swallowed a toad, Ben. Anything wrong?"

Irritated, Ben asked, "What do you think Mrs. Winthrop would say if she discovered how long you lingered at the teacher's house?"

The notion that Liza and Jon had reached a level of familiarity in so short a time riled him. Jon always had been an affable communicator. Never mind that most women swooned at his good looks. Undoubtedly, Liza was just as taken.

"I doubt Iris Winthrop is overly concerned about a man with a preacher's license breaking any laws of propriety. You might better worry what she'd say if she learned the teacher had supper with you—a widower." Jon reclined even further into the leather chair. A wide smile curved his lips. "Now, that would make for fine dinner conversation, Ben Broughton."

"Don't be smart," Ben said, shifting in the chair, his long legs stretching out until they reached the middle of the room, hands clasped across his thick chest. "Nothing happened."

"No? I saw you standing close to her, touching the side of her face just before I knocked."

Ben's gut lurched. He'd been afraid of that. "I might have known."

"What are you thinking, Ben?" Jon's face sobered.

"What do you mean?"

"You're not seriously considering marrying that woman you sent for, are you?"

A moan shoved past Ben's throat. "I've already told you, my daughters need a woman in their lives. The mail-order bride seemed like a good solution."

"That's hooey. You've managed fine for the last year and a half."

"You haven't walked in my shoes," Ben blurted.

"True." Jon readjusted his lanky body, the leather squeaking and whining under his weight. "But I saw something tonight that I hadn't noticed in you since Miranda was alive."

Ben bit down on the wall of his mouth. "What are you talking about?"

"You watch her in a particular way. I see something light up in your eyes when you look at her."

Ben guffawed. "Now who's talking hooey?"

"You better think long and hard about what you're doing, Ben. And then you best pray even harder."

The words hit Ben right where Jon intended—square between the eyes. What was he suggesting, that Ben had feelings for Miss Merriwether, feelings that went beyond friendship? Horse hockey! He'd as much as proposed to another woman! Blazing bluefish! She could arrive any day.

❋ ❋ ❋ ❋ ❋

Talk of the big thunderstorm filled every store, the post office, the little bank, and the main street. It was unheard of that the school doors would close after just one day of school, but close they did for three more days.

Days of nonstop rain drenched the walkways to and from school, making passage for even horses nearly impossible. Little Hickman Creek swelled to levels higher than even the old-timers could remember.

The bridge went out sometime during that first night, but the men and boys joined efforts and erected two new bridges in record time, one in its original spot, and a brand new one directly off the Broughton's property. Fortunately, as soon as the rain stopped, the creek leveled off, making bridge construction more manageable.

While the men worked, the women prepared food and drink, using Liza's cabin as a central point for food preparation and serving. Long tables with makeshift benches made from unused wood from the bridges, draped with red and white checked tablecloths, sat in the beating sun. Fresh lemonade and cider flowed aplenty, as did cold well water. Cold-cut sandwiches, fried chicken, roast beef, and a variety of salads kept the men charged with bounteous energy.

In the late evenings, rather than head for home, many folks, including the children, lingered for a time of singing and dancing, laughing and joking, and pleasant conversation. It was a treasured time for Liza, as it gave her the opportunity to connect with people that she might never have had the chance to meet otherwise.

On Friday, the last day of August, school resumed, but it wasn't until the following Monday that the students seemed ready to jump into their lessons. Liza was just as weary of the stop-and-start launch to the school year, and so she understood the lethargy that resulted. It would take a few days for the students to re-acclimate to the school routine.

With the sturdy new bridge in place, Liza found herself walking to town in record time and well ahead of her students, thankful that she did not need to rely on Ben Broughton for transportation after all.

Benjamin Broughton, the man she'd now come to think of secretly as *Ben*, had had little to say to her over the past days, even though he had sat at her table and eaten the food provided by the women. Only on occasion had he glanced her way, and then with looks that seemed filled with petulance and irritation. Was he angry with her? If she hadn't been so busy running back and forth to refill containers and platters, she might have asked him what it was that had him so rankled.

Just when it seemed they'd reached a plateau in their friendship, a kind of common ground on which to converse, he had to grow as cantankerous as a tiger with a toothache. To make matters worse, whenever Jonathan Atkins came near, charming the other ladies, as well as herself, with his tomfoolery, Ben's sullenness seemed only to multiply. She'd thought they were such good chums, Ben and Jon, but if that were the case, why did Ben allow the man to bother him so?

The church service the Sunday after the storm had been full of praise and thanksgiving, the singing exceptionally enthusiastic, and the people particularly friendly. As guest speaker, Jon Atkins had delivered a fervent message about righteous living. He was well versed, highly animated, and passionate in his delivery. Liza thought she could easily listen to him preach every Sunday and saw by the way folks received him afterward that they all felt the same.

She'd also thought the service a perfect example of the way a community pulls together in the face of adversity, counts their blessings, and realizes anew what truly matters in life. Thankfully, the only mishap anyone suffered from the storm was the loss of a rickety bridge. And because of the rain, families stayed in their homes and became reacquainted, played games, ate, and enjoyed the fellowship of friends and neighbors. As soon as the rain subsided, men and boys seemed to come from out of the woodwork to begin the work of building the bridges. It was community at its best.

By the end of the first week of September, Liza had learned the names of all of her students, picked out which ones she could count on to give her their best effort, which ones lagged behind, even though their efforts seemed unsurpassed, and which did not begin to reach their potential. Her primary focus became meeting the individual needs of all of her students and challenging them to go beyond the mediocre.

It was Wednesday afternoon. More than a week had passed since the storm. Life seemed finally to have reached a level of sameness—that is, until Liza heard quiet whimpering coming from somewhere in the front of the classroom.

"Miss Merriwether, Eloise Brackett is crying," Lili informed her. She might have told her she could see that, but she appreciated the concern in Lili's voice, so she kept the remark to herself.

"Eloise, come up to my desk, please," she said softly. Liza had been correcting essays by the older students while the class worked independently on various morning assignments. As soon as the forlorn-looking child stood to her feet, a round of snickers came from the back of the room. Liza's senses awakened as she scanned the faces of each boy. Rufus Baxter and Clement Bartel sat in their usual slumped-over positions, their lazy grins in place.

Ever since the noon recess incident in which she'd learned the identities of the culprits behind the outhouse lock-in, there'd been no real unpleasantness for her to deal with. In fact, she'd thought the waters far too calm, and Eloise's tears proved her theory right. She mentally geared up for what would come next.

When the child drew near, an offensive odor overtook Liza so that she had all she could do not to turn her face away. It was evident the child had not bathed in days nor changed her underthings.

"Can you tell me why you're crying?" she quietly asked, subconsciously holding her breath, then breathing only when necessary.

The child's wet gaze turned downward as her lower lip trembled. Head shaking from side to side, it was obvious she didn't intend to talk. It was then Liza noticed a piece of paper sticking out of Eloise's tight little fist. Liza reached down and pried her fingers open so that she could seize the note.

Unwrapping the small wad, she smoothed out the wrinkles and read:

Hey littel girl—you ever here of a bathtub or don't yer old man own one? In plane werds—you stink!

Liza closed her eyes to fight back her own batch of tears. Words could sometimes wound more deeply than physical hurts. Hastily, she silently prayed for wisdom.

"I'm sorry you were hurt by this note, Eloise," she whispered, drawing the child into a warm hug, suddenly unconcerned about her offensive odor. "Try to ignore it if you can."

Eloise's eyes welled up even more as she fought to stay brave. Then, speaking loud enough for the classroom to hear her, Liza added, "If it will make you feel any better, Eloise, the person who wrote this note is a terrible speller. And the handwriting is nothing to brag about."

That brought snickers from several students, particularly those who recognized themselves as innocent. A quick scan of the back of the room helped her narrow down the guilty party.

Neither Rufus nor Clement saw any humor in her comment.

Liza made a point to give them both a stern look.

At the close of the day, Liza packed up her schoolbag, which contained uncorrected essays, arithmetic problems written by the younger children, and algebraic equations by the older. On top of that stack of papers, she packed her class registry book, her grading book, and, last of all, her lesson book. By the time she pulled the strap over her shoulder, she heaved a sigh under its weight. It was still better than hauling a tall stack of slates, she told herself. Ever since the mass production of paper, the need for slates had greatly decreased, even though the children still enjoyed scribbling on them every chance they got.

Once outside, she closed the door behind her and locked it, pulling on the knob to assure herself she'd done the job. Then she headed for Sam's livery to see about obtaining a rig for her ride out to the Brackett farm.

It was time she paid Mr. Brackett a visit.

Chapter Thirteen

The Brackett farm wasn't much more than a square piece of land with the remains of dried cornstalks, a ramshackle barn, and a falling-down shack. A sagging porch with broken steps leading up to it seemed to say, "Go away," rather than, "Welcome." Chickens roamed freely throughout the yard, poking in the earth in search of scraps. Liza's stomach knotted at the thought of Eloise Brackett living under such conditions.

When she called the team of horses to a halt, an unleashed goat came around the corner of the house to investigate her arrival. Instinctively, she wrinkled up her nose at the smell and the sight.

Climbing down from the rig, she threw the reins over a nearby post.

"Teacher!" Eloise stood just outside the door, a smile as wide as the Mississippi on her round little face. "Pa, it's the teacher."

The bulbous-nosed man appeared behind Eloise, the door slamming behind him, crooked on its hinges. Immediately he put a hand to his daughter's shoulder. "What's my Eloise done?"

The child tilted her face upward to see into her father's eyes. A look of worry crossed her freckled expression. Liza smiled in order to put Eloise at ease. "She's done nothing, Mr. Brackett. She is the perfect little student. Very smart, too."

He seemed to relax. "What can I do fer ya then?"

"I'd like to speak with you privately, if I may," she answered, coming to the bottom of the porch steps, praying he wouldn't invite her inside. Outside would suit her just fine. "How about you scoot along, Eloise? I'll talk to you later." Eloise remained grounded in place, her

167

large blue eyes pools of concern. "Don't worry, honey. I simply want to speak to your father. Nothing more."

"You heard her, El. Scoot."

In spite of his rough appearance, deeply etched face, and lack of top teeth, there was gentleness in the manner in which he spoke to Eloise.

"Say yer piece," Mr. Brackett said once Eloise disappeared inside the house, resuming his rough tone. Liza saw it as his only means of defense. How many people had made him feel incapable, if not worthless? She recalled Mrs. Winthrop's accusatory words when she'd insisted she and her husband would make better parents for Eloise than Mr. Brackett himself, despite the fact he was the child's own father. She wondered how Eloise would feel if she knew about the controversy surrounding her father's ability to parent.

"There was an incident at the school today."

"I thought you said Eloise was a good student."

"Oh, she is. It's nothing like that."

"Then what?" he asked, his impatience mounting as he rubbed at his scruffy, unkempt beard. Even from a distance she could smell his body odor. The urge to cover her nose was strong.

Out of her dress pocket she drew the note and handed it to him. "Someone passed this note to Eloise in class today."

Mr. Brackett stared at the wrinkled piece of paper, then frowned. For just an instant, Liza worried that he couldn't read, but then her doubts cleared. "Who would write such a mean thing to my little girl?" he asked, his face a picture of rage.

"I have my suspicions," she said, "but no real proof. I'm afraid the important thing here is not so much who wrote it, but seeing that it never happens again."

"Yer right about that, miss," he said.

"And the only way to ensure that it doesn't happen again, Mr. Brackett, is to see that Eloise comes to school in clean clothing every day—and thoroughly bathed."

Surprisingly, the man said nothing for several moments, simply stared instead at his barren fields. Afternoon sun beat down on Liza's shoulders while unmoving air seemed to steal away her breath, adding to the discomfort of the awkward moment. Overhead, a lone bird chirped a melodious string of notes.

Liza watched him carefully, wondering what he would say and *when.*

Finally, his words came out, shaky at first so that he had to start again.

"I—I know I'm not the best pa for my Eloise."

"No one can love her more than you do. It is not my intention to try to convince anyone otherwise."

His watery, murky eyes seemed to peer inside her soul, shaming her for no apparent reason.

"I'm glad you see it that way," he said, his shoulders slumping momentarily before he gave them a prideful, determined lift. "I'll see she takes a bath tonight."

"No need to make an issue of the matter," Liza assured. "But I don't want to see Eloise hurt again. If you could have seen the pained look on her face today, you would know exactly what I mean."

"I reckon I do. I'm not so good at keepin' house, either, as ya can see." He eyeballed his surroundings.

"I'm sure things have not always been easy, but I should think you could get Eloise to help you with the household chores."

"She does lend a hand whenever I ask. She's a good girl." Liza studied the rise of his proud shoulders.

"She certainly is, Mr. Brackett." She took a step back. "I would think one or two baths a week should suffice—using soap of course." She might have suggested he do the same but thought better of it. Lifting the reins from the knotty post, she heard Mr. Brackett clear his throat.

"Ain't no other teacher ever come out here." She read gratitude in the simple statement. "I'll do my best with cleanin' my girl up, but I can't do her hair so good."

Just as Liza was about to take the first step up to the rig's high seat, an idea planted itself in her head. "How about you drop Eloise off a few minutes early every morning so I can comb her hair and put it in a braid?"

A light seemed to travel across Mr. Brackett's otherwise dark expression. "I figure my Eloise would like that plenty—that is, if yer sure it's no trouble."

Liza felt a smile explode on her own face. "I would consider it a pleasure, Mr. Brackett. All you have to do is see to it that her hair is washed at least once a week."

He looked thoughtful. "I 'spect that's the least I can do."

She took the first step up, then turned. "You're doing the best you can, Mr. Brackett. Don't forget that."

"Thank ya, ma'am," he said in a raspy voice.

Ma'am? She'd come a long way with Mr. Brackett since their first encounter, and the notion rather pleased her. Letting out a breath, she climbed the rest of the way up and seated herself high atop the rig. Then, taking up the reins, she gave them a gentle flick to turn the horses.

"Good day, Mr. Brackett."

He gave a simple nod, then reached over the porch railing and pulled a long blade of grass out of the ground. Popping it into his mouth, he began to gum the blade, and Liza noted how his whiskery upper lip kept hitting the underside of his nose. The sight made her giggle aloud as she rolled on down the slight incline toward town.

✳ ✳ ✳ ✳ ✳

Ben patted the scented envelope in his pocket to assure himself that it was still there. He wanted to read the missive privately, and that meant escaping the postmaster's curious eyes. It had been well over three weeks since he'd sent money to the bridal agency requesting passage for a mail-order bride. He'd been ready to accept the fact that he'd been duped when the letter arrived in this morning's delivery. Now he wondered if he'd find a refund enclosed in the envelope. Perhaps Miss Sarah Woodward had already accepted another offer for marriage. Was it wrong of him to hope?

"Howdy, Ben!" Ben turned his horse around at the sound of his name and was pleased to discover Rocky Callahan just leaving Johansson's Mercantile, his arms loaded down with what looked like a new saw, a hammer, and perhaps a bag of nails or screws.

"Rocky, good to see you." He directed Tanner to the side of the street in order to allow approaching wagons a clear enough passage. "Looks like you have a project underway."

Rocky took off his hat and beat it once against his bulky thigh, then plopped it back atop his head of thick, dark, wavy hair. By the look of him his square jaw hadn't seen a razor in several days. "Mending some fences on my back forty. Lost a couple head of steers last week. Wandered off my property."

"Did you get them back?"

"I did. With the help of our old buddy Jon Atkins."

"Ah, Jon. He does get around."

Rocky grinned. It was the first time Ben had seen his friend truly smile in a long while. Then again, if anyone could bring a smile to a forlorn face it was Jonathan Atkins.

"You can say that again. You seen much of him?"

"Here and there," Ben answered. "I have a hunch Reverend Miller will ask him to fill in at the pulpit. Jon gave a rousing sermon Sunday after the storm."

"So I heard from several folks. Kind of wish I'd have heard him myself. Imagine Atkins a preacher," Rocky said, kicking a stone clear across Main Street. "Don't seem possible. Wasn't it just yesterday we were breakin' into old man Sumpter's barn in search of some of that illegal brew, Atkins leading the way?"

Ben couldn't hold back a spurt of raucous laughter. "We were thirteen at the most back then—bratty kids. It was pure luck that we didn't get blistered for pulling such shenanigans."

Rocky nodded and smiled, revealing straight, white teeth. It was good to see his friend looking halfway human again. "Bratty kids, you say? Little devils might better describe us," he muttered, lightheartedness lining his voice.

Tanner shifted his long legs and stomped an impatient hind foot. Ben reined him in and spoke his name to gentle him. "I might still be going down the wrong road if it hadn't been for Miranda's Christian witness. That woman calmed me down."

Rocky sobered. "I guess I would have to say the same about my Hester. 'Course it didn't hurt none that Ma stayed on her knees most nights when I was growing up."

Both men shared a short-lived laugh, their minds taking them back to sweeter times.

"Speaking of women, you think Jon's got an eye out for that new teacher?" Rocky asked, squinting into the sun.

 172

Ben's stomach knotted without warning. "Might be. Why do you ask?"

Rocky chortled. "Just listen to the guy talk about her. I've yet to meet the woman, but when I do, I get the feeling she'll be wearing a halo."

Ben forced a smile, but decided not to comment.

Jon wasn't alone in his admiration of Liza. Apparently, the whole town was warming to the teacher. She'd been making the rounds, visiting the families of each of her students, and making a fine impression. He saw no harm in it, he supposed, but he didn't like the idea of her traveling out to the Baxter or Bartel farms, and he meant to tell her so the next time he saw her. Both farms were male dominated and unsuitable for a woman's visit.

"Well, I best get back out to the house. Got fields waiting on me," Ben said, turning Tanner around and giving Rocky a smile and a nod of the head.

Halfway between Little Hickman and his farm, he reined in Tanner and retrieved the letter from his pocket.

Sweaty fingers perused the fancy handwriting on the outside of the envelope.

Miss Sarah Woodward. The finely crafted letters that made up her name and her Massachusetts address made his nerves rattle.

The envelope was too thin to have held a refund of his money. If anything it contained only one piece of fine parchment stationery.

Broad shoulders slumped in premature defeat.

His thundering chest told him if he didn't open the envelope he could remain clueless as to its contents. On the other hand, he'd started something from which he couldn't very well back away. If he had any scruples at all he would follow through on his commitment to wed this unknown woman.

What if Mr. Atkins marries Miss Merriwether before you get the chance? Why did Lili's words of warning keep drumming in his head?

Sure enough, one sliver-thin paper fell from the envelope. Unfolding it with shaky hands, he held it up to read the beautifully penned words.

My Dear Mr. Broughton:

It is with gratitude and pleasure that I write to inform you of my deep yearning to come to Kentucky.

Ben's heart seemed to plummet like a rock to the earth, and he let the letter slip from his fingers. He swallowed down a bitter taste and uttered a hasty prayer toward heaven. "Oh, Lord, what have I done?" Forcing himself to follow the letter to its conclusion, he picked it back up and continued.

Believe it or not, I have always wanted to visit Kentucky, and now I have been offered the chance to reside there. I cannot tell you how pleased this makes me. I feel certain that God has His hand in this entire transaction.

She made it sound like some sort of business deal, Ben thought, as he mopped a hand across his sweat-covered brow, then over his entire face. Of course, he was the one who had sent the money. If that wasn't a business deal, he didn't know what was.

It has become necessary for me to leave the state of Massachusetts, so your offer to move me to Kentucky will be a welcome respite. I understand that the greenery and glorious hillsides are indeed picturesque.

I do have a slight hitch to our arrangement, and so I hope this will not pose too large a problem for you and your family. My mother has taken seriously ill, and so I am required to see to her needs. Therefore, I must beg off coming to Kentucky immediately. I shall be along as quickly as possible, and that is all I can say for now. I hope that you will be patient with me concerning this most pressing matter.

Since I will be traveling to Maryland where my mother resides, please address any questions or concerns you may have to the Marriage Made in Heaven Agency.

I look forward to the day of our meeting.

Yours truly,
Miss Sarah Woodward

P.S. You sound like a very nice Christian man. And your daughters sound lovely, as well.

Ben sighed, refolded the letter, and placed it back inside the envelope.

What was he to do? The woman was coming. He momentarily felt relief that she would be delayed to care for her mother, but he realized that she would eventually make her way to Little Hickman Creek.

If Jon were here he would call him every kind of name for a fool. On the other hand, perhaps he'd rejoice anew that his competition for Liza had vanished.

❋ ❋ ❋ ❋ ❋

It was the third week of September. True to his word, Mr. Brackett began bringing Eloise to school fifteen minutes early every day. Almost from the start, Liza saw a change in the students' attitudes toward the little girl. It was as if the anonymous note had struck a chord in all their hearts, giving them an extra dose of compassion for a child who lacked a mother's touch. To top matters off, she'd been arriving at school every morning clean as a pin.

Of course, it wasn't long before Lili learned that Liza was braiding Eloise's hair, and so one morning after coming into school, she asked if Liza might braid hers, as well.

"I would love to, Lili, but you must come a few minutes early every morning so that it doesn't interfere with our class time."

175

"I'll tell Papa," she'd announced.

The next day she came to school at the regular time, her hair in its usual crooked part and with the rather imperfect golden braid down the middle of her back. "Papa says we mustn't *umpose* on you," she said, her mouth droopy with disappointment, "that you already have yer hands full enough."

"I see." She had half a mind to tell Mr. Benjamin Broughton he could jump off a cliff. Of course, seeing him these days was a rarity, so telling him anything would be difficult. The man had avoided her like the plague ever since the major thunderstorm, always dropping Lili off a good distance from the door so he wouldn't be forced to speak a greeting. If she were a good shot, she might have picked up a small rock and aimed it straight for his noggin, but then what kind of example would that be for the children?

She didn't know what to make of Ben Broughton. Apparently, she'd misconstrued his actions when he'd brushed his hand across her cheek, even gazed at her with those intensely inky blue eyes. *I think God has brought you to Little Hickman for a reason*, he had said in a quiet voice just before Jon Atkins came knocking at the door.

What did it matter anyway? Ben had sent for a bride, so her worrying about what he thought of her made no difference. In fact, that doubtless explained his cold shoulder these past days.

Liza marveled at how easily the children had adapted to the classroom routine. Every day began with the Pledge of Allegiance followed by The Lord's Prayer. Soon afterward came the grade-level morning recitations.

Since her classroom consisted of students between the ages of six and fifteen, it became necessary to adhere to a schedule so that she could meet at least once a day with each child. While the rest of the class worked at their seats on individual assignments, she listened to smaller groups recite their lessons, whether it be math problems, spelling words, or quoting something they had learned from a geography or history assignment. The ringing of her handbell would indicate when the next group should come forward to the recitation bench.

Liza trained her ear to listen for restlessness. When it seemed the students could sit still no longer she had them stand and do body stretches, take a drink from the water crock, and speak in low whispers. After a few minutes of this, most were ready to resume their lessons until it was time for the morning recess.

She had devised a schedule of jobs for the students, the older ones tending to the younger, assisting with difficult assignments, and watching out for them on the playground. Other tasks entailed cleaning the slate boards and pounding the erasers, straightening and organizing bookshelves, keeping the water crock filled with fresh water from the outside pump, dusting shelves daily, sweeping the floors during the lunch-hour break, and maintaining their own workspace. When colder weather set in, she would enlist the help of the bigger, stronger boys to fill the coal bin daily for fueling their potbelly stove.

Discipline problems had so far been kept to a minimum. She'd discovered early on that the Hogsworth twins were not nearly as difficult to handle if she kept them hard at work. Ever since the incident in which she'd discovered their guilt at having locked her in the outhouse, they'd toed the line, perhaps counting their blessings that she hadn't seen fit to punish them, or, more importantly, inform their parents.

In fact, one afternoon, immediately following the recess break, she'd found a folded note sitting on her chair. Upon opening it, she discovered a hurriedly scrawled note that said simply, *I think yore very perty and exter nice. And yu teche us good things. Sam Hogsworth.*

Immediately warmed clear to her toes, she'd smiled at Sam,

noting the crimson blush that crossed his face. Taking great care, she refolded the torn piece of paper and stuck it in her dress pocket for safekeeping. It was her first note, and she intended to cherish it.

Gus Humphrey was another boy she'd heard tales about and had worried would give her trouble. Instead, she found him easily bored when not challenged to reach beyond the ordinary. She suspected his former teachers had difficulties with him because they didn't recognize his early signs of boredom.

One day she discovered him examining the classroom's ancient globe. She asked him if he might be interested in taking home the atlas and then reporting back to her five facts he'd learned about his favorite continent. His face lit up like a firecracker. "You really mean it?"

She nodded. "Of course I mean it."

"You mean I could actually take home the big atlas, the one donated by the school board?"

"Don't look so surprised."

"But it was never allowed before. Neither Mr. Lofthouse or Mr. Abbott would hear of it. And I don't think Mrs. Winthrop would approve, either."

She gave him a reassuring smile. "Well, as you can see, I am none of those people, and since I trust you to take extra special care of the volume, I have no concerns about your borrowing it."

"Can Lenora look at it, too, and my parents?"

He seemed enthralled with the idea of turning it into a family affair. She laughed with glee. "Of course! In fact, you can all work together on the assignment. How would that be?"

"Great! Ma and Pa will be happy. They never got much schoolin' when they was young, but they still like ta learn," he'd exclaimed, his expression a picture of enthusiasm she had stored away in her memory bank for evoking later.

The only students that truly troubled Liza were Rufus Baxter and Clement Bartel. Sour expressions were usually found on their faces, with Clement seeming to be the leader of the two and Rufus following his dour example.

Both fifteen, neither appeared interested in learning. Their favorite body positions in the classroom seemed to be with shoulders sagging, legs stretched out, and arms sprawled every which way across their desks. So far, Clement had handed in only half of his assignments, with Rufus showing him up just slightly. Much was required of the older students, and from what she'd observed, Clement was the one who struggled the most academically.

There was something else about Clement Bartel that worried Liza, and that was the way he watched her with keen, hungry eyes. Every time she passed his desk, his gaze traveled the length of her, a lazy smile curving his small mouth, his pimpled cheeks flushed with desire. How could she teach the boy if he refused to stop this game of intimidation? The way he'd been acting, she dared not lean over his desk to offer him assistance, and if anyone needed assistance in learning, it was Clement Bartel.

Of course, her superior was Mrs. Winthrop, but she felt no more comfortable in bringing the problem to her than she would handling a prickly porcupine. No, this was a problem for which she simply had to find her own solution.

It was a beautiful sunny afternoon and Liza had just sent the children out for their afternoon recess. Tired and sweaty, she mopped her damp brow and replaced a book in its rightful place on a high shelf near the window overlooking the playground.

Gazing out at the students, she observed a few engaged in a game of baseball, others sliding down the ancient, well-used slide, and still others perched in swings, awaiting an older student's willing push. A smile of approval crossed her face. For the most part, they were learning to live as a sort of family, viewing each other with respect and consideration.

"Giving yourself a breather?" asked a deep, smooth voice.

She whirled around at the familiar sound and blushed at the sight of Ben Broughton standing in the doorway, his tall, imposing frame taking up a great deal of space.

Determined not to let on how pleased she was to see him, she turned back toward the window to regain a measure of composure. "I was watching the children at play and benefiting from the afternoon breezes. We're certainly enjoying a fine Indian summer." Satisfied that she had gathered her wits, she faced him once more. "Is there something I can do for you, some message you want me to give Lili?"

He took off his hat and ran his fingers through his head of thick, black hair, but it stubbornly fell back across his forehead in several directions, making her stomach knot with edginess. Simply put, the man was far too handsome for his own good.

He walked the rest of the way into the classroom. "Where does Lili sit?" he asked, still not stating his purpose in dropping by. For reasons she couldn't explain, his English brogue seemed especially pronounced today.

She pointed to the front row. "Right there. Closest to my desk."

"The one with the bunch of wilted flowers, I take it." He gave her a slanted grin.

"That's the one," she said, noting the sorrowful looking bouquet of weeds Lili had picked that morning.

"Her mother always liked flowers. I assume Lili is no different."

"All women love flowers," she answered too hastily, praying he wouldn't view the comment as a hint.

He walked across the room to stand beside her at the window. His giant presence loomed over her, making her want to stretch to her full height, small as she was. What was he doing here, and why, after making himself scarce for days on end, would he suddenly appear and act as if no time had passed?

"Is that Lili over there?" He bent at the shoulders to get a better view of the children at play.

Liza tried to determine where his eyes looked. "Yes. She is pushing little Erlene Barrington in the swing. I notice she watches out for her a lot. Erlene is so tiny compared to the others. And Lili is big for her age."

"She thinks the world of you, you know," he said, his throaty whisper massaging her taut nerves.

"Well, the feelings are mutual," Liza said, meaning it sincerely. "You haven't told me why you stopped by." She figured the quicker he stated his purpose and left, the sooner she could regain her normal heart rate.

Moving to her desk, she began to shuffle through some papers. The pendulum clock seemed to have slowed its ticking.

He stepped closer to her desk. "Actually, I hear that you've been visiting the families of your students, and I came to see when you might be going out to the Baxter and Bartel farms—that is, if you haven't already done so."

"No, I haven't. Why would you ask?"

"They're a rough bunch, the Baxters and Bartels. When you decide to go up there, I'd just as soon drive you myself."

Chapter Fourteen

I assure you I don't need you driving me to the Bartel and Baxter farms. I've managed all the other home visits without your help." Liza gave Ben a self-reliant look, but he didn't buy it.

"That may be so," he told her, his own back stiff with stubbornness, "but there aren't many families in these parts as vindictive as those two. There's moonshining and who knows what else going on up there in those parts. For all I know they might greet you with a shotgun. It's just plain not safe for a woman."

Ben could see by her obstinate look that it wouldn't be easy convincing her, but he'd be hog-tied before he'd let her go alone.

"I don't see…"

"Liza, tell me what day you're planning to go."

"What?"

"I'm going to drive you, so you may as well stop arguing with me." Exasperated by her willfulness, he took a couple of calming breaths and waited.

When she still didn't give an answer, he stepped closer, finding her too irresistible to ignore a second longer, her light blue dress drawn in at the waist to reveal how tiny she was, her golden hair pulled back into a tight little knot, several loose strands falling about her glowing cheeks in gentle ringlets.

Beads of perspiration dotted her idyllic little face. Without forethought, he took a folded kerchief from his back pocket and dabbed her cheeks and brow. "I don't want anything to happen to you," he said, shocked by how much he meant it. "And that's why I insist on taking you."

"Oh."

Obviously taken aback by his gentleness, she gazed at him, her blue eyes uncertain. He couldn't say he blamed her. He'd done everything possible to avoid her for the last several days, too afraid of what might happen if he didn't. But now here he was doting on her like some kind of teenaged fool. And if he didn't watch himself, he'd be kissing her flower petal lips before the sun went down.

"When I say those families aren't safe, I mean what I say. Some folks around here have had run-ins with them. Personally, I haven't, but I don't want you taking any unnecessary chances."

"Oh," she repeated in a feather-light voice.

He refolded the kerchief and put it back in his pocket, then unthinkingly tucked a couple strands of her golden hair behind a delicate ear. Standing so near, he couldn't help but notice she smelled of lavender. He wanted to move closer to see if the scent came from her face—or perhaps behind one ear.

"Ben, you mustn't…"

"That's the first time you've called me by my first name," he said, suddenly warmed by the realization.

"Yes, well…"

"What were you going to say?"

She moved away from him, taking up the big handbell on her desk. "I'm going to call the students in. I'd rather you weren't here when they come in."

"You wouldn't want anyone getting the wrong idea?"

"Exactly."

"I'm afraid I can't leave until you tell me what day you plan to go up to the Bartel and Baxter farms."

Sighing, she let her shoulders slump in resignation. "How is Wednesday?"

He gave her a victory smile. "I'll be waiting outside the school with my rig. I'll see if Emma will watch Lili until we get back."

"Fine," she said, keeping a careful distance.

He grinned. "Tell Lili I stopped by to see her, but she looked like she was having too much fun for me to interrupt."

She nodded curtly. "I'll tell her."

"Good-bye, Teacher."

With that, he walked outside wearing, he knew, a silly grin on his face. And just like that, the name of *Sarah Woodward* popped into his head—like a nagging ache for which he couldn't find one ounce of relief.

✳ ✳ ✳ ✳ ✳

As promised, Ben was waiting outside the schoolhouse on Wednesday afternoon. Climbing down from his rig, he offered up a smile warm enough to match September's sun. Liza's insides fairly melted when she saw him, but lest she allow her feelings to show, she gave him a stiff smile and turned her back to him to lock the school-house door.

"Papa, Miss Merriwether got flowers today!" Lili bounced down the steps to greet her father.

"Did she now?" Ben asked. "Does she have a secret admirer?"

"I don't know if it's a secret," she answered, climbing aboard the runabout.

Liza approached the smiling man and took his outstretched hand, feeling a gentle squeeze when he helped her up to the high seat. "An admirer, Miss Merriwether?" His tone was low and guarded. "I'm not sure I like the sounds of that."

Liza found herself giggling, charmed by the wary look in his eye. Was he toying with her?

"Tell Papa who gave you the bunch of flowers, Teacher." Lili sat in the seat behind and leaned far enough forward to wrap her arms around her father's solid neck. Liza couldn't help but notice the continuing smile on Ben's sun-bronzed face as he set the horses at a slow trot down Main Street heading for Emma Browning's place. The clip-clop of their feet against the hard earth competed with the birds overhead. Out of the corner of one eye, she saw him reach a hand up to gently pat Lili's wrist, and the simple act filled Liza's heart with some kind of unknown longing. Was she coming to *love* this family? She'd known them for such a short time, but already they'd touched her heart in more ways than she dared admit.

"Well?" Ben said, turning his gaze on Liza. "Who is this secret admirer?"

Liza gave a light laugh. "I suppose it's no secret that one of my students seems to have a slight crush on me."

Ben lifted a thick black eyebrow. "It's easy to understand why he would."

His gaze swept over her until she was forced to look away. She was enjoying the repartee far too much to be considered proper. After all, wasn't Benjamin Broughton betrothed to another? Perhaps she would bring up the matter later if his flirtatious overtones continued.

"Who is it?"

"Sam Hogsworth."

"Sam? I thought he and his twin brother were troublemakers. What have you done to turn poor Sam into a love-struck noodle head?"

Both Lili and Liza laughed now. "It's 'cause she's so pretty, Papa. Everyone says so. You should see how the boys watch her, as if they was old 'nough to court her."

"Oh, Lili, such talk," Liza cried, deeply embarrassed by the added attention. "That's plain silly. Besides, you're the pretty one. Now, may we please discuss something else?"

Lili rattled off any number of tidbits pertaining to her school day on the way to Emma's place. As usual, Ben gave her his full attention, even though his watchful eyes kept trailing back to Liza.

Once at Emma's, he instructed Lili to be on her best behavior, promising to come back for Molly and her as soon as possible.

"You don't have to do this, you know," Liza said after they started on their way up the mountainside.

Ben's gaze moved over her face until the palms of both her hands turned sweaty and she had to wipe them on her skirt. "Oh, but I do, Liza," he whispered, his voice carrying its usual mellow tone. "I told you before; I won't risk anything happening to you. Now, sit back and relax."

Warmed, Liza closed her eyes to the breezes and allowed herself the luxury of enjoying the ride.

Her visit with the Baxters was unusual, to say the least. Mrs. Baxter showed her face briefly, long enough to present Liza with a cup of lukewarm iced tea, offer her a shy smile, and then scoot back into the kitchen at Mr. Baxter's gruff orders. The poor woman appeared worn to the bone. Stringy brown hair fell upon scrawny shoulders, while her smudged, gaunt face, although devoid of deep wrinkles, looked old beyond her years. Something in the woman's eyes ached for recognition.

"Oh, but I would love to have Mrs. Baxter join us, sir," Liza had said, aching for the woman and annoyed that her husband would dismiss her when he knew good and well that the teacher had come to introduce herself to the family. Of course, where the *family* was remained a mystery. Either Rufus had conveniently hidden himself, or his father had purposely sent him and the rest of the clan to another part of the house. Rufus was the youngest of ten children. It crossed

Liza's mind that as soon as the children reached age sixteen they probably skedaddled. Maybe it was just Rufus who remained.

"Ain't a bit necessary," he'd answered, losing a wad of spittle in the pronouncement.

"But I would like to talk to both of you about what Rufus can expect to learn in school this year. Perhaps Mrs. Baxter could assist him in his studies."

He laughed outright at her suggestion. "That woman ain't got the brains of a butterfly. Anythin' pertainin' to ar son's educatin' best go through me."

Liza seriously doubted that Rufus had acquired an ounce of intelligence from his father's genes.

"But—" At that, Ben had jabbed her hard enough in the side to nearly knock her off balance. She took the poke as a clear warning to leave the matter alone. Still, it did little to settle down her anger at Mr. Baxter's impertinence.

For the next few moments, she and Ben sat on straight-backed chairs while she tried to initiate pleasant conversation between hasty sips of her iced tea, Ben's promise to leave the talking to her an instant regret on her part. To make matters worse, the visit lasted only as long as the iced tea, after which Mr. Baxter stood to his feet and shuffled to the door, his way of shooing them on their way.

Liza had barely begun discussing her expectations for the school year, let alone her early observations about Rufus's lack of interest in learning and Clement's negative influence. She'd had a nagging feeling from the first day of school that Rufus would be a different boy were it not for Clement's poor example.

"Thank ya fer stoppin' by. I'm sure my boy won't be givin' ya no trouble. If he does, well, ya have my permission to hit 'im 'longside the head." To this, he tacked on a throaty laugh.

"Let's be going, Miss Merriwether," Ben said evenly. He took her by the elbow. "Thank you for your time, Mr. Baxter." Then Ben steered her toward the door with both hands on her shoulders.

"I don't resort to physical punishment," Liza said, half turning.

"Humph! My boy's accustomed to rough handlin'." He puffed his chest up at the remark, as if it were something of which to be proud. "Can't imagine what the school board was thinkin' in hirin' a lady not much bigger than a pea pod."

He threw his head back and laughed at his own remark. Liza opened her mouth to say more, but Ben stopped her with his cool, "We're leaving now," and pushed her out the door.

Once Ben took the horses' reins in hand and headed up the trail in the opposite direction, Liza let him have it. "What was that about, Benjamin Broughton? You were supposed to accompany me, not thrust me out the door before I finished what I came for."

"I didn't thrust you. It was more like a gentle nudge. And the man had finished listening to what you had to say as soon as you said hello."

"But I'm his son's teacher."

"True, but not all parents place as much importance on their child's education as you might wish."

"Poor Rufus."

Ben turned to look at her. "You're something."

"What do you mean?"

"I believe you'd have pushed that man to his limits if I hadn't been here. No telling what trouble you might have found yourself in."

Liza swept a bothersome strand of hair out of her eyes. "He's pig-headed and obnoxious. Anyone could see that. I feel sorry for his wife."

"I'm sure she doesn't know any other way of life," he supplied.

"He as much as said she was stupid. I hope she didn't hear him."

 188

"She's heard worse, I'm sure. One thing you should know about these hill people is that they live by their own set of rules, and you best respect them for it."

"What do you mean?"

"A lot of things go on up here that not even the law will get involved in, Liza. Until we have lawmakers that are willing to risk life and limb, I suppose it will continue for generations to come."

"What kinds of things are we talking about?"

"Bootlegging, thievery, all forms of abuse. Even incest. Everyone in these parts carries a gun. Didn't you see the pistol Baxter had tucked away in his hip pocket?"

Liza gasped. "No! I saw the rifles on the wall, but I assumed those were for hunting game."

Ben chortled, looked both ways when they arrived at a fork in the road, and then guided the rig to the right. He seemed to know exactly where he was going. "They hunt game all right. Trouble is it's not always the four-legged kind."

Liza put a hand to her mouth to stifle a shriek. "Is murder another one of their vices?"

"They wouldn't call it murder. They would call it self-defense, protecting their property and their rights as citizens. They don't consider themselves criminals, and for the most part, they're not. Most folks up here are as law-abiding as the next; however, there are some who rule their land as if they were kings, going to any lengths to keep people off it.

"They treat their women, daughters included, as second-class citizens, more like slaves. Most of the wives up here grew up in similar situations. They look at it as a way of life."

"These people need the Lord," Liza said, her heart suddenly fallen clear to the tips of her high-top shoes.

Ben looked straight ahead. "You're right on that count."

❊ ❊ ❊ ❊ ❊

The Bartel place sat on a large stretch of land. Ben had no idea how much property Angus Bartel owned, but he'd heard from some that it was close to a hundred acres, and probably more. How he'd found the money to acquire it was another matter. To Ben's knowledge, he'd never held a job, at least not in town. Some thought he made brew of the strongest kind and sold it to the underground market. Ben had seen men of every known description come and go in these parts, most slickly dressed, wearing guns under their long, dapper coats.

This was dangerous ground to be on, but Liza was a stubborn woman. There was no way he would have allowed her to make the trip alone.

"Is that it?" Liza asked after they rounded a bend in the trail.

"It is."

"It's not much more than a big, run-down shack. The Baxters' farm was better than this."

The yard, littered with waste, created a potluck for roaming chickens and goats to pick at. A nearby barn looked ready to topple. Tall, unmowed grass bent to the gentle breezes while an array of soaring wild flowers grew up helter-skelter, untouched, a stark contrast to the peeling white paint on the ramshackle, clapboard, two-story house.

"Most of the men in these parts make their money, then squander it on gambling and such. They patronize Madam Guttersnipe's hangout on a regular basis, I'm afraid. They're not much for taking care of their possessions, unless someone tries to steal away what's theirs."

Liza visibly shuddered and Ben put a hand to her shoulder. "You should let me do the talking, Liza."

"But I'm Clement's and Rosie's teacher." Her pert little chin jutted out in defiance. He couldn't help but admire the little spitfire. And maybe what he was feeling went even deeper than admiration. Whatever it was, he knew his heart was in trouble.

"Okay, you do the talking, but if I need to cut in, I will," he said.

"That seems fair enough."

"And when I say it's time to go, don't argue with me."

Liza gave him a dubious look before relenting. "All right, I suppose you know more about what to expect than I do."

"Believe me, Liza, I do *not* know what to expect, and that's what makes me nervous."

"Hold it right there!"

Ben halted the team in the middle of the road and looked all directions before he spotted Angus Bartel's approach from behind a decaying shed. How long had the burly man with the scruffy, graying beard been watching from his hiding place? Denim overalls hung loosely over a dirty shirt, and a tattered felt hat perched sideways on his head of longish hair added to his already coarse appearance. What stood out the most, however, was the shotgun he held at the ready.

"Mr. Bartel, we'd be obliged if you'd put down the gun. We mean no harm," Ben said, determined to stay calm for Liza's sake.

"Can't ya read? Sign says, no trespassin'."

"We saw the sign but figured you wouldn't mind if..."

"Well, would ya lookie there, Paw?" From the barn came a sauntering Clement Bartel, as big as his father, if not taller and huskier. Instinct told Ben the boy was trouble. Greasy strands of long, sandy-colored hair lay across his pimpled forehead. Baggy, torn pants fell haphazardly below his exposed waistline. "It's my teacher. Ain't she a perty one? Didn't I tell ya she was a looker?"

Ben's gut twisted to the point of nausea.

191

"Shut yore mouth, boy." Angus spat on the ground. "Show some respect." But even as Angus spoke the order, it was obvious by the glint in his eye that his son's remarks had humored him.

Liza shifted, and Ben put a hand to her thigh to still her. "The teacher here would like a word with you and Mrs. Bartel. This is a social call, mind you. Miss Merriwether has been making the rounds to all her students' families."

"Well now, ain't that nice?" With that, Angus lowered the rifle to his side, allowing Ben to breathe easier. Still, the shrewd look in his eye did little to ease his suspicions about the two of them.

"Yeah, it's mighty nice," echoed Clement, his gaze resting exclusively on Liza.

"Are your wife and Rosie nearby?" Liza asked. "I would like to see them."

"The woman's busy makin' ar grub. Rosie's helpin'. They can't be bothered," Angus said, pulling at his unkempt beard.

Clement let his gaze fall to the ground, then kicked a stone with the toe of his boot, a sly smirk present on his face.

"Oh, but I'll only take a minute of your time."

"Let 'er stay, Paw," Clement urged, the whine in his voice exaggerated. "It ain't ever' day sech a perty thing comes across ar land."

Angus opened his mouth to respond at the same time that Rosie came bounding onto the porch. "Teacher! Mama, it's my teacher! Come quick."

Liza's face lit up at the sight of the ten year old. "Rosie!"

"Miss Merriwether!" the child cried, running toward their wagon, bare feet caked with dirt, knee-length dress faded and holey. Instinctively, Ben moved the horses closer to the house, something he was certain Angus would find objectionable.

"I heard you was visitin', but I din't think you'd really come to my house."

"She comed to see me, too, brat," Clement asserted.

Liza started to climb down, but Ben snatched hold of her arm. She turned a sour look on him before giving the child her full attention. "I would not have left you out, Rosie," she said, taking care not to look Clement's way.

"I got all my homework done," the child announced. Clement sneered audibly.

"Good for you. I'm proud of you," Liza said.

"You hightail it back in the house, and tell your maw there ain't no need fer her to be steppin' out on the porch," Angus said with undue harshness.

Too late, Mrs. Bartel opened the door and stepped outside, shielding her eyes from the afternoon sun to get a better view. Her discolored cotton dress hung just past her knees, and, like her daughter, her feet were bare. Although just as pale and gaunt looking as Mrs. Baxter, this woman wore a certain kind of defiance that showed up clear as glass in her intelligent eyes.

"Git back in the house, woman," Angus Bartel ordered.

But the woman's chin came out at the same time that she pulled her shoulders back. It was then that Ben spotted the large bruise about the size of a fist on the underside of her jaw. He tensed as he thought about how and where she'd acquired the ugly bluish mark. Had it come from her brutish husband or, worse, her son? Tempted to ask, yet knowing the stir it could cause with Angus, he waited for a dose of spiritual wisdom.

The gasp that came from Liza's throat told Ben she'd also glimpsed the bruise.

"I would like to meet the teacher, Angus. Rosie has told me so much about her," Mrs. Bartel said in a quiet voice. She rested her hands on the wobbly porch railing and squinted up at Ben and Liza. "Afternoon. May I interest you in some lemonade?"

The woman had grit; Ben had to give her that much.

Angus transferred his weight from one foot to the other, stuck a thumb in one hip pocket, still holding to the rifle with the other hand, and released a low growl. He moved his murky eyes from the poor woman back to his son. Some hidden message lay buried in their depths, and Ben didn't like the grim feeling it produced. He leaned his heavy frame in closer to Liza, willing her to sit still.

"A glass of lemonade would be nice, ma'am," Ben answered, "but I'm afraid we can't stay. Dusk is falling in, and I have to get Miss Merriwether back down the mountainside."

"Oh," said Mrs. Bartel, her face dropping with disappointment.

"I would love a glass, thank you," said Liza, scooting off the high seat before Ben could nab her. With lightning speed, Clement was there to capture her hand, his hungry eyes taking in the length of her as she hopped down. Ben's gut twisted with dread. What was the young buck trying to accomplish by flirting with his schoolteacher? Just as quickly, Ben's own feet hit the ground, after which he raced around to Liza's side and seized her by the elbow.

Moments later, Mrs. Bartel and Rosie returned with a tray of mismatched glasses and a tall pitcher of lemonade. At this proximity, Ben caught a better view of the woman's facial contusion, and the mere sight of it made his stomach reel. If he were a betting man, he would wager his last dollar that she hadn't gotten it falling. Had the bruise resulted from an act of defiance on her part? What would she face when they left for disobeying her husband and bringing out lemonade? How many other such wounds lay hidden beneath her clothing?

Angus Bartel huffed in anger as he climbed the porch steps and plopped into a warped rocker, his eyes never leaving the small gathering, his rifle lying at the ready across his lap. It didn't take a genius to realize he wanted Ben and Liza off his property, and the sooner the better. Ben prayed for both wisdom and protection. Men such as Angus Bartel were as dangerous as dynamite. One false move and you might not live to tell about it.

Chapter Fifteen

*L*iza watched Mrs. Bartel with keen eyes. The poor thing tried her best to play the hospitable hostess, but with a husband such as she had, vulgar and undignified, and a son with the manners of a loutish bull, she was hard-pressed to pull it off. Still, she lifted the pitcher with ease and, with Rosie's help, poured the lemonade into the empty glasses, plastering a smile on her face as she did so.

"I want to thank you for makin' the trip up the mountain, Miss Merriwether," the woman said, handing over a full glass of lemonade to Liza and then one to Ben. Ben lifted the glass and, to Liza's amazement, swallowed the entire contents in one gulp. "It ain't an easy trip. My Rosie rides down with Mr. Chalmers ever' mornin'. He works at Grady Swanson's sawmill. Clement here finds his own way," she said, giving Clement what looked to Liza like an iniquitous stare.

"Oh, you have Mr. Broughton to thank for driving me," replied Liza, lifting her face to gauge Ben's expression and finding it incensed. Something told her she should have remained in her seat. She hugged the cool glass between her palms, praying for the correct choice of words, wanting to keep the visit cordial and Ben's displeasure in check.

"I'd have been happy to drive you, Teacher. All ya needed to do was ask." Clement grinned with his syrupy offer, revealing two oversized, yellowish front teeth Liza had never noticed before, perhaps because he rarely showed them unless it was to sneer.

"I appreciate the offer, Clement, but it wasn't necessary," Liza said. "Mr. Broughton insisted."

"That so?" Clement's eyes fell to Ben. "You sweet on my perty teacher, Mr. Broughton?"

"Clement, that's enough," Mrs. Bartel said, turning a trembling chin upward, something in her eyes indicating distress at having to discipline her son.

"Miss Merriwether, I believe we should go." Ben's fingers clenched Liza's elbow until she nearly winced, but her feet refused to budge. Angus rocked back and forth on the porch, the chair squeaking loudly with every pass. "The boy ain't meanin' no harm, Broughton," he said with a husky laugh. "I think he has a soft spot fer the teacher. Can't say I blame him none. She is a perty thing."

"Mama…" Rosie's soft voice interrupted the exchange, her face a picture of worry and embarrassment as she pulled on her mother's skirts.

"I think it's obvious you aren't interested in what the teacher has to say, Angus," Ben inserted roughly, looking from father to son. Liza stiffened at the harsh tone his words carried. "Come on, Liza." He yanked at her arm again.

Risking Ben's anger, Liza said firmly, "I came to talk to the Bartels, and I would dearly like to do just that."

Angus's sour-sounding laugh rose up from his round, meaty gut. "I can't say I got the time, miss."

"Are you saying you're not interested in your children's education?" Liza faced him head-on, determined not to give in to his intimidating glare.

"I'm saying I ain't got the time," he pressed.

"What say we leave the women to their own talk, Angus?" Ben suddenly offered. "You and Clement can show me around your place." He handed his empty glass back to Mrs. Bartel, his steely eyes never leaving Angus's face in the process.

197

Mr. Bartel ceased his rocking and beard pulling, his beady eyes filling with suspicion. "Ain't nothin' around here you'd be interested in seein', but it can't hurt to give you a tour." With that, the man stood. "Come on, boy." He motioned at a reluctant Clement to lead the way.

"Ben," Liza whispered, worrying her lower lip with her teeth as Angus and Clement started meandering down the path and Mrs. Bartel and Rosie walked up to the porch.

"You'll be fine," he quietly assured. "Stay on the porch where I can keep my eye on you. I won't go far."

She nodded. "All right, but what about you? What are you...?"

He bent down close to her ear, sending a ripple of shivers up her spine when his breath tickled her lobe. "I'm big enough to take care of myself, but bear in mind we're leaving in ten minutes, you hear?"

"I'll be ready," she promised.

Ten minutes passed and Ben did not return.

Liza glanced out at the shed to which the three had entered while Mrs. Bartel kept up her chatter. "It's been so long since I talked to another woman, ma'am. And one as pretty and refined as you makes it extra special."

"Thank you, Mrs. Bartel. I'm happy to talk to you, as well." She looked at Rosie, whose cheeks were beaming with delight. "You should be very proud of your daughter. Rosie is a fine student. She attends to all her lessons and minds her manners perfectly."

Mrs. Bartel smiled with pleasure. "She always has been a fine child. I—I'm sorry about Clement."

Liza paused before responding. "Yes, well, I'm afraid your son has some difficulties in school—both academically and socially."

"He ain't my son. I want to make that clear right off." The words came out sounding cold and hard as stone. "He comes from another woman, one of Angus's, well, you know." Liza *didn't* know, and she felt too stunned by the information to pry. "The woman had no money, you see, so when Clement was five, she dropped him off on ar porch. Never come back fer him, neither. That was ten years ago. Clement ain't seen her since.

"I tried to raise the boy best I could, but he is terrible cruel. By the time we got him, he already had a mean streak blacker than sin; kilt ever' little animal he could get his hands on, kittens, puppies, even wild bunnies. Strangulated 'em, he did, then left 'em to rot on my doorstep like he was proud or somethin'. I can't abide his awful temper and disrespect for the feelin's of others." That said, she put a flat palm to her wounded jaw.

Liza gasped. "Did Clement do that to you?"

Mrs. Bartel shrugged. "Weren't nothin'. He's always knockin' me or Angus around."

"Angus too?"

"Angus is gettin' older. He can't stand up to the boy the way he used to. When Clement gets in one of his fits, there ain't no stoppin' 'im, and pity the person who gets in his way."

She shook her head in a show of defeat. Rosie's perceptive gaze said she wasn't a bit surprised by her mother's words. "My mama's never done nothin' to Clement 'cept be nice to him." She wrapped an arm around her mother's tiny waist.

"Oh, Rosie, has Clement ever hurt you?" Liza asked.

Rosie nodded, frowning. "A couple times, Teacher, but mostly I walk away from him 'fore he gets too mad. Mama stands up to him. That's what gets her in trouble."

"Why doesn't Mr. Bartel make him leave?" cried Liza, her heart reeling with untold misery.

The woman shrugged again, then let go a frail-sounding chuckle. "That man has no backbone. Truth be told, I think he's scared o' his own boy. Clement's powerful wicked when someone sets him off, Miss Merriwether, so Angus caters to the boy, anythin' to keep from gettin' struck."

"Oh, Mrs. Bartel," Liza said.

Mrs. Bartel turned her gaze to a distant field. "Angus ain't sech a bad man, miss." She spoke in so soft a voice that Liza had to lean in to her to catch the words. "Oh, I know he comes across like an ornery fool, and heaven knows he ain't good fer much, but he ain't in bad with the law like most are up here, and that's somethin'.

"That woman, the mother of Clement, she was a bad seed; worked at Madam Guttersnipe's place 'til Clement was born. After that, she left for greener pastures. I thought we'd seen the last of her until she come back five years later. She left Angus's bawlin' kid on ar porch along with a note claimin' she couldn't handle the boy, nor afford 'im.

"It weren't no secret that the boy belonged to Angus. Anyone could see it. 'Sides, I knew Angus had it bad fer her back then."

Mrs. Bartel tossed her head back, and Liza took note of yet another small bruise hidden beneath the front flap of her fallen collar. Suddenly the woman turned her delicate face toward Liza. Deep-set, hazel-colored eyes watered at the corners. "Angus says he ain't been back to Guttersnipe's since, and I believe 'im."

Liza wasn't interested in hearing about the illicit activities that dotted Angus Bartel's past; however, she was concerned about Rosie's welfare in light of all she'd learned regarding the girl's half-brother. It was not a healthy or safe situation for anyone, let alone a ten-year-old child.

"Mrs. Bartel, I'm worried about Rosie and you."

Mrs. Bartel flipped her skinny wrist. "Don't bother yerself about us, ma'am. We've made do till now. I 'spect we'll be fine."

"Have you talked to anyone else about this? What if I went with you

200

to talk to the sheriff? Mr. Broughton says he's a fair man. I'm sure if…"

"No! Angus would never stand fer that. Clement's still his flesh and blood. I got to respect my husband's wishes."

"What if *I* was the one to report him?" Liza suggested.

Mrs. Bartel's eyes roamed over Liza's face in disbelief. "You ain't got nothin' to gain by doin' a thing like that. You could get yer own self in a heap o' trouble. Clement could…"

"I care about you and Rosie," Liza interrupted, "and I don't want anything to happen to you. By the look of those bruises, Clement has a fierce temper."

"Yes, and he could use it on you."

Liza ignored the retort. "If I simply walked away today and disregarded what I've learned, then I'd feel responsible if something even worse happened to you."

"But it ain't yer problem, ma'am."

Liza smiled at the forlorn-looking mother and child. "But it *is* my problem. We are all God's children, put on this earth to love Him and care for others. I would be disobeying my heavenly Father if I simply walked away and did nothing."

A distant rustling of leaves alerted Liza to the men's and boy's return. Frustrated by her sudden lack of time, Liza hurried to say, "I am going to talk to Mr. Broughton about this. He will know what's best. Don't worry." But Mrs. Bartel's trembling mouth said that she would do just that. Worry. "And whatever you do, do not tell Mr. Bartel about our—ahem, discussion."

"But Angus don't like no secrets."

"This isn't really a secret. It's simply unnecessary for you to tell him everything we discussed."

"Oh." That seemed to clear the matter up, for Mrs. Bartel's shoulders visibly relaxed.

"You womenfolk done with yer yappin'?" Angus called out, chomping on a blade of grass while he approached, his gnarled, bearded face a picture of outright tension.

"We are." Liza looked Ben over carefully, thankful to discover he looked no worse for the wear. Clement, however, wore self-absorption like a coat of many colors, his usual brash manner standing out in the way he sauntered toward her, as if he owned the universe, giving her a cocky half-grin.

"Good," Ben said in a curt tone, "because it's time we headed back."

❄ ❄ ❄ ❄ ❄

"Why didn't you let me do the talking?" Ben asked, gripping the reins to keep from strangling the little woman sitting beside him.

"We didn't actually agree to that—did we?" Her voice faltered.

He gave her an incredulous stare. "It was the last thing we discussed before we reached the house."

"I thought we decided I would do the talking and you would cut in if necessary."

"I notice you were stingy on your end of the bargain, then," he said. "I told you it was time to leave and you balked."

"But I wanted to talk to Clement's mother," she argued.

"You—it—oh, what's the point; it's done, and you're not going back there." Ben wasn't sure which emotion had him most riled, anger that she'd been so stubborn, or relief that they were both in one piece. The tour of Angus's farm had turned up no evidence of bootlegging that Ben could see, but fifteen minutes of keeping company with him and that foulmouthed son of his had him convinced that Clement's middle name was Evil.

Liza's shoulders straightened. "We have to go to the sheriff, you know."

"What?"

Liza turned blue, moist eyes on him, and Ben's insides nearly fell in a heap at his feet. She was really something.

"It's our Christian duty," she pressed.

"Liza, did you see the rifle? It was cocked. Do you know what that means?" He felt his patience dwindling.

"Of course I know. I'm not entirely brainless. But it was just there to scare us. Mr. Bartel wouldn't have used it on us. His wife told me Angus is not in bad with the law," Liza said in a rush.

At the bottom of the mountain, Ben pulled the horses to a halt under a shady patch of trees and shifted in the seat in order to look into her eyes, taking care to breathe normally, praying at the same time for patience and a gentle spirit, even though his blood seemed at the boiling point.

"You don't know these people the way I do. They're not to be reasoned with—or trusted," he managed.

"Don't you see? Mrs. Bartel said Angus never laid a hand to her. All those bruises came from Clement. She said that Clement roughs up his own father when his temper goes sour because Angus is getting too old to defend himself. She said…"

Ben put a hand to Liza's mouth and kept it there. Her blue eyes bulged at the act, but at least it was enough to silence her. "And you believed her?"

He waited to remove his hand until she gave a slow nod. Several strands of golden hair blew into her face, blocking her vision. It took a great deal of restraint on his part not to remove them. He wanted to take the silky strands between his fingers and roll them around, test them for their smoothness. Fortunately, she tucked them out of the way before he had the chance. "She also told me Clement is not her son."

Ben sat back. "Really."

"Apparently, Angus met some woman at Madam Guttersnipe's place and, well, you know."

Ben groaned. He *did* know, and the knowledge turned his gut inside out. "I don't know why the people of Little Hickman don't run that woman and her evil establishment out of town."

"That's beside the point," Liza cried. "What's important is that we report what we know to the sheriff."

"I'm not sure Will can do anything," Ben replied.

"Why not? You saw the bruises."

"I did, Liza, but without Mrs. Bartel's cooperation, I doubt there's much the sheriff can do. He'll need solid proof."

"But we saw the proof with our own eyes."

"Will Mrs. Bartel back you up on that?" he asked.

Liza's face held instant panic. "Don't you see? She wouldn't have told me about Clement if she wasn't afraid and desperate. If you could have seen how she trembled while she was talking about it, well, you'd understand. Something else, I spotted another bruise beneath her collar." Ben's stomach clenched. *Another bruise.* "If we don't do something to help them, who will?"

He turned his gaze outward, watching tall blades of grass dance to the gentle breezes. An unexpected chill in the air warned of changing temperatures once the sun settled into the horizon. He bit unconsciously at his lower lip, contemplating what he'd learned.

"You're right about one thing," Ben confessed.

"What?"

"It is our Christian duty. We can't pretend nothing is going on in that house."

Liza's shoulders dropped in relief. "I'm glad you see it that way. When should we go see the sheriff?"

He gave her a thorough look. "*We* are not going to go to the sheriff."

"What? But you said…"

He put a hand to her mouth again. It seemed the only way to quiet her. "*I* will go see Will Murdock. *You* will sit tight and mind your manners, Miss Merriwether."

She slapped at his hand. "I will not. I have just as much right…"

"You're the town's one and only teacher. You have your safety and that of your students to consider."

"I don't see how my going to the sheriff is going to endanger…"

"Listen to me. If Clement ever got wind that you went to the sheriff on Rosie's and Mrs. Bartel's behalf there could be real trouble in store."

"Perhaps you're right, but that's a chance I'm willing to take." There went her stubborn little chin again.

"Well, I'm not," he stated.

"You have no say in the matter." Now her lip went out in a pout, and suddenly he wanted to kiss it. The realization threw him for a loop.

"You are a pigheaded woman. Has anyone ever told you that?"

Only a hint of a smile revealed itself. "Aunt Hettie, I suppose, but not in those precise words," she relented.

"And how would your aunt feel about your getting involved in a potentially dangerous situation?"

Now she crossed her arms and leaned against the straight, hard back of the wagon seat. "That's not a fair question."

He sighed. "Liza, you know I'm right."

"Oh, for goodness' sake, go to the sheriff without me, then, but I expect you to tell me how he plans to handle the matter." Her stubborn look told him she wasn't one to concede defeat, but this time common sense overruled.

He touched a finger to her chin and guided it around until her gaze met up with his. For a change, she sat mute, her large, round eyes full of curiosity and something else he couldn't quite decipher. Uncertainty? Trepidation?

He carefully cupped her perfectly designed face with both his hands, readjusted himself on the seat so that he faced her more squarely, and then slowly moved in, deliberately, drawing her closer. When their lips first met, it was with feather-lightness, a tentative kind of touch, unsure, wobbly. After all, she was the first woman he'd even looked at, let alone touched, since Miranda.

He moved his hands from her warm cheeks to her shoulders and then up and down her arms. Finally, he went to the small of her back to pull her closer. There his hands temporarily rested while he continued to taste her sweetness, lose himself in the moment.

She seemed to do the same as her own arms moved to the back of him, his bulk making it difficult for her to reach around, her breathing snagging and catching with each intake.

His heart thumped out a rhythm that rumbled through his head, drowning out the sounds of testy whip-poor-wills and scolding chipmunks from the tree overhead, the earthy creatures obviously angered by their invasion of privacy.

Her softness so mesmerized him that it wasn't until she pushed away from him, gasping for air, that he came to his senses in one fell swoop.

"What did you do that for?" she cried.

"Pardon me?"

"You shouldn't have done that," she insisted, looking at her lap.

He grinned. "Why not?"

She scooted to the far side of the seat, as if that would keep him from snatching her up into his arms once more.

"You know why not," she insisted.

"Refresh my memory."

Her blue eyes narrowed into mere slits and her slender arms went into their usual stubborn cross. "It wasn't proper or fitting."

Now he chuckled outright. "You seemed to enjoy it."

"Be serious," she said, her lower lip extending just enough to resemble the beginnings of another pout.

He had never been more serious about anything in his life. "Liza…"

"What happened to your—bride?" The pointed question stabbed him in the side like a pitchfork. "I thought you were betrothed. How could you—you kiss me like that—when you're devoted to another?"

"I am not devoted. For your information, I won't be marrying Miss Sarah Woodward after all," he announced, knowing it to be true the second he spoke the words. He would contact the agency first thing in the morning.

"Oh? And why not?" She kept her gaze straight ahead, her crossed arms rigid.

"Because I have feelings for you."

Suddenly she turned shocked eyes on him. "But that's impossible."

He smiled down at her. "Why is that impossible, Liza?"

"Because you barely know me."

"I think I'm off to a good start."

"Besides, I've just begun my teaching job," she said, breathless. "Mrs. Winthrop would never approve. My contract clearly states I am to have no inappropriate contact with anyone of the opposite gender.

Apparently, she considers Jon Atkins safe since he's a preacher, but no one else."

"She doesn't know Jon Atkins," he mumbled between his teeth.

"What?"

"Nothing."

She worried both sides of her lower lip with her bright, polished teeth, and then threw him one of her determined looks. "We must never look upon each other's faces again, do you understand?"

Now he laughed straight from his belly. "That will be hard to do, considering you are my daughter's teacher—and, don't forget, my neighbor."

She stiffened. "Then I shall move back to town."

"No, you won't." This time, his back went up.

"I will."

"Not after all the work the men and I put into that place. You're staying put."

"You cannot order me around, Benjamin Broughton."

He attempted steady breathing. "No, I'm beginning to see that about you."

Lord, what is it in this woman that draws me? She is nothing like my mild-mannered Miranda—steady, compliant, meek and gentle Miranda.

With Miranda, life had always been simple, uncomplicated... Liza, on the other hand...

"For ye have need of patience, that, after ye have done the will of God, ye might receive the promise." He'd read the passage from Hebrews just that morning. Why now was God bringing it to mind? *What promise?* And what was this about patience?

"—not a child." Somehow, in his quiet meanderings, he'd missed what she'd said.

"What?" he asked.

Loving Liza Jane

"Never mind."

Choosing not to push, he asked, "Anyway, what would people think if you moved back to town?"

"What do you mean?"

"Wouldn't folks turn suspicious if you simply up and left the cabin? Someone is bound to put two and two together, Teacher."

She looked thoughtful. "I see what you mean. Well then, we'll simply forget about this—this entire episode."

"We will?"

"Yes, we will. We will forget that—that ridiculous kiss ever happened."

To this, he chuckled and picked up the reins, suddenly jerking the horses and, in turn, the wagon, into motion.

"Sorry, Miss Merriwether," he said quietly, turning his gaze on her. "I don't think I'll be forgetting that kiss anytime soon."

Chapter Sixteen

When Liza determined to forget about the kiss, she hadn't planned for it to be so difficult. Necessary as it was to blot it from her thoughts, the reminiscence kept returning each time she spotted Ben walking out to his barn on a cool, crisp morning, milk pail or egg basket in one hand, lantern in the other. He never failed to lift his head to gaze toward her cabin, but she kept herself hidden in the shadows, always taking care to light her own lamps after he'd made it safely inside the dark barn.

Three times, he'd stopped her on her early morning trek into town to offer her a ride, but each time she'd refused. "Do you plan to buy a horse or at least rent one?" he'd asked one particular frosty morning. "I heard Sam got in a couple of nags. This walk will be cumbersome once winter sets in. I've an extra stall, if you've a mind to use it."

She'd managed to keep her eyes trained on the path ahead, her chin high, her shoulders straight. "I've put too much money into furnishing my cabin to purchase a horse just yet. Maybe I'll be ready in the springtime. Until then, the walk is good for me."

"I'm thinking I'll drive you when the freezing temperatures arrive."

"And I'm thinking I'd just as soon walk," she'd replied.

"Stubborn woman," he'd muttered under his breath, loud enough for her to hear, however. Piloting his rig alongside her, he'd added, "I talked to Will Murdock about the Bartels."

Liza's ears had perked at that, and so she'd turned her gaze upward, hopeful. "What did he say?"

 210

"As I suspected, there's not much he can do unless Mrs. Bartel is willing to press charges against Clement."

"She won't do that. She said Clement is still Angus's flesh and blood."

"Well, then…" he'd started.

Frustrated, she'd said, "There must be something he can do."

"He's promised to visit and look for a chance to talk to Mrs. Bartel privately, but aside from that, his hands are tied," Ben had told her.

"Angus will never leave her side."

Ben had shrugged. "It's the best Will can do, Liza."

She'd walked along, waiting for him to slap his horses into a faster pace and leave her behind. But he hadn't. Instead, he'd continued in a mellow tone, melting her bones in spite of the brisk, biting air. "I want to talk about what happened between us, Liza."

She'd swallowed down a hard lump. "Nothing happened."

"What do you mean? I kissed you, and you kissed me back. That's something."

"I told you I don't want to speak of that. I'm doing my best to forget it ever happened, and I'll thank you to do the same."

"And I told you I won't be forgetting it anytime soon."

"Well, you best train your mind otherwise. Now, would you kindly leave me to my walking? I'm working out my day's lessons in my head."

He'd given her a heavy sigh and a dark look to match. "We will discuss this, Liza. If not today, then soon."

"Good day, Mr. Broughton," she'd replied.

After that, he'd shaken his head and turned his team around. She'd thought he was going to town, but apparently, he'd only meant to drive her to the school.

211

She'd been harsh with him, but she didn't have the time to consider either of their feelings. It was entirely true that Mrs. Winthrop wouldn't approve were she ever to discover Liza with Ben. Why, Liza could lose her job on the spot, and then where would she be?

A female teacher never compromises herself, the contract clearly stated. *Marriage or other unseemly behavior by women teachers is strictly forbidden.* Not that she had done anything unseemly with Benjamin Broughton. God Himself knew she had nothing for which to feel guilty, unless it was the fact that she might very well be falling in love with the English farmer.

Late fall was upon them. The leaves had turned many shades of oranges, yellows, and brownish hues, transforming the rising and falling terrain of northern Kentucky into a magnificent arena of color. Never had Liza seen such beauty. Although Boston's rural areas boasted similar colors, the city where she'd grown up provided no match when it came to Kentucky's leafy display.

Autumn sunshine cast its warm glow on Liza's shoulders as she made the after-school hike up the path toward her cabin. Shifting the weight of her satchel to her other shoulder, Liza strode over the newly built bridge that spanned Little Hickman Creek. Once across, she spotted her cozy cabin at the top of Shannon's Peak, nestled amongst two tall pines, several oaks, some flowering bushes, and numerous evergreens. It was a welcome sight after a long day of teaching, the square little dwelling with its smokestack chimney, new curtained windows, and cheery front door seeming to call out a greeting. What a change from the first time she'd seen it in early August.

The weight of her bag reminded her of the stack of papers that awaited correcting once she finished her supper of stew. Just because the school day had come to an end didn't mean her work had also finished. Often, the mountain of papers to correct at the close of the day kept her up into the wee hours of the morning.

"Miss Merriwether!" Lili Broughton waved her arm and ran down the front steps of her own house.

"Hello, Lili," Liza called out, waving back. The child had earned a warm place in Liza's heart, one that no one else came close to filling. She knew it wasn't right for any teacher to choose one child over another, but in Lili's case, it had happened before she had the chance to prevent it.

"Papa said I should invite you to supper. Can you come? Please?"

Liza stopped in her tracks while Lili kept up her fast approach, finally screeching to a halt in front of her, breathless, freckled face aglow.

"Oh, Lili, I…" Leave it to Ben to send Lili in his place. He knew she would decline an invitation coming from him, but one from his daughter, well, that was another story.

"Please…" begged Lili, one long, crooked braid slung over her shoulder.

"Well, honey, I've already planned my supper. In fact, it's been stewing all day on a low flame."

"But can't you eat it tomorrow?"

Lili laughed at the eager-faced child, her blue eyes bright and intelligent.

She patted her heavy schoolbag. "Look at all the papers I have to correct."

"I can help—and so can Papa."

It was then she saw Ben Broughton saunter out onto his porch and wrap a muscled arm around one of the porch columns, his legs crossed at the ankles, his eyes, even from this distance, scrutinizing. On his lips, he'd planted one of his infamous slanted grins, the kind that seemed to heal her tired, achy joints, smooth her jagged emotions.

"Well, I suppose I could wrap the kettle up tightly and store it in a cool place until tomorrow."

Instantly, Lili went into a sort of happy dance, spinning circles until her long cotton skirt extended in a bell.

"You'll get dizzy, and then you won't feel like eating," Liza said, realizing how like a mother she'd just sounded. The realization struck her so that she glanced in Ben's direction once more, only to find him smiling wider.

What was she doing? Certainly, Mrs. Winthrop would have her job if she discovered Liza taking supper in the presence of a gentleman, worse, in his home. Rather than consider the consequences, however, Liza took the small hand offered her and allowed the child to pull her in the direction of the Broughton house.

The afternoon and evening turned out more than pleasurable. After supper, she'd helped with the cleanup, just as she had the other time she'd shared a meal with them. This time, however, it was Ben who worked alongside her while Lili tended to her baby sister.

"Thank you for the supper. You're turning into quite a cook," Liza said to Ben while she washed the dishes and he dried and put them away.

He chuckled. "My chicken 'n dumplin's with mashed potatoes is one of only two specialties I lay claim to. After that, I'm afraid my cooking skills are almost nil."

Liza smiled. "And what is this other specialty, if I may ask?"

"Why, beef dodgers and baked beans, of course."

"Beef dodgers? What are those?"

Going still in a show of disbelief, Ben cried, "You, my dear, have not lived until you've eaten my beef dodgers."

"Oh? I'll be the judge of that." She giggled. "What are they?"

"Little corncakes filled with minced beef. The recipe followed us over on the ship from Europe."

His mention of the ship spurred on questions about his family, which he freely answered, and before she knew it, he'd told her about his parents and grandfather, and their dreams for coming to America.

After they had washed, dried, and put away the last dish, Lili talked her father into taking his violin down from a high shelf and serenading them with songs. His deep, resonant voice carried throughout the small house while Lili played with her sister on the floor and Liza watched and listened, warmed to the tips of her stocking-clad feet by the sweetness of it all.

Next, Lili pulled down a checkerboard, and the three of them took turns playing checkers, laughing and teasing the entire time. Although Lili beat Liza on more than one occasion, neither could triumph over Ben, so with chagrin, they eventually declared him checker champion of the night.

"Papa never lets me win," Lili said in a near pout, pushing back from the table. "He says I have to learn to be a good loser."

"He's right," Liza said, smiling. "That way, when you finally do beat him in the game, he will have learned from you how to take his loss graciously."

Ben laughed at that, his eyes freely roving over Liza's face, lingering for a moment on her mouth. Liza felt her face go red as a beet and so she quickly looked at Lili, who was stretching to put away the checkerboard.

"I can't wait for October Fest!" the child suddenly announced when she turned to face both adults.

"I've heard it's quite an affair," Liza said, clasping her hands together and resting them on the table. Although the event wasn't

215

scheduled for at least another week, the townsfolk were already abuzz about it. The Friday of the festival even warranted a day off school. Mrs. Winthrop had made that clear right from the start when Liza signed her contract and the woman had given her a calendar of holiday events and vacation dates. "What shall I expect at this—festival?"

"Oh, all the kids get balloons, there's pie eating contests, three-legged races, running relays, pumpkin carving, baseball games, and lots of food."

Lili seemed up on everything and Liza laughed at her childish enthusiasm. "It sounds like a wonderful time."

"Oh, it is. Mostly the kids play the games and the big folks stand around and visit until some man announces it's time for the baseball game."

Liza pictured it. It would be her first-ever community picnic, and she found herself catching Lili's excitement and anticipation. She'd even set the older students to work on constructing signs to advertise the occasion. That very afternoon they'd gone out attaching them to store windows and lampposts.

"It's actually a celebration of harvest," Ben offered.

"We missed last year's fair 'cause Papa and me was sad," Lili chimed. "Ar mama..."

"Lili, why don't you get Molly set for bed?" Ben hastily interrupted. The baby was sitting on the floor not far from Liza, growing crankier by the minute while the rest of them visited.

Without forethought, Liza pushed back her chair and extended her arms to the child. Molly's whining ceased as she considered Liza's silent offer, then quickly accepted it.

Her pudgy warmth soon dissolved any doubts in Liza's mind about freely loving this child as much as she did the older one. Instinctively, and almost as if it were second nature to her, she soothed the child's tears by wiping them with the pad of her thumb and speaking into her velvety ear.

Moreover, when she looked out the corner of one eye she glimpsed Ben watching and thought she detected a glimmer of something in his expression that she dared not evaluate too closely.

What am I doing, heavenly Father? The prayer tripped through her mind like an autumn leaf breaking free of its branch and drifting to the earth below. *Have I gone too far to turn back?*

"If thou canst believe, all things are possible to him that believeth."

Believe? All things are possible? Exactly what was God trying to tell her?

"I'm afraid I really must be going," Liza announced out of the blue, walking to the other side of the table and placing the baby into Ben's capable arms.

Ben's eyes went wide with surprise. "Already? But..."

"Yes," she announced, feeling on the verge of tears—and for no good reason other than that she was a woman fighting a battle with her fierce emotions. "I'm sorry. Thank you for the supper and—and the hospitality. I'll see you at school tomorrow, Lili."

"Tomorrow is Saturday," Lili said happily.

"Oh, silly me, how could I forget something like that?" Ben's eyes followed her every move, hastening her need to escape. "Then I guess— I'll see you at church on Sunday," she added, turning toward the door.

"Wait, I'll walk you up the hill," Ben offered, suddenly pushing his chair back and creating a loud scraping sound along the planked flooring.

"No!" she said, turning to give him a look she could only hope and pray he would read as willful determination. "I can manage on my own, thank you."

Taking a step backward, he shook his head ever so slightly, sending her a silent message of annoyance. She knew what he was thinking; *she was running away*. Well, perhaps she was.

Outside, she scampered up the side of Shannon's Peak and made for her tiny cabin, all the while biting back autumn's chill and the notion that she was fast losing control of her heartstrings.

❄ ❄ ❄ ❄ ❄

"Papa, look at all the people. Do you think Miss Merriwether is here yet?" asked Lili, her high-pitched tone a sudden annoyance to Ben's weary ears. She'd gabbed all the way into town about October Fest while he'd bounced a fussy Molly on his knee. What is more, now that they'd arrived, she expected him to know the teacher's whereabouts, which was funny indeed, since Liza had made a great effort all week to avoid him.

Ever since her hurried departure last Friday night, he'd seen nothing but glimpses of her out his window or on the way to his barn. He'd even tried to visit her at her cabin, but she'd refused to open the door, saying it wasn't proper—never mind that she'd visited *him* twice now.

"Look, there's Mr. Callahan." Lili's announcement drew him out of his secret musing.

"Well, I'll be," Ben muttered, surprised and pleased to see Rocky. Rocky looked up and waved a sturdy arm, his face solemn but friendly.

"Ben, hello," he called. "Came into town for some feed and a few supplies. I forgot about the festivities. Busy place around here."

"It is. Why don't you join my family later for some lunch? I packed plenty."

"We'll see. I have a cow that needs rescuing from a sink pit. 'Spect she'll be there awhile unless I lend her a hand."

 218

"Need some help?"

"I'll manage, but thanks for the offer. I think between my horse and me, we can pull her out."

Ben studied the fellow's face and thought he detected unspoken concern hidden somewhere in its depths. "How have you been?"

"Guess I can't complain. It's my ailing sister that has me worried."

"Elizabeth?" Ben remembered Rocky's older sister only vaguely, her marrying and leaving the area before Rocky reached his teen years.

"Yeah. She's bad off. Doctors don't expect her to live through the winter."

God, not more sadness. How much could one man handle in a lifetime?

"I'm sorry to hear that, my friend." Helpless to say more, Ben just steadied his team of horses and waited to see if Rocky would elaborate.

"She wants me to take her kids—after—you know..."

"You're joking." Ben couldn't imagine how Rocky would manage. "What about the kids' father?"

"He left them high and dry nearly five years ago, right after Seth was born. The girl, Rachel, was only a couple years old at the time. Then he up and died from a head injury two years ago. Got kicked by an angry steer. He never cared a whit about his own flesh and blood, though, so it was mighty hard feelin' sorry for the guy when I heard the news."

A sudden chill ran the length of Ben's backbone. "What about your parents? Can they help with the kids?"

Rocky shook his head and briefly glanced at his shoe. "Ma would like nothing more than to bring the kids into her own house, but she admits she and Pa are getting too old. To tell you the truth, my pa's not well. I think this thing with Elizabeth has taken its toll on him."

"Rock…I don't know what to say other than God has the answers. He's there for you."

"Yeah, well…I best get a move on," he answered, noticeably eager to avoid any further discussion, particularly anything pertaining to God.

Frankly, Ben couldn't blame him. The guy had a lot on his plate. Probably the last thing he wanted to do was rehash his troubles—or hear about how much God loves him despite it all.

Lord, go with him, Ben silently prayed, watching as the tall, muscular figure sauntered down the sidewalk and into Eldred Johansson's Mercantile.

※ ※ ※ ※ ※

Fortunately for the town of Hickman, Mother Nature provided glorious weather for the fall celebration. Liza shifted on the porch swing that she and Emma Browning shared.

"Thank you for inviting me to sit," said Liza, bending her head back to allow the warm breezes to tickle her throat.

"Well, thank you for accepting the invitation," Emma said. "I was hoping for some company. Seemed a shame to let this comfortable swing go to waste."

Liza smiled. "I agree. I'm sure with summer's end you're wishing now you'd spent more time on your porch."

Emma nodded knowingly. "Summers do have a way of speeding right on by, don't they? Before you know it the snowflakes will be flying."

"Oh, I hope not. I dislike the cold weather."

"We don't get a lot of snow here, but once every decade or so we've been known to get a blizzard. We're about due, I'd say. Winds

 220

can be bitter coming down from those hills," Emma said, glancing out over the rise and fall of the countryside.

The two sat in comfortable silence, both using their feet to keep the swing moving.

Liza glanced through Emma's door. "Seems awfully quiet around here. Where are all your boarders?"

"I 'spect most are boozing it up at Guttersnipe's about now. They'll look for any excuse to drink and call it a celebration. Tonight should be interesting. They'll make a racket after midnight looking for their rooms."

A young couple Liza didn't recognize waved at Emma. She returned the gesture.

"How will you sleep?" Liza asked.

Emma batted a slender wrist. "Oh, gracious, I'm used to it by now. Been doin' this business for nigh onto ten years. If the fool ruffians have nothin' better to do with their lives than throw 'em away on booze, then I have no sympathy."

"But that's so sad. Don't any of these men have families?"

"Most are drifters. They might've had families at one time, but they've lost track of them, or they're purposely running away. I don't ask questions. Long as they pay their rent, they're safe with me."

Liza nodded and looked out over her surroundings. Here and there, children scampered about between their parents' protective gazes, excited about the day's activities, asking for candy or an ice cream cone from one of the many booths set up on Main Street. Merchants and townsfolk displayed their wares, anything from homemade soaps, candles, and liniment, to handcrafted quilts, kitchen towels, and homegrown produce and baked goods.

"Miss Merriwether!" Liza turned in the direction of the greeting. Thomas and Erlene Barrington were approaching from the other side of the street. She waved at them. "Have you seen Lili?" Erlene asked in her usual shy manner when they reached the bottom of the porch steps. Erlene had gotten used to Lili looking after her on the playground.

"I'm afraid I haven't," she answered. Liza had been avoiding the Broughton family, Ben in particular, leaving this morning at dawn to do a few things in her classroom. She'd come to realize that even socializing with Benjamin Broughton put her on dangerous ground. In time, he would look into her eyes and recognize her feelings for him, and then where would she be? No, it was best to keep her distance from him altogether.

"Well, we'll be on our way then," Thomas said, taking his sister by the hand. "Have a nice day."

"You as well," Liza said, "Have fun."

"Nice kids," Emma stated as the two children headed back across the street.

More easy silence followed as both women watched the gathering crowds of townsfolk.

"I understand that Ben Broughton decided against sending for a bride," Emma said, startling Liza with the pointed declaration. Emma's eyes dropped to Liza's face, as if searching for a reaction.

"Really?" Liza asked, pretending disinterest.

"He's asked if I'll continue watching Molly until he can decide what to do," Emma said. "I told him I would. The extra money comes in mighty handy."

"I'm sure you helped take a load off his shoulders with your generosity. Molly's a dear, isn't she?" Liza said, feeling wistful.

Emma nodded. "Easy as pie, too, but let's admit it, Ben needs a wife and those little girls need a mama."

"Why don't you marry him?" Liza asked on a dare, sneaking a

peak at Emma to see if there were any chance the woman carried feelings for him.

"Me? Ben and I are friends, but that's as far as it goes. He's always respected my privacy, and I 'preciate that about him. But I'd never marry him. Men are a bother. I 'spect even Benjamin would wear on my nerves after a while." To this, she gave a little chortle. "The plain truth is, most men can't be trusted."

Liza detected a bitter edge to Emma's words and wondered what had put it there. Was it her father who had made her life so unbearable? Worse, had he treated her cruelly, thereby putting a sour taste in her mouth for all men?

Liza had few words to offer, her own sheltered life certainly making her less than wise when it came to relating to Emma's vindictive world. She did have God, though, and His promise of faithfulness. Hastening with a quick prayer for guidance, she challenged, "Have you ever considered what your heavenly Father can do for you?"

Emma turned a questioning look on Liza. "You mean God?"

She bit back a grin. "Yes, God."

"Can't say I have. God and me don't seem to be a mix."

"You shouldn't be so quick to decide something like that. What if I told you He loves you more than you know and wants to be your friend?"

"Then I guess I'd have to say I'm not interested." This time her tone went cold, approaching icy.

Liza looked off into the distance and listened to the delighted squeals of children, a barking dog, approaching horses' hooves, and the whir of turning wagon wheels. Closer, she overheard neighbors conversing on the street, a whistling passerby, and the rasping chatter of a squirrel as he darted from one branch to another on a nearby elm.

"I meant no offense," Emma hastened.

"Oh, none taken, believe me," Liza replied. "It's just that God has done so much for me, and I thought maybe you…"

"I prayed once when I was a little girl."

"You did?" Liza's ears perked up at that confession. "What happened?"

"I asked Him to make my father disappear." She laughed at the absurdity of her own remark.

"Oh." A sort of helplessness moved in. "I don't mean to poke my nose where it doesn't belong, but your father, well, I caught a glimpse of him once."

"Yeah? I'm certain you don't frequent Madam Guttersnipe's vulgar establishment."

Liza forced a nervous giggle. "Absolutely not!"

"Then when?"

"You were shooing him off your porch that first day I arrived in Hickman." To Liza, it seemed like years ago and not mere months.

Emma squinted into the sun as if trying to recall the instance. Then light seemed to dawn. "Oh, that time. Yes, every so often the old coot tries to persuade me to open my doors. He has no idea that I will never welcome him, not inside my hotel, and certainly never again into my life. He's done too much damage for me ever to forgive him."

"I'm sorry," Liza said, once more feeling at a loss.

"Don't be. What's done is done," she said with a gentle flick of the wrist and a smile to cover up any trace of emotion.

"Good afternoon, ladies." Jonathan Atkins's pleasant voice broke into their quiet conversation.

"Jonathan. Or should I say, Reverend? How are you?" Liza greeted happily.

The sandy-haired fellow helped himself to the porch, then approached an empty wicker chair and plopped himself into it, as if it sat idly by, purposely waiting for him. His ready smile was enough to melt most any woman's reserve, certainly Liza's, even though he'd never had to work hard to charm her.

"Have a seat," Emma said coldly and pointedly after the fact.

Nothing about her face looked welcoming, and for the life of her, Liza couldn't figure out why. What had Jonathan ever done to her? Surely, she couldn't find fault with him, a man of the cloth.

"Please, Reverend sounds too stuffy," he replied, snatching a quick glance at Emma before allowing his eyes to rest on Liza. Stretching out his long, sturdy legs so that they took up the better share of the porch, he gave a relaxed sigh. "Ah, I must say, you ladies do add an extra ray of sunshine to an already beautiful day."

Liza laughed at his forward behavior, having come to recognize him as one who never put on airs; instead, taking life as it came to him, enjoying and relishing in its offering, whether good or bad.

He could teach Emma a thing or two.

One glance at Emma, however, put a halt to that thought. The woman sat stiff and unmoved, obviously put out by the preacher's sudden emergence.

Eager to right the situation, Liza attempted conversation. "I have enjoyed your sermons the last two weeks, Jon. They've been so challenging and inspiring."

"Thank you, Liza. I had hoped for that. I'm afraid too many sermons these days serve only to satisfy the egos of the regular attendees rather than confront the issues. I hate to think of the church sinking into oblivion when we are surrounded by a world in need."

"I agree," she answered, casting a wary look at Emma and finding her unresponsive and clearly annoyed.

"Are you ladies planning to join in the festivities or simply watch them from afar?" Jon asked, his sandy hair blowing off his forehead, drawing attention to his finely chiseled face. Despite his rather long and lanky body, he exuded masculinity, easily dispelling all preconceived notions that men of the cloth couldn't be handsome and fun loving.

"Oh, we are planning to enjoy it, right Emma?" Liza said, hoping her overdone cheery spirit wouldn't give away her uneasiness at Emma's sudden overcast mood.

Jon trained keen, heedful eyes on Emma, tipping his head to one side as he studied her. A hint of a smile played at the corners of his mouth. Liza thought he looked like someone who held the answer to some vague mystery. And maybe he did.

"Yes, of course," Emma answered. Then, standing, she blurted, "Would anyone care for something to drink?"

"Don't worry about me," Jon said, a touch of humor sneaking past his deep blue eyes. "I merely stopped by to say hello." With that, he stood to his feet so that his eyes met up with Emma's tart stare.

Hesitating at the door, Emma matched his gaze. "Well, all right then."

Liza felt a chill run the length of her spine at Emma's cheekiness. Did she have no respect—even for a minister of God's Word?

Apparently not, for the next thing she did was escape into the house, allowing the door to slam behind her.

Hurrying to make amends, Liza stood as well. "Jon, I don't know what got into her. I was speaking with her earlier about spiritual matters. Perhaps I…"

He touched a hand to her elbow and gently squeezed. "Don't worry about it, Liza. Ben thinks she is a woman running scared, and I tend to agree with him."

"Ben?" Confusion set in.

"Yes, and speak of the ugly fiend himself..." Jon looked up and waved his free arm toward the street, keeping the hand at her elbow firmly in place.

Liza looked up in time to catch Ben Broughton's icy stare along with the tirelessly joyful reception of his eight-year-old daughter.

Chapter Seventeen

Ben swallowed down an invisible lump and fought to stay calm. What was Jon doing holding so possessively to Liza's elbow, looking for all the world as if he'd already laid claim to her? Furthermore, what had they been discussing when he'd drawn the buggy to a halt in front of Emma's place, their heads close, both serious and contemplative? Moreover, why was it not fitting or proper to be seen with *him*, Ben, but perfectly acceptable when it came to Jonathan Atkins? Jon may be a minister, but Ben knew him to be just as red-blooded as the next guy.

A kind of panic ran through his veins, the kind that created havoc in his gut and made him hot under the collar. Apparently, Liza had been serious when she said she intended to forget about the kiss they'd shared. From the look of things, she'd more than forgotten it.

"Hello, my friend," Jon hollered, his smile more annoyed than pleased. "Are you butting in on my private time with this pretty lady again?" His good-natured tone made Ben's teeth clench.

Molly stirred in Ben's lap. He readjusted her, then handed her over to her older sister. "Just driving by," he announced. He wasn't about to admit he'd had his eye out for the schoolteacher ever since he'd arrived in town an hour ago. It hadn't occurred to him that he would discover her at Emma's place.

"Miss Merriwether, I'm about to do the sack race. Are you planning to come and watch?" His daughter leaned over his lap to shout the question, and Ben had all he could do not to cover his ears.

"I wouldn't miss it, Lili," Liza replied. "By the way, Erlene Barrington was looking for you a while back."

"Oh, goodie," Lili shrieked. "Sarah Jenkins and me are gonna be partners in the three-legged race. Can you watch us?"

 228

Liza's golden hair, tied back in its usual bun, looked looser today, the side strands blowing in the wind. As always, Ben longed to brush it from her flawless oval face and twist a couple glistening wisps around his forefinger. A blue calico dress, gathered at the waist with a wide belt, accented her womanly features. If he had been a man bent on anger, he might well have told Jon Atkins to remove his hand from the teacher's elbow and make it snappy. Instead, he resolved to sit still on his high perch.

Liza laughed. "I will cheer you on, as I will any other of my students who might be participating, but I shall secretly wish you the winner."

Lili clapped and then took Molly's hands and patted them together as well. The baby giggled with glee. Ben, however, had to force a smile. Liza had yet to look his way. Jon on the other hand seemed bent on rubbing in the fact that he'd reached Liza ahead of him.

"I think I'll join you if you don't mind," Jon said. "I love a good contest, don't you, Ben?" Ben offered Jon an empty smile.

"That would be lovely," answered Liza, looking up at Jon. "Just let me talk to Emma to see if she'll meet us at the site of the race."

Emma? "I'll talk to her," Ben said. And just like that, Ben climbed down from his rig, instructed his girls to stay put, and walked up to the house to invite Emma Browning to join him.

If Ben's secret ploy in inviting Emma to join him was to make Liza jealous, it was childish and foolhardy. Yes, she'd accepted, but from a sense of duty, and for that, Ben regretted inviting her. She was a friend, already distrustful of men, and he'd used her as a means for getting back at Liza.

"I best get my evening meal on the table," Emma announced after having watched a few events from the quilt they all shared on the large grassy field overlooking the masses of people that had shown up for the festival. Ben knew she felt uncomfortable, although why that was, he couldn't say.

"Want me to walk you back?" Ben offered, sitting straighter, one knee drawn up so that his arms rested lazily over it.

"Don't be silly, Ben," she said, standing to her feet.

"How about me?" asked Jon, eyes filled with merriment. He was the only one lying straight out on the blanket, his hands serving as cushions for his head. He chewed idly on a foot-long blade of grass.

She produced a brittle smile and an upturned brow. "I'm sure I can find my own way back." Then to Liza, "Stop in and see me anytime."

"I will. Bye, Emma," Liza said from her corner of the blanket, Molly sprawled out asleep on her lap. The sight of woman and child caught Ben in the gut and squeezed till it hurt.

"That woman despises the ground I walk on," Jon said. "And I can't for the life of me figure out what I did." Oddly, he wore a grin at the pointblank assertion, apparently unmoved by her lack of responsiveness. Extraordinary coming from a man who defied all odds when it came to his number of admiring acquaintances. In fact, Ben never had met a person who didn't crave Jon's company. And Liza didn't appear to be the exception, much to his chagrin.

"You probably didn't do anything. She's not fond of men in general unless they're old and crusty—and not related to her."

Jon scoffed. "You being the exception, I take it." He pulled himself into a sitting position, one hand still holding to the long blade of grass, guiding it in and out between his teeth, and the other going behind him for support.

Here and there, folks milled about, waving greetings. Games and races of all types had been stationed in various places. Lili, still breathless from her last two contests, both of which she'd placed in but not won, returned and leaned her tired body into Ben's broad chest and mopped continuously at her sweaty brow.

"We've formed a safe alliance over the years. I guess she knows I pose no threat," Ben said.

"And I suppose I do?" Jon said, his brow knit with confusion. "What is there about me that threatens her?"

Ben tipped his head to one side to study Jon's expression. Somehow, it'd gone from blithe and unconcerned to perplexed in the space of a second.

"She was hurt bad as a kid; that much I know, although even I don't know the half of what went on behind closed doors. There were bruises. A cut lip here, a scratch there. Once I saw a scald mark on the side of her neck, which she told me she'd gotten as a result of dropping a frying pan. I remember thinking it seemed an unlikely spot for a burn, but, shoot, I was just a kid. What did I know?"

Jon made a sound of disgust deep in his throat. "That pitiless excuse of a man. How dare he treat his own daughter like some kind of—of mongrel. What is wrong with him?" Jon's anger seemed more rooted in the personal than the righteous, which Ben found interesting.

"He's a worthless drunk, plain and simple," Ben answered. "Always has been—far back as I can remember."

Moments of silent deliberation ticked by before Liza spoke. "Seems to me that the plain and simple truth here is that Emma and her father need the Lord." Her statement put Ben to shame, and doubtless Jon as well. "I think we should make a pact to pray for them."

"You're right, Liza," Jon said. "Rather than talk about it, we should be praying."

A thoughtful smile curved Liza's mouth. "I spoke with her about the Lord today, but she quickly let it be known she is not interested in

God. It made me think of the woman at the well who was afraid to let Jesus see her for who she really was."

"That's insightful," Ben said, giving a nod while simultaneously shooing a fly from his face. "Perhaps if anyone can reach her, you can, Liza."

Liza nodded, and the three adults fell into another state of quiet reflection.

Finally, having had enough of the adult conversation, Lili sat bolt upright, her strength renewed, and shot a frustrated glance at everyone. "Well, this has turned boring," she announced, jumping to her feet and pulling Ben with her.

Taken aback by his daughter's boldness, Ben looked down at Jon, who hadn't moved so much as a neck muscle, and Liza, who gently rocked his sleeping child where she sat. "How about we all go for a walk?" Ben suggested.

Jon shook his head. "No thanks. I believe I'll just sit here and enjoy this wonderful autumn breeze." Glancing in Liza's direction, Jon added, "It'd be a shame for Liza to move the baby, don't you think?"

"Come on, Papa," Lili said, tugging on his arm. "You can buy me an ice cream."

"An ice cream?" Ben gave Liza a look he hoped she would read as yearning.

But she merely flicked a free wrist at him. "Go on. Molly and I are fine. I think it's good that she's getting this nice nap, don't you?"

"Sure, but…" He continued gazing down at her, wishing she could read between the lines. "I wouldn't mind carrying her."

"Nonsense. She'd awaken. Jon's right, the weather is too perfect not to sit a spell longer. You and Lili go have fun."

That was it, then. She wanted to be alone with Jon.

Ben shot Jon a warning look, but if the guy detected it, he didn't let on. Instead, he reclined again, squinting up at the clear blue blanket of warmth and sighing with contentment.

Later, Ben's hand holding tightly to Lili's as they picked their way through mobs of townsfolk on their way to the ice cream stand, he blurted, "For someone afraid that Mr. Atkins is going to get to Miss Merriwether before I do, you sure were anxious to leave the two of them alone together."

Lili looked up at him with knowing eyes. "Oh, Papa, don't you know anything?"

"Huh?" he asked, dumbfounded by the tenor of her voice.

"The way Miss Merriwether was looking at Molly, I don't think she would want to marry Mr. Atkins."

"Why would you say a thing like that?"

She stopped in her tracks, forcing him to do the same. "Miss Merriwether likes us. Can't you tell?"

"She does?"

"Papa, you're silly," she tacked on. "Come on. We both need ice cream."

❄ ❄ ❄ ❄ ❄

Abbreviated days meant less sunshine and cooler air. Once brightly colored, leaves of every shape and size had turned a crisp brown and fallen to the cold, hard earth. During recess breaks, many of the students gathered the dry leaves into piles and took turns diving into them, sometimes burying the younger students, to their great delight. However, even they complained of the temperatures and were contented to come inside and linger by the potbelly stove.

With October Fest a thing of the past, Liza busied herself in her classroom, arriving earlier than usual on frosty mornings to stoke the fire and haul in fresh drinking water. When the big boys arrived, she enlisted their help to carry in the large buckets of coal to keep the fires burning throughout the school day, always hoping that someone other than Rufus Baxter or Clement Bartel would turn up first.

With every passing day, both boys had become increasingly more difficult to handle, and she feared what would happen when the day came that she couldn't handle their rude innuendos. She still held to the opinion that it was Clement who led in the escapades and Rufus who followed. If she could just convince Rufus to think for himself, she was sure he would blossom academically. Of course, with the obvious abuse his father had doled out, what chance did the boy have for thinking positively about himself?

Liza shifted her backside in the teacher's chair, then reached up a hand to sooth her aching neck muscles. She'd decided to stay later today and correct a week's worth of assignments, enjoying the warmth of the potbelly stove and its remaining glowing embers. The only sounds she heard were those of the ticking clock above her head and the dead leaves that whispered past the window nearest her.

On her desk sat a letter from Aunt Hettie, finely penned. She frowned as she perused her own careless handwriting, feeling guilty for having rushed through her response. However, the clock on the wall registered half past six, and she didn't relish walking home in the dark. Still, she'd wanted to take the time to write her. So much had happened, and it seemed a shame not to keep her aunt and uncle informed of her dealings.

Quickly, she scanned the missive, checking one last time to see if she'd missed anything important.

Dearest Uncle Gideon and Aunt Hettie,

How wonderful it was to receive your latest letter. As always, I love to hear from you. I am happy to find you are in good health and faring

well in my absence. I trust the weather there in Boston has been warmer than usual. It has been a typical fall here in Kentucky, according to the citizens of Little Hickman.

I wish you both could pay me a visit. You would be proud of the way I have fixed up my little cabin, Aunt Hettie. It has turned out to be a fine dwelling for me, neat as a pin, and decorated in just the way I like it. As you know, I was not so pleased when I first laid eyes on it. However, the gentleman who owns the place did a fine job of fixing it up, with the help of the townsfolk, of course. It is actually beginning to feel like home, particularly since all of the furniture I ordered finally arrived just over two weeks ago.

I am pleased to tell you that I am enjoying my time in the town of Little Hickman. My students as a whole are wonderful; that is, if I don't count two particular boys who always seem to want to cause me problems. I have been looking for ways to discipline them that will not increase their hostilities, although that is indeed a tough assignment for this young, rather inexperienced, teacher.

I'm afraid I have done the unthinkable as a teacher, Aunt Hettie. I have picked my favorites among all of my students, one of which happens to be the daughter of the man who owns the cabin I live in. He is a widowed man with two young children, but I told you that in an earlier letter.

Liza frowned at herself for having included that last paragraph. Would Aunt Hettie now think her interest in the child resulted from the fact that Lili's father was a widower? No matter, it was too late to change it, and she surely could not blot out the lines with ink. She'd written rather sloppily as it was.

She turned her eyes back to the letter, and then stopped when she heard a rustling sound from outside the window. She glanced up and caught the slightest hint of movement, a shadowy figure lurking and then instantly pulling away when she'd lifted her head.

Without hesitation, she folded the letter, deciding not to read what remained, and stuffed it into the already addressed envelope. Next, she extinguished the kerosene lamp on her desk. Dusk had settled, leaving her surroundings dimly lit, but another lamp at the back of the classroom created enough light to see her out.

A feeling of unease made its home in the pit of her stomach as she began gathering up her belongings. The trek home would be cooler than usual, not to mention unnerving now that she'd heard someone—or something—lurking.

Common sense told her she need not worry. The silhouette could have been anything, a neighbor walking his dog past the school, curious as to why the schoolhouse light was on. Perhaps he'd chanced a peek inside and left upon seeing the teacher at her desk. Then there was the possibility of a pesky raccoon or opossum making a racket while climbing the large oak next to the building. The scavengers were always scrounging for things to eat.

She scolded herself for having allowed her imagination free rein and went about tidying up the rest of her desk, suddenly realizing how late the hour. As if to accentuate that point, her empty stomach grumbled in protest.

As she pushed her chair back, the legs screeched against the floor, startling her. She laughed nervously at her own jumpiness. Liza gathered up her satchel, stuffed it with the items she wished to carry, and took it to the back of the classroom where her coat, hat, and scarf hung from a hook. Her back to the door, she didn't hear a sound when it opened, and was stunned to turn around, one arm in her coat sleeve, and find Clement Bartel gawking down at her.

"Clement, what are you doing here?" The boy towered over her like a full-grown man.

"I seen the lights on, Teacher. Thought I'd pay you a kindly visit."

She didn't like the low quality to his voice, nor the fact that he'd closed the door behind him.

"I'm sorry, Clement, but we'll have to visit during school hours. Perhaps during the recess period we could…"

He moved in closer, his dark face reflecting bold desire.

"Clement, it is not appropriate for you to be here at this hour."

"It ain't very appropriate for you, either," he returned. "No tellin' what could happen to one so perty as you."

She bristled when he touched a clammy hand to her arm. "Need help puttin' this coat on?" he asked, giving her a grin. The stench of his sour breath hung in the air like untended garbage, while his dirty hair lay in separated clumps across his pimpled forehead.

"I can manage, thank you. What brings you here?" It was best to remain calm and controlled, she reminded herself.

Lord, please give me wisdom to say the right words so that I don't create a bigger problem for myself than I am able to handle.

"Comed into town to buy a few supplies fer Paw," he said, a feral grin planted across his thin lips. "Saw the lights on in the school and thought I'd check on ya. Wondered if you was lonely."

"Actually, I'm just leaving, Clement, but I appreciate the thought. You best head back up to your place."

"What's the hurry? Ain't no school tomorrow." He took a step closer, and her nerves tangled.

"It's getting late, Clement," she said, swallowing hard.

Dear Lord, please see me through this predicament.

✳ ✳ ✳ ✳ ✳

"Where is that fool woman?" Ben muttered to himself, climbing aboard his rig and heading for town. He hadn't wanted to leave the girls, but since he'd already put Molly to bed a half hour ago, he was sure Lili would tend to things just fine until he returned.

He told himself repeatedly it was not his place to worry about Liza, but he couldn't stifle his worry when the clock pushed seven and she had not come home. Dusk was no time for a woman to be roaming these parts, and he meant to tell her so just as soon as he laid eyes on her. Of course, she would balk at his protective nature, but he didn't care.

He steered the horses over the familiar rise and fall of the well-trodden dirt track; not that they needed steering; the beasts could have gotten to town without the help of reins. The brisk night air nibbled at his nose and cheeks, but sheer adrenalin kept his blood running warm.

The school and yard were dark when he approached, but something told him to stop anyway. This time he would check the outhouse *first* rather than last on the chance that someone had played another prank on her. It didn't seem likely, however, since, despite all the odds, she was maintaining good rapport with her students, even the Hogsworth twins, wonder of wonders.

He drew the horses to a halt, jumped down, and heaved the reins over a hitching post. That was when he noticed a pale glow of light trailing a path under the school door. A strange kind of premonition slithered through his veins, cautioning him. He took the entrance steps slowly, stealthily.

"Just because yore my teacher don't mean we can't be special friends," said a male voice, not quite husky enough to qualify as manly.

"Clement, I would like you to leave now. We'll talk another t-time."

"What say you give me a little…"

Ben wrenched open the door and crossed the room in less time than it would take to drop a pebble in a pond. The young man had both his hands on a flailing Liza, his strong grip on her arms preventing her escape.

"Unhand her," Ben said coolly, fighting with every ounce of staying power he could muster not to toss the lad clear to the other side of the building. He could do it, he told himself. He could bloody him up quicker than it would take the boy to beg for mercy.

The faintest glint of terror rose in the young man's eyes at the shock of facing someone bigger and stronger than he was, but the look was short-lived. With sadistic eyes and posture to match, he dropped his hands to his sides, releasing his teacher, and then made a grunting sound. Liza moved to Ben's side, her short, heaving breaths clear indication of her fright. Ben longed to look her over carefully, but he couldn't allow himself that luxury just yet, not until he took care of this rabble-rousing teenager.

"Well, lookie here, Teacher. It's yore boyfriend," Clement said. "I'm downright jealous."

"Keep your mouth shut, Clement. Are you okay, Liza?"

Her yes came out more in the form of a simple nod and a faint little squeak.

"Ain't nothin' wrong with her," Clement said, raising both hands in a show of peace. "I was merely bein' friendly."

"Didn't look too friendly to me," Ben issued.

Clement laughed, a guttural sound from down deep. "Oh, it was approachin' on mighty friendly. She was likin' it, too. Matter o' fact, we was startin' to get real cozy. Another minute and…"

Ben's fist came up as if it had a mind of its own and planted itself squarely on Clement Bartel's jaw. The boy went down without a fight, the impact sending him several feet backward and knocking him down, but not until his shoulder made contact with the corner of a desk, and he'd pulled over a chair en route to the floor. Squawking like a rooster who'd lost all its tail feathers, the boy lay there rolling around and holding his face.

"Ben!" Liza shrieked in fright. Her hand went to her throat while she looked from him to Clement and back to him with boulder-sized eyes. "You hit him."

Ben half grinned. "I did, didn't I?" He walked over to the boy and yanked him to his feet by the scruff of his collar. "Hasn't anyone ever taught you the proper way to treat a woman?" At that, Clement cleared his throat and hurled a wad of bloody spittle into Ben's face.

When he might have been enraged at the act, Ben merely chuckled, wiped his cheek with the back of his sleeve, and said, "Well now, I guess you could say we're even. Come on, we're going to pay the sheriff a nice little visit."

"I ain't goin' to no sheriff."

"Oh, but you are," Ben assured.

"I done nothin' wrong," Clement wailed in protest, even as Ben shoved the boy's arms behind him and led him in the direction of the door. Clement's shaky, crooked gait indicated his inability to put up much of a fight.

"No? I'd say manhandling the teacher qualifies as a criminal act."

"There weren't no manhandlin'. I told you she liked it. Matter of fact, she's been askin' fer it." With that remark, Clement threw Liza an angry, if not sultry, look, and Ben tightened his hold on the boy's wrists, deciding to ignore the crude remarks and praying for a large dose of old-fashioned self-control.

The notion that Clement meant to harm Liza turned Ben's stomach inside out. What might have happened if he hadn't arrived when he had? The bruises Ben had seen on Clement's stepmother were clear proof that he was capable of crime at its worst.

At the door, Ben turned to find Liza still standing like a statue. "Come on," he issued. "You have a complaint to file."

240

Chapter Eighteen

*A*re you sure you're all right?" Ben asked on the ride back home. A barrier of silence had stretched between them until he finally broke it down.

"Yes," she managed shakily.

"The boy should be sitting in jail," Ben muttered through clenched teeth.

"I think it's enough that he not be allowed to return to school," Liza said, her hands folded around her handkerchief. "The truth is, he drags the other students down with his cruel taunts. He wasn't interested in learning anyway."

"If you'd pressed charges, Will would have thrown him in a cell, Liza. He told you as much."

"And what would that have accomplished? He couldn't keep him there forever, and chances are Clement would have come out even angrier. Besides, it wasn't as if he truly hurt me. In fact, the only thing he really accomplished was to frighten me."

"What if I hadn't come when I did?" Ben asked, turning his gaze on her. Liza felt his eyes bearing down on her, his anger still fresh and close to the surface. Never had she witnessed such a violent reaction as she had when she'd seen Ben trounce on Clement.

"I don't want to think about it," she answered.

The absence of warmth combined with the events of the evening caused a shiver to run the length of her body. Ben sensed it and put a big steady arm around her shoulder. "Come here," he said, drawing her close.

241

She should have resisted his touch, but the fact of the matter was she was too cold and exhausted to do much about it. Thus, she folded into his embrace, dropping her head against his expansive chest, her cheek soaking up the heat of his rough woolen jacket.

"Why did you come?" she asked into the inky blackness. Cloud-covered skies prevented the moon from showing its face on this colder than normal evening.

Whether intentional or not, he tightened his grip on her. "I got worried when you didn't come home," he said with a touch of gruffness. "What were you thinking by staying so late?"

"The time got away from me. I had a mound of assignments to correct and after that a letter to write and…"

"You couldn't have done that in the safety of your cabin?"

"I was comfortable where I was. I didn't feel like leaving immediately after school."

"You need to use some common sense," he said with a hint of anger. "It's not safe for a woman to be roaming these parts after dark."

"But…"

"There are wild animals of every kind out here, not to mention the hill folk I've warned you about. Clement is a good example of what can go wrong when a defenseless woman is…well, you see what I'm saying." He made a huffing sound, then charged ahead with, "Until you get a rig or a horse of your own, I intend to drive you back and forth, that's all there is to it."

"What?" Now her own ire went up, as did her back. "That's completely unnecessary, and I am not defenseless," she wanted to make clear. She pulled away from his warmth. "Many of my students walk greater distances than I do. Why should I have the luxury of riding?"

 242

"You're being silly, and you appeared quite defenseless to my eyes when Clement had his hands on you."

It was hard to argue with that, so she closed her mouth up tight and dropped her shoulders.

"It doesn't make sense for you to walk when I can just as easily pick you up when I pick up Lili." His voice had dropped in tandem with her shoulders. She sensed his watchful eyes as they darted from the dark trail ahead back to her face.

"Oh, I suppose," she finally relented. "But on nice, sunny days I shall continue to walk."

"As long as you come home right after school," he ordered.

"Why are you so bossy?" she asked with folded arms.

He leaned over until his hot breath touched her earlobe. "Why are you so stubborn?"

And since she had no answer for that particular question, she closed her mouth up tight again.

❄ ❄ ❄ ❄ ❄

Clement's absence made a remarkable difference in the classroom dynamics. Many students' expressions went from sullen to bright, closed to open. Liza interpreted the change in atmosphere to mean they felt safer, happier. Without knowing it, many had refrained from expressing themselves at the risk of hearing a snide remark from the back of the room. Clement's taunts and jeers had earned him many reprimands, but they had only served to quiet him temporarily, his crossed arms and smug looks an indication of his obstinacy. Moreover, Liza had surmised he enjoyed it when she disciplined him, for that meant he'd gained her full attention.

One noticeable change in the classroom came from Rufus Baxter. Just as Liza had suspected, Rufus began to emerge a different boy in

Clement Bartel's absence. Apparently, his self-esteem suffered to such a degree that he'd failed to reveal his identity outside of Clement's influence. So intent had Rufus been on replicating Clement's every act that, without him there, he seemed at a loss how to misbehave, one incident yesterday proving Liza's observation.

It had been an unusually lovely day, the kind that came so rarely at November's onset, so Liza had allowed an extra five minutes of afternoon recess time. An energetic game of baseball had ensued, despite the chilly air, with even the younger children allowed their times at bat. Liza paused at the back entry to watch, proud of how they had all learned to accept each other's differences. Had Clement been amongst them, he'd have had a fight going for certain—someone complaining about the little ones playing, their slower reflexes holding up the game, or their incompetence affecting the score. Yet these children seemed not to care about age or size differences, everyone laughing and enjoying the temporary freedom from their confining little classroom.

When Liza waved the big handbell signaling the end of recess, Thomas Barrington put up a fuss. "Aw, can't we stay outside just five more minutes, Miss Merriwether? Our score is tied."

"Yeah," the Hogsworth twins begged in unison. "Five more minutes can't hurt none."

Liza laughed. "You're lucky I gave you the extra five minutes to begin with. Now hurry inside. We have more work to do before the day's end."

Someone moaned, and it seemed the entire class had turned a hopeful look on her, as if their pleading eyes might change her mind. That was when Rufus spoke up. "Come on, you guys. Teacher said it's time to go in. 'Sides, ain't nothin' wrong with a tie. Jus' means both teams won."

With that, Rufus had made his way toward the building and past Liza with, wonder of wonders, the younger children following suit.

She'd known from the start there was goodness in Rufus. Now it was a matter of making him believe it.

If there was one thing that troubled Liza about Clement's ban from school, it was Rosie Bartel's strange behavior. Rather than blossom in her older brother's absence, she'd taken to distancing herself, replacing her usual cheery smile with a somber face. When Liza had asked her if she was all right, she'd merely nodded, saying she was tired.

"Aren't you getting enough sleep, Rosie?" Liza had asked.

The child merely nodded her head and asked, "Can I go back to my seat now?"

"Of course," Liza had told her, fighting dark thoughts as she'd watched the child trudge back to her desk, shoulders slumped.

Lord, I can't help but feel that something is amiss. Please keep Rosie safe. I don't trust her father, and I certainly don't trust Clement. I saw what he was capable of when I met his stepmother.

Yes, something was amiss all right, and with God's help, Liza meant to find out what it was.

Cold winds blew in from the west. Liza shivered at her desk while correcting today's assignments and reflected on the change one day could make in the weather. Yesterday the sun had shone; today the clouds prevented any hope of even getting a glimpse of rays.

Her students' voices carried over the tempestuous winds, their shouts of cheerful play during the noon break making the gloomy weather inconsequential. She smiled to herself, pleased that they didn't seem to mind the cold temperatures. She must remind them at close of day to begin dressing more appropriately, however. Many were still arriving at school in thin jackets and sweaters.

245

Liza dipped the end of her pen into the inkwell and penned the words "well done" at the top of Sarah Jenkins' essay on the life of George Washington. Just as she laid the paper down and reached for the next, the front door opened, forcing Liza to look up.

"Mrs. Winthrop! What a pleasant surprise," she fibbed.

The woman moved with her usual confidence, her lovely gown of navy blue topped with a jacket of the same color, its fur collar wrapped snugly around her neck, a fine, plumed hat arranged nicely on her head. Despite the winds, not a hair on Mrs. Winthrop's head had gone astray. The only thing that indicated she'd been in the elements was the faint glow of her round cheeks.

As the woman began removing her navy woolen gloves, one finger at a time, Liza couldn't help but think about the contrast she made to her scantily dressed students.

"To what do I owe the honor of your visit?" she asked while standing and pasting a smile on her face. She held to the edge of her desk with both hands, something about the woman's presence always making her feel wobbly on her feet.

Lord, help me keep my wits about me even though this woman makes me unduly nervous. The hasty plea floated on the wings of a cold draft, the result of Mrs. Winthrop having left the door ajar.

Mrs. Winthrop's nose seemed to point a bit higher as she scanned the contents of the classroom, her eyes going from floor to ceiling as if to assess the purpose of each teaching tool. "Rocks in the classroom?" she asked, signifying the tin bucket containing a hundred or more pebbles.

"They make fine counting tools as the children work on their sums."

The woman snorted. "They can't memorize their facts?"

"Well, yes, but concrete objects are handy for teaching them the concepts."

She huffed again but failed to respond. Then she turned toward the window that overlooked the playground. "I see that they seem to be playing well."

"Yes, I have done my best to instill in each of them a sense of respect."

"With the exception of Clement Bartel, I assume?"

Liza's stomach did a strange twist as she eyed the woman's demeanor, trying to discern the purpose for her visit, let alone the crude comment.

"Obviously Clement is a hard case. He is a very stubborn and rebellious young man," Liza said to Mrs. Winthrop's back, the woman's gaze never wavering from the children at play.

"So you admit that you could not handle him."

"I—I will confess his disruptive behavior made teaching difficult. He also interfered with my students' ability to learn." Liza loosened her grip on the edge of the desk when she glanced down at her white knuckles.

At last, Mrs. Winthrop cleared her throat, skimmed a hand across one of the desks as if to check for dust, and then turned to face Liza. "I understand you had a run-in with Clement a few weeks ago."

Liza felt heat rush to her face. "I sent you a complete report."

"And I have reviewed it carefully. I'm sure it was all quite unpleasant for you."

Why now did the woman comment on the matter? Since Liza had not heard from her in response to the incident, she figured Mrs. Winthrop had dismissed it entirely, having assumed Liza had handled it correctly.

"Yes, very unpleasant," Liza said. "And it would have been much worse had it not been for Mr. Broughton's timely appearance. Sheriff Randolph commended Ben, uh, Mr. Broughton's quick actions. Why,

I…" Liza halted her next words when she spied the lady's pinched look.

"Now you've hit upon something that concerns me," Mrs. Winthrop said. "Why would Mr. Broughton come checking on you in the first place?"

Liza didn't like her snappish tone, but she tried not to let it show. "He noticed that I hadn't come home yet."

"Does he make a habit of keeping his eye out for you?"

"Yes, I mean no. He is my neighbor, after all."

"I had wondered all along at the wisdom in that," Mrs. Winthrop stated simply.

"Pardon me?"

"When Mr. Broughton offered his place, I balked at first. It didn't seem proper, but there was little else we could do, you see. After all, his offer seemed more than generous."

"My living arrangements should be of no concern to you, ma'am."

Lord, give me patience with this woman. And please add some unconditional love while You're at it.

"Oh, but they are. I understand from several of the townsfolk that Mr. Broughton has been seeing you to and from school on a daily basis. Surely, you can see the inappropriateness of such an action."

"His children accompany us."

The woman squeezed her lips in a tight line. "You're not suggesting they serve as qualified chaperones."

"Mrs. Winthrop, I don't need a chaperone."

"Are you forgetting the conditions of your contract? No unseemly behavior with anyone of the opposite gender will be tolerated."

"There is no unseemly behavior."

Mrs. Winthrop threw a halting hand in front of Liza's face. "I must insist that you not accept any more rides with Mr. Broughton. To do so would be to put you in breach of contract and could very well cost you your job. In addition, I will not have you flaunting your presence in this classroom after hours."

"Flaunting? I have not…" Fresh anger swam to the surface, blurring her vision.

"And one more thing," Mrs. Winthrop said, her chocolate eyes swirling with ire. "Little Lili Broughton has whispered to her friends about your personal visits to her home. It seems the word has gotten out to several parents. I'm sure you recognize how unacceptable this sort of behavior is."

Liza could scarcely blame Lili for talking to her friends. Naturally, she thrilled at Liza's visits. Still, she would have to speak to the child about the downfalls of boasting. "I have paid a visit to all the homes of my students," Liza said, forcing calmness.

"But Mr. Broughton is the only widower. That is one visit you could have forfeited for the sake of decency."

"I also visited Mr. Brackett. As you know, he is a widower, as well."

To that, Mrs. Winthrop nearly toppled. Putting a hand to her throat, she made a show of coughing. "I can assure you my brother-in-law poses no threat to your respectability."

"And Mr. Broughton does? What of Jonathan Atkins? Would it be inappropriate to be seen with him?" Liza asked, sudden boldness running through her veins.

"He is a minister," Mrs. Winthrop said in haste. "That is quite different."

"But I don't see…"

"I believe this conversation has ended, young lady," Mrs. Winthrop said with abruptness. "I shall let myself out."

Liza counted her breaths, taking care not to say something she would later regret, while Mrs. Winthrop donned her cold-weather gear and made for the door. Laying her hand to the doorknob, she said without turning, "You would do well to pay heed to what I've said, Miss Merriwether. There are other teachers about should you have difficulty adhering to the demands of your contract."

✻ ✻ ✻ ✻ ✻

Ben drove the team home, Molly bouncing happily on his lap and Lili engaged in her usual ceaseless chatter.

"How come Miss Merriwether didn't ride home with us, Papa?"

"She said she preferred walking tonight."

Actually, she'd insisted, but Ben kept that tidbit of information to himself. The look of utter determination on the woman's face, along with something else quite indiscernible, had warned him against arguing. He'd seen a similar look plenty of times before and learned the futility in trying to change her mind. Of course, he would watch for her lantern to come on later, and if it didn't, he would go looking for her. He wouldn't let her off the hook that easily, not after her recent encounter with Clement Bartel.

There was to be a meeting of the church assembly that evening concerning the hiring of a full-time minister. Reverend Miller had announced just two Sundays ago that his failing health prohibited him from continuing his circuit. It was past time that the community sought a full-time minister, namely the very qualified Jonathan Atkins. Support had risen up all around, with Ben being Jon's number one supporter. No one else was better suited for the position, or had greater vision. The people of Little Hickman would do well to hire him on the spot. If they didn't, some bigger congregation was sure to grab him.

After supper, Ben would knock on Liza's door to see if she wanted a ride to the meeting. If she refused, then she would have to stay at home. He would not have her walking three miles to a meeting after dark, and that was all there was to it.

✳ ✳ ✳ ✳ ✳

Liza heard the nicker of approaching horses and glanced out the frosted window in time to see Jon's wagon coming over the crest. After school, she'd spotted him talking to Doc Randolph outside his office on her walk toward home. As soon as he'd glimpsed her, he'd waved farewell to Doc and come bounding across the street to greet her, his boots kicking up dust. Laughing at his antics, she'd welcomed his presence, happy that should Mrs. Winthrop see them together, there'd be no objection. *That is quite different*, she'd said, *he is a minister.*

Piffle. Minister or not, he was still a man, and a fine-looking one at that, never mind that she wasn't attracted to him in a romantic sense. And she was beginning to see that Jon viewed her similarly. Somehow, they had fashioned a friendship that required little in terms of obligation, which suited her just fine. Perhaps he sensed her heart was elsewhere. Whatever the case, the casual way in which they treated one another had made it easy for her to ask him for a ride to tonight's meeting.

"I would love to escort you to the church tonight," he'd said, looping an arm through hers. "I need the support of friends, and I consider you one of my best."

She'd laughed. "You have more friends than I can hope for in a lifetime, Jon."

He'd tipped his head at her as they walked along. "I doubt that. From what I hear, you are doing a fine job as Hickman's school-teacher."

Without her realizing it, her shoulders dropped. "Tell that to Mrs. Winthrop, would you?"

"What do you mean?"

"Oh, I don't know. I get the distinct feeling she doesn't approve of me." There'd been no point to dragging the young preacher into her tale of woes. Best to keep this particular problem between her and the Lord. God would see her through, of that she was certain. He had brought her to Little Hickman for a reason, and she was sure it was for teaching its children.

"Being confident of this very thing, that he which hath begun a good work in you will perform it until the day of Jesus Christ."

The verse from Philippians had nearly stopped her in her tracks when it came to mind, but she'd managed to keep pace with Jon.

"Don't worry about Iris Winthrop. She and Clyde tried for years to have a family of their own. When they couldn't, she made it her mission to make everyone around her equally unhappy. Poor Clyde; I don't know how he sticks with her but for the grace of God and the sweet distraction that must come from running his store."

Liza had covered her mouth to stifle an iniquitous giggle. "Reverend Atkins, you shock me."

He'd laughed. "Iris is not a bad person, really. She's just had some hard knocks. Unfortunately, she's never learned that God can take the ugly things of life and turn them into beautiful. Until she does, she will do everything in her power to make everyone miserable."

"You seem to know her well."

"Not really, but I treat her with as much kindness as I can muster, and every now and then I have to ask God for an extra dose."

Again, she'd giggled, happy that he'd managed to redirect her otherwise gloomy thoughts.

"Jon!" she now called, opening her cabin door and letting in a gust of cold night air. "I'll be right there!" He waved a friendly greeting from his high wagon perch as she closed the door again.

She threw on her long wool coat, secured her matching hat, and then doused the single light in her window before pulling on her mittens.

Taking a satisfied look around her cozy cabin, she reopened her door and bumped headlong into Ben Broughton's brick-hard chest.

Whistling winds did little to calm her frayed nerves at the sight of him, his dark eyes running the length of her, the absence of a smile setting her off balance.

"I came to offer you a ride," he mumbled, "but I see it wasn't necessary."

Her gaping mouth couldn't come up with a suitable reply.

"Ben!" called Jon, his voice barely reaching them due to the hard, driving winds. "You're welcome to hitch a ride with Liza and me."

"No!" Liza objected loud enough for Jon to hear. Ben's frown grew, as did his obvious hurt and confusion. "I mean, Ben, I don't mean to hurt your feelings," she said, quieter now, "but I, well, it might not be appropriate if both you and Jon, well…"

"I see what you mean," Ben said, stiffening before her eyes. "Three is a crowd, right?"

"What? No…I don't mean…"

"Don't try to explain, Liza. I understand that you want to be alone with Jon."

With a prompt turn, and before she could manage another word of denial, Ben waved a hand at Jon and called, "I'd just as soon drive my own rig. Thanks anyway."

"You sure, Ben? I've plenty of room."

But Ben had disappeared into the darkness without another word.

Chapter Nineteen

The vote had been almost unanimous—almost, but not quite. Most surmised it was the elderly Mrs. Crunkle and her counterparts, the widows Jacobsen and Marley, who opposed the appointment of a full-time minister, claiming they'd managed all these many years with Reverend Miller, and what use was it to hire someone on a permanent basis? Of course, it mattered little to them that the Reverend Miller had recently resigned his position as circuit rider, and they would therefore be without a minister if they failed to vote in Jon. Ben had no idea where their thinking took them, so he chalked it up to old age.

The meeting had been brief, as church assemblies go. Most were eager to see the young Jon Atkins become their pastor. He had fresh ideas, a vision for the future, compassion for people, and a deep love for the Lord. Add to that the fact that he could preach their socks off, and he was a shoe-in for the job.

Ben had fought down a bitter taste most of the night. Despite his excitement at Jon's appointment, he couldn't help but feel a sense of loss at the same time. Since it was obvious that Liza had feelings for Jon, and who could blame her, the time had come to back away from her, forget the fact that he'd already given her his heart. He would just have to rein it back in, regain control. Lili would be disappointed, but so be it. Some things were not meant to be, and God help him, this was one of them.

"Ben, good to see you," Jon said, offering a hand at the school's front door. Several people stood in a long line, each waiting for his turn to welcome the new preacher.

"Congratulations, my friend. I'm proud of you. You'll make Hickman a fine minister," Ben said.

"It's not about what I can do, Ben. It's about what God can do through me," Jon said.

Ben took the hand offered him, ashamed for the jealousy that hovered so close. *God, he is a spiritual giant next to me.* The sudden insight made Ben withdraw his hand.

"A new heart also will I give you, and a new spirit will I put within you."

Why did it seem that the short passage from Ezekiel that he'd read that very morning had now come back to taunt him? Did he need a new heart? Was God trying to tell him something here?

"You okay?" Jon asked.

"I'm fine. I best be getting home to my girls."

Ben started to go through the door. When he glanced back, he saw Liza approach Jon with a smile on her face and two of her older students on both arms.

Not far behind Liza stood Iris Winthrop, her normally downturned face actually donning a halfway pleasant look.

❄ ❄ ❄ ❄ ❄

It was Saturday morning. The sun came over the horizon like a bride about to meet her groom, dazzling and perfect. It was enough to take Liza's breath away as she busied herself in her neat little kitchen, canning the last of her applesauce and peaches and sipping on her morning cup of coffee.

Something about Saturday mornings brought out the domestic side to Liza, making her want to dust everything in sight, beat the rugs until they nearly fell apart, wash every last garment she owned, and cook up a storm on her refurbished cook stove. Now, she ran a hand over its smooth, clean enamel and blessed the day that Ben and his friends had not only scrubbed the stove and sink until they sparkled, but also helped to make her cabin livable.

She scanned her surroundings with loving eyes and, as was often the case, allowed her gaze to fall upon the painting that hung next to the bedroom door.

Patience Is a Virtue. She liked to think she was learning the meaning behind those words, but every once in a while, she got hit with a fresh dose of reality and knew with certainty she had not. Her stormy reaction to Mrs. Winthrop's recent classroom visit exposed her weakness when it came to patience. Even now, she stewed over the harshly spoken words.

A sudden knock at her door drew her up short. She dropped the wooden spoon she'd been using to stir her applesauce back into the kettle and tugged the belt of her nightdress securely around her.

That would be Lili, she decided with a smile, begging to help her with the canning. And she would welcome her company.

However, it wasn't Lili but Ben who stood just on the other side of the door, his overwhelming stature making her heart pound in her chest.

She peered at him through the shiny glass pane, having opened all the curtains as soon as the sun began to rise. She'd wanted to experience its loveliness from every window. Now she wished she hadn't been so hasty, for he could easily see every move she made. In fact, she wondered just how long he'd been watching her before he'd even knocked. *Such foolishness.*

Ben peered back, his stare unreadable. "Open the door," he ordered, and none too softly.

She turned the knob with care. "I'm not dressed yet," she murmured, intending to open the door a matter of inches, dismayed when he managed to push it fully past her.

He inspected her. "Then get dressed." His tone demanded notice.

"What?"

The sound of a nickering horse on the other side of the house forced her head past his broad frame. Ben's beautiful stallion stood shackled to a pine tree like some raging fiend unable to contain his fury. A hind foot beat out a rhythm into the hard, cold earth, vibrating everything around it. Liza could only imagine once sleeping ground moles now scattering about in their underground tunnels.

"You once told me you could ride."

"Yes."

"Put on some riding clothes then," he said. "You're going to prove it."

"Now?" Anger suddenly replaced confusion. "I'm busy right now."

"Busy? Or scared?"

"What? How dare you?" *Lord, here I am again, requiring patience.*

Ben gave no response this time, just arched eyebrows asking a silent question.

"Oh, all right. Give me a minute," she said, "but I don't understand the point of this."

"You will," was all he said by way of response.

Brisk morning air chilled her to the bone. Of course, she could blame her sudden chill on the air or she could blame the man and his wild horse.

"You know how to mount?" he asked when she faced him wearing a pair of Uncle Gideon's overalls and work shirt. To say that she felt like a fool was putting it mildly. She worried about what he must be thinking, then gave that up when she realized he'd barely even looked at her. What was wrong with him?

"Of course I know how to mount. I grew up riding at Uncle Gideon's sister's ranch."

"Then I suppose you know all about riding wild stallions?"

"I've ridden a few—I think," she added for general purposes. She hadn't really been told of the horses' genders.

His lower lip twitched just slightly, and she thought he might have smiled were it not for his sour mood. "This guy needs to know right from the start that you don't intend to give him any slack. Let him know who's boss," Ben said, indicating the horse.

"Like you're doing now, you mean?" she asked, hoping to pry a smile out of him with her facetious comment.

"This is no time for joking."

"No, I can see that," she answered, turning down her mouth. "Don't worry, I can manage."

He gave her a slanted glance. "Don't be so sure of yourself."

Liza breathed heavily and the stallion sidestepped, giving Liza a start. "Why'd he jump like that?"

"Because you breathed. Steady, Tanner," Ben said in a soft voice, rubbing a hand along the horse's muscled neck.

"Because I breathed?"

"Sudden moves or noises spook him. When you walk him, be on guard for chipmunks, squirrels, anything that might run across his path. If he jolts, you'll need to be prepared."

Her heart stepped up its beating, and she sucked in a silent breath of air, taking the reins that Ben handed over to her.

When she lifted her foot to place it in the stirrup, she realized her need for help. Without prompting, Ben stepped up and lifted her at the waist until her booted foot connected with the stirrup, and she managed to swing her other leg over. He had already adjusted the stirrup heights, placing them in the last loops so that they would be at the shortest distance from the saddle. He must think her such a child, she mused.

"Comfortable?" he asked. He seemed miles away from her.

She nodded, thankful that the horse had barely moved when she mounted. She felt his giant body quiver and quake beneath her when she made an adjustment in the saddle, heard the steady roar of each dragon breath as he pranced in place.

"Take him slowly. You'll need to pull back or he'll take your slackness to mean you want to run."

"Maybe I do."

He gave her a scorching look. "Don't even think about it."

As soon as she clicked her tongue to her teeth to nudge the horse along, he gave a powerful jerk, a thrust of his body that set Liza's mind at attention. She pulled for all she was worth on the bulky leather reins, the friction burning clear through her heavy gloves.

"Easy now," she heard Ben whisper, the familiarity of his tone immediately quieting the manic beast. "Liza, maybe this wasn't such a good idea," he said, his voice suddenly gone shaky.

For some reason, Liza delighted in the thought of worrying him. "Too late now," she said with a fastened grin.

Again, she nudged the horse forward, prepared this time for any sudden moves. As expected, Tanner lurched and snorted, but she rode it out, moving in the saddle in accordance with his gait, familiarizing herself with his power and might, gaining Ben's respect with every passing second. Her childhood riding lessons were paying off.

After several minutes of walking, Liza stepped Tanner up to a slow-paced canter.

"Liza, I said to keep him walking," she heard Ben say, his voice low and calm so as not to spook the horse. So far, she'd stayed within Ben's parameters, between the cabin and the main house, with him staying close by, issuing quiet orders from behind.

"I think we're starting to get used to each other," she said, pleased when Tanner didn't jerk forward at the sound of her voice.

"That's no reason to get overconfident," Ben replied.

She supposed he was right, so she pulled back on the reins, proud with the way Tanner reacted to her silent command. "Whoa," she added for good measure.

Everything seemed to be going smoothly until Lili burst from the house, all spunk and spirit. "Miss Merriwether, you're riding Tanner!" she squealed with delight. At that, Molly let go a different kind of squeal as she toppled off the porch steps and rolled to the ground. Liza witnessed it all from the corner of her eye, but that was all the time Tanner gave her before he bolted off toward the open field and Little Hickman Creek. The wind in her face, Liza felt the bun in her hair fall apart, her long hair flying behind her.

"Whoa!" she bellowed until her throat wrenched in pain. "Whoa!"

Her body bounced like a rag doll atop the raging, locomotive-like creature. She fought to stay upright, yet forced herself not to go rigid lest she lose her footing.

Stay with the animal; contemplate his every move; talk to him; breathe with him; and above all else, never, never, never let him smell your fear. The words of a childhood instructor came into her mind.

With all her might, she pulled back on the reins. "Dear Father in heaven, please make this horse obey," she shouted to the heavens, gripped by terror when Tanner leaped over a small ravine, pleased when she managed to right herself by grabbing hold of the saddle horn and sliding back into place.

Talk to him. "Easy, boy, that's it. Whoa." After what seemed like several minutes, her gentler talk seemed to slow his pace. Pulling the reins tighter, she kept up her talk. "That's a boy. Easy. Now you have it," she continued, hoping he was listening. "Slower now. No need to hurry," she said, noting that her yanking had given way to gentle tugs.

With ears directed outward, Tanner released several loud, angry snorts from his giant nostrils as he slowed to a canter and then an unhurried walk. She reached down a hand to rub his sweat-strewn side, realizing her own frantic breathing coincided with that of the horse. "Calm down," she issued, as if she were someone worthy of his attention.

"Thank You, Lord," she whispered toward the heavens.

Approaching hoofbeats forced her gaze toward home, where she spotted one of the draft horses, carrying Ben, leaving behind grey clouds of dust. Ben rode bareback, a magnificent sight, man and beast.

For a moment, Liza feared Ben's approach might spook Tanner again, but at the sound of Ben's voice, the horse remained in place. "Liza, are you all right?" he asked, bringing his horse to a dead standstill next to Tanner. Both horses let go a string of snorts, enough to match two fiery dragons standing side by side.

"I'm perfectly fine," she said, calm as could be. No point in letting him know what terror she'd just encountered.

"Good," Ben said, hiding any show of emotion. "You'll be riding Tanner to school every day from now on."

✳ ✳ ✳ ✳ ✳

Ben met Liza at the barn the next few mornings, reacquainting her with the procedure for readying Tanner for the ride to school. He showed her where to find the tack, how tight to pull the belly harness, and how to station herself in the stall when saddling him up. In the event that Tanner should rear or sidestep, Ben had built a permanent

261

ladder against the wall for making a hasty exit. "I've had to use it a couple of times myself," he'd admitted. "Tanner doesn't realize his might. When he objects to something, it's not usually out of spite but fear."

"I'll manage," Liza had said, her shoulders straight, her stance determined.

"After what I witnessed, I've no doubt you will," he'd said with a grin, assessing Liza from top to bottom, still amazed at the grit she'd displayed when the stallion had bolted.

How could he fault Jon for his attraction to her? She was a woman to admire and cherish. And since Liza appeared to be equally charmed with Jon, he had no choice but to wish them both the best. Hadn't she as much as said she'd rather ride alone with Jon to the church meeting? Sure, the truth had hurt, but better to find it out now than later.

He and Jon had been friends for years, and the last thing Ben wanted was for a woman to come between them.

"Do all things without murmurings and disputings."

If that verse from Philippians hadn't been clear enough about what God expected of him, he was sure there were plenty more where that came from.

"You'll have to lead Tanner over to that wooden bench so you can mount him without my help from now on," Ben had told her on the third morning. "I won't be out here most mornings." In fact, he'd make it a point not to be.

She'd given him a strained look. "Of course. You have more important things to see to than—well, you're very generous to allow me to borrow Tanner."

"You'll have your independence," he'd reminded.

She'd nodded. "I'll be safe on Tanner, and you won't have to bother with driving me."

"It was never a bother, Liza."

"No, but—this is much better—for everyone."

He'd taken a step back then to get the full view of her. She wore no riding pants, but her long skirts covered most of her legs, and her high-top boots took care of what they didn't. Her hat covered her neatly pinned golden hair, a shame since now he knew how those locks looked when flowing freely in the wind. Her pink cheeks flushed at his perusal. "Well, I'll be off, then," she'd said, turning the already prancing stallion in the direction of town.

"I don't need to tell you to be careful."

"No, I suppose you don't," she'd said, turning to glance at him, but not really looking into his eyes.

"Well, Sam will be expecting Tanner at the livery," he'd added, laying a hand to Tanner's rump.

"Yes, and thank you again. I appreciate this."

That marked the end to their conversation, as Miss Merriwether had by then kicked the stallion into a slow canter. As she did, her bonnet, tied under her chin, came loose from her head and flew behind her. No doubt, her hair would do the same.

❋ ❋ ❋ ❋ ❋

November ushered in December, and with it came Kentucky's first snowflakes. The children couldn't contain their joy when they spied the silvery flecks.

"Miss Merriwether, can we get a closer look?" asked Lili, her big blue eyes round with hope and wonder.

But before Liza could nod her approval, the Hogsworth twins had already beaten a trail to the window closest to their desks. The rest of the class stood at the ready.

She laughed. "Take five minutes."

You'd have thought she'd just announced the end to the school day the way the children leaped from their seats and headed for the tall windows on either side of the room. When they'd gotten their fill of looking out one window, they raced across the room to another, as if the flakes would fall any differently on the opposite side of the building.

Liza couldn't help but catch their excitement as she nuzzled in between Eloise Brackett and Rosie Bartel to peer up at the snowy clouds emitting the frosty crystals. Placing an arm over both girls' shoulders, Liza was alarmed to discover a large bump at the base of Rosie's neck, just under her right ear. Her high collar did a good job of covering most of it, but when Liza's arm had rested atop the child's shoulder it had managed to pull away a bit of the material.

"Rosie, what happened to you?" she asked, bending to get a better look at the black-and-blue mark, alarmed at its protruding size.

The child's hand went to the spot, then yanked her collar back in place. Her downcast eyes seemed filled with worry and torment. "'Twas nothin'," she said, turning away and heading for her desk. The rest of the children talked in excited tones about the snow and barely noticed when their teacher took Rosie aside.

"Rosie, how did you get this mark?" She knelt beside the child's desk when Rosie took her seat.

"I fell," she muttered. "I fell off the porch and hit a big rock."

Liza gasped. "Did your mother have Doctor Randolph look at it?"

She threw wide her eyes. "'Course not. We never go to the Doc. Mama says we're too poor."

"I'm sure the doctor would understand if your parents couldn't pay immediately. Would you like us to walk over there during the lunch break?"

"No!" She seemed clear on that.

Liza leaned in closer. "Sweetie, is there anything you're not telling me? How did you fall off the porch?"

"I tripped. Clement says I'm very clumsy."

"Clement?"

At that, Rosie curled her lips under and pinched them tight together, an indication that she'd already said more than she intended. Hands folded at her desk, she stared straight ahead, as if to study the origin of some speck on the wall.

Liza watched closely, not wanting to push, but concerned for the child's safety. "Rosie, did Clement have anything to do with your falling off the porch?"

"I tried to help Mama," she said, her voice so low that Liza had to put her ear up close to the little girl's mouth to hear. "Clement was beatin' on her. Clement got fierce mad and comed runnin' after me. He told me to...I can't say the word, Miss Merriwether, 'cause it was bad," she said, her large eyes turning toward Liza and filling with tears. "That's when he pushed—I fell off the porch."

Liza wrapped an arm around the child and drew her close, her own stomach whirling and churning. After a minute she asked, "Is your mother all right?"

Rosie nodded in slow motion. "She fixed my breakfast this mornin', but she had to be careful not to move too fast."

"Where was your father—during...?" She knew she was asking questions that the sheriff should be asking, but it worried her that Rosie might not share the same information with Will Murdock.

"Out in the fields. He was cuttin' hay."

"I see." Liza sat back on her heels and pondered her next words. "Did your mother tell your father?"

Rosie accompanied her nod with a faraway look. "Papa can't do nothin' 'cause Clement's bigger 'n him."

Suddenly, Liza knew what she had to do. "After school I am going to visit the sheriff." Rosie's boulder-sized eyes filled with fright. "You are not to worry, do you understand? Everything will be just fine. The sheriff will know what to do. In the meantime, I want you to do everything in your power to avoid your brother."

"He ain't my brother," Rosie said, crossing her arms in front of her.

At the close of the school day, Liza strode down Main Street with a great sense of purpose, taking care to wave at folks along the way, but failing to stop and chat as some might have liked. She hoped they would suppose her brusqueness was due to the uncommon cold and not lack of kindliness. Regardless, she hadn't the time to worry what folks thought. She had devised a plan of sorts, and the sooner she got to it the better.

Dear Lord, don't let me race ahead of You. If this plan comes from You, may it work accordingly. And if it's not, then please turn my thoughts elsewhere.

"I will instruct thee and teach thee in the way which thou shalt go: I will guide thee with mine eye."

Thank you for that blessed reminder from the Psalms, Father.

After a satisfying visit with Sheriff Murdock, in which he'd promised to haul Clement in for questioning, Liza hurried her steps toward her next desired stop.

Rounding the bend on Main Street, she turned down one of Little Hickman's few cross streets, Washington Avenue. She laughed at the rather formal title and wondered if it hadn't been Mrs. Winthrop herself who had named it. Somehow, a narrow gravel road seemed hardly worthy to carry a fancy word like *avenue* behind its name.

Each house along Washington had its own character. Simply built, the tall clapboard structures boasted front porches, albeit warped in most cases, and narrow paths leading from the houses to the street.

 266

An assortment of mostly withered plants and shrubs hugged the fronts and sides of each house, a reminder of days gone by when they'd flourished in the warmth of the sun.

The grandest house on the street stood out from the others, its white, two-story structure, green-shuttered windows, and covered front porch with four massive columns seeming to beckon passersby. *Nothing warped in those fine boards*, Liza mused. She gawked for several minutes at its stately presence before she set off up the heavily trampled pathway toward the porch.

Large pots of still blooming chrysanthemums situated on either side of the wide staircase added color to the otherwise overcast day, as if to lend strength and support as she climbed the freshly painted steps. A white wicker couch with matching rocker and side table adorned the far side of the porch. Had she not known the woman inside, she might have felt welcomed enough to sit a spell and drink up the simplistic beauty.

At the front door, Liza sucked in a breath, whispered a prayer for courage and the proper words, and lifted a gloved hand to knock on the enormous front door. Hurried steps inside produced more jitters within her.

She recognized Clyde Winthrop as soon as he flung wide the door. He'd always been more than friendly to her whenever she'd visited Winthrop's Dry Goods. Small boned and sporting a mostly bald head, his unsubstantial appearance gave way to his friendly smile, making his otherwise frail exterior seem inconsequential. Even now, his smile seemed to stretch from cheek to cheek.

"Well, if it isn't Miss Merriwether. Iris, come quick; it's the teacher," he called toward the back of the house. "Won't you come in?"

He ushered her into the parlor, where imported furniture of the finest quality filled the room. Velvet draperies covered the front and

267

side windows, and a finely woven European rug lay atop the shiny wood flooring.

Mr. Winthrop pointed her to a chair where she was about to sit when the lady of the house flitted in.

"Well, my goodness…" was about all Mrs. Winthrop could offer by way of a greeting.

Liza stifled a giggle, turning it into a puny cough instead. "Hello, Mrs. Winthrop. Mr. Winthrop. I hope I'm not intruding on your supper, but I promise you I shall only be a minute."

"Not at all. Please, sit." Mr. Winthrop pointed her to the chair again, while his wife, tongue-tied, remained frozen in place. Apparently, she'd been recalling her last encounter with the teacher and marveling at the fact the young lady even had the nerve to show up on her doorstep.

"What can we do for you?" Clyde Winthrop asked, taking up a chair across from Liza while ignoring his still standing wife.

Liza folded her hands and put them in her lap, lifting yet another silent prayer heavenward. "Well, I would like to present you with a proposition."

Chapter Twenty

W hat sort of proposition?" Mrs. Winthrop guided herself to a chair and dropped into its softness.

"I was wondering if you might be open to, well, allowing someone to live with you—for a time, that is."

"What?" Mrs. Winthrop bristled where she sat, her pointed chin jutting out.

"It's a woman and her daughter," Liza said, hurrying to get the words out before they both put her out of the house. "They are suffering untold abuse at the hands of a cruel young man, and they have nowhere else to go. At first, I thought to invite them to my own cabin, but then I realized my place is far too small." Neither spoke a word, so she hastily carried on. "It won't be forever, mind you, just until the sheriff can work through the details of the..."

"The sheriff?" Mrs. Winthrop shrieked. "Now see here, young lady, I..."

"Iris!" The little man's sudden outburst shut the woman up on the spot, making Liza wonder how many times he'd had to resort to that particular tone. Not many, by Iris Winthrop's stunned expression. "Let Miss Merriwether continue. I would very much like to hear about these people in dire need of help."

Liza proceeded to tell them about her student, filling them in on every detail but the child's name, until Mr. Winthrop choked with tears and even Mrs. Winthrop showed a measure of emotion.

"Sheriff Murdock agrees that they should not continue living in the same house with their offender, and when I suggested I might ask you to house them temporarily, he thought it was a fine idea."

"He did, did he?" Mrs. Winthrop said, giving a little sniff.

"Yes, he pointed out that you do have the biggest and finest house in the entire town and surrounding area, and that since you have never had children of your own, perhaps you would enjoy having a little girl around."

To that, Mr. Winthrop's eyes clouded even more. He turned to face his wife.

"Well, I think the situation is one that warrants little consideration on our part. We have plenty of room and resources by which to offer our assistance."

"Clyde." His wife's panicked tone would have stopped any other man, but perhaps this man was so accustomed to his wife's rantings that he'd learned to pay them little heed.

"Iris, we have the three extra bedrooms upstairs. They are all fully furnished and well equipped. The bedding needs shaking and the furniture dusting for lack of use, but there is no reason why we should decline this very sensible suggestion."

"Well, I...who are these people?" Mrs. Winthrop suddenly asked.

It was the question Liza had been waiting for. If Mrs. Winthrop were even half unconvinced, the revelation of their names would wipe away all Liza's hopes. Was this where she should prepare herself for a fast exit?

"It's—Rosie Bartel and her mother."

"What?" Mrs. Winthrop squealed, standing to her feet. "You expect us to take in those—those unfortunate hill people?"

Mr. Winthrop allowed his wife her minute's worth of fury, and then he calmly said, "It matters little to us where these folks hail from, Miss Merriwether. The important thing is that they arrive at a place of safety."

Liza sighed with relief that she'd at least managed to bring Mr. Winthrop over to her side.

"Clyde." The woman's voice had dropped considerably, perhaps from shock.

"Now, how shall we go about making the arrangements?" the kindly man asked, approaching Liza and offering her his arm.

Taken aback, Liza stood to her feet and followed his lead to the door. "I believe Sheriff Murdock will be in touch with you. He intends to pay the family a visit tonight or early tomorrow morning. I suppose you could expect them as early as tomorrow. This is providing that Mrs. Bartel even agrees to leave."

"Let us pray that she will," Clyde whispered.

"Thank you, Mr. Winthrop. I hardly know what to say."

"No words are necessary, my dear. In fact, I should thank you for thinking of us. I've wanted a little excitement around this house. It's too quiet around here most times." He winked at her and gave her arm a little squeeze. "I know it's hard to believe."

Liza glanced over his shoulder at Mrs. Winthrop, who now held a kerchief to her mouth. Was the woman crying?

"Mrs. Winthrop. Will she be all right?"

He nodded and released a low chuckle. "Most don't know that underneath that tough façade is a warmhearted woman. Perhaps this Mrs. Bartel and her daughter will be just the ticket for drawing out a little of that warmth."

"Good night, Mr. Winthrop."

"Good night, my dear."

❋ ❋ ❋ ❋ ❋

She had done it again. It was well past dusk, and Liza had not arrived home from school. Ben mucked out the stalls, calling himself every name in the book for caring so deeply. Two stalls over, Charlie, one of the draft horses, snorted, as if to respond to Ben's mutterings. If it weren't for the fact that Tanner wasn't in his stall, he might well have taken himself to bed and forgotten Liza altogether. But even as he nurtured the thought, he knew it wasn't true. He wouldn't sleep until he knew the schoolteacher was safe.

The clip-clop of approaching horses had him tossing his pitchfork in the air, picking up a lantern, and walking to the barn door. In the distance, he distinguished the silhouettes of two horses and their riders, one Tanner and Liza, and the other—he discharged a heavy breath and fought down the hostility that naturally rose—Jon Atkins, who else? She'd spent the supper hour with him.

"Ben, is that you?" Jon's voice carried over the still night air, awakening a distant owl.

Ben leaned heavily into the doorway and crossed his arms, allowing the lantern to dangle from one arm. "Who else would it be?" Ben asked. It was too late to hide his impatience. It came out clear as could be in the tone of his voice.

Jon laughed his usual good-natured laugh, obviously ignoring Ben's jibe.

"Look who I ran into on Main Street. I didn't think it safe to allow her to ride back from town unaccompanied."

Ben took a moment to study Liza. Her hair had come undone, and she looked nothing like the prim and proper schoolteacher she claimed to be.

"It's late—and dark," Ben mumbled, his eyes trailing a path back to Jon.

Jon's gaze tipped upward. "So it is. Sky is black as coal. Would you have a look at that harvest moon?"

Ben kept his gaze pinned on Jon. He'd be hornswoggled before he'd look at the moon at Jon's suggestion. However, he did notice Liza sigh in wonder when she caught a glimpse of it. "It's absolutely beautiful, Jon."

The three wrapped themselves in a fifteen-second blanket of silence until Jon poked a hole through it. "Liza had quite a day today. She went to see Sheriff Murdock after school and..."

"What? Why did you go to the sheriff? Did Clement Bartel..." Every nerve ending jumped to life as Ben lurched forward, spooking Tanner with his sudden movement. Liza steadied the untamed brute like a regular pro.

"Why don't you let her tell you?" Jon suggested, dismounting and leading his horse toward Ben's house. "And since I've already heard the story, I'll just go inside and help myself to your coffeepot, if you don't mind."

"Fine. But keep the noise down. My girls are sleeping." Where had all this gruffness come from? But he should have known the answer to that without asking.

He was jealous, plain and simple.

✳ ✳ ✳ ✳ ✳

Ben loosened Tanner's belly strap.

"I could do that, you know," Liza said, nervous in Ben's company, particularly when he seemed so hot under the collar.

"I'm here, I'll do it," he muttered. "Tell me what this visit to Sheriff Murdock was all about."

Liza stood at Tanner's head, rubbing his velvet muzzle, while Ben worked. "I spotted a bad bruise on the side of Rosie's neck today."

Ben's head shot up. "Clement?"

She nodded.

A cussing man would have inserted an emphatic expletive at

273

that particular point, but instead Ben issued a silent prayer for protection over anyone that came across Clement Bartel's path.

"So you reported the incident to Will?" he asked, hauling the saddle off of Tanner and heaving it on the tack box.

"I did. He intends to pay the Bartels a visit tonight."

"Good. I hope he throws that boy in jail."

Liza shivered at Ben's acidic tone. "I agree he deserves punishment."

"But?" Ben pinned her with his midnight eyes, and she went as still as death itself, forgetting even to breathe.

"Nothing. It's just that you sound so, I don't know, cold and unforgiving."

"You want me to forgive all that Clement's done to Rosie and her mother?"

"Well, we should all have it in our hearts to forgive. Ephesians 4:32 says, **'And be ye kind one to another, tenderhearted, forgiving one another, even as God for Christ's sake hath forgiven you.'**"

Ben lifted his gaze to the rafters, then directed it back to her. "That was good, Teacher. Was that verse situated anywhere close to 'Patience is a virtue'?"

She stepped around Tanner and slapped Ben playfully on the forearm, knowing he toyed with her. "You will never let me forget that, will you?"

"Not if I can help it," he said, adding a chuckle.

"Want to know what else happened?" she asked. When he nodded, she spilled the entire story about her visit to the Winthrop home, how Mr. Winthrop had been eager to help Rosie and her mother, and even how Mr. Winthrop had craftily put his wife in her place.

Ben laughed. "Well, what do you know? The man does have a way of getting through to that hard-nosed lady, after all."

Liza giggled shamelessly. "He claims that under her tough façade there is a soft-hearted woman, and I think that once she finds there is joy in helping others, we will all begin to see a different Mrs. Winthrop."

"Ah, so your plan was twofold." Ben looked around Tanner and caught Liza up with his dark eyes. "You're something."

He'd told her that before, and she never did quite know how to take the remark.

"Thank you. I think."

"So—you and Jon..."

"What about me?" asked Jon, entering the barn at the mention of his name, tin cup in hand, steam emitting from the top.

Ben looked up, his face suddenly serious again. "Nothing. I see you found the coffee."

"This stuff is so strong it almost walked to me when I called its name. Did you make this yesterday?" Jon asked, tipping the cup up to take another drink.

"Nope. I believe it was three days ago."

Jon spat, and the black liquid flew across the barn, leaving a wet trail on the opposite wall.

❋ ❋ ❋ ❋ ❋

As Liza began to tick off the days of December, she sensed an underlying current of excitement among her students with the approach of Christmas. Although the citizens of Little Hickman were mostly plain in appearance and lifestyle, there was certainly room in their hearts for the tradition of gift-giving and holiday joy.

"Can we make a paper chain to hang across the doorway, Miss Merriwether?" Lili asked over lunch one Tuesday.

Liza looked up from her desk to see more than a dozen pairs of eyes awaiting her reply. She laughed. "We'll start this afternoon."

"What color shall it be?" asked Samuel Thompson.

"All colors. Christmas doesn't have to be just green," answered Eloise Brackett, her braids still holding from when Liza had fashioned them three hours ago. Without fail, Mr. Brackett continued to drop his daughter off ten minutes before the start of each day so that Liza could see to her long brown hair. True to his word, he'd even seen that she was clean most days.

"Who's going to hang the chain?" asked Rufus from his place in the back. Now that Clement was gone, Rufus had been slowly inching his desk forward. But now he'd reached his limit as he butted desks with Andrew Warner.

Liza picked up her cold beef sandwich and took a bite. "I would think someone tall. Why not you, Rufus?"

"Me?"

"You are the biggest and the tallest," said little Todd Thompson.

Rufus smiled, then gulped down the rest of his water.

It was working. As Rufus Baxter's self-worth improved, so did his grades. Liza had just finished correcting his English paper. Instead of the usual failing grade, she happily penned a large C+ at the top of his paper, and beside that, the words *Fine Job*!

"After we make our paper chain, can we make more decorations?" Lili asked before sinking her teeth into a shiny apple.

Liza laughed. "If I didn't know better, I'd say you were trying to escape your assignments."

That remark produced a hearty laugh from several students, Lili included.

"I'd like to make a Christmas angel," offered a quiet Rosie Bartel. "I would hang it on my desk to remind me."

A kind of hush fell over the classroom with her petal-soft words. "To remind you of what?" asked Lenora Humphrey.

"That God's angel was watching over me and Mama. That's why I come to live with Mr. and Mrs. Winthrop, because an angel told us that we should go there."

"No kidding?" asked Gus Humphrey, his green eyes big as the round tin plate on top of his desk. "Is she joshin' us, Miss Merriwether?"

"If she says an angel guided her to the Winthrop's, then I will be the last to argue with her," Liza said, praying her words were the right ones.

One thing Liza did know for sure; Rosie and her mother had never been happier, and truth was folks were talking about the change they'd seen in Mrs. Winthrop. "Why, she's been smiling and greeting us on the street," Liza overheard one lady say to another at Johansson's Mercantile. "It's a marvel what that Bartel woman and her daughter done brought out in Iris's face. All this time, I think she wanted to feel needed."

Although the eavesdropping hadn't been intended, it had put a warm spot in Liza's heart; but it also made her wonder how Mr. Bartel was faring with his boy. Since Mrs. Bartel still failed to file a complaint against Clement, the boy continued to roam free. Was he now turning his rage on his own father? But Liza supposed she couldn't carry the weight of everyone's burdens on her shoulders. She would have to leave some of the load to her heavenly Father.

"Then I think you should make an angel," Lili told Rosie, her comment forcing Liza back to the present.

Liza finished off her sandwich, then urged everyone to clean up his or her area before donning winter gear and going outside for a brief play period.

At the end of the day, Liza straightened her desktop, stacked her writing tools in her ribbon-trimmed canning jar, bent to pick up several pieces of paper from the floor that the students had missed during the clean-up period, and then moved to the closet to retrieve her coat and scarf. While slipping her arms through the sleeves of her long woolen coat, she surveyed the hastily made paper chain that hung above the doors and windows.

Hanging down the front of Rosie's and Lili's desks were white-robed angels, looking tattered and lopsided. A sigh and a smile slipped past her lips. Liza thought they were perhaps the prettiest sight she had ever seen. Who but children knew best how to celebrate the Savior's birthday?

She bit her lip to chase back a tear at the thought of spending Christmas without Aunt Hettie and Uncle Gideon. Limited expenses had simply prohibited it, most of her excess monies having gone into making her cabin a home. And she was just now beginning to build up a meager savings for herself. No, she simply could not afford a train ticket back East, and she certainly couldn't imagine riding all that way to the station with Mr. Brackett again.

In truth, if she were to cozy up to anyone on a wagon seat, she would want it to be Benjamin Broughton.

She stepped out into the brisk December air and watched her hot breath form a cloud, then quickly dissipate. It was almost Christmas, a time for rejoicing. Why then did she suddenly have to fight down a lump the size of the apple Lili had brought to school that day? Moreover, why could she never seem to get the image of Ben Broughton out of her mind?

She hurried her steps to Sam's Livery, head down to ward off the biting winds. Very few shoppers milled the streets on this particularly cold afternoon and Liza couldn't blame them. Kentucky, although its snow accumulation was scant, could certainly boast its frigid temperatures and icy winds. She drew her collar up more snugly about her neck and started across the little alleyway that separated Little Hickman's Post Office from Sam's Livery. Suddenly, a giant tug on her arm jolted her backward, and the next thing she knew she was being dragged into the shadowy confines of the narrow alley.

Gasping and panting, Liza fought down bile when she glimpsed Clement Bartel's evil eyes and sniffed the stench of stale liquor on his acidic breath. "Clement," she cried, "let go of me."

"Not a chance, Teacher," he laughed hoarsely. "Not until I'm done with you." The excited timbre of his voice, accompanied by his evil grin, scrambled her senses. She wriggled against his powerful hold but realized when he slammed her up against the wall of the livery, sending shards of pain up and down her spine, that her strength was no match. A glimmer of hope washed over her with the thought that Sam might have heard, but it quickly disappeared. With dozens of horses inside, all beating and stomping and snorting, why should Sam think a little thump against the wall was anything unusual?

"You disappoint me, Teacher. I had you figured for bein' nicer than you turned out to be." He cleared his throat and hurled a wad of spit at her shoe.

Liza turned her face away to avoid their close proximity. "I—I don't know what you mean, Clement."

He snarled and pressed her up against the wall again, his face coming so close that she felt his hot breath on her ear, smelled its acrid odor. "You went to the sheriff."

"I had to. You pushed your sister off the porch, Clement."

Now he cursed. "That little pig is always gettin' in my way. She gets what she deserves. You didn't have to go to the sheriff."

"You beat your own mother, Clement," Liza spat out.

"She ain't my mother!" he shrieked, planting his fist into her jaw before she had time to dodge it, jarring her wits. "And that's for what your boyfriend did to me." His clipped words dispersed traces of spittle across her face. Razor-sharp pain cut clear to her jawbone, as waves of light-headedness washed over her. She tried to scream, but a filthy hand covered her mouth, blocking her airflow, increasing the dizziness. When he readjusted his hold, she eked out a tiny sound.

One more blow to the eye region had her moaning with gut-wrenching pain.

"Dear Father," she whispered as she felt herself slither down the wall and fall into a heap on the cold, hard earth, "help me."

She had no idea how long she lay there in her semiconscious state, but when she opened her eyes, she felt the sting of cold and pain, swallowed down a commingling of blood and bile, and sought out her offender. Waves of relief coursed through her when she realized he was gone. "Lord Jesus…" But the two-word prayer was all she could handle as she pulled herself slowly to her feet, grabbing hold of the wall to steady her, fighting down the urge to heave. *Must get help, must get help…Lord, take me to safety.*

It took every bit of concentration she could gather to put one foot in front of the other, her blurred vision making the trek all the harder, so when she first laid eyes on Sam Livingston's glorious approach, she wondered if her eyes were playing tricks on her, or whether she was looking into the face of a toothless angel. It didn't matter, for when he reached out his arms to her, she lost her footing and fell into his waiting embrace.

✳ ✳ ✳ ✳ ✳

The pounding of approaching hoofbeats halted the Broughton's evening meal. Even Molly dropped her spoon and squealed with delight at the thought of a visitor. Ben looked across the table at Lili and pushed back his chair, its shrieking legs protesting against the wooden planks.

He drew back the curtain to peer out the window, then threw wide the door. "Emma, what in the world?"

"Ben, you have to come quick," said a winded Emma. "Liza's been hurt."

Ben pulled her inside and closed the door against the biting air. "What?"

"She was beat up in the alley between the post office and Sam's Livery. Sam practically carried her into my place. Doc Randolph is with her now. Sheriff Murdock's out investigating."

Clement Bartel. Untapped rage boiled to the surface as Ben went for his coat and hat. On impulse, he yanked his rifle off its high perch. Turning his gaze to a frightened Lili, he battled to stay calm. "Lili, you clean up the supper dishes. I'll be back as soon as I can. See to your sister." Then to Emma, "Drive out to Jon Atkins' place. He'll want to know."

"Jon Atkins?" asked Emma, her expression draped in confusion.

"Just do it, Emma." He stared at her until she offered him an empty nod.

"Papa!" Lili's scream punched him in the gut. When he whirled around, he bumped flat against her. Quickly he dropped to one knee and took the hysterical girl into his arms. By now, Molly had joined in the chorus, her screams echoing that of her sister.

"Stay with them for a few minutes before you head out to Jon's," he said to Emma over Lili's head. She gave him another vacant shake of the head.

He kissed a salty tear on Lili's cheek as it made a fast trail downward, then rocked back on his heel and cupped her face in both his hands. "Everything will be fine, sugar. You stay calm, you hear me? Your sister needs to know that she's safe."

"But who would hurt my teacher?" she asked between sobs. Her seven-year-old mind couldn't possibly grasp the ugliness of such an attack.

"That is not for you to worry about." What else could he say?

"Are you going to kill him?" she asked, eyeing the rifle under his arm.

Rather than answer the question, he eluded it. "I'm taking this for protection. Don't worry. Everything will turn out fine. God is in control."

So why was it, he wondered, as he made fast work of harnessing the team to the rig, that it felt like everything had suddenly spun wildly out of control?

He drove the rig with frightening speed, taking each bump with a wince, praying the wheels wouldn't suddenly have a mind to go flying off their axle.

At Emma's, he leaped down, threw the reins over a hitching post, and pounded a trail up the porch steps and into the house.

Several men whose names he didn't know stood in solemn, hushed circles. Tenants? Ben tipped his hat at a shorter fellow.

"You Broughton?" the man asked.

"I am."

"Albert Dreyfus," said the gray-haired fellow as he offered a hand. "Mighty big shame. Who would want to hurt such a pretty little lady?"

"Where is she?" Ben asked, his breaths nearly matching the rate of his pounding heart.

"In there. Doc's with her." Albert pointed to the small room with closed door. It was the same room where Molly napped in a crib during the day. He remembered there being a small daybed off to one corner.

Ben sent up a hasty prayer and approached the room, knocking lightly before he turned the knob and entered.

Doc turned at the sound. "Ben, she's sleeping now. I gave her laudanum for her pain."

At first glimpse, Ben barely recognized her for the red, swollen cheek, split open at the jaw and covered with a bandage.

"I had to stitch the wound. It should heal with barely a scar," Doc said, knowing full well where Ben's eyes had fallen. "I have good, steady hands."

The tender skin around her puffy eyelid had blackened where the blood vessels had burst with the impact of the blow she'd taken. Her usual neat head of hair lay in a mass of twisted curls around her head, dried blood adding to the tangle. Ben gasped in shock and dropped to one knee at her bedside. Without thought for what the doctor might think, he picked up her hand, finding it limp and lifeless, but taking comfort in the fact that her skin was still soft and warm. He kissed the top part of her hand, then gently turned it over and did the same with the palm, finally bringing her hand between both his hands, where he cupped it as he would a treasure.

"She looks much worse off than she is, Ben," Doc Randolph whispered. "She took a beating from that Bartel fellow, but she's feisty enough to be up and around before you know it."

Ben turned his gaze upward. "How do you know it was Bartel?"

"She confessed it to Emma before drifting off into a restless sleep."

"Emma failed to tell me that part."

"It's Will Murdock's job to handle things from here, Ben," Doc said in soft tones. "Emma probably saw no point in telling you."

He'd known all along that Clement was the guilty one, but this simple confirmation from Doc only fed his fury. No doubt, Emma had guessed how he'd react and decided to keep the information to herself.

"When will she wake up?" His eyes went to Liza's motionless body.

"She'll be out for a while. Best not to disturb her."

Ben nodded, relieved to see the steady rise and fall of her chest beneath the down comforter. "I'll stay with her."

"Good. I'll be on my way, then. I'm due out at the Johnson's farm. Myra is about to deliver her sixth." Doc shook his head and gave a low chuckle before he sobered again and put a hand to Ben's shoulder. "The teacher will be fine, Ben."

"And then what? Bartel attacked her. What will keep him from coming after her again?"

Doc frowned. "I'm just as frustrated by that as you, Ben, but Will Murdock is a good man. He will see that justice is served. Probably on his way out there right now to arrest him."

Ben counted Liza's breaths from the chair that he'd pulled up next to the bed. Every so often, he picked up her limp hand and gently squeezed in the hopes of reassuring her she was not alone. When she didn't respond, he rubbed gentle circles into her forearm with the tips of his calloused fingers and whispered comforting words. "I'm here, Liza. I want you to know you're safe and you're not alone. He won't hurt you again, honey."

But even as he spoke the words, he wondered how he could make such a promise. Unless someone stopped Clement Bartel, he was bound to strike again.

A good hour passed before Ben heard the stomping of feet just inside the house and then the quieter approach of footsteps. Ben's head went up when the door opened and Emma stepped inside, followed by Jon's towering presence.

"How is she?" Emma whispered, her face consumed by worry.

"She's been sleeping the entire time. Were my girls okay when you left them?" Ben asked, still haunted by Lili's frightful scream.

"They had calmed down considerably. I didn't take off for Jon, uh, Reverend Atkins' place until I felt comfortable in leavin' them."

"Thank you. I appreciate that."

Jon's eyes fell to Liza's still frame as he stepped in closer. Not surprisingly, he reacted in much the way Ben had; he dropped to one knee and took Liza's small hand in his. "Oh, sweet Liza," he whispered.

Ben stood. "Here, have a seat." He supposed it was only right that Jon usurp his position as caregiver now that he had arrived.

Without acknowledging Ben's generous maneuver, Jon sat, holding to the teacher's small, lifeless hand, deep concern etched in every aspect of his expression.

"Who would do this, Ben?" Jon asked.

Ben eyed Emma. "You didn't tell him either?"

Jon forced a burst of air through his closed-up mouth. "I couldn't get much more than a few words out of Miss Browning. Did you expect her to tell me who did it?"

"I didn't think it was necessary," she said, her face pinched.

"It was Clement Bartel," Ben told Jon. Then to Emma, "Did she give you any details, Emma?"

She wrung her worried hands. "No, just that Clement Bartel dragged her behind Sam's Livery and delivered her a few blows. She said he mumbled something about paying her back for the way you'd hit him in the schoolhouse."

"Why that…" Ben sauntered to the door, his purpose revived.

"Where are you going, Ben?" Jon asked, placing Liza's hand atop the blanket and standing.

"Out to find that no-good piece of crud. Any coward who hits a woman to get back at a man isn't worth a barrel of cow dung."

"Ben, wait a minute."

Jon bolted out the door behind Ben, leaving Liza with Emma.

Ben started to climb aboard his rig when he realized Tanner was over at the livery. "Would you mind driving my rig home and checking on my kids a bit later? You can tie your horse to the back."

"Sure, but Ben, listen to reason. Let the sheriff handle this. He's better equipped…"

"I'm equipped," Ben said, lifting his rifle out from under the floorboard and setting off across the street.

"Ben, listen," replied Jon, keeping step with him. "Just this morning I read from Proverbs that we are not to take matters of judgment into our own hands. **'Say not, I will do so to him as he hath done to me: I will render to the man according to his work.'** Don't you see it's out of your hands? God will see that justice is done, if not in this world, then the next."

Ben paused to eyeball his friend. "And I mean to see that it happens in this world."

"It's not your game to play, Ben."

Ben's gut recoiled. "This is not a game."

"Look—I'll go with you. How would that be?"

Ben stopped midstride. "Stay with Liza for a while, Jon, and then drive my rig home."

Chapter Twenty-One

*B*en urged Tanner to take each turn in the road with care. Nightfall was always a challenge, even to an experienced rider, but the glow of a full moon and a sky stocked with stars made the jaunt easier. A quick stop at Will's office had told Ben all he'd needed to know. The sheriff wasn't in. And since he might need help in arresting Clement, Ben meant to be there for him.

Halfway up the mountain, however, he ran into Will Murdock himself, alone.

"Ben, what are you doing up here?"

"Come to lend a hand. Where's Clement?"

The sheriff ran a gloved hand over his scruffy face. "Disappeared."

"What do you mean disappeared?"

Will Murdock reined in his horse on a piece of flat terrain. Ben followed suit. "Angus said he ran off a couple of days ago. I made a thorough search of the property, Ben, the barns, sheds, and every room of the house. The room that the boy slept in is missing all of his clothes and personal belongings, along with several blankets.

"Angus said Clement took off with most of the food supply and his best horse. I don't need to tell you the old guy seemed more put out with that than anything else. 'Course that might be due to the black eye Angus was sporting. Figured on the inside the old fella was saying good riddance. Yep, my guess is the boy's skipped town for good."

One side of Ben felt relieved that he wouldn't have to kill the punk tonight, but another went through untold anguish at the thought of him roaming the hills.

287

"So that's it, then?"

"Not exactly. I'm putting together a posse first thing in the morning. We'll scour the hills and surrounding farms, but my guess is the kid's hightailed it out of here by now. Even Clement Bartel isn't stupid enough to wait around for us to catch him. He'll know after what he did to the town's beloved schoolteacher that everyone will be on the lookout for him."

Ben wanted to believe that was true, that they had seen the last of the villainous delinquent, but something told him it couldn't be that easy.

"What time are you heading out in the morning?"

"First light of day," Will answered.

"Count me in," Ben said, turning Tanner toward home.

"I figured as much. See you in the morning," Will answered.

❄ ❄ ❄ ❄ ❄

"Ouch, that hurts," said Liza, jerking backward when Doc Randolph touched a tender spot under her eye.

"I'm sorry," he answered. "Just making sure that your jawbone isn't cracked. I'm fairly certain it's not, but it's mighty hard to tell with all that swelling. In truth, you look a bit worse today than you did yesterday." He sat back on the bed and tipped his balding head at her, as if studying her from a different angle might result in some change.

"Would you hand me a mirror?" Liza asked, sliding up on the pillow Emma had provided.

"You don't need a mirror, Liza," Emma cut in. "You look just fine."

"I would like to be the judge of that," Liza said. "Hand me a mirror—please."

Emma's eyes went to the doctor. Finally, Doc nodded. "Something tells me she'll get her hands on a mirror whether we give her one or not. Do you want her prowling around your house all hours of the night, Miss Browning?"

"Oh, all right." Emma yanked a mirror from the top drawer of the little dressing table behind her. "Don't say I didn't warn you."

"But you said I looked just fine," Liza reminded, taking the mirror and placing it facedown on her lap, too nervous to look just yet.

"I lied," Emma said, biting her lip.

When Liza tried to smile, it turned into a wince, even the simple act of smiling too painful a task.

She lifted the mirror after a hurried breath for courage and gasped outright. One eye stared back at her; the other one was fastened shut, its surrounding tissues black and blue and swollen beyond recognition. A large gash, stitched to perfection, filled her with a sharp reminder of yesterday's attack.

"I don't foresee any scarring," Doc said when he realized she was studying the tear where he'd had to stitch. "I'll re-bandage that now if you'll allow me, Miss Merriwether."

"Call me Liza, please," she told the doctor.

"Fine. Have you seen enough, or would you like to keep the mirror handy, Liza?" The glint in his eye told her he enjoyed teasing.

She handed off the mirror to a nervous Emma. "Thank you."

Emma pushed the mirror back in the top drawer. As soon as she turned around, Jon Atkins presented himself in the doorway.

"Jon," Liza said, peeking around Doc while he set the new bandage in place. Once done, he stepped back, making way for her visitor. "Come in." Because of the swelling, she found she had to talk through her teeth.

Jon stepped inside the small room, and as soon as he did, Emma took flight. Jon watched her go and shook his head. "She hates me."

"She doesn't hate you."

"I've never had a woman hate me before. I don't know how to handle it."

A giggle bubbled up, but she had to force a frown. "Don't make me laugh, Jon Atkins. It hurts."

Doc Randolph zipped his bag up after having stuffed it full of his stethoscope, a bottle of laudanum, and the bandaging materials. "I'll be on my way now, miss. I'll stop in tomorrow. After that, I would think you'd be well enough to head back to your own place."

"And my teaching job?"

"I would suggest you take off the remainder of this week. You don't want to take any chances on bumping that cheek or eye area. It could create some internal bleeding." When Liza opened her mouth to protest, he continued, "From what I hear, Bess Barrington is having the time of her life. And I'm sure Thomas and Erlene are proud of the fact that their mother is acting as their temporary teacher."

The sly man, Liza thought. He did know how to quell a protest, that was for sure.

Jon pulled up a chair as soon as Doc Randolph said good-bye.

"Are you doing okay?" he asked, taking her hand in his and giving it a gentle squeeze. She recognized the innocent act for what it was—a show of friendship.

Liza turned up her mouth at the corners to generate a faint smile. "That's as far as I can go," she said through her teeth while pointing to her pathetic attempt at a smile.

Jon chuckled. "I'll accept it as the full-blown thing. Now, tell me how you're doing."

"I'm fine. Is Clement in jail yet?"

Jon stiffened and gave her hand a little extra squeeze. "Not exactly, but I don't think he'll be bothering you anymore."

Liza frowned. "What do you mean? Where is he?"

"That's the problem, Liza. No one seems to know. But it's a sure thing he's nowhere around these parts. There's been a posse out scanning the entire area since daybreak. I rode with them a few hours myself, and I daresay not a rock was left unturned. Will organized a good search, Liza, breaking up the lot of us into smaller groups and scattering us every which direction for miles around. Last I heard everyone's returned empty-handed."

Instant dread gripped her on all sides, closing in on her until normal breathing seemed a chore. *He's still out there. Oh, God...* Drops of sweat popped out all over her skin, making her lightweight cotton garment feel like prickly wool.

"Liza, take it easy," Jon soothed, running a comforting hand up her arm. "Take some deep breaths."

She tried but found it took surprising effort. Tears fell like rain from the corners of both eyes, stinging the wounded one in particular. Jon yanked a kerchief from his hip pocket and clumsily dabbed at her tears.

"Will said even Clement isn't stupid enough to hang around town," he offered in a soothing voice. "The kid knows he's cooked if anyone catches him. It's a sure bet he's far away from here, and you'll never have to lay eyes on him again, Liza."

"What's going on?" Ben's voice snapped her out of her panicky state.

"Ben." Relief flooded her at the sight of him, his larger-than-life body seeming to fill up the doorway. She lifted her hand to him, then dropped it when all he did was step the rest of the way through the door and come to a stop at the foot of her bed. Suddenly she ached to have him hold her hand as Jon was doing, whisper comforting words. She'd dreamed that he had done just that yesterday, calmed her with his mellow voice, told her she wasn't alone. Couldn't he suggest to Jon that he give up his chair?

291

"Is she all right?" Ben asked, directing the question at Jon as if she wasn't even in the room, or worse, too dim-witted to answer on her own.

"She's fine. Just a little shook up with the notion that Bartel's still on the loose."

Ben's face went from worried to annoyed in the span of a second. He looked as if he wanted to come nearer, but something held him at bay. Surely, Mrs. Winthrop hadn't approached him as she had Liza about the matter of his "unseemly behavior" with regard to the teacher's sense of propriety. It would be mortifying if she had.

"Liza, I want you to stop worrying over Bartel's freedom. If I wasn't convinced before, I am certain now that Clement has skipped town completely."

"Are you sure?"

"I'm sure. And to remain on the safe side, the posse will scour the area again tomorrow. There isn't a man in town who wants that young felon roaming these hills."

Somehow, the reassurances meant more coming from Ben than Jon, although she couldn't say exactly why.

She breathed a sigh and nodded.

"Feel better?" Ben asked.

"Yes."

"Good. Now I best get home to my girls. Mrs. Bergen up the road watched over Molly today so that Emma could tend to you."

"I heard that," Liza said. *Do you have to leave so soon?* But to ask the question would be selfish on her part. For now, it was enough that Jon seemed willing to keep her company.

"I'll be on my way. I merely wanted to check on you."

Merely? The word itself denoted lack of interest.

"Take good care of her, Jon."

Jon's face, although normally jovial, drew into a slight frown at Ben's parting words. "I'll do my best," he said. Then to Liza, "Hm, that was an interesting visit."

＊ ＊ ＊ ＊ ＊

"Are you sure Miss Merriwether is okay, Papa?" Lili asked for at least the tenth time that evening. She'd been sitting at the table studying her spelling list, and he'd noted she'd had just as much trouble concentrating tonight as he had.

Ben closed the book he'd been trying to read, thankful when Lili's question forced him to give it up. His mind had taken him in a million different directions, and this book on American history was not one of them.

"Yes, she's fine." Actually, she was far from fine, but he decided to hold off on the gruesome details of Liza's appearance. Her face looked worse today than it had yesterday.

"Can I go visit her after school tomorrow? I want to tell her how much everyone misses her. Mrs. Barrington is nice, but she ain't no Miss Merriwether."

Ben laughed outright. "Lili, you know better than to say ain't."

"I know. It's a slang word and highly improper. Miss Merriwether taught us that."

Ben studied the crackling fire just feet away. "Doc Randolph said she can probably come home tomorrow, but I expect she won't be up for your visit just yet. Maybe the next day. We'll have to see how she's doing by then."

"If I wrote her a note, would you deliver it to her?"

Molly toddled past, and Ben reached down a hand to pat her downy head. She gave him one of her cheery smiles, sputtered something in baby lingo, and kept on walking.

"I suppose I could do that," he said, already leery of the idea, especially in view of the way Jon had latched onto her, sitting at her bedside, holding her hand, wiping her tearstained cheeks with his handkerchief, speaking in low, comforting tones. Liza belonged to Jon, and the sooner Ben accepted that, the better off he'd be.

With a sigh, he placed both hands atop his knees and stood. "Come on now; it's time for bed."

❋ ❋ ❋ ❋ ❋

It was lovely to walk into the warmth of her friendly cabin. Thankfully, Ben had banked a roaring fire for her earlier today, making her coming home that much pleasanter.

"Thank you so much for offering to bring me home today, Emma. You're such a sweet friend. I'm afraid you've spoiled me rotten."

"It was nothing. Are you okay?" Emma asked, helping Liza to a chair.

"I'm perfectly fine. You are like a mother hen. Has anyone ever told you that?"

Emma tossed her a blanket. "Oh, piddle," she said, pulling up a straight-back chair from the nearby table and sitting while Liza dropped into the snuggly warmth of one of the chairs she'd ordered through the Sears and Roebuck Catalog.

Her back still suffered strain from when Clement had thrust her up against the wall, but she'd managed to hide it from the others, even Doc Randolph. She figured her facial injuries were bad enough without adding fuel to the fire by mentioning her twisted back muscles.

"You would make a fine mother," Liza said, still striving to find a comfortable position. "You've certainly had plenty of practice with Molly."

Emma blushed crimson. "I don't have a mind to marry—ever, so babies are out of the picture for me."

"So you say," Liza said, getting no further response on the matter even though she gave Emma plenty of time.

"Can I get you something to drink before I head back to town?"

"Oh, do you have to leave so soon?" Liza glanced out her curtained window in time to see Ben walk from house to barn. She noted how his gaze seemed to travel in the direction of her cabin. Her heart took a leap and might have landed on her sleeve had she not reined it in.

"I have a hungry crew of scalawags waiting for their supper," Emma said.

"They were so kind to me," Liza said, directing her eyes away from the barn and the big English farmer.

Emma's face lit with a smile. "I never saw such a bunch of softies as when you came in on Tuesday night. I don't think a one of them slept through the night. Every so often I'd hear a creak on the stairs and knew that someone was comin' down to check on you."

Liza put a hand to her heart. "That's so sweet. They've shown that they're capable of having a softer side. God put that there, you know, that softer side. It's in us all, but we have to open our hearts to His Son Jesus in order to experience it completely."

Emma shifted in her seat and harrumphed. "Don't think they'll stay that way. Now that you're gone, they'll be up to their old tricks again, drinkin' and carousin'."

Liza felt the invisible wall come down at the mere mention of God and couldn't help but wonder what hurts her friend had suffered that would so close her up to the possibilities of inviting Jesus Christ into her life. Better to let it rest for now, Liza thought. One day soon, she will see the truth of God's love.

Emma rose to her feet and moved to the kitchen. "Looks like Benjamin filled your bucket with fresh drinking water."

Liza's heart tipped precariously at the mention of his name. "That was kind of him."

"I think he's sweet on you," Emma said. "Matter of fact, I know he is."

"Oh, Emma, don't say such things."

"Why?" Emma filled a tin cup with the clear liquid and brought it to Liza.

Liza swallowed deep and relished in the thought that Ben had filled her water bucket. "Because I'm the schoolteacher. I'm not allowed to display any outward feelings toward a man, or vice versa."

"I should be the schoolteacher," Emma submitted. "Then folks would never question my wish to remain single."

Giggles rose up. "Don't be so sure. You are a beautiful woman. Some man would still chase you down."

She gave a laugh herself and carefree flip of the wrist, then moved to the door. "Well, all I know is what I see. And I saw plenty of doting from that man when you were at your worst."

"What do you mean?"

"You slept through most of it, but he was right there next to you, holding your hand, well, until Mr. Atkins and I arrived. Then he moved aside for him."

"Oh. Jon is a good friend, nothing more."

"No need to explain that to me."

※ ※ ※ ※ ※

Well, at least she was safe and sound at home, Ben mused, glancing out the barn window at her darkened cabin as he finished the milking and the gathering of a few more eggs. He'd wondered how she'd done on her first night back home, but he'd guessed she'd fared quite well considering all the guests she'd received.

Every time Ben had glanced out his window, another rig had pulled up. First, there were the Bergens bearing baskets of food, far more than Liza could consume in her lifetime. Next, the Barringtons, Elmer and Bess. It looked like Bess carried an armful of flowers. Probably picked them up at Johansson's Mercantile. Every so often Eldred happened upon a peddler who'd received a shipment from some Southern growers.

Flowers. Why hadn't he thought of that? All he'd done was build a roaring fire and fill her water bucket. She'd have appreciated flowers more.

An hour or so later, he'd spotted the Jameses, and after that, Ralph and Mary Thompson, each bearing a gift.

He could only imagine how exhausted Liza had been at the end of the day. In fact, he'd had half a mind to put out a "No Visitors" sign at the base of Shannon's Peak and wished he had when he'd seen Jon Atkins come riding alongside Mr. and Mrs. Humphrey. And wouldn't you know it, that threesome had stayed the longest of all.

Of course, Jon would recognize the propriety issue for what it was. Although he'd seen Liza to her door before, there'd be no point to visiting her alone now while she was so much in the public eye.

"Papa, can you deliver this letter to Miss Merriwether for me?" Lili asked, giving him a start when she appeared in the barn doorway.

"You're up early," Ben said, walking over to drop a light kiss on the top of her braided head. She was becoming quite adept at braiding, a skill he'd never quite mastered.

"I had to finish my letter."

"Ah." Ben set the milk bucket down and looked at his daughter.

"Well, since she had so many visitors yesterday, perhaps you can deliver it yourself—after school, I mean."

"Yippee!" At that, she turned and made a dash for the house, the letter flying through the air at the end of her arm.

After transporting Lili to the schoolhouse and Molly to Emma's, Ben decided to make a stop at the post office. He received so little mail that weekly stops were usually sufficient.

As soon as he entered the post office, George Garner gave him a wave from the back room. "I was wonderin' if I was gonna have to come lookin' for ya."

"Why is that?" Ben asked.

"You've had a letter sittin' in yer box for nigh onto a week."

"Thanks," Ben said, walking to his box and flipping open the little glass door to retrieve the posted missive.

Like a meteor falling from the heavens, Ben's heart fell when he caught a glimpse of the letter's origin. *Sarah Woodward.*

All the way home, Ben wondered how to deal with this new set of problems.

Since he'd sent word to the Marriage Made in Heaven Agency requesting they put a halt to the proceedings, he hadn't heard one word of reply. Enough time had passed, he'd figured, and so he'd clung to the assumption that the woman he had sent for had indeed received his message. In fact, he'd put the matter out of his mind.

But apparently, that wasn't the case, for she'd written of her mother's sudden death after months of caring for her, and how she hoped her move to Kentucky would help to alleviate her untold grief. She made no mention of Ben having cancelled his end of the bargain. Moreover, she explained that the bridal agency had folded some weeks ago due to poor management of funds. Apparently, they'd failed even to forward Ben's message.

If all goes well, she'd said at the close of her letter, *I should be leaving for Kentucky via train by the end of the week.*

The end of the week? If his figuring were right, she would arrive within the next ten days.

Oh, Lord, I've made a mess of things.

"The Lord is good, a strong hold in the day of trouble; and he knoweth them that trust in him." The verse from Nahum 1:7 went through his mind.

Ben searched the heavens as he clicked the horses on their way over Hickman's new bridge and up the trail toward home. Work awaited him on the farm. He still had bales of hay to haul in from the north field, a couple stretches of fence to repair, hinges to replace on the barn door, stalls to muck out, and a lame horse to tend. And that didn't even count the daily chores that running a farm entailed.

He needed a wife, yes, but marrying a woman out of a sense of duty? How did that fit within God's perfect plan?

But what were his choices? A woman whose fare he'd prepaid was coming to Hickman with the purpose of wedding him. Did he have sufficient funds to send her back East? Moreover, would she balk at returning? She'd mentioned in her letter having sold her possessions. After all, they'd struck a bargain of sorts, hadn't they?

And what about the kiss he'd given Liza some weeks ago and the declaration that he wouldn't marry Sarah Woodward after all. Would it matter in the end if he changed his mind? Despite his deep affection for Liza, it appeared that Jon had won her heart.

He passed Liza's cabin on his way to the barn, scoffing at his predicament. Smoke swirled from her little brick chimney. Was she sitting in front of the fireplace, soaking up its warmth, perhaps curled up in her Sears and Roebuck chair enjoying a good book? He dropped his gaze. No point in dwelling on what went on inside her cabin.

299

"Lord, I've been a fool," he prayed as he led the team into the barnyard. "I think I know so much and then discover I know nothing. Your ways are perfect, Father, and yet I continue to set about making a mockery of them.

"First, I send for a mail-order bride without putting the proper amount of prayer into my decision. Surely, You don't mean for me to marry a stranger, someone I don't even love.

"Next, I fall for a woman who seems to have set her eyes on someone else. I can't blame her for her attraction to Jon. He's my best friend, after all, full of love for You and compassion for others. Naturally, his warmth and personality would draw her.

"But in her attachment to him, I've grown bitter and sometimes hateful, not only toward Jon but toward the entire situation. It is true I need a heart adjustment. Shoot, Lord, I need a life adjustment. I've grown cranky and irritable.

"Not only did I want to catch Clement Bartel for what he did to Liza, I wanted to kill him. I believe I might have if the boy hadn't turned tail and run the other way. Jon was right, I had a mind to take matters into my own hands, and it wasn't right, Lord. Yes, I want Clement brought to justice, but I don't want to carry a heart of hate in the meantime.

"Forgive me, Lord, for allowing my humanness to once again control my thoughts and desires. Please renew my spirit and my longing to serve You. Make me all that You have designed me to be.

"And, Lord, please show me exactly how to handle this matter of Sarah Woodward."

And with that, he jumped down from the rig and set about removing the harnesses. The horses nickered in appreciation. At least he'd managed to make them happy.

Chapter Twenty-Two

Monday morning couldn't come early enough to suit Liza. After five days of rest, she needed to feel alive again, needed to feel useful. In the past days she'd come to rely too much on the help of others, having received a total of seventeen visitors, all bearing gifts of food, flowers, baked goods, and even a treasured ladies' magazine, something she hadn't laid eyes on since living in Boston.

She'd been thrilled to see the Barringtons, the Bergens, the Jenkins, and so many more families concerned for her welfare. Perhaps most surprising, however, was her visit from Mrs. Bartel and Iris Winthrop.

Mrs. Bartel had shed crocodile tears upon first seeing Liza. "Oh, it's all my fault," she'd cried, dropping into a chair that Liza had directed her to, Liza winding up more the comforter than the other way around. "If only my Rosie hadn't told you about the beatin's and Clement's pushin' her off the porch. Clement has a powerful bad temper. I just wish you hadn't had to suffer at my expense, Miss Merriwether. I'm sure he was fightin' mad when you went to the sheriff." Her crying had continued, so Liza quickly had handed her a handkerchief.

At first, Mrs. Winthrop had been aghast at all the tears and words of despair, but soon she'd offered her own brand of encouragement.

"You mustn't blame yourself for another's willful actions," she had said, standing just behind Liza. "It's not your fault that Clement turned out as he did. He's made his choices in life."

Liza had thought Mrs. Winthrop's reasoning uncommonly sensible and compassionate until the less-than-tactful remark that followed. "If you want to lay the blame to someone, you could start with that deplorable husband of yours. Why, if he'd stayed home instead of patronized that—that awful establishment when he did, then Clement would never have been born!"

Mrs. Bartel had cleared her throat, wiped her eyes with her sleeve, and simply stared at Mrs. Winthrop, evidently unsure how to handle the coarse comment.

"I think what Mrs. Winthrop is trying to say is that you shouldn't carry the guilt for Clement's wrongdoing. He is the one responsible and he alone."

With that, Liza had served the women tea and cookies, pleased that the balance of the visit was cordial.

Her favorite visits had come from Lili. At first, the little girl had seemed horrified by Liza's bruised face, but in a short time, she had disregarded the contusions altogether, as they chatted about Lili's school day, her lessons and activities, and various students in the classroom.

"Sam Hogsworth misses you," Lili had said over cookies and fresh milk. "He hasn't been very nice to Mrs. Barrington."

Liza had gasped. "Oh dear. What has he done?"

"He told her that she had a big nose."

"What?" Liza could barely believe her ears.

"Well, it's true that she does," Lili had said in Sam's defense. "Have a big nose."

"But he never should have made such a cruel statement, and to the teacher, no less. I'm sure it hurt her feelings, not to mention that of Thomas and Erlene. Erlene is so sensitive. I hope he didn't make Erlene cry."

"Huh-uh. Well, I mean, he told Mrs. Barrington she had a big nose, but not to her face, of course. He just said it to the window what sits next to her desk when him and me was outside. He was mad when Mrs. Barrington made him do his sentences over 'cause they was so messy."

Liza had sighed with relief and chased the last bite of cookie down with the last of her milk. "I would have made him do the same," she'd said.

"But Sam is in love with you. He's not in love with Mrs. Barrington," Lili had reasoned.

Liza had bit her lip to keep from smiling. "I will have to have a talk with Sam when I get back."

"Are you coming back soon?" Lili had asked.

"Monday."

"Yippee!"

From Friday on, Lili had made a point to visit often, bringing Molly twice. It had been such fun watching the baby toddle from one place to another, enraptured by all there was to see in this strange new place.

On Saturday, Liza had happily fixed them a lunch of tomato soup and strawberry preserve sandwiches while Ben drove into town. He'd instructed the girls to eat at home, but, of course, Liza wouldn't hear of it. Who could pass up strawberry sandwiches? Even she had caught herself lapping at the corners of her mouth, checking for any remains of sweetness.

The only thing that had put a damper on Liza's long days at home was Ben's lack of visits. Lack of *interest* was more like it, she'd mulled more than once.

The only time they'd talked was at a distance, once when she'd stepped outside for a breath of fresh air and had spotted him walking across the yard to his house. "Ben!" she'd called, waving wildly.

"Hello!" he'd returned, stopping midway between the house and the barn.

She'd have given the moon for him to walk just one step closer to her house so she could gauge his expression, but instead she'd had to guess by the timbre of his voice.

"How are you?" she'd asked over the distance, fishing for words to keep the conversation running, even though the bitter air had her shivering.

"I'm great, but the better question is, how are you?"

"I'm fine," she'd returned.

"Glad to hear it. Then you're healing?"

"Yes. I'm going back to work on Monday."

"So Lili tells me. She's excited about that."

"Ben, I want to thank you for—well, everything you did, you know, joining the posse, coming to see me at Emma's place, making sure I had a fire when I came home—and filling my water bucket." There was so much more she'd wanted to say, but it stopped there.

"You noticed that, huh? Well, don't mention it. What are neighbors for if not to lend a hand?"

He'd looked like a giant standing there in his big wool barn coat, arms crossed, and his dark hair blowing in the wind. And was that a shadow of beard growth on his chiseled face?

"Yes—you're right."

"You've had a good deal of visitors," he'd said.

She'd wanted to ask him why he hadn't been one of them, but then remembered how she'd chased him away the other times, her fear of Mrs. Winthrop's discovering it making her wary. She'd nodded. "Yes, people have been so kind and generous. I have enough food to feed an army." That would have been a good occasion to invite his family over for supper, but that would have been playing with fire.

After a moment's lull, he'd waved her off. "Well, you best get inside before you catch a cold." And that was where the conversation had ended.

Then there was yesterday.

She'd wanted to give her body one more day to heal before facing her students, and so she'd foregone church. Besides, without Ben's offer to drive her into town, she'd been hard-pressed to know how to get there unless she called on Jon Atkins, who was certain to be busy preparing for his Sunday sermon. She doubted arriving at church on Tanner in her Sunday dress would look good to the general populace. No, it was best this way.

As Ben and his family had ridden over the crest on their way back from services, Lili had waved a greeting at her from the wagon seat. "Miss Merriwether! Want some help beating that rug?"

Liza had put the rug to her side and waved. "I'm finished now, Lili, but thank you for offering." Lifting a hand to her eyes to block the sun, she'd noted the strained look on Ben's face. Anyone could see he was avoiding her. "How was the church service?" she'd decided to ask.

"Mrs. Farnsworth sang a song that didn't come out so good," Lili had offered, "and Mr. Atkins talked about—I forget—what did he talk about, Papa?"

Liza had smiled at the child's candidness, then waited for Ben's response, hoping it would earn her at least a look.

"He spoke on the importance of forgiveness," he'd supplied, giving Liza a hasty inspection before returning his gaze to the barn straight ahead.

"Forgiveness. That seems timely," Liza had answered, "in light of all that's happened. I wish I could have heard it."

"It was a good reminder for us all." He'd seemed to put particular emotion into the words, making Liza wonder. "I thought Jon might have come for you this morning, but I see you decided on another day of rest."

His remark about Jon had confused her, but she'd passed it over with a nod. "Yes, I figured tomorrow is soon enough to frighten my students with how bad I look."

"You don't look bad, Teacher. In fact, I think you look beautiful," Lili had offered.

Her overindulgent kindness had brought tears to Liza's eyes. "Lili, you would think a cat with two heads was beautiful," she'd teased.

Lili had laughed. "You're silly."

After a second's pause, Ben had turned and pinned her with a thorough look. "I'd say you look a might better than you did five days ago. Everything seems to be healing nicely from what I can see. I don't think your students will be too shocked. Besides, many of their parents visited you and have no doubt put their children's minds at ease."

"Thank you for that, Ben," she'd said. "I feel better already."

"Well, good." Suddenly he'd tapped the horses into a walk, indicating an end to the short conversation. Liza couldn't help but feel cheated.

"Want me to visit you today?" Lili had asked over her shoulder.

"Lili, don't invite yourself," Ben had scolded.

"I would love nothing more," Liza had replied. "And please bring Molly."

"Send them home when they get to bothering you," Ben had called after, his gaze pointing straight ahead.

"Then I'll never send them home," she'd returned, hoping for a chuckle from Ben but getting none. Only Lili had laughed with glee at the outlandish remark.

The barn was dark when Liza entered it the next day. She wanted to get an early start on this frosty morning. After all, there was much to do in preparation for her return to school. First, her students would want to know the details of her absence. She'd carefully thought the matter through and decided to be truthful if they asked about the attack, but careful to omit the gruesome details. In other words, she would tell them only what they needed to know. No point to filling them in on everything, but no point, either, in denying that it'd happened. Children needed to know that they lived in an imperfect world where danger lurked—even in a small town such as Little Hickman.

Next, she would need to learn where Bess Barrington had left off with the lessons so she could resume and, hopefully, make a smooth transition.

She lit the big lantern that Ben kept on a shelf near the door, thankful that it provided plenty of light.

Tanner whinnied from his stall and kicked with impatience at the sound of her voice. She smiled at the notion that they'd formed a kind of companionship during their walks to and from the livery. Often she would tell him about her plans for the day, and he would nicker in return, toss up his powerful head, tip back his keen ears, and step up his self-important prance.

"Good morning, everyone," she called, passing Charlie and Lucy, the draft horses, and then poor Maggie, the lame pony. Ben said she wasn't good for much but looking at these days, but he didn't have the heart to put her down. She liked knowing that about him. She stopped for a moment to rub a hand along her muzzle. "You're a good ole girl," she whispered before resuming her steps.

A stray chicken had escaped her coop and startled Liza by strutting across her path. "Shoo!" Liza said, putting a hand to her throat to calm herself, noting how her heart had instantly leaped into double-time with the unexpected movement. The past week had been a lesson in training herself not to jump at every little sound. She supposed the attack had done a number on more than just her exterior. It seemed she also had a jumble of nerves to deal with on top of everything else.

Because her back still bothered her, she moved a bit slower than usual as she readied Tanner for their trip to town.

"Need any help?" said a nearby voice.

She knew it was Ben immediately, but her brain failed to send the message to her rigid, taut nerves in time to keep her from jolting backward and then losing her balance on the big wooden box she stood on. In less than a second Ben leaped forward and grabbed her with both his arms to steady her.

"You okay? I should have called to you from the door. I'm sorry if I gave you a scare."

She noticed that his big hands hadn't moved from the top part of her arms where they gently squeezed, and because she stood on the box, their eyes met one-on-one, his nearness pressing in on her and making breathing a chore. Tanner edged over, making room for Ben's unexpected presence and giving a gentle snort of welcome.

"I—I don't know what's wrong with me," she said, her voice faltering as tears crept dangerously close to the surface.

Seeing him like this, sleep still evident in his sapphire eyes, his scruffy, unshaven appearance lending to his gruff look, filled her with some raw, untapped emotion. Maybe it was a culmination of the past week's events and the idea that she'd butted heads with the ugly side of life. Or maybe it was that she stood in the presence of the one who had the ability to soothe her frayed nerves without even trying, heal her shattered emotions with a simple touch of the hand.

"Liza," he whispered, turning her into an embrace, lifting her from the box and tenderly placing her feet squarely on the solid floor. "You've been through a lot."

She took in his musky scent, her cold nose rubbing up against the roughness of his woolen coat, and released a jagged sigh that kept her tears at bay. Her fists caught and held the fabric where his jacket came together, his rock-hard body pressing against hers until it seemed he would squeeze every last bit of air from her lungs.

Tanner turned his head to nuzzle the two of them, but neither seemed to notice, Ben's ministering to her tattered emotions a distraction to them both.

A light kiss on the top of Liza's head made her long for more of him, and so she tilted her face upward just slightly, hoping that the move might encourage him to journey to her lips. Suddenly, it mattered little what Mrs. Winthrop might think. Yes, she'd signed a contract, but she couldn't very well control the pounding of her heart and the urgent need to love this man.

But just as she issued the silent invitation, his hands traveled down her coat sleeves and stopped at her wrists. He set her back from him and gazed into her eyes, his face a picture of perplexity. How could she set him straight, erase his confusion, if she couldn't explain the changes that had taken place within her own heart? No, it was best to allow him to speak first.

"I'll finish saddling Tanner," he said with curtness, unexpectedly dropping her hands to her sides and spinning around to face the impatient stallion.

Disappointment raced through her veins, leaving a trail of regret. Words failed her, for she couldn't begin to express her feelings without first knowing what he thought. He'd kept distance between them for the last five days. Was he even now kicking himself for having touched her? And had his feelings for her so changed that the mere thought of kissing her lips left him cold?

Silence filled the gap until she mounted Tanner without Ben's assistance, standing on the box and putting her foot in the stirrup, and then throwing her other leg up and over.

"Have a good day," he issued from his place on the floor, broad legs positioned a foot or more apart, his stance straight and intractable.

"And you as well," she replied, turning Tanner around and nudging him into a slow walk. Outside, she urged him into a canter.

Better to be completely out of sight before she let the tears flow.

❊ ❊ ❊ ❊ ❊

The time passed rapidly, too fast to suit Ben. With each day's passing, he came that much closer to having to face the person of Sarah Woodward, and still he wasn't one step closer to knowing what to say to her when he did lay eyes on her.

How would she handle his immediate rejection, his suggestion that she head back East? He couldn't marry someone he didn't love, he'd decided, couldn't even court her in his present state of mind. He'd added up his funds and decided he could offer her a cash settlement for her trouble, but would it be enough?

Would she rant and rave about having made a useless trip, complain that he'd wasted her time, or worse, melt into a pool of tears, her disappointment mingling with the grief of having already suffered a great loss, the death of her mother?

To say Ben felt like a heel would be putting the matter in gentle terms. Perhaps saying he felt like a brainless, coldhearted, worthless idiot would be slightly closer to reality.

"Papa, it's Friday," Lili said, coming out of her bedroom dressed in her Sunday best, Molly trailing in her cotton dress, barefoot and unkempt.

"Yes, it's Friday, so why are you dressed as if you were heading for church and not for school?"

"Miss Merriwether said we could read a Christmas play today and I'm to read the part of Jesus' mother. I think I should look my best."

"Ah," Ben said, "I agree." He touched the hot mug of coffee to his lips, then took a long, slow sip of the brew, watching Lili over the rim.

"Todd Thompson will be Joseph." She scowled and wrinkled her nose. "But just because he's going to be my husband doesn't mean I have to like him."

"Of course not."

"Rufus, Gus, and Freddie are the wise men." Lili took the piece of buttered bread Ben offered her along with the cup of milk. After taking a good-sized bite and chewing it down, she said, "Christmas is only two weeks away, Papa. Ain't that thrillin'?" Ben arched an eyebrow. "I mean, *isn't* it thrillin'?"

For the life of him, he couldn't muster her enthusiasm. Too many things weighed heavy on his mind. "Absolutely exhilarating."

"Oh, Papa, you're silly. Can't you be serious?"

She had no idea how truly somber was his mood. What would Lili think if she learned a woman was coming, one he'd sent for, no less, with aspirations for being his wife and the mother of his children?

Later, after dropping an energized Lili at school and Molly at Emma's, Ben headed for Johansson's to buy a new saw, some nails, and a post digger. Grady Swanson's sawmill was his next stop, where he picked out some boards for finishing off the fence repair. On his way out the door, he bumped into Rocky Callahan.

"Rock, how you been?"

The man's dark features seemed to give away his sour mood.

"Wonderful, just wonderful," he answered, the sarcastic tone hard to miss. "My niece and nephew are coming in on today's stage."

"The stage? You serious?"

"Yeah, ain't that something? It's not often the stagecoach comes to town, but I hear it's carrying an assortment of people."

Ben's gut tightened at the news. Would Miss Sarah Woodward be among its passengers?

"That so?" A moment passed before Ben continued. He dreaded to ask the question. "How is your sister?"

Rocky shifted his weight as his face went sullen, a streak of emotion flashing across it. "She passed on. Time came quicker than anyone expected."

"I'm sorry to hear that, Rocky. Really sorry."

"Not as sorry as me," the fellow said, kicking a stone with the toe of his boot.

"No, of course not."

"Liz and I weren't all that close. That's why I'm dreading taking in her kids. They'll be like strangers to me."

"It'll be difficult at first, but time will begin to close in that gap of awkwardness," Ben said, as if he had a clue of the vastness in Rocky's assignment.

"Maybe so, but that isn't what I'm worried about."

"What do you mean?" Ben asked.

"I haven't time for these kids. Haven't time to see to their physical needs, let alone the emotional ones they're bound to carry with the loss of their only parent."

Ben turned thoughtful. "I see what you mean." He laid a hand to Rocky's hard shoulder. "I'll keep you in my prayers, Rock. God has an underlying plan. I'm certain of it."

"Yeah, well, I've heard that before," he muttered. "I best get moving. I've a lot to accomplish. Plan to add another room to my cabin."

Ben might have offered his help were it not for the fact of his own level of responsibility. The notion that he'd bitten off more than he could chew weighed heavy. "Let me know if you need help with the

 312

new room," he replied, feeble as it was, watching as Rocky gave a weak smile and strode off.

"Father, go with him, give him a sense of hope in the middle of his circumstances," Ben quietly prayed.

"Behold, the eye of the LORD is upon them that fear him, upon them that hope in his mercy."

The comforting words from the Psalms lent peace even to Ben as he ambled back to his wagon.

✳ ✳ ✳ ✳ ✳

Anticipation lingered in the air like the smell of fresh-cut pine bows. The students hurried through their lessons, knowing that when everyone had accomplished his or her assignment, they would set about reading the Christmas play. Everyone had some job to carry out, whether it was moving a prop or reading an important line of a designated character.

The children had worked hard this week, making Liza's return to the classroom not only a pleasure, but also easier than she'd have expected. To her delight, Bess Barrington had done a fine job in her absence. She'd left a glowing report of the children's efforts with nary a remark about any ill behavior, and had even assisted the class in designing pretty "welcome back" cards, which she had placed on Liza's desk. Bess had written a note that she'd left alongside the children's cards:

> *I have always longed to be a teacher, but with Thomas coming early in my marriage, followed later by Erlene, it seemed impossible. This past week has been wonderful for me, although I'm sorry for the horrible circumstances that made it possible.*
>
> *Having Erlene and Thomas in the classroom, and watching their bright minds at work, only made my experience all the pleasanter.*
>
> *I trust you are doing well.*

Liza folded up the missive, which she'd already read at least a dozen times that week, and stuffed it between two standing books on her desk.

"Is it almost time for the play, Miss Merriwether?" asked Lili in a high-pitched whisper. Of course, the rest had heard her, their enthusiasm equally matched.

Liza checked the clock on the wall. Two more hours of school hung between them and their weekend. "I should think it won't be long now."

"I wish our parents could have watched us," offered Lenora Humphrey from her desk situated halfway back. Liza noticed that she, along with most of the girls, had copied Rosie and Lili in fastening a Christmas angel to the front of her desk. Apparently, the boys would have none of it, however.

"It would have been nice, but I'm afraid our building isn't big enough to host a play. Besides, it isn't as if we've had much time to prepare. Why, you don't even have your lines memorized."

"Besides, our props stink," said Rufus.

The barn had been drawn with crooked lines and smeared with bits of charcoal to give it a rugged appearance, then fastened to the front of the room. It was less than perfect, but the children had given it their all. Then there was the manger, crafted from crates that Mr. Johansson had donated when Freddie Hogsworth had inquired about obtaining extras. Under the makeshift manger was the straw that Sam Livingston had contributed to the cause.

"I think your props are quite fine," Liza encouraged, to which Rufus visibly relaxed. The poor boy needed constant reassurance. "Now, let us quickly finish our assignments."

Outside, the sounds of approaching hoofbeats and the squeaky turn of wheels rumbled up Main Street, coming to a stop across the road from the schoolhouse and smack in front of Johansson's Mercantile.

Rufus, being tall enough to see, poked his head up high to peer out the window. "It's the stagecoach," he announced.

A gasp rose up all around. "Can we look, Teacher?" came the small voice of Erlene Barrington. It wasn't every day the stage rolled into town.

"Of course. In fact, I'm just as curious as you," she stated.

In a flash, they dashed to the window overlooking town and watched the exit of several passengers, the first an elderly fellow Liza recognized as Mr. Morgan, who'd visited his daughter's family for Thanksgiving. Then there were Mr. and Mrs. Jameson, who'd taken a trip south and were now returning. After them was a middle-aged man that Liza failed to recognize, followed by two school-aged children.

"Who are they?" whispered Rosie.

"I don't know, but they look like they'll be comin' to school," replied Thomas Bergen.

"Do we got room for them, Miss Merriwether?" asked Lili.

"Of course, we have room for them, honey. There's always room for one more."

"You mean two more," corrected Gus.

"Well, we don't know that they'll be coming to school. Perchance they're only visiting relatives," Liza said, studying their sagging shoulders and dour expressions.

A vaguely familiar man approached them then, his own dour expression matching that of the children. "That's Mr. Callahan," said Andrew Warner. "He's my neighbor."

Mr. Callahan. The name came back to her now. He was the widowed friend of Ben. But why would he be shaking the hand of the young lad and nodding nervously to the tiny girl?

"Look at *her*," said Lili in hushed whispers, watching as a finely-put-together woman stepped down from the coach, her every movement poised to perfection, her long neck straight, her manner trained to demonstrate self-confidence and dignity. She reminded Liza of the fancy women of Boston's upper region, those who came from the Imperial district and reeked of wealth and finery. Wrapped in a cashmere coat trimmed with mink collar and wearing a matching hat over glistening red curls, Liza could only dream of such extravagance.

"Who is it?" asked a choking Freddie Hogsworth.

"I wouldn't know," answered Liza, equally interested.

"Maybe she's the kids' mama," said an ever practical Sarah Jenkins.

"Naw," said Andrew Warner, his nose pasted to the windowpane, emitting steam and fogging the glass. "She don't look like no ma to me. 'Sides, she ain't hoverin' over them."

While the lot of them watched in open curiosity, Liza more fascinated with the forlorn children now than with the woman, Lili let out a shriek. "What's my papa doing talking to that—that woman?"

Liza's eyes trailed a path to the source of Lili's bewilderment and discovered Ben conversing with the beautiful lady.

A fierce ball of fire rolled around inside her stomach, as if she had license to concern herself with whom Ben chose to talk. Nevertheless, the bitter taste of resentment simmered.

It seemed impossible, even highly unlikely, Liza reasoned. She leaned into the glass as if to get a better view. Could it be? No, Ben had told her himself that he'd changed his mind about the notion of marrying Sarah—what was her name?—Woodward. Still, it would explain his untold lack of friendliness and his apathy toward kissing her. Oh, to think she'd encouraged that kiss!

 316

Another hurried look across the road found him taking the woman by the elbow and leading her off the street, bending now to speak into her ear.

"What is he doing?" Lili shrieked again.

Fresh anger boiled to the surface, burning Liza's lungs and throat.

"I—I don't know, Lili," she answered, jealous ire mixed with blinding disappointment. "I suppose you'll have to ask him when you get home."

Chapter Twenty-Three

*S*he definitely wasn't happy with him. That much was clear. Ben sat across the table from Sarah Woodward in Emma's kitchen, Emma having taken Molly and scooted out the door to allow the two their privacy, but not before supplying them both with hot cups of tea and a plate of warm cookies.

"I'm deeply sorry for the inconvenience I've caused you," Ben told Sarah. "I know that your journey couldn't have been easy, particularly in this cold weather and then following on the heels of your loss."

The woman twisted a flaming red curl around her index finger, her rosy cheeks, once blushing with delight at having finally met Ben face-to-face, now flushed with something altogether different—outright anger? "You might have let me know."

"Believe me, I tried. When I failed to hear back from the agency and received no further letters from you, I assumed you'd gotten the message. It's been months."

"Well, as I told you, the agency folded some time ago." She fingered a cookie with her finely manicured hands, then went for her cup of tea instead.

"Yes, you told me that in your recent letter. Until then, however, I had no way of knowing."

She pursed her lips and blew air through her nostrils, putting Ben in mind of a fierce tiger. Blazing red hair curled around her cheeks, and when she huffed again, a lock shot straight out like a red-hot flame.

She looked too much for him to handle anyway, he decided. Of course, he'd thought the same when first meeting Eliza Jane Merriwether.

"What changed your mind, if I might ask?" Sarah inquired, leaning forward, now hugging the cup of hot tea between both her hands.

There was no denying the woman's beauty. High cheekbones etched to perfection and framed by the lovely red curls drew attention to her larger-than-life hazel eyes, blue in the light of the sun, but now green in the light of Emma's kitchen.

And her elegant garments. Although clothing never defined the person, the way Sarah Woodward dressed hinted at her lineage. Wouldn't Iris Winthrop have a fit once she realized she'd met her match in Hickman's skimpy world of fashion?

Why would a lady of this caliber apply at such a place as the Marriage Made in Heaven Agency when, by all intents and purposes, she could have any man her heart desired?

Ben pondered her question. "I was hasty in sending for you. In truth, I didn't truly pray about my decision as I should have."

"Well, I did, and I still believe I've made the proper choice in coming here."

Ben struggled in his heart and mind, on the one hand feeling sorry for her, and on the other, knowing with certainty that he wasn't to marry her. Whether it did him any good or not, he was in love with another woman. Marrying this one wouldn't solve the problem of his bleeding heart.

"Again, I'm sorry."

"You're in love with another, aren't you?" she said.

Her words halted his next breath. "Pardon me?"

"Oh please, I've seen the look before. You can't tell me that you haven't been snagged by someone else."

He closed his eyes. Was he that transparent? "It doesn't matter. She's taken with someone else."

"Married, you mean?"

"No, of course not."

"Well then, what's the problem? Go after her."

Ben couldn't believe the candidness of this stranger. He found himself pushing back in his chair and laughing, her smile offering him a measure of relief. At least it didn't appear she'd be tarring and feathering him.

"Look," he finally said, pulling a thick envelope from his pocket, "I'll put you up at Emma's. You can stay as long as you care to, after which I've provided you with enough money to go back East to your friends and family." He dropped the envelope on the table under her flawlessly formed nose.

She pushed the envelope back at him. "I have very few friends and family back East," she stated simply. "I'll stay on here, find something to do, somewhere to work."

"What?" How could he tactfully tell her she would never fit in? He measured his words with care. "By the look of you, you've never even seen a speck of dust before. This town is built on dirt."

"I can handle dirt. I'm staying and I don't want or need your money."

No, he could see she didn't need his money. But why she would want to stay when Little Hickman had nothing to offer a woman like her was beyond him.

He angled his face at her, then inched the envelope back in her direction. She promptly shoved it back. "Please, Mr. Broughton, I believe God sent me to this town, if not for the purpose of marrying you, then for something else far greater, and I shan't go back on that conviction. Now, if you'll be so kind, could you carry in my trunk?"

❈ ❈ ❈ ❈ ❈

At close of day, Liza scanned her quiet, vacant classroom, the last of her students having rushed out the door just fifteen minutes ago. Everything was in its place, papers picked up, books neatly stacked.

The Christmas play had helped to take Lili's mind off the incident she'd witnessed on the street, her father with the beautiful stranger, as she read her lines with rapt enthusiasm. "What manner of salutation is this, O angel?"

And when the angel Gabriel, played by none other than Rufus Baxter, told her with snickers that she was to bear a child, she solemnly replied, with great dramatic flair, "But how shall this be, seeing I know not a man?"

Gabriel, fighting to regain his composure, said, "The Holy Ghost shall come upon you, and you shall bear a—a child, for with God nothing shall be impossible."

Then a blushing Mary hastily replied, "Behold thy handmaid; be it unto me according to thy word."

All the students clapped at the final curtain, tickled by their achievement, tickled further when Liza surprised them with homemade cider and cookies. If her heart hadn't weighed so uncommonly heavy, Liza might have been more apt to join in the excitement, but as it was, she'd had to paste a smile on her face the entire time.

Just as Liza pushed her chair up to her desk and stepped off the tiny platform to head for the coat closet, the door blew open, and in its wake stood Clement Bartel.

"Clement!" Her heart went into immediate double-time, pumping out a pace that made her feel like fainting. His figure so shocked her that at first she stood frozen in place, unable even to think rationally. But the slammed door, along with his fiery eyes and hard-faced expression, snapped her back to attention.

"You are not to come anywhere near me, Clement Bartel. You've been banned from school property," she said, stepping backward.

He laughed, the malicious sound chilling her as he eased forward. Without forethought, she made a mad dash for the back door, figuring if she moved fast enough she could make it to safety.

But her hopes all shattered when he seized her just before she touched the doorknob and dragged her painfully by the hair across the room, tossing her like a rag doll into a chair. "Sit there, witch!" he roared.

With little consideration for the consequences, she released a bloodcurdling scream, to which he rewarded her with a slap across her stitched jaw.

Untold pain wreaked havoc with her senses as she felt fresh blood make a pathway down her face. A tingling sensation came over her with the shock of it, made tears gush without warning and her eyes go blurry.

"Ha! Blood, just the result I was looking for." He lurked over her, madness in his eyes. "Got me a rope, see?" He withdrew a ball of twine from his hip pocket and stuck it under her nose.

Amidst the excruciating pain, she knew the importance of maintaining a measure of calm if she was to come out of this alive. "I thought you ran away," she managed, her throat tight and painful.

"That's a laugh. These hills are filled with caves. I'd know 'em with my eyes closed. Fool sheriff thought he had me figgered out. I even overheard 'im tell a group o' other idiots that even one as stupid as Clement Bartel wouldn't stick around these parts." Clement cursed. She lifted her hands to her ears to blot out the evil words.

"Stick yer hands out," he ordered hoarsely, showing her the twine.

"Clement, don't do this," she said, even as she extended her hands, anything to avoid another blow to her face. When he began to wrap her hands with the twine, she felt a twinge of pity for the boy. "God loves you, Clement. You don't have to prove yourself to Him or anyone. He wants to come into your heart and…"

Another bluster of rage made him strike her in the mouth, knocking her sideways, threatening to land her on the floor were it not for Clement's yanking her back into place. "Shut up! Ain't no God in these parts."

Indescribable pain shot through her face as she felt blood trickle from a split lip. "Dear Father in heaven, please…"

"Shut up, I tell you!" he bellowed, bending down until his face came even with hers. At least he didn't strike her, and she counted that a blessing.

"Please keep me safe, dear Father, and help Clement…"

The school door flew open, hitting the wall and bouncing back. Rufus Baxter stood in the entryway, feet apart, hands at his sides.

"Rufe, you're just the man I was lookin' fer," Clement said, turning with nonchalance. "Come lend me a hand."

Rufus walked inside, giving a wary eye to Liza, who by now could barely make him out due to her mounting wooziness.

"You okay, Miss Merriwether?" he asked. "I came back for my lunch pail."

"Rufus, you must leave immediately. Go!" she issued, hoping he wouldn't try to involve himself. Clement would think no more of killing him than he would of crushing an ant beneath his boot.

Clement laughed and made fast work of using the twine to tie her to the chair.

Next, he withdrew something from his pocket and struck it against his shoe, then tossed it in the air, where it landed on a stack of papers. A match?

Blinded by a sudden flame, Liza screamed again, then watched as Rufus tried for all he was worth to stamp out the fire before tearing into Clement like a madman.

Rushing him like a bull would his worst enemy, butting him in the stomach with his head, Rufus knocked Clement to the floor, shouting and growling nonstop, beating Clement's face to a pulp, while flames curled up around their rolling bodies, shooting higher in the room.

Fear coiled like a serpent in the pit of Liza's stomach as she watched first one chair go up in a fiery blaze and then its accompanying desk. It seemed a cruel twist of fate that her parents should perish in a fire, and now she would, as well. A raspy cough expelled from her lungs as she looked about the cloudy room, realizing the closed up windows would not allow for any fresh air. The school door, slightly ajar, seemed only to feed the flames.

With alarm, Liza realized they were in the middle of an inferno, and it wouldn't take long for the flames to consume them all.

"Dear Father, help us!" she screamed to the heavens.

❋ ❋ ❋ ❋ ❋

Ben sipped a cup of coffee on Emma's porch, Molly on his knee, a blanket covering her. Lili was in the house with Emma, helping her and Little Hickman's newest citizen bake a batch of Christmas cookies.

Jon had joined him, coat collar flipped up to cover his exposed neck. "It's cold out here. What are you doing?" he asked, taking a seat beside Ben.

"Just getting a dose of fresh air, enjoying December's sunshine."

"Heard a beautiful lady arrived on today's stage." Jon took his time settling into the chair.

"So that's why you're here," Ben said with a chuckle.

"Just curious is all," he answered.

"Yeah, well, it's a long story, but the mail-order bride I sent for and then reneged on just happened to arrive today."

Jon bolted upright, then turned to gape in the window behind him. "You aren't going to—"

"No, I'm not going to marry her," Ben interrupted, thinking it strange that a man who was bent on gaining the schoolteacher's full attention wouldn't want to marry off every other eligible man in town.

"Well, praise the Lord," Jon exclaimed, looking toward the heavens. "It's time you concentrated your efforts on the woman you really love, anyway."

"What do you mean?" Ben asked, leaning forward.

"Anyone can see that you have eyes for Liza. Why are you dragging your feet with her?"

Confusion ran deep. "I thought you…"

Jon laughed. "Liza's a wonderful friend, yes, but I think God has another woman better suited—"

"Fire!" A young lad came running up the sidewalk, his eyes full of panicked excitement. "The schoolhouse is on fire!"

❈ ❈ ❈ ❈ ❈

All was quiet, save the roaring flames that hissed and sizzled everywhere, consuming everything, including Liza's will to stay awake. *Hot, so hot.*

Amazing Grace, how sweet the sound…

Her throat, parched and dry, failed to swallow.

Lord, I'm coming home…

There was no air left to take into her lungs, only hot, burning, gray clouds.

Yea, though I walk through the valley of the shadow of death…

325

"Miss Merriwether." The strangled voice came from somewhere nearby. "It's me, Rufus. We have—to—get out of here."

When Liza struggled to see, she glimpsed the poor boy lying at her feet.

Father, help—us.

Door slamming open, pounding footsteps, earsplitting yelling, and—what? Was it the angel Gabriel come to take her home?

Big arms, so big, lifted both her and the chair, as if they weighed little more than a few measly pounds. This *was* the angel Gabriel. Sweet peace filled her soul.

"Gabriel—please—you must—go back for—Rufus."

But those few words were all she managed before her world went black as night.

✳ ✳ ✳ ✳ ✳

"Any change?"

Ben turned his head in the little room off Doc's office to find Jon looming over him.

He shook his head in response. It was all he could manage due to the exhaustion running through his veins.

It'd been two days of continuous sleep for Liza and unbroken vigilance for him. Even though Doc and everyone else who'd stopped by had told Ben to go home, he'd refused.

Even Mrs. Winthrop, who'd hovered briefly in the doorway, ringing her hands with worry and something else, had told him he should get some rest. "I don't intend to leave the woman I plan to marry, Mrs. Winthrop."

"Oh my!" she'd gasped. "Well…" Perhaps it was for purposes of shocking her that he'd made the hasty announcement. Whatever, the look on her face had afforded him a brief thrill. But then she'd smiled and softened. "Well, that's good news then, isn't it?"

He'd eyed her with suspicion. "For me it is. I hope it will be for her."

She had granted him a clueless look. "You haven't asked her yet?" He'd shaken his head. "Well, I wouldn't worry. It will all work out as God sees fit."

To that, he'd blinked his eyes in disbelief. "I thank you for that, Mrs. Winthrop." Then, "Mrs. Bartel and Rosie…"

"They've gone on back to Angus now… As much as I tried to talk that woman out of going home… Well, I suppose she loves him…in her way."

"Yes, I suppose."

She'd left soon after.

"No signs of pneumonia?" Jon asked, breaking into his thoughts.

Again, Ben shook his head. "We're turning her often, putting sips of water down her throat, forcing her to expel the soot."

Jon placed a hand to Ben's shoulder. "Courage, my friend. Courage. God didn't bring her this far to let her go. I'm confident of that."

Ben nodded and ran a hand along the back of his neck.

"You should let me sit with her awhile," Jon offered.

Ben tipped a glance upward to eye his friend. "And take the chance that when she wakes, you will be the first man that she sees? Forget it." To that, he managed a weak chuckle.

Jon gave a knowing smile. "How are your girls faring?"

"They're staying at Emma's, and between her and Sarah Woodward, they're faring quite well. Turns out Sarah's a mighty fine lady," Ben said, surprised himself by her untold benevolence.

"God truly does work out all things for His good and in His time frame."

"Now if He would just wake her up," Ben said, eyeing his sleeping princess.

"Patience is a virtue, my friend. Ever hear that?"

Without forethought for the sleeping patient, Ben burst into riotous laughter, a culmination of all his pent up emotions and his bundle of tightly drawn nerves.

Although Jon failed to see the humor, he entered into the situation with gusto.

❋ ❋ ❋ ❋ ❋

Laughter, Ben's laughter, made Liza's heart flutter with hope and expectancy.

Had she entered heaven's gates by way of Gabriel's strong arms with Ben following close behind? The last thing she remembered was those powerful arms carrying her away…away.

"Ben…" she muttered through closed, dry lips. So hard to move, impossible even to swallow for the fire burning deep in her throat.

The laughing ceased, but oh, how she missed its melodious pitch, reverberating her being, making her feel vibrant, making her long to open her heavy eyelids and view her surroundings.

"Liza? Are you waking up?" Ben's voice massaged her ear, tickling her lobe.

"Liza, can you open your eyes? It's Jon."

Jon? Surely, he had not followed through heaven's gate, as well.

"How is she?" This second voice brought her up short. Where was she, and why was she reclining on a—hard mattress?

"She seems to be trying to wake up, Doc," said Ben, the tenor of his voice changing, lifting.

"That's good. Liza? It's Doc Randolph. You're in my office and doing just fine. You've been resting since the fire. But you'll soon be feeling good as new."

His words trailed off as she pondered that one word—fire.

Fire? So hot, so parched. Need help, oh, God, please—help—us.

"Water." The need to quench her thirst swiftly surpassed everything else, her curiosity, her pain, even her need to escape.

"Water, she wants water," Ben cried. Sudden movement rocked her bed, made her eyes flutter and her fingers tingle. *Fingers.* Yes, there they were on the ends of her hands—feeling, touching—the woolen fabric of her—blanket.

A strong hand, familiar and real, reached behind her head and gently lifted.

"Here's some water, sweetheart."

Wet and wonderful, she lapped it up, leaning into its source, longing for more.

"That's enough for now, honey."

Sweetheart? Honey? If she'd had any doubts before, they were gone now. She *was* in heaven, and Ben was at her side.

Again, she tried to lift her eyelids, but they seemed immovable, heavy.

"Here, how's this?"

A soothing cloth, cool and moist, trailed a delicious circular pattern over her face, relieving cracked lips and encrusted eyelids, slowly but surely bringing her back to a place of sameness. She made a slit in her eyelids, then closed them up tight again. *Too bright.* Then just as slowly, she tried again, this time going a little further until she made out the shape of three figures, all hovering close, shadowed by the overhead light.

"She's waking up," said Ben, his voice now taking on a husky quality, packed with emotion. "Liza?"

"Ben?" she said, choking with the use of untested vocal chords.

"Water. Here, try another sip," he suggested, lifting her head just slightly again and tipping the cool tin cup to her lips. The liquid slid down easier this time, refreshing her parched tongue and throat.

Coming fully awake now, she lay there in the strange little sterile room surrounded by glass-enclosed cabinets housing bottles of every size on one side of the room, and on the other, bookshelves. A stethoscope hung on a hook near her bed, along with various other medical supplies and equipment. Next to her bed was a tray with a variety of paraphernalia—bandaging materials, scissors, tape, and some sort of antiseptic ointment.

Satisfied that she was among the living, she took in a raspy breath. "There was a fire," she stated simply.

"Yes, there was." This from Jon. Ben sat next to her, holding her hand and making little circles on it with the pad of his thumb.

"The s-school?" she managed.

"The school is gone, Liza," Doc Randolph said.

Waves of regret swept over her. "Oh, dear. All the s-supplies and books and…" Her gaze traveled to Jon. "…our Sunday meeting place."

Jon smiled and leaned forward. "Believe it or not, the Winthrops have offered their expansive house as a means for meeting on Sundays. It will be crowded, but we'll make do until we erect a new building."

With the realization that she was truly alive came a fresh flood of memories, all washing over her at once, filling her head with unanswered questions.

"Rufus?" she asked, dreading the answer yet needing it more than anything.

"Rufus is young and strong," said Doc. "I'm on my way out there now. His mother and father are doing a fine job of caring for him."

"Mr. Baxter?" Liza asked. "Has he been good to Rufus?"

"Far as I can tell," Doc said. "Can't always predict how these hill folk will act, but I do believe they're proud of Rufus for the stand he took against Clement. Some might call him a hero."

Panic thundered through her body at the mention of Clement. Ben must have sensed it, for he squeezed her hand and looked at Jon and Doc. "I'd appreciate some privacy."

"Oh, absolutely," Jon said. Then to Liza, "You get well, darlin'."

"Thank you," she managed, confused as to Ben's request for privacy.

Next, Doc laid a gentle hand to her forehead. "I'll return later to check her vital signs," he said to Ben.

When the room fell silent, Ben pulled his chair closer, leaning in until she felt his breath caress her face. He studied everything about her until she felt near blushing. "You scared me nearly to death, do you realize that, young lady?" His words came out on a tender whisper.

She shook her head in reply.

"Well, you did. I thought I'd lost you. When I heard there was a fire in the schoolhouse, I grew wings and flew there."

To this, she managed a weak smile, trying to picture the whole episode.

"The place was so smoke-filled that I had to feel my way along," he said. "Thank God He led me straight to you. I picked you up chair and all."

"I thought you were the angel Gabriel, ushering me into heaven," she admitted.

He grinned. "It wasn't your time for going home yet, sweetheart."

Sweetheart? His words were like warm honey traveling the length of her.

"How is Clement?" she decided to ask. So far, no one had mentioned where or how he was.

The blue of Ben's eyes seemed to go a shade darker with her question, his answer taking so long in coming that Liza wasn't sure she wanted to hear it after all. "Clement—didn't make it out of the fire, Liza. After I got you out, I went back in for Rufus. I never did see Clement. It would have been impossible to get him, though, because the roof collapsed after I pulled Rufus to safety. They found Clement's body under one of the rafters."

Liza shook from the veracity of his words. "I'm glad you didn't risk your life by going in a third time, Ben."

Although her heart broke for Clement and all the poor choices he'd made along the way, she had to let it go, had to remember that the choices he'd made were not her responsibility. And something she could be thankful for was the change she'd witnessed in Rufus. Truly, God had brought something good out of the whole mess.

"Where will we hold school?" she asked, suddenly concerned for her students.

"The school will have to close until we build a new one in the spring," Ben said, soothing her with the way he gently rubbed her hand.

"I don't have a job." Reality struck her square between the eyes.

"No, I don't suppose you do." His voice took on a tranquil quality.

"But that means I will have to move back to Boston. Without a job I can hardly continue living in the cabin, expecting the town to pay my salary, supply my needs, and…"

Ben silenced her with a gentle kiss on the mouth. "You're not going back to Boston."

Ripples of pleasure ran from head to toe. "I'm not?"

He shook his head and gave her a slanted grin. "No, you're not."

"But where will I go, what will I…"

"You're moving in with me," he said, simple as you please, touching his lips to her forehead now.

A picture of Ben and the *beauty* she'd spotted him with by the stagecoach rematerialized in her head. "But I saw you with a very lovely lady."

"Yes, Lili told me all about that, how you watched from the classroom. My, my! Curious little bunch, aren't you?" His eyes shone with humor. "For the record, that was Sarah Woodward."

"I knew it," Liza said, gritting her teeth, bracing herself for what would come next.

"Jealous, Teacher?"

She simmered internally. "So you sent for her after all?" she asked, ignoring his taunt.

"She never got the message that I'd changed my mind about the marriage bargain. I offered her money to send her back East, but so far, she's declined."

"So you're forced to marry her after all?" she asked, unnerved.

Suddenly sober, he replied, "Actually, I'm marrying someone else altogether, if she'll have me."

The way his eyes traveled over her face as if to drink in everything about her made her tremble all over again.

Dear Father, what is he saying?

"Would you have me, Liza?"

"Me?" she asked. Even her toes quivered under the covers when she glanced down at them.

"Would you make me happy by becoming my wife and a mother to my daughters?"

The idea tempted her. A wife? A mother? "But I thought you weren't interested in me…I thought…"

333

"Forget what you thought. I was a fool to think you'd fallen in love with Jon Atkins."

"Jon? I appreciate him as a dear friend."

"He set me straight, believe me. Anyway, will you?" he asked again, visibly on edge.

"But who will teach the children come fall?"

The students would have lost an entire semester of learning. They would require someone patient and kind, someone with a great deal of compassion and understanding.

Ben gave a sheepish look. "It won't be you. I've already told Mrs. Winthrop I intend to marry you—if you'll have me," he added.

A gasp hurried past her mouth. "Oh my, that must have thrown her."

"Will you?" he asked a third time.

Something like joy welled up inside her. And suddenly everything seemed to fall into its proper place. The words from John 14, **"Let not your heart be troubled, neither let it be afraid,"** held new meaning, seeming to wash over her as a gentle reminder that God was in control. He had His plan worked out well in advance, even down to why she should give up her life in Boston and take up residency in a scant town known as Little Hickman Creek, Kentucky. What if she had failed to listen to His still, small voice?

Yes, she'd served as the town's teacher, but she wasn't the only qualified person for the job. Bess Barrington had proven as much. To say Liza had come to Hickman for one reason only, to be the teacher, was to put God in a box, to place limits on all that He'd intended for her—and for Ben and his girls.

"Yes!" she said with joy and gladness. "I will!"

To that, Ben's face lit with relief as he bent close to drop another tender kiss on her lips.

He embraced her, careful of the open wounds she'd suffered at the hands of Clement Bartel. The shadow of those attacks would linger, fading only with time, but the memory of God's generous gift of love and grace in the midst of cruelty and despair would forever live on.

To everything, there was a purpose, even to the burning down of the town's precious schoolhouse. In some way, God would make even that catastrophe work for the good of all.

After a minute, Liza tried to pull herself into a sitting position. Ben put his arm around her back and drew her up, then stacked a few pillows behind her. "How's that, honey? Comfortable?" he asked.

"Yes," she said. "It's wonderful." The fresh use of endearments had her swooning with pleasure.

He tipped his face at her and smiled. "Have I told you that I love you, Miss Merriwether?"

She settled back into the pillows and sighed. "No, but you may at any time."

"I love you, Miss Merriwether," he supplied, placing a kiss on either cheek.

She giggled with sheer giddiness. "And I love you, Mr. Broughton."

And then he leaned forward to kiss her again. When he pulled back, he whispered close to her mouth, "What say we change that to Mrs. Broughton in the next couple of weeks?"

"A Christmas wedding?" she asked, drinking in the comfort of his nearness.

His big hands took her face and held gently. "I can't think of a better time to make you my bride, and since my house is big enough to invite several guests, we'll do it there, with Jon officiating, of course."

Without a moment's hesitation, she said, "I want to invite Rufus and his family." Ben looked only slightly curious. "He tried to save my life, Ben. With time, perhaps we can convince the family of their need for the Lord." Now he rewarded her with a full-mouthed smile.

"I think it's a great idea, sweetheart. In fact, I really don't mind if you invite the entire town—just as long as you agree to become my wife."

Shivers of delight scrambled through her veins. "Oh, Ben, I love you so much. I don't think I can wait two weeks."

He kissed the tip of her nose and chuckled. "Patience is a virtue. Ever hear that?"

She brought her hand up to stifle a giggle. "Yes, I believe you'll find it in the Bible."

Now their laughter combined, and with the fusing of two hearts, they soared as one.

About the Author, Sharlene MacLaren

*B*orn and raised in western Michigan, Sharlene MacLaren attended Spring Arbor University. Upon graduating with an education degree, she traveled internationally for a year with a small singing ensemble, then came home and married one of her childhood friends. Together they raised two lovely daughters. Now happily retired after teaching elementary school for thirty-one years, "Shar" enjoys reading, writing, singing in the church choir and worship teams, traveling, and spending time with her husband, children, and precious grandson.

A Christian for over forty years and a lover of the English language, Shar has always enjoyed dabbling in writing—poetry, fiction, various essays, and freelancing for periodicals and newspapers. Her favorite genre, however, has always been romance. She remembers well the short stories she wrote in high school and watching them circulate from girl to girl during government and civics classes. "Psst," someone would whisper from two rows over, and always with the teacher's back to the class, "pass me the next page."

Shar is a regular speaker for her local MOPS (Mothers of Preschoolers) organization, is involved in KIDS' HOPE USA, a mentoring program for at-risk children, counsels young women in the Apples of Gold program, and is active in two weekly Bible studies. She and her husband, Cecil, live in Spring Lake, Michigan, with Dakota, their lovable collie, and Mocha, their lazy fat cat.

The acclaimed *Through Every Storm* was Shar's first novel to be published by Whitaker House. *Loving Liza Jane* is the first in the Little Hickman Creek trilogy.

You can e-mail Shar at smac@chartermi.net or visit her website at www.sharlenemaclaren.com.

Sarah,
My Beloved
the next novel in the Little
Hickman Creek Series

by Sharlene MacLaren

ISBN: 978-0-88368-425-2
Trade • 352 pages

Sarah Woodward has come to
Kentucky as a mail-order bride. But when she
steps off the stage coach, the man who contacted her
through the Marriage Made in Heaven Agency informs her
that he has fallen in love with and wed another woman.
Sarah is disappointed, but she feels that God led her to
Little Hickman Creek for a reason. With her usual stubborn
determination, she refuses to leave until she finds out what
that reason is.

Rocky Calahan's sister has died, leaving him with two
young children to take care of. When he meets the fiery
Sarah Woodward, he proposes the answer to both their
problems—a marriage in name only. Sarah soon comes to
love the children, but Rocky is afraid that she'll never survive
as a farmer's wife with her privileged upbringing.

Can Rocky let go of the pain in his past and trust God's
plan for his life? Will Sarah leave him or will they actually find
a marriage made in heaven?

**WHITAKER
HOUSE**
www.whitakerhouse.com

An excerpt from Sharlene MacLaren's next novel:

Sarah, My Beloved
Second in the Little Hickman Creek Series

~ *Chapter One* ~

January 1896

"It was the nicest, pertiest weddin' I ever did see." The woman's high-pitched voice soared across the room like an overzealous blue jay.

"You're right, Mrs. Warner. Never saw a sweeter couple," another woman chirped in reply.

"And so in love," someone twittered.

"Why, the bride fairly glowed."

"Hmm, indeed."

The ceaseless nattering of female voices forced twenty-seven-year-old Sarah Woodward to find a hiding place in a far corner behind a bolt of purple gingham in Winthrop's Dry Goods, her presence in the store yet unknown since she'd entered ahead of the others and while the owner was in the back room. Too embarrassed to show her face now, she longed to slump to the floor and disappear between the slats in the worn wood. After all, the aforementioned bride should have been *her*.

It seemed a cruel twist of fate that the man she'd agreed to wed by means of the Marriage Made in Heaven Agency out east, and had traveled halfway across the country to meet up with, had fallen in love with the town's schoolteacher before Sarah had even had the chance to lay eyes on him. She should have known better than to seek the assistance of a mail-order bride service for the sake of adventure, never mind that she'd felt certain God had led the way.

Of course, the man had been a gentleman about it, apologizing profusely for the mix-up in communication, his message to halt the proceedings not reaching her in time, and offering to pay her for her

339

trouble, namely sending her back to where she'd come from, Winchester, Massachusetts.

Naturally, she'd refused his offer for compensation. She didn't want his money. Besides, she wouldn't go back to Winchester—not as long as Stephen Alden, Attorney at Law, lived there. The man seemed bent on marrying her, and it was truly the last thing Sarah wanted.

It wasn't as if her heart had broken over the news of Benjamin Broughton's plans to wed another. She scarcely knew the man. No, it was more regret than heartbreak, regret that her plans had failed. After all, without the benefits of a marriage license, Stephen would still consider her open territory—might even chase her down—and she couldn't have that.

Lord, there has to be another way, she'd prayed in earnest that first night she'd arrived in Little Hickman, Kentucky, and learned of her fate—that her trip to Kentucky had been in vain. But if there was, He had yet to reveal it to her.

"And to think that poor Woodward woman traveled all the way from Massachusetts to marry Benjamin," someone tittered.

Sarah's throat went dry as she covered herself more fully with the bolt of cloth, praying no one would notice her. So far, her luck had held, but if the women didn't vacate the place soon, she felt certain she was in for more humiliation. As if she hadn't already taken the prize in that department.

The ring of the cash register's drawer opening and closing floated through the air.

"Yes, it's a shame she made the wasted trip," said one woman. "Of course, what would one expect? Imagine! Calling on a marriage service to procure a husband. It's beyond me why any woman would resort to such measures. It makes one wonder."

A round of concurrence rose up amongst all the yammering.

"Mighty pretty thing, she is. Looks like she comes from wealth," said Mrs. Warner, the only woman whose voice Sarah recognized.

"Yes, doesn't she," agreed one. "She wears such fine clothing."

"But that hair," rattled another. "Seems to me she ought to do something about that awful mass of red curls!"

Sarah instinctively seized a fistful of hair and silently rebuked her mother for having passed it down to her. It was true. Her thick, unruly, garnet-colored mane had been akin to a curse. For once, she would like to walk into a room and not feel the stares of countless eyes—as if she'd grown two heads and three arms.

"I agree. It looks like a ball of fire most of the time. Even hats don't seem to cover the worst of it." Sarah recognized that particular voice as belonging to the proprietor, Mrs. Winthrop, a woman seemingly determined to discover everyone's biggest fault.

Sarah swallowed hard and adjusted her feet, still ice-cold from her jaunt over from Emma Browning's Boardinghouse, while awaiting the dispersing of the small gathering of gossipy women, taking care to keep her head down and her eyes on her leather tie-up boots.

About the time she thought the last woman had made her purchase, the bell on the door tinkled softly, indicating the arrival of a new customer. At the door's gaping, a blast of cold winter air skittered past Sarah's legs, generating an unexpected shiver that ran the length of her five-foot, five-inch slender frame.

Voices stilled at the newest customer's arrival, making Sarah crane her neck from curiosity. Ever so carefully, noiselessly, she peered past aisles and shelves crammed with stitching supplies, everything from embroidered tapestry to threads, scissors to needles, and luxurious velvet to sensible cotton. With interest, she surveyed the source of the women's sudden hush, thankful that the Winthrop's large inventory made hiding easy.

Skulking in the doorway, looking uncomfortable if not overtly out of place, was the man Sarah instantly recognized as the uncle of the two young children she'd come into town on the stage with three weeks ago. Alone and forlorn looking, the poor little urchins had lost their mother to some fatal lung disease and been shipped to an uncle that, she'd learned later, didn't want them. Her heart had gone out to them almost immediately, for she knew how feelings of rejection could play upon the psyche of a small child.

Although she didn't know the man, and certainly didn't care to, she'd surely wanted to give him a piece of her mind. How could anyone deny small children the affection due them, particularly when the subjects were family members who had just lost a loved one?

Her blood had boiled then, and it fairly simmered even now. *Lord, forgive me for despising someone I don't even know.*

"Afternoon, ladies," came the cavernous voice of the powerfully built man, his shoulders so broad it surprised her that he'd passed through the door without having to shift sideways.

A woolen cap pulled low over his head shaded his eyes, making their color imperceptible, but failing to conceal his granite-like stare. Black hair, gleaming in the light, wavy and unkempt, hung beneath the cap's line, skimming the top of his collar. A muscle clenched along his beardless, square-set jaw, automatically triggering a response from Sarah to recoil. What exactly were his intentions for coming into the dry goods store?

"Why, Mr. Callahan, I don't believe you've ever graced our store with your presence," said Mrs. Winthrop, her buttery tone making Sarah grimace. "What can I do for you?"

"I'm lookin' for some fabric for my niece, Rachel," was his curt reply. "She needs a new dress or two; warm, serviceable ones mind you. I'm also needin' someone to sew them. I was hopin' you could make a recommendation."

"Oh my, well, I do believe a seamstress for hire is something we dearly lack in this town. Most make do with their own meager talents."

"Well, I don't happen to be too handy in that department," Mr. Callahan snapped, his tenor indicating his lack of humor at the situation.

"Yes, well, I have a few ready-made dresses in stock if you'd care to look. Or you could place an order if you'd like to glance through a catalog. What size would your niece...?"

"I could have gone to Johansson's Mercantile if I'd wanted a ready-made dress," he cut in, fingering a piece of woolen material under Mrs. Winthrop's nose. "But I'm not of a mind to pay for such an unnecessary extravagance. That's why I came here—seeing as you have so much cloth in

 342

stock." His eyes scanned the place, and for a heart-stopping instant, Sarah feared he'd spotted her lurking in the gingham. But then his gaze traveled back to Mrs. Winthrop.

"Oh, I see." Mrs. Winthrop's hand went to her throat, no doubt offended by the mention of her competitor, Eldred Johansson. The other women each took a step back, feigning disinterest, but Sarah knew better. They wouldn't be leaving the premises until Mr. Callahan did, for fear of missing the excitement. And neither would they be offering their help by the look of them.

"How are your niece and nephew?" Mrs. Winthrop asked, folding her hands at her waist, her chin protruding.

"Rachel and Seth are surviving just fine," he replied in a gruff tone.

"It was a shame—about their mother," Mrs. Winthrop offered.

"My sister, you mean," he said.

"Of course," Mrs. Winthrop answered. "It must have been a shock to—well, everyone."

"Not a shock, no. She'd been ill for some time. Now, what about that seamstress?" His curtness seemed to add an icy dimension to the already chilled room.

"Well, as I said, I don't happen to know of anyone offhand."

"Any of you sew?" he asked the women, turning an assessing eye on each of them.

"I stitch for my family, but I'm afraid I'm quite pressed for time right now what with all my youngins' runnin' every which direction," one woman answered while nervously fingering her parcel.

Mr. Callahan nodded and looked to the other two women. Both shook their heads. "I'm afraid I can barely make do with my own pile of mending and darning, Mr. Callahan. You'd best order somethin' ready-made." This from the woman referred to as Mrs. Warner.

"Well, since I don't intend to spend the extra money on such a frivolous expense, I 'spect my niece'll have to make do with what she has, holes or not."

Sarah's blood had fairly reached its boiling point when she stepped forward, her camouflage no longer important. "I can sew," she stated quite calmly despite her inward seething. Perhaps it was her hasty prayer for self-control that kept her from throttling the man the second she came out of hiding. A little girl who'd just lost her mother deserved a new dress. How dare he call such a purchase an extravagance?

"Well, saints above, M-Miss Woodward," Mrs. Winthrop stammered. "W-where—?" Her eyes went round as the harvest moon while the other voiceless women bystanders merely gaped. Shamefaced and clearly mortified, each one, with the exception of Mrs. Winthrop, began her hasty retreat toward the door, filing out one by one, failing even to proffer a respectable good-bye. Icy air snaked into the room with the open door, adding to the already cold atmosphere Mr. Callahan had ushered in by his mere presence.

"You say you can stitch a dress?" Mr. Callahan asked, his eyes, a piercing shade of blue now that Sarah had the chance to see them up close, coming to rest on Sarah's face, then carefully sweeping the length of her.

Determined not to allow the man's intimidation to ruffle her, Sarah replied, "I said I can sew, didn't I?"

"But can you stitch a dress for a girl?" he asked with a good measure of impatience.

Under his scrutiny, she felt her neck muscles go stiff. "I've never made a child's dress," she admitted begrudgingly, "but I've made plenty of other things. I expect with proper measuring and planning I can make her a fine dress."

He gave her another hasty once-over. "You make what you're wearin'?"

She looked down at the blue satin gown peeking out from under her long cashmere coat. Her mother had purchased it for her as a gift before taking ill a year ago. It would be her final gift from her. An unanticipated wave of sadness threatened to divert her attention until she regained control of her wobbly emotions.

"No, but I've fashioned some of my own clothing."

"Really." He tipped back on his heels and gave her a disbelieving look. "You don't appear to be the sort who would stoop to such menial tasks."

Taken aback, she prayed for the right choice of words. "I'll have you know there is nothing menial about sewing. It's a fine hobby and one that does a great deal to alleviate stress, Mr.—" The man was nothing if he wasn't a dolt.

"Callahan. Rocky Callahan." He tipped his head a little by way of a greeting, and she noticed that one corner of his mouth curved slightly upward. "But then you already knew that, didn't you, Miss—?"

"Sarah Woodward," she put in, deciding to ignore his impudence. "I met your niece and nephew on the stagecoach a few weeks back, and I saw you take them away."

No point in trying to hide the fact that she'd noticed him. She wouldn't admit to having studied him at close range, however.

"I assumed you were the uncle in question," she added. *But not because you overflowed with love and compassion.*

He glanced at Mrs. Winthrop who'd failed to move from her place behind the counter. Upon receiving a red-hot glare from him, she took up a bundle of papers and moved to the back room, expelling a loud gasp of air on her way. "I'll let you know about the fabric," he called after.

Once again turning his dark gaze on Sarah, he said, "You're the woman Ben Broughton sent for."

Sarah's stomach tightened. The last thing she intended to do was discuss her personal reasons for coming to Little Hickman.

"I suppose you would need to alleviate some stress about now," he said with a mocking grin, making Sarah's back go straight as a pin, her chin jut with resolve. "Must have been a bit of a shock to travel all that way and then find the man you came to marry had set his cap for the schoolteacher."

"I'll need to measure your niece—is it Rachel?" she asked, trying her best to ignore his callousness.

He pointed a thumb over his shoulder. "She's out on the buckboard if you've a mind to measure her right now."

"You left her sitting in the cold?" Sarah exclaimed. "And the boy as well?" Picking up her skirts, she scooted around his broad frame to see out the window. Sure enough, two unfortunate little souls sat huddled together high on their perch, plainly frozen by the way they both hugged themselves. "They're freezing."

"What is wrong with you?" she asked, whirling around to face him, no longer thrown off balance by his tough exterior. "The wind is brisk today, cold enough to bite off the tips of their little noses."

"I told you I invited them in," he said, as if that should fix the matter.

"Well, you should have insisted." Without waiting for his retort, she went to the door and flung it open. "Come in out of the cold," she called over the wailing winds.

Like lifeless statues, the pair sat rigid. Finally, the boy gave his sister a hopeful look, but she rewarded him with a slow shake of the head.

"Come in," Sarah called again, lowering her voice so that it came off sounding less demanding. Again, the boy looked to his sister; his bare little fingers finding a place to warm themselves between his skinny legs.

"They're not wearing mittens," Sarah hissed in disbelief.

"Couldn't find them when it was time to leave. The girl is absent-minded. I've no idea where she put them and neither does she. I figured it would teach them both a lesson to go without."

"What? How old is she, six, seven? What do you expect?"

"She's seven, and I expect some level of responsibility," he answered.

His impertinence angered her so that she made a huffing sound before traipsing out into the frigid air and coming face to face with the poor little imps. Eyeing them both with equal amounts of compassion and firmness, she looked from one to the other. "Hello, Rachel and Seth. My name is Sarah, and I would like you both to come inside now. I'm to make a dress for you. Isn't that nice, Rachel? If you'll please come inside I can measure you."

The child turned cold eyes on Sarah and folded her arms in front of her. "I don't need no dress," she stated.

"Just the same, you should come inside. It's bitter cold today."

"Is it going to snow?" asked the boy, his teeth clattering as he spoke. His sister knocked him with her elbow, indicating he wasn't to ask questions.

"It certainly feels cold enough," Sarah replied with a smile. "Do you like snow?"

He nodded readily but at his sister's silent admonition, chose not to elaborate.

"Do you remember me? We rode into town together on the stage."

A simple nod was all she got from Seth. Rachel remained bravely staunch. "Ar mother died," he said simply.

"I know, and I'm ever so sorry. Did you know my mother died about the same time as yours? If you come inside we can talk about it."

Rachel's cold stare intensified. "I don't want to talk about it."

"Fine then, we won't. I do need to measure you, however, so it's best you hop on down. You might help me pick out the cloth as well, how would that be?"

Only slightly intrigued with that notion, the girl looked at the doorway from where her uncle waited, his dour expression matching hers. "Ar uncle hates us," she declared.

Sarah digested the girl's words and planned her response with care. "I don't think he hates you." Her hasty glance backward signified he couldn't hear them over the whistling winds.

"Well, it don't make no difference anyway," Rachel clucked. "'Cause we don't like him neither."

Rachel shivered and offered a hand to the angry child. Begrudgingly, she took it, jumping to the hard earth below and taking care to keep her frown in place. Next, Sarah held her arms out to the boy who went to her with no prodding, his icy fingers clinging to her neck until they stepped inside and Mr. Callahan closed the door behind them.

At the pinging of the door's little bell, Mrs. Winthrop appeared around the curtained doorway. Sarah set Seth's booted feet on the floor. "Have we made a decision on the fabric yet?" she asked.

"Not yet, Mrs. Winthrop, but I would appreciate a tape measure if you have one," Sarah said. "I need to take Rachel's measurements."

"Yes, of course." She headed for a drawer near the cash register, pulled out a long cloth tape, and then hurried to deliver it. She seemed anxious to be rid of them.

After removing Rachel's coat and tossing it to the side, Sarah saw why the girl needed dresses. This one was tattered beyond repair, the hem hanging crooked, holes in the sleeves, and a three-cornered tear on the back of the skirt, revealing a portion of her petticoats. Stains from lack of washing had fixed themselves down the front of her. To make matters worse, the material was nothing more than thin cotton, wearing and fraying at the edges. Sarah cast an eye at Mr. Callahan and hoped he read her disapproving look. If he did, he didn't let on. Instead, he shifted his weight from one foot to the other while she measured, as if to communicate his agitation. The act only made Sarah want to dawdle.

Once finished measuring, they moved to the various bolts of cloth, Mrs. Winthrop following on their heels, Mr. Callahan and the boy standing near the cash register. Sarah steered the girl in the direction of the warmer weaves, her eyes seeming close to bursting at the variety of colors and patterns. Finally, her gaze landed on rose-colored, heavy, brushed cotton. Soiled fingers came out to judge its texture. Sarah watched in rapt wonder as the girl's expression went from hesitancy to sureness.

"You like this one?" Sarah whispered.

A simple nod of the head followed. Had she never had the opportunity to choose before? Moreover, had she never owned a new dress? By the looks of the one she wore, it was a hand-me-down, perhaps previously worn by more than one girl. Sarah's heart squeezed at the notion, for she couldn't begin to count the number of brand new dresses she'd owned in her lifetime.

Mrs. Winthrop removed the bolt and hurried to a long table where she laid the material out to prepare for cutting. "Do you need thread?"

"I believe I have plenty of color choices back in my trunk. I'll check my supply before purchasing," she said. The woman looked across the table at Sarah, clearly intrigued.

"Fine," she managed, taking up with the huge piece of cloth.

Just then, Mr. Callahan approached, the young boy on his tail. "How soon before you finish the dress?" he asked.

"I've nothing better to do with my time. I should think I'll finish it in the next day or so."

He lifted a dark eyebrow and then removed his woolen cap before running long muscled fingers through his thick mass of black, wavy hair. "Nothing better to do, huh? You staying over at the boardinghouse?" he asked, his bottomless voice resonating off the walls.

"Yes." Best to keep her answers short, she determined.

"And how long will that last?"

Bemused, she angled him a curious stare. "What sort of question is that, Mr. Callahan?" Mrs. Winthrop's hand movements slowed, as if she wanted to make certain not to miss a beat in the conversation.

"A simple one. You came here to marry Benjamin Broughton, right? Since that didn't pan out for you I was curious as to how long before you go back to wherever it is you came from." A shadow crossed his face, indiscernible in nature.

She hid her anger beneath a forced smile. "Not that it is any of your business, sir, but I shall remain in Little Hickman indefinitely. I sold most of my possessions while still in Winchester. To return now would be most futile."

"Winchester?"

"Massachusetts. Just outside of Boston."

He cocked his dark head. Sarah found she had to crane her neck to see into his face, making her believe his height exceeded six feet. "Ah, no family or friends up there?"

"Friends, yes, but none worth staying for," she confessed, immediately put out with herself for divulging such personal information. As if that weren't enough, she added, "My parents are both deceased and I have no siblings."

To that, he gave a perfunctory nod. "How long you staying at Emma's place?"

She couldn't help the little huffing sound that slipped past her lips. What did he care where she resided and for how long? "For the time being," she offered. "In time I hope to…" It wouldn't do to mention that her financial resources sat in a trust fund back in Boston, awaiting her marriage as per her mother's final will and testament, so she buttoned her lip and left the sentence unfinished.

Creased brow raised, mouth slightly agape, he waited for her dangling sentence to reach its conclusion. "What? In time you hope to what?"

The children had wandered away out of boredom and had taken up with looking at various items about the store. Finished cutting the fabric, Mrs. Winthrop carried it to the cash register and pretended busyness, then took up a writing utensil with which to jot some figures.

"Find some suitable place in which to live," she finished, miffed at herself for being so forthright.

"In Hickman?" He grunted in disgust, trailing it with a cold chuckle. At that, Mrs. Winthrop gave a mighty sniff, causing both adults to turn their gazes on her. Hastily, she resumed her figuring. Mr. Callahan looked down his nose at Sarah. "In that case, you might be lookin' a while. You'll not find much finery in these parts, lady, and from the look of you, you've been conditioned to enjoy life's finer offerings."

His mocking manner unnerved her, the way he perused her from top to bottom, as if she were some piece of furniture he'd been pondering buying and couldn't quite determine whether it would mesh with his older pieces.

"I'll have you know I'm quite adaptable, sir!"

As if he had good reason to disbelieve her, he gave a half-nod. "No need to be snappish," he chided. Then with a twist of his head, he glanced at the children who'd wandered to the back of the store. "Don't touch anything," he ordered. At the harsh tone, his niece and nephew jolted to attention.

"Now who's the snappish one?" she asked, sticking out her chin.

Clearly irritated, he ignored the remark and moved to the cash register where he pulled out a sheaf of bills from his pocket. Sarah examined the roll of greenbacks from where she stood.

A palpable tightwad, that's what he was.

Mrs. Winthrop stated her price, and Mr. Callahan frowned. "You sure about that? Seems high to me."

"It's extremely reasonable, Mr. Callahan," Sarah inserted. Mrs. Winthrop's shoulders sagged with gratitude.

"Oh, fine," was his annoyed response, passing the proprietor a single bill then waiting while she made change. Once she slipped it to him, she gathered up the paper parcel containing the rose-colored material and handed it over to Sarah.

Man and woman faced each other as rivals. "Bring Rachel by Emma's tomorrow afternoon," she issued. "I should be ready for her first fitting by then."

"Tomorrow?" His brow gathered into a frown. "Don't know as I'll have the time tomorrow."

Rather than react, Sarah merely gave her head a little toss. "Well, I can't put the finishing touches to the dress without first fitting her."

Broad shoulders went into an impatient shrug. "Oh, all right—tomorrow."

"Good." Then to Rachel, she bent just slightly and placed a hand on her tattered, wool bonnet. "See what you can do about finding those mittens, okay?"

The girl nodded, her expression bleak. Sarah smiled at both unfortunate waifs. Clearly, they needed attention.

As for the man, he deserved nary a glimpse backward as she tugged open the heavy door and marched out into January's harsh breezes.

✳ ✳ ✳ ✳ ✳

Courting Emma

Third in the Little Hickman Creek Series
Sharlene MacLaren

Twenty-eight-year-old Emma Browning has experienced
a good deal of life in her young age. Proprietor of Emma's
Boardinghouse, she is "mother" to an array of beefy, unkempt,
often rowdy characters. Though many men would like to
get to know the steely, hard-edged, yet surprisingly lovely
proprietor, none has truly succeeded. That is, not until the
town's new pastor, Jonathan Atkins, takes up residence in the
boardinghouse. The whole town will witness the miracle as
Emma begins to experience God's transforming power at work.

Trade • ISBN: 978-1-60374-020-3 • 368 pages
Available Spring 2008

WHITAKER
HOUSE

www.whitakerhouse.com